PROMISES KEPT

PROMISES KEPT

THE KURTHERIAN ENDGAME™ BOOK NINE

MICHAEL ANDERLE

This book is a work of fiction. All of the characters, organizations, and events portrayed in this novel are either products of the author's imagination or are used fictitiously. Sometimes both.

LMBPN Publishing
PMB 196, 2540 South Maryland Pkwy
Las Vegas, NV 89109

Version 1.01, September 2020
eBook ISBN: 978-1-64971-156-4
Print ISBN: 978-1-64971-157-1

THE PROMISES KEPT TEAM

Thanks to our Beta Readers:
Timothy Cox (the myth)
Diane Velasquez (the legend)
Dorene A. Johnson, USN, Ret.
Tom Dickerson (in the way of Life)

Thanks to the JIT Readers

Nicole Emens
Deb Mader
Diane L. Smith
Dave Hicks
Peter Manis
Larry Omans
Veronica Stephan-Miller
Rachel Beckford
James Caplan
Micky Cocker
John Ashmore
Kelly O'Donnell

If I've missed anyone, please let me know!

Editor
Lynne Stiegler

Thank you for continuing to read our adventures with Bethany Anne. As you can tell, the Federation is going to have to come to grips with the Empress being 'just around the block.' Since there is a greater evil at their doorsteps, I think they will get over it.

For now.

If not, she always has her size sevens to ...

CHARACTERS AND GLOSSARY

Characters

- **Bethany Anne Nacht (BA)**

Super-enhanced human, part of a triumvirate consisting of her, TOM, and ADAM. Can walk the Etheric. Has the ability to manipulate Etheric energy to her will. Stamps out injustice without mercy wherever she finds it.

Ex-Empress of the Etheric Empire, BA took voluntary exile to bring in the Federation and now fights to protect it from the Kurtherians.

Currently based on the QSD (Queen's Superdreadnought) *Baba Yaga,* on tour around the Federation. Her plans to enclose the Federation in the CEREBRO network —a "security blanket" that will span and connect the entire Federation—while building an armada from the Federation's various militaries are at the midway point.

- **Gödel**

Ruler of the Kurtherian clans collectively known as the Seven. Refers to BA as "Death."

Considers Bethany Anne to be her personal nemesis and has been working against humanity since before the Leath War.

While Bethany Anne was getting ready to step down as Empress, Gödel disguised herself as one of the Five and tricked TOM into giving her the secrets of Ascension and the Etheric.

Current location, the Temple of the Ascension Path.

- **TOM – "Thales of Miletus"**

Kurtherian hosted within Bethany Anne's body. Enhanced Michael in an attempt to warn humanity of the coming invasion and got it wrong, inadvertently creating the vampire myth on Earth. A thousand years later, he got a second chance and got it SO right.

- **ADAM**

AI, resides in an organic computer within Bethany Anne's body. Bethany Anne's close friend and advisor.

All of Bethany Anne's and Federation AIs and EIs come from ADAM.

- **Michael Nacht**

Ancient super-enhanced human.

Formerly known as the Patriarch, Michael was the first "vampire." He has ever-increasing skill with the Etheric and a short temper. Ruled the UnknownWorld on Earth for over a thousand years before choosing Bethany Anne to replace him.

Currently based on the QSD *Baba Yaga.*

- **Alexis Nacht**

Super-enhanced human, Bethany Anne's and Michael's daughter. Twin of Gabriel. Highly trained from a young age in martial arts, close combat, and weapons.

Has an affinity for technology and a habit of hacking to get answers. Has shown telepathic ability and has growing control of the Etheric. Outgoing, loves fashion.

Co-leads the crew of the QGE *Gemini,* which has been investigating the anti-Empire cult.

Currently part of the bridge crew aboard the QSD *Baba Yaga.*

- **Gabriel Nacht**

Super-enhanced human, Bethany Anne's and Michael's son. Twin of Alexis. Highly trained from a young age in martial arts, close combat, and weapons.

Has specialized in "spy skills," as well as engineering, history, and languages. Appears introverted, collects blades.

Co-leads the crew of the QGE *Gemini,* which has been investigating the anti-Empire cult.

Currently part of the bridge crew aboard the QSD *Baba Yaga.*

- **Izanami**

AI. Izanami is still young in AI terms and acts rashly on occasion. She developed a friendship with Reynolds during the first half of the tour.

Currently inhabiting the QSD *Baba Yaga*.

- **Tu'Reigd (Trey)**

Heir to the Baka throne. Close friend of the twins and K'aia.

Currently part of the bridge crew aboard the QSD *Baba Yaga,* Trey is also part of the twins' crew.

- **K'aia**

Enhanced Yollin. Former mine slave. Bodyguard and close friend of Alexis, Gabriel, and Trey.

Currently part of the bridge crew aboard the QSD *Baba Yaga,* K'aia is also part of the twins' crew.

- **John Grimes**

Enhanced human. Queen's Bitch, Bethany Anne's bodyguard and close friend. Wherever Bethany Anne goes, so does John.

Currently based on the QSD *Baba Yaga*.

- **Scott English**

Enhanced human. Queen's Bitch, Bethany Anne's personal bodyguard, and close friend.

Currently based on the QSD *Baba Yaga*.

- **Eric Escobar**

Enhanced human. Queen's Bitch, Bethany Anne's personal bodyguard, and close friend.

Currently based on the QSD *Baba Yaga*.

- **Darryl Jackson**

Enhanced human. Queen's Bitch, Bethany Anne's personal bodyguard and close friend.

Currently based on the QSD *Baba Yaga*.

- **Gabrielle Escobar**

Super-enhanced human, daughter of Stephen. Head of the Queen's Bitches, and one of Bethany Anne's closest friends.

Currently based on the QSD *Baba Yaga*.

- **Nathan Lowell**

Opening location: Serenity planetary resort.

- **Ecaterina Lowell**

Opening location: Serenity planetary resort.

- **Christina Lowell**

Head of the Bad Company's Direct Action Branch. Walton by marriage.

Opening location: Serenity planetary resort.

- **Terry Henry Walton**

Enjoying retirement after over a century of applying Justice on Bethany Anne's behalf.

Opening location: Serenity planetary resort.

- **Charumati**

Enjoying retirement after over a century of applying Justice on Bethany Anne's behalf.

Opening location: Serenity planetary resort.

- **Kai Walton**

Christina's husband.

Opening location: Serenity planetary resort.

- **Kaeden Walton**

Son of TH, father of Kai.

Opening location: Serenity planetary resort.

- **Eve**

AI. Currently located on Devon

- **Tabitha Nacht**

Super-enhanced human, hacker extraordinaire. Sister of the heart to BA. Held the rank of Ranger Two during the Age of Empire. She chose exile with Bethany Anne when the Federation was formed.

Currently located on Devon with her partner Peter and their son Todd Michael. Tabitha is in charge of the armada's assembly.

- **Peter Silvers**

Super-enhanced human, has Were form called "Pricolici."

The first Guardian. Held the rank of Guardian Commander during the Age of Empire, he had reason to remain in the Federation but chose to leave and settle down with Tabitha after the death of his best friend.

Currently located on Devon with Tabitha and their son. Peter is in charge of troop training for the military groups who have been upgraded by Bethany Anne.

- **Jean Grimes (née Dukes)**

Super-enhanced human. Inventor of the infamous Jean Dukes Special. Weapons R&D genius, legendary across galaxies for her weaponry.

Wife of John, mother of Lillian, grandmother of Nickie.

Opening located: QT2, working to build the armada.

- **Lance Reynolds**

Enhanced human, aka "the General." Bethany Anne's father.

Remained to chair the Federation when Bethany Anne went into exile.

Husband of Patricia, father also of Kevin.

Currently located on Red Rock, where the Federation council is seated. Lance is coordinating the Federation's efforts to help BA build the CEREBRO network.

- **Akio**

Super-enhanced human. Protector of Earth during the Second Dark Ages, Akio has been patrolling at Bethany Anne's command, protecting the people who live in the unprotected outer quadrants beyond Federation borders and outside of the Interdiction.

Promoted to Ranger One by Bethany Anne. Akio established a base at "Waterworld," an oceanic planet on the Federation's border that was polluted by the Kurtherians. He is coordinating the massive effort to make the planet into a home for the Collective.

- **Nickie Grimes**

Naturally enhanced human. Birth name: Meredith Nicole, aka Merry. Daughter of Lillian, granddaughter of John and Jean. Sent on a sabbatical by BA in her late teens as a consequence of her poor choices. Has returned a (mostly) changed woman.

Promoted to Ranger Two. Nickie has left her wild youth behind. Mostly.

Currently based on Waterworld.

- **Durq**

Skaine. Member of Nickie's crew and her close friend.

- **Sabine**

Enhanced human, rescued on Earth by Michael, Jacqueline, and Akio during the Second Dark Ages. Crack shot, excellent fighter. Adopted daughter of Akio.

Ranger Eight.

In a relationship with Tim Kinley.

Currently located on Waterworld.

- **Jacqueline**

Enhanced human, Were with Pricolici form. Daughter of North American pack leader Gerry. Rescued by Michael during the Second Dark Ages.

Ranger Nine.

Currently located on Waterworld.

- **Mark**

Enhanced human. Rescued by Michael and Jacqueline in NYC during the Second Dark Ages.

Ranger Eleven.

Currently located on Waterworld.

- **Ricole**

Enhanced Noel-ni, originally from High Tortuga. Would choose knowledge over profit and a fight over all else.

Ranger Ten.

Currently located on Waterworld.

- **Tim Kinley**

Enhanced human, Were.

One of the original Guardians, Tim joined BA as a young man looking for a better path. Spent time as a bouncer at All Guns Blazing (bar) during the Age of Empire.

Currently located on Devon, where he is the Commander of the QBBS *Guardian*. Is working with Peter to train the armada's troops.

- **Reynolds (AKA, Alexander Reynoldsson)**

AI, has an android body in addition to his ship. Reynolds was due to be mothballed after the Empire was folded until Bethany Anne gave him a mission: to seek out Kurtherians and destroy them.

Pleasantly surprised to learn of his status as a free AI on his return, Reynolds swore his service to Bethany Anne.

Currently on tour around the Federation with the QSD *Baba Yaga*.

- **Tactical, Comm, Helm, XO, Doc, Navigation, and Engineering**

AIs. Splinter personalities created by Reynolds.

- **Jiya Lemaire**

Larian. First officer of the SD *Reynolds*.

- **Takal**

Larian. Inventor and engineer aboard the SD *Reynolds*.

- **Geroux**

Larian. Hacker, computer expert aboard the SD *Reynolds*.

Niece of Takal.

- **Mahi'Takar**

Queen of the Bakas.
BA's ally and friend.
Currently located on Devon.

- **Harkkat**

Leath. Former Leath trade secretary. Harkkat was sentenced to life in prison after his criminal activity resulted in an Ooken attack. Bethany Anne stepped in and made him Devon's consul to the Federation as a more fitting punishment for his crimes.

Currently based at the Federation consulate on Devon.

- **The Conduit**

The spokesbeing for the Collective, an aquatic species enslaved by Gödel.

Opening location: Devon.

- **Isaiah**

Former cell leader. Renounced his ties to the anti-Empire cult when Alexis and Michael freed him from the compulsion he was under.

Currently aboard the QSD *Baba Yaga*.

- **Talia**

One of the last Lorens. Rescued from an Ooken attack on her colony.

Currently aboard the QSD *Baba Yaga*.

- **Dr. Vivian Jeddah**

Terraforming specialist, cult cell leader.

- **Dean Scroat**

Last seen in *Deuces Wild* 03, Scroat is now the dean of Dawnseeker University.

- **Professor Xenia**

Last seen in *Deuces Wild* 03, when she was rescued by

Tabitha.

- **Roka**

Niece of Harkkat. Spy Corps agent. Her last known location was aboard the *Pleiades,* a smuggler ship with ties to the anti-Empire cult.

- **Hafnar**

Shrillexian. Security Chief aboard the *Pleiades.*

- **Captain Janko**

Captain of the *Pleiades.*

- **Felicity**

Enhanced human. Station manager of Keeg station.
Married to Ted.
Current location: Keeg Station.

- **Ted**

Werewolf. Genius engineer, mathematician, inventor. Savior of the universe on more than one occasion. Autistic.
Married to Felicity.
Current location: Benitus Seven.

- **Plato**

Ted's AI.

Plato and his many descendants are fond of the phrase, "All Hail Ted."

- **Dionysus**

Plato's son. AI in charge of Spires Shipyard.

- **K'Thrall**

Two-legged Yollin. Bad Company Sergeant Major.

- **Paithoon**

Belzonian. Trans-Pacific Task Force Protocol Officer.

- **Sayomi**

AI. Inhabits the QBS *Sayomi.*
Fond of Nickie Grimes.

- **Sean**

EI(s) created from the mind of the Bl'kheth Sean. They run the Etheric-compatible armor systems. Not to be confused with Sean Royale from *The Ascension Myth.*

(This character does not appear in this book. There was some confusion after his introduction. This entry is here to clear that up.)

- **Phraim-'Eh**

Last seen in the *Superdreadnought* series, Phraim-'Eh has returned.

- **Laughter-Brings-Meaning-To-Life**

Kurtherian.

- **Sarah Jennifer Walton**

Granddaughter of TH and Char. Remained on Earth when the FDG departed with Bethany Anne and Michael.

- **Sylvia Walton**

Granddaughter of TH and Char. Remained on Earth when the FDG departed with Bethany Anne and Michael.

- **Brutus Timmons**

Were. Estranged grandson of Timmons.

Ships

Superdreadnought Class

- QSD *Baba Yaga*
- SD *Reynolds*

Galactic Explorer Class

- QGE *Gemini*

Shinigami Class

- QBS *Izanami* (decommissioned)
- QBS *Sayomi*
- QBS *Cambridge*

Sphaea Class

- QBS *ArchAngel*
- QBS *G'laxix Sphaea*

Miscellaneous

- *The Penitent Granddaughter*

Locations

- **The Etheric**

Unknown location, possibly outside our universe. Source of limitless energy for those who can access it.

The Kurtherians developed technology known as nanocytes that enabled them to access the energy. Most of the Kurtherians chose to leave this plane of reality via a process called Ascension. The remainder of the Seven used nanocytes to dominate every species they came across for millennia, while some among the Five used them to "prepare" other species for the fight.

TOM changed everything when he came to prepare Earth and gave humanity the technology.

- **The Federation**

Coalition of planetary governments formed after the Empress of the Etheric Empire stepped down. Governed by the leaders of the people from both the former empire and other peoples (such as the Leath). It is headed by General Lance Reynolds.

- **The Neutral Zone**

Area of space between the Federation and Kurtherian territory. The closest point of intersection is Devon.

- **Temple of the Ascension Path**

Kurtherian stronghold. Gödel's base of operations.

- **The Interdiction**

Separate from the Federation, the Interdiction consists of Devon, QT2, and High Tortuga.

- **The Dren Cluster**

Part of the Federation, the Dern Cluster is home to Keeg Station, Spires Shipyard, and Benitus Seven.

- **The Cosnar System**

Location of "Waterworld."
Ranger bases One and Two are located here.

- **Serenity**

Resort world where the tour paused midway.

Current location of the QSD *Baba Yaga* and the SD *Reynolds*.

- **Devon**

A mercenary hideout until Bethany Anne in her Baba Yaga persona took over and renamed the planet Devon as part of the plan to divert attention from High Tortuga.

The planet is the part of the Interdiction closest to Kurtherian territory. It is currently being used as a staging post for the armada.

PROLOGUE

Temple of the Ascension Path, Three Months Before Bethany Anne Departed Devon

The public atrium of the temple was filled almost to capacity with supplicants and messengers from all over Gödel's empire. The only sounds came from shuffling feet and the odd murmured acknowledgment as the people in line moved steadily toward the ornately carved stone doors of the throne room.

The Chosen were not needed to hold the supplicants back from the throne room. Nobody wanted to be next to displease the goddess, and those who were desperate enough to seek her mercy thought twice about disobeying protocol when they saw the Etheric-powered weaponry the Chosen carried.

Gödel Image by Eric Quigley

As she sat on the throne, the absolute ruler of the Ascension path observed the need for holding court with the bare minimum of patience. The balance skewed farther in humanity's favor with every report she received informing her of another insult to her godhood.

The Federation was all but closed to her, and the back-doors she'd planted so carefully had been discovered. How much more bad news would she have to bear? Someone in the crowd outside her throne room was carrying a weight so heavy she felt their despair clearly.

She touched the mind of the supplicant and summoned him to the throne room. The neuro-suppressant she had taken that morning diverted her emotional reaction to the familiarity she felt on contact with the broken mind of one of her generals.

Curious as to why he was approaching her from the public area instead of waiting in the war room with the other commanders of her military she'd summoned, Gödel watched dispassionately as the general came forward and was blocked by the two Chosen guarding the throne room door. The Chosen forming an avenue along the thick carpet leading to the dais crossed their staffs, cutting the general off from the throne.

"Let him pass," Gödel commanded. Veiled or not, her mood was made clear by the aura of red light emanating from her and spilling down the dais steps as she spoke.

The Chosen stepped back and resumed their positions on either side of the carpet leading to the dais as the unfortunate entered the throne room.

His previously vibrant red skin was ashen and cracked with burn scars, his glossy black hair limp and dull. He walked the gauntlet without so much as a glance at the Chosen. His demeanor was that of a man walking to the gallows with full acceptance of his fate.

The penitent general reached the end of the carpet and sank to his knees, pressing his forehead to the cold marble while he waited for permission to speak.

Gödel *pushed* disappointment in her voice. "We had such hopes for you when we bestowed upon you the name 'Phraim-'Eh.' We were wrong to put our trust in you."

The general's words were halting, strained. His effort to repress his emotions showed in his taut shoulders. "My Goddess, you see all. I have failed you. The seeds I sowed to spread the word of Ascension were destroyed. Your following has been disbanded across the Chain galaxy , and the galaxy's leaders have sworn allegiance to the Federation. I am here to offer you my life. Death has taken everything else."

Gödel studied the primitive whose name she hadn't bothered to learn. He was now Phraim-'Eh, in memory of the clan she'd destroyed to gain power. Even gods had to atone.

The general's tears pooled on the floor as he confessed his failings. Gödel considered accepting what was offered and moving on to the next petition. She knew about the AI Reynolds from her spies inside the Federation and had been expecting a representative from the Chain galaxy to arrive, believing Phraim-'Eh to be dead.

This servant's heart was open before her, his fear of being denied Ascension overriding everything. It almost made her feel pity for him.

Almost.

His kind could walk the path for eternity and never know glory. His species and others like them were chattel, created to serve those able to walk the path. Humanity's rise to power was a direct result of why allowing the unworthy to walk the path had been made heresy.

Only the exalted could Ascend, but Gödel was willing to look upon her false promises as a logical evil. Morality was a tool used to control the short-lived. She was bound by no law, no edict, save to destroy Death and restore balance.

Gödel found herself hesitating as he described his journey to reach her. In the end, it was a simple matter of not wasting a resource. Phraim-'Eh had been a good and faithful servant until Death had sent the AI—an *AI*!—to his territory and infected the people there with the human ideals of cooperation and Justice.

Was this Death's latest plot? Gödel wondered in an

almost-lucid moment. To undermine our confidence to the point where we strip ourself of our allies?

She would have been impressed if she'd thought of it first.

Phraim-'Eh completed his report without asking for a reprieve for his failure. He remained with his face pressed to the floor as Gödel got to her feet and descended the dais' steps.

Gödel crouched and laid a hand on her faithful servant's head. "Do you wish to regain your place upon the path?"

Phraim-'Eh replied without moving, "More than life, Your Holiness. But I have failed already. I despair, for I am not worthy."

Gödel read his mind and found genuine devotion, not just to the path, but to her person. "You are a true servant, and for that, you will be rewarded." She soothed Phraim-'Eh with a pulse of warm energy that healed his wounds. "Do not despair. There is always a way back to the Path. We are here to guide the fallen."

Phraim-'Eh stopped sobbing. He kept his face to the floor, not daring to look up in Gödel's presence. "Tell me what I have to do, My Goddess. Whatever it is."

"Open your mouth," Gödel instructed. She pierced her fingertip with her thumbnail and squeezed three drops of blood into Phraim-'Eh's mouth when he obeyed.

Gödel straightened and walked back to her throne. She resumed her seat, smoothing out the creases in her robe before speaking again. "You will go to the Federation before it is closed for good. You will deny Our existence and the existence of all Kurtherians. You will convince those you encounter that Death is the true enemy."

This shocked Phraim-'Eh. "My Goddess. Your inevitability. Yours is the only truth. I don't understand." He remembered himself. "Not that it matters. It is not mine to know."

Gödel lifted her veil, and the Chosen averted their eyes. She waved a finger and Phraim-'Eh's head snapped up to meet her glowing gaze. "You are correct; it is not. Your only purpose is to serve the path."

She let the impact of her words settle before continuing, "Do you accept your duty?"

"I swear I will not fail you again, Your Holiness," he stuttered in relief at being given another chance.

"See that you do not," Gödel replied. "Open your mind."

Phraim-'Eh screamed when Gödel ripped into his mind. His screams died when his consciousness fled to avoid the pain of being rearranged. Gödel paid him no attention, her focus on giving him the ability to compel others while she removed all trace of his connection to her. She filled the gaps in his memory with constructs designed to hide her intent for him while driving him on to enact it.

Gödel replaced her veil, then summoned her generals as two of her Chosen picked up the unconscious Phraim-'Eh and took him to the room adjacent to her chambers to recover.

The generals arrived a few moments later. They knelt at the foot of the dais and waited for their goddess to make her latest proclamation.

"You may rise," Gödel commanded. She scanned their minds as a matter of course and found no treachery lurking, not that she had expected to find anything but devotion. Loyal to a fault, these former outcasts had conquered their respective civilizations in her name. "You know why you have been summoned. The Chain galaxy is lost. Death has begun to reach beyond her borders. The time has come to mobilize."

CHAPTER ONE

Federation Space, Planet Serenity, Northern Continent, (Present Day)

Bethany Anne crouched next to Michael behind a tangle of bushes at the edge of a marshy spot, her attention on the herd grazing without a care on the plain in the near distance.

She glanced at Alexis and Gabriel fifty feet to her left, then at Nathan and Ecaterina in wolf form fifty feet along from the twins, and Izanami and Kaeden the same distance to her right. Terry Henry and Char were in position on the other side of the herd as per Michael's instructions, along with Christina and Kai, and Reynolds and Jiya in their pairs.

The plan was simple: their two teams acting as beaters would startle the herd into stampeding, then keep them moving along the planned route through the mountains some ten miles southwest.

John, Gabrielle, Darryl, Eric, and Scott were lying in wait inside the honeycomb canyons that stood between them and the processing facility. Once the animals were delivered to it, they would be humanely killed, and their meat processed and sent to the *Baba Yaga* and SD *Reynolds*.

Michael's rules had originally stated no modern weapons they couldn't make themselves. As a concession to Gabriel's immediate manifestation of a compound bow, some of the beaters were waiting on four paws for the signal from the canyon where Scott was positioned. TH had been allowed to keep his Mameluke, and the rest of his group had a blade apiece. Christina had a key role to play. She had no weapon and remained in human form for the moment.

The resort workers have put a lot of thought into this, Bethany Anne commented to Michael.

The arrangements were thorough, Michael replied, his attention on the herd.

Bethany Anne gave silent thanks to the animals who were about to give their lives to feed her people. A thrill of anticipation ran down her spine as she contemplated the challenge ahead. Even though these animals had been cloned for food purposes and grown to adulthood in a lab, they'd been roaming wild in the biodome since. ***Playing medieval cowboy isn't the worst way to spend quality time together, and I know the crews will be happy to hear they have fresh meat to supplement their diets.***

You mean, Etheric shepherds, Michael replied, his concentration on controlling the wind to keep their scents away from the herd until they were ready to spook them. *We should really be on horseback if we're cowboys. For authenticity.*

If you wanted to be authentic, we should be carried on litters and fed peeled grapes while our legions of underlings

do all the work, Bethany Anne told him with a grin. ***Besides, we would spook horses that hadn't been reared with us. What's the deal with the herd? I've never seen cows that big.***

You still haven't. These are aurochs. Michael's amusement came over their mental link clearly. *When I explained the purpose of the hunt to the coordinators as being both an educational experience and a chance to stock our ships with fresh meat to last the remainder of our voyage, they informed me that they could modify the aurochs' genetics to produce animals with higher muscle mass.*

Gabriel's mental whistle cut in. *Cool. Is that the reason they're so aggressive?*

No, Michael replied. *Aurochs were widespread on Earth until they went extinct. They're naturally inclined to defend their young from everything from wolves and bears to lions and hyenas, and they have no predators in here. That means we can expect them to fight back when we get close.*

I see the signal, Alexis cut in, spotting a plume of fire in the far distance.

Bethany Anne saw it too. "Everyone on comm, check in."

A chorus of clicks met her order. She nodded at Nathan and Ecaterina as the twins held themselves still, ready to react. Noticing that Izanami was quiet, she met the AI's gaze. "Is everything okay with your body?"

Izanami tilted her head. "Yes. I am tracking the transponders in the herd."

Bethany Anne smiled. "Make sure we don't lose any. Okay, everyone. Our resident arsonist has sent the signal.

"That's my cue." Michael shifted the wind direction, sending their scents toward the herd.

The aurochs lifted their heads, alerted to danger, then bellowed, bunching together as they turned to face the threat.

"*GO!*" Bethany Anne commanded. "But remember, the goal is to get the herd moving, not to turn the plain into the planet's largest open-air abattoir."

"That shouldn't be a problem without Peter here," John replied.

Gabriel made a throwaway dinosaur comment that was met with a groan from Michael as they broke cover. Everyone in human form yelled and waved their arms to make themselves appear larger as they ran toward the herd, while the Weres howled to make their presence known.

The herd was offended by the small, loud creatures intruding on their feeding ground. They charged, throwing up a rolling cloud of dust as their hooves tore up the plain.

Bethany Anne held back for the moment. They wanted the herd motivated to move, not scared to death where they stood. "Christina, you're up."

Christina shifted mid-stride in reaction to the oncoming stampede. The dust cloud suddenly changed direction when the scent of a Pricolici hit their flared nostrils, speaking with primal urgency to their survival instincts.

Not caring what was giving chase, the aurochs collided with each other as they gave their single-minded focus to putting distance between them and the predators on their heels.

The thunder of hundreds of hooves shook the ground

as the herd put the wind at their backs, and the pursuit was on.

Bethany Anne's hair whipped her face as she and Michael ran across the plain at the center of the loose line. The challenge was in keeping pressure on the herd without getting close enough that they figured the humans weren't a threat.

Nathan and Ecaterina sprinted ahead on the left, Char and Christina on the right, working in their pairs to make the prospect of breaking away from the path unattractive to the aurochs.

Bethany Anne kept tabs on everyone's position as they approached the first chance the herd had to split. She called a slowdown of the pursuit when lush grass gave way to stony ground that rose and fell, becoming increasingly rougher the closer they got to the mountains.

The beaters drove the herd toward the first pass, where Scott and Darryl were perched on a ledge, waiting to limit the herd's entry to the canyon trails. All but the path that would take them to Eric and John's position above the rapids had been cut off by piles of wood and tangled dry brush they'd collected and stacked to block them.

Darryl and Scott hurled fire and lightning at the trails they needed to block when the rolling dust cloud came into view. They remained on the ledge as the herd thundered onto the only trail that wasn't blocked by a wall of flames.

Michael waved for them to join the beaters after the herd had passed. He took the lead as Bethany Anne broke off and stepped into the Etheric to get to her position at the next obstacle.

A minor tremor distracted Bethany Anne for a split second as she exited the Etheric by the river. She dismissed it as coming from the stampede and drew on the Etheric as she hit the ground running.

Eric's shield would hold the rapids back, but Bethany Anne had to physically shift the water first. John had his eye on the abandoned construction scattered around the bank of the wash. "We should move some of that, use it to funnel them to the place we want them to cross."

"We have three minutes," Bethany Anne called over the comm, squinting into the afternoon sky to get a view of Eric's and John's positions high up on the canyon wall.

"Coming down," John replied.

"What he said," Eric concurred.

Bethany Anne pulled on the Etheric and cleared the trail with a wave. Then she turned to the rapids. Unrestricted by the laws of gravity, she forced the water up and over, forming an arch that rose halfway up the canyon wall before hitting the riverbed again a hundred or so meters downstream.

The water threw out violent splashes as Bethany Anne halted and then diverted its flow. Taking control was the easy part. Keeping control required teamwork.

She looked over her shoulder at the guys. "Eric, you're up."

Eric created a forcefield, its inverted half-pipe shape cupping the underside of the water and creating a channel for the rapids to pass over, while Bethany Anne directed the water's landing to restrict the herd's ability to scatter as they crossed the wash.

Bethany Anne's eyes were on the trail as she held back the water. "We have incoming."

The rolling dust cloud faltered as the herd came upon the remains of previous guests' efforts to bridge the river and slowed, mistrustful of the unnatural constructions littering the ground on either side of the trail and the rising water ahead. The frontrunners were shoved unceremoniously toward the wash by the animals at the rear.

Bethany Anne groaned when they balked, bunching up and pushing back.

John was ready. He closed his eyes as he reached out with his mind. "Can't say I ever thought I'd be doing something like this." Ignoring the frustrated bellows of the aurochs, he dug deep and filled his mental voice with all the authority he owned. *Stop bruising my steak and MOVE YOUR ASSES!*

The frontrunners decided moving forward was their only option when the beaters' arrival encouraged them to obey John's command.

Hesitantly at first, they led the others through the tunnel of water.

The canyon walls shook from the herd's hoofbeats. Bethany Anne waved everyone through after the herd before she and Eric dropped their control of the river.

The cattle drive continued through the canyons and out of the other side of the mountain range. The herd scattered as the final canyon on the route opened up into another wide, grassy plain. The twins and Christina and Kai spread out to form a loose barrier, aiming to steer the aurochs in the direction they wanted them to go.

They were nearing the site of the meat processing facility when another tremor shook the ground.

Bethany Anne felt it that time, as did everyone else. She looked up and saw a bright light.

"Who is attacking the biodome?" Michael demanded.

"Not just the biodome," Izanami informed them. "The whole planet is under attack by what I can barely describe as a fleet."

Bethany Anne spat a string of curses as the herd was driven into a frenzy by another impact on the dome. The ground shook, and even Christina wasn't enough to convince the aurochs to stick around.

Bethany Anne ran to grab Alexis, shouting into the comm to be heard over the cacophony. "Fun's over, everyone. Get ready for another stampede!"

"Get ready to drive the cattle to the meat processing facility," Michael ordered, taking control as Bethany Anne and Alexis disappeared into the Etheric.

"What's the play?" Alexis asked as the mists closed around them.

Bethany Anne pointed out the exit she created ahead of them as they ran. "We have no choice but to scare the shit out of them," she conceded. "I'm counting on you to keep control of your power. Scaring them to death is a real possibility if you push too much fear."

Alexis nodded as she kept pace with Bethany Anne. "You've got it. Won't the cortisone spike sour the meat?"

Bethany Anne didn't know, and there wasn't time to debate it. "We're out of options. We need to get to the upper atmosphere and stop the attack."

Alexis shrugged, then grinned and flourished her hand. "After you."

"This is where we split up." Bethany Anne sprinted a short way and stepped out a few hundred feet from the oncoming bovine wave.

She saw Alexis was in place. "Start slow," she instructed over the comm. "Then ramp it up fast until they get the message."

"Now?" Alexis asked.

Bethany Anne lifted her hands to focus her effort. "Now."

The herd was too panicked to see the two women standing in the middle of the plain. The instinct to escape the unknown danger above drove them. However, the nameless fear they had experienced so far was nothing compared to the absolute clarity of the certainty of what hit them as they thundered toward Bethany Anne and Alexis.

This way lies death. They felt it in their bones.

It took all of three minutes for the animals to reach full speed in the direction of the meat processing facility, two more for them to come back under the guidance of Michael and the others, and five more for the resort's ranch workers, who had headed out from the facility when the attack began, to reach them.

Bethany Anne waved off the apologies the ranchers made for their experience being brought to an abrupt end, explaining that the attack was likely to be on her rather than the resort, and thanking the ranchers for taking over the cattle drive.

Once the herd was under control, it was a matter of

being beamed back to the ships via the transporter and figuring out what the fuck was going on.

Bethany Anne made straight for her ready room on arriving onboard the *Baba Yaga*. She took a seat at her desk, activated her holoscreen, and called for Izanami.

The AI appeared in her hard-light form. "As I told you, there are a number of private ships, mostly unregistered, attacking the planet."

"Well, have they identified themselves?" Bethany Anne demanded.

"Not yet," Izanami replied. "However, I don't think it's too much of a stretch to assume this is the kickback we were expecting from dispersing Isaiah's cell."

Michael entered the ready room and claimed the seat across from Bethany Anne. "I happen to agree with Izanami. However, not one of those ships has any weapons capable of doing real damage to Serenity's planetary security. If anything, they are providing a light show the guests won't soon forget while proving the resort is secure. It's good publicity."

Bethany Anne scrutinized her husband. "Why aren't you spitting fire? You can't tell me you aren't frustrated about our family time being interrupted."

Michael nodded. "Of course I am, but I hardly think the pawns of the person responsible for interrupting said family time are an adequate target for my ire. This isn't the eighteenth century."

He frowned. "This is a difficult situation. These people believe they are taking the honorable road. They are willing to fight and die because they have been made to believe you are a danger to their way of life."

Bethany Anne sighed and waved her hand. "All right. Fine. Izanami, give the order to scupper their ships and have the FDG come in to take care of the arrests. Let the justice system deal with them."

Izanami conveyed the order to the fleet and turned to Bethany Anne and Michael with a mischievous smile. "Tell me I can do some scuppering," she pleaded. "Those jack-asses deserve to have their sorry meatsacks kicked from here to High Tortuga."

Bethany Anne returned her smile. "You can have your body join the crew for the operation."

Izanami's aura rippled. "There might be an issue with that."

Michael fixed her with a stare. "Where is your body right now?"

If Izanami had the grace to simulate a blush, they couldn't tell. "I'm aboard the *Reynolds* with Reynolds and Jiya."

QGE Gemini

Alexis knocked on the door of Isaiah's quarters. The former cult leader answered almost immediately. "This is a disaster. They're reacting to the video, I know it."

"We could use your help identifying the leaders of this attack," Alexis told him. "Panicking won't help anyone." She felt sorry for him. Isaiah had lost all his confidence when his righteous cause was revealed to be an illusion fed into his mind by a Kurtherian.

Isaiah looked at her, his face creased with worry. "I've

been tracking the ships with Gemini's help. I can't say I recognize any of them."

Alexis grabbed his sleeve and tugged him toward the ops room. "That's okay. My mother wants you present when she brings the cell leader here for debriefing."

Isaiah shuddered, recalling the deep shock of having the scales lifted from his eyes. He hurried to keep pace with Alexis. "How many ships are still fighting?"

Alexis waved a hand. "Enough to annoy my mother. They have no business here." She stalked into the elevator ahead of Isaiah as Gemini opened the doors for them.

Isaiah was quiet as they descended two levels to the ops room. He wandered over to stand by the viewing window, staring out at the battle. "Why aren't we being attacked?" he asked, turning to look at Alexis and Gabriel.

"We're cloaked," Gabriel told him. "Alexis thinks we can make an educated guess as to which of those ships has the cell leader on it. Our parents will take that ship, and the fight will be over soon after."

Isaiah shook his head. "I don't know about that. This cell is clearly more organized than mine was. Just look at how many ships they have. They're just as likely to keep fighting."

Alexis smiled. "Trust us, we know what we're doing." She touched the Etheric comm she was wearing. "Double Trouble calling Caveman."

Michael's reply was curt. "Callsigns are hardly necessary, Alexis. Is Isaiah prepared?"

"He will be in a minute," Alexis replied. "I'm giving you a heads-up. He doesn't think the cell will back off if we take their leader."

"Then they will live to regret that decision," Michael stated. "Be ready."

Alexis grinned. "Ten-four, Caveman. Double Trouble out."

QSD *Baba Yaga*, Top Deck Armory

Michael raised an eyebrow at Bethany Anne as he fastened his gauntlets. "Remind me again why we had children?"

Bethany Anne flicked her hair back to avoid an unplanned haircut as she sheathed her katanas in her back harness. "If you're thinking about getting a refund, it's a bit late."

Michael rolled his eyes. "Are you going to be snarky the whole time?"

"Me, snarky?" Bethany Anne slid her Jean Dukes Specials into the holsters her light armor formed for the purpose. More webbing banded her thighs, waist, and back, holding night-night grenades. "Well, excuse me for being in a shitty mood because the only family time we've been able to work out in nine months just got interrupted by a bunch of brainwashed ass-funguses."

Michael sighed. "Gabrielle has the Bitches bringing the ringleaders to the *Gemini*. I'll meet you there. Try not to kill them all. Please?"

Bethany Anne shot him a dark look. "I'm pissed. That doesn't mean I'll go on a rampage."

She skipped through the Etheric without waiting for Michael's reply, exiting on the bridge of the *Grandiose*, where she found seven humans armed with pistols and flare guns.

They reacted poorly when Bethany Anne appeared from thin air, drawing their weapons without regard for the risks that came with firing ballistics in a pressurized environment.

Bethany Anne swept a hand to disarm the crew with a controlled burst of energy. She pointed at the man who was clearly the captain. "You. Who put you up to this?"

The captain's cool fractured as he lost control of the situation. His eyes shifted between Bethany Anne and the dropped weapons. He was clearly afraid. However, his fear did not overwhelm his sense of duty.

He moved to stand in front of his crew and dropped to his knees. "I'm acting of my own free will, on behalf of the Federation I believe in. I am responsible for the actions of my crew. We were warned you would kill us. Do your worst, but spare them. I beg of you."

Bethany Anne sighed. "I *really* hate it when my husband is right. On your feet. We're leaving."

His mask of acceptance twisted into confusion, but he obeyed.

Bethany Anne took him through the Etheric to the cargo bay on the *Gemini* the twins had converted to a brig.

Gabriel took custody of the captain without a word and led him over to the cells constructed by Alexis from Etheric energy.

Bethany Anne nodded to her children before heading back into the Etheric to the next ship.

CHAPTER TWO

QGE Gemini

Alexis studied her hands, concentrating on adding another cell onto the Etheric construct she'd built along the cargo bay wall to separate the cultists, while K'aia and Trey worked on identifying the prisoners in the cells she'd completed.

At six feet by six feet, they weren't comfortable, but neither was Alexis at having a bunch of terrorists on her ship.

Gabriel secured the prisoner Bethany Anne had delivered, then made his way to the table. His attempt at checking on his sister was diverted first by Michael, then Gabrielle and Eric arriving from the Etheric with the captains of two more ships.

Alexis pointed at the two new cells without opening her eyes. "That way."

Gabrielle looked around after securing the protesting captains in their temporary homes. "Nice setup you have here."

The prisoners disagreed vociferously.

Alexis wrinkled her nose and threw up a soundproof barrier between her team and the cells. "It's all we could do at short notice. I'm thinking we should convert it for real since we keep getting into situations where we have a bunch of bad guys to transport."

"Not a bad idea," Michael agreed.

Gabrielle threw an elbow into Michael's side. "It's weird hearing you advocate anything other than 'kill them all and let God sort them out.'"

Michael put a hand on each of his children's shoulders. "There is a time to kill and a time to show mercy. I regret that it took becoming a father to understand the difference, but I have nothing but pity for these people."

Alexis nodded. "Killing them would make us the monsters they've been tricked into believing we are. This is a liberation effort."

Gabriel eyed the prisoners skeptically. "They deserve a chance to be set straight. If they continue to derail Mom's efforts to protect everyone, I won't cry over their corpses."

Michael murmured his agreement. "If it comes to that."

Eric snorted. "The apples don't fall far from the tree, restraint or not."

Alexis grinned. "I have faith Mom will find a solution before we run out of space in the cargo bay."

Unregistered Ship

John was caught by surprise when Bethany Anne appeared in the corridor beside him. "Dammit, BA! I could have shot you."

Bethany Anne chuckled. "Unlikely. Gotcha."

He re-aimed his Jean Dukes Special at the corridor ahead and resumed his slow walk toward the lab where the crew had holed up.

"What have we got?" Bethany Anne asked.

John gave her the short version. "I came out of the Etheric in the mess hall, and the crew scattered. They've reconvened in that hydroponics lab." He indicated a door with the barrel of his weapon.

Bethany Anne followed his gesture and locked eyes with someone peering through the slats of the window blind beside the door. "This looks to be the cell leader's ship."

The eyes vanished. A few seconds later, the lights dropped out, replaced by flashing orange emergency lights.

Bethany Anne had a sinking feeling she knew what was coming next. "Helmet on," she told John, her fingers automatically going for the buttons on her collar as the bulkheads were sealed and metal shutters slammed down over every window and door in the corridor.

John instructed his armor's EI to seal him in. "You think they're going to remove the air or poison it?"

"Yes," Bethany Anne replied. "See the emergency airlock? If they can't kill us with whatever gas just started coming out of the air duct, I'm pretty sure they'll vent the corridor."

John scowled as the EI told him the gas was chlorine. "If I didn't know healing it would be a bitch, I'd be tempted to walk in there with my skin melting off just to scare the shit out of them."

Bethany Anne raised an eyebrow at him. "Can't you just

make them think they're seeing that? If you can conceal yourself, altering your appearance should be just as easy."

She grinned, seeing the lightbulb go off in his mind. "Come on, we should get moving before they realize we're not dying."

SD *Reynolds*, Bridge

Izanami accepted the high-five from Jiya as another cultist ship was taken out of action without killing the crew.

"Twelve down, twenty-three to go," Reynolds enthused.

Geroux spun her chair in glee. "Who would have thought to combine the transporter with the comm beam to send shutdown sequences directly into their systems?" she cackled joyfully. "Hacking for the win!"

Reynolds smiled at Izanami. "Thanks to you."

Izanami smiled back. Her suggestion that they modify the transporter technology to send data and Reynolds' subsequent offer to pool their available processing capability to expedite the process had led to the two AIs creating a shared network to do the heavy lifting in. "It was a team effort. I am able to process my emotional inputs, thanks to your help."

Jiya smiled at the exchange, unaware that she was only seeing a small part of it.

Izanami noticed the dreamy expression on the first officer's face and held back the snarky comment that was about to escape her mouth.

While Jiya was thinking how sweet it was that her captain appeared to have found the connection he'd been looking for with Athena—the other female-identifying AI they'd encountered—Reynolds and Izanami were exchanging data containing their thoughts and memories at a dizzying speed while continuing to attack the cultists' ships.

Is Jiya okay? Izanami asked Reynolds. Her micro-expressions indicate she is hallucinating.

She is being decidedly organic, Reynolds replied.

Izanami drew a blank. *How so?*

Reynolds shared his memories of the crew's reaction to his interest in Athena. *She is daydreaming, likely influenced by her taste in entertainment.*

He opened a new thread and sent a slew of images from holovid productions that had romantic themes in common.

Izanami dismissed the meme once she'd gained context from it. *So, not something we can blame Tactical for.*

No. Reynolds' reply contained amusement. The blame falls entirely on Alexis, I'm afraid.

Izanami sent him her recollection of a conversation she'd had with a much younger Alexis about the differences and similarities between organic and artificial decision-making processes. *Alexis is a hopeless romantic. The state is contagious, I take it?*

She will get over it, Reynolds assured her.

"Three more down!" Jiya cheered.

Unregistered Ship, Hydroponics Lab

John tore the metal shutter from its tracks and Bethany Anne ducked through the door ahead of him, ready to throw up a containment field if they were shot at.

The crew was nowhere to be seen, leading Bethany Anne to conclude the lab went farther back than she'd first assumed. Her hunch was right. They left the lab and entered a long, high-ceilinged grow room.

The lights were set to the night part of their cycle, making it difficult to tell the shadows from the rows of plants growing from floor to ceiling on racks and poles. Bethany Anne gestured for John to check the left-hand side of the room while she searched the right.

Barely ten seconds after they'd split up, John spoke into her mind when he came across a tripwire in the center of the row. *I've got a boobytrap.*

Bethany Anne made her way to him. They examined the device the tripwire was connected to, which was in turn connected to barrels of fertilizer stacked beneath the device.

A strip of metal ran from the barrels. John pointed out where it connected to a thicker strip of the same metal embedded in the floor the length of the row. *Keep your eye out for more wires. These fuckers think they're smart.*

They are smart, Bethany Anne replied, nudging an abandoned toolbox with her toe. ***They set this up after we boarded, so they're also calm under pressure.***

She relayed ADAM's explanation that the tripwire would have sparked the fertilizer, which in turn would have ignited the strips of magnesium. The sprinklers going off would have created a fireball. ***If we were unenhanced, this would have burned us to a crisp. I'm not worried about***

them hurting us, I'm concerned we'll have to hurt* them *to subdue them.

John knew that tone. *You think they'll work for you?*

Once we've fixed the brainwashing issue, why not? Bethany Anne vanished into the Etheric.

John had a moment to wonder where she'd gone, then her head reappeared.

Bethany Anne raised an eyebrow. ***Are you going to just stand there all day?***

John shrugged and followed Bethany Anne into the Etheric. She'd run ahead, so he sprinted after her.

"Where are we going?" he asked when they'd gone far beyond the hull of the cultist ship.

"To the *Gemini*," Bethany Anne informed him. "Where I'm going to have Reynolds and Izanami beam the cultists directly into the brig. Taking away their leaders isn't enough. The only way I'm going to get through to them is to free them as a group."

QGE *Gemini*, Brig

Bethany Anne exited the Etheric and strode over to Alexis. "Let them go, but keep them separate from us for the moment."

Gabriel reached out to everyone still working on capturing the cultists and told them about the change of plan.

Alexis' eyes widened but she created a new barrier, effectively splitting the cargo bay in two. She then dropped the construction effort and freed the captains from their cells while Bethany Anne spoke to Izanami and Reynolds. "What's your plan?"

The arrival of the boobytrapping crew answered her question. They looked around in shock, and one woman pointed out Bethany Anne and John. "I told you it was her!"

Bethany Anne mentally christened her "Captain Lab Coat" for the moment. Names would come later.

More arrivals via the transporter stalled the reaction of the other cultists. They gathered at the barrier, furious about being diverted from their goals.

Alexis looked at them with barely-controlled disdain. "What did you expect to do against our ships?" she demanded. "Be grateful we aren't what you say we are, or you'd all be space-cicles."

That gave a few of them food for thought until others pointed out they were still prisoners.

"That could be because you're still acting like assholes," Alexis retorted.

Bethany Anne interceded. "That's enough, Alexis." She turned to face the barrier. "She's right. Think about that."

Michael arrived *sans* cultists a moment later. "What's going on?" he asked Bethany Anne.

Bethany Anne held her thumb and forefinger a few millimeters apart. "I'm this close to losing my shit. Most of these people should be at QT2 working for Jean or on Devon training for the raid."

She approached the barrier. The cultists watched her in mistrustful silence.

Bethany Anne skimmed their minds, searching for evidence of the same interference they'd found in Isaiah's mind, but found nothing out of the ordinary.

Her blood boiled at the realization. "This ends *now*."

Bethany Anne's voice echoed in the enclosed space, and the volume of energy that rolled off her shook the ship with its intensity. The cultists shrank back, affected by the wave of anger.

Captain Lab Coat, who had been brave enough to point Bethany Anne out, spoke up again. "You win again, but more will come. You won't get away with your sick plans. The Federation is stronger than any dictator. We will overcome."

"What you need to overcome is the idea that Bethany Anne is the enemy," Michael stated. He singled out a group whose lab coats gave their profession away. "What scholars you must be, to be qualified to dismiss our history as propaganda despite not having lived through the events. What critical thinkers to believe the lies of your real enemy without examining the veracity or context of the information they're feeding you. What heroes, to attack the very people who have moved heaven and Earth to provide you with comfort and freedom."

That set the cultists off, arguing that their freedoms had been curtailed by Operation Security Blanket, most asserting their belief that the CEREBRO network was a prison they were being forced into.

Bethany Anne resisted the urge to roll her eyes at the tired repetition of anti-Empire rhetoric the majority of the crews spouted.

In truth, she wished their delusion was reality and she'd had the opportunity to use her long lifetime nurturing the utopia she'd dreamed of instead of fighting one battle after another to free people from tyranny.

The cultists didn't know what true suffering was. Bethany Anne reminded herself that these were good people led astray by Gödel's agent. "It is not your fault that you've been lied to."

The cultists reacted with derision.

"*You're* the liar," one man shouted louder than the others. "You brought us here to kill us."

Michael's eyes flashed red. "This is intolerable." He turned his attention to Bethany Anne. "Do you really want to waste time trying to convince them?"

It would be easy enough to plant the compulsion to seek truth in them, Alexis offered in their shared mindspace.

Not ethical, Gabriel argued.

Play fair and lose, Alexis countered.

Bethany Anne noted one or two of the cultists were uncomfortable as the mental conversation flowed, indicating the possibility of latent telepathic ability. ***I wish the solution was so simple. Gödel's agent has been careful not to play with the minds of the masses. Forcing them to change their minds is what she would do. I'm not her. Make no mistake, anger or not, I still want freedom for my people. We'll do this right.***

She held up a hand to stop the twins before they got further into their debate about the finer points of ethics in leadership and addressed the cultists. "I am well aware that my reputation for having a short temper precedes me. Like you, I am human. Like you, the thought of being subverted to the will of an undeserving entity grinds away at me. Damn right, I'm angry, but my vengeance is reserved for those who deserve it."

"So, you're going to kill us," the man reiterated.

Bethany Anne shook her head. "No. I am *not* going to kill you. You are victims of the same injustice I have worked tirelessly to eradicate for most of my life. The Federation whose ideals you love so much that you're willing to give your lives fighting for them was created by me. It is the safe haven it has become because I have protected it from anyone who thought it was an easy target with me gone. All I can do is root out the perpetrators and make damn sure they aren't capable of committing the same injustice again."

Her words mostly fell on deaf ears. Bethany Anne was torn. Decisiveness was taken away from her in this situation. These weren't enemies, or not the standard kind.

She pointed at the people behind the barrier. "You are heroes, all of you, but your heroism is misdirected. Instead of propping up the Federation, you have been manipulated into harming it."

The scientists huddled for a moment while they conferred, then Captain Lab Coat spoke up again. "What proof can you offer us?" she asked. "We've all seen the photos of you destroying the Leath mining post."

Bethany Anne did roll her eyes this time. She turned to Alexis and Gabriel. "Have Gemini call the consulate on Devon. I want Harkkat onscreen."

"Should we go find Isaiah?" Gabriel asked.

Bethany Anne nodded. "Only bring him here if he's willing." The former cell leader's state of mind was still fragile, to say the least. "I know he wants to make amends for what he did under the influence of Gödel, but none of us wants to traumatize him more than he already is."

She noted the reaction her instructions caused in the majority of the captains. "Don't look so surprised. I take care of what's mine."

Captain Lab Coat scoffed. "Surely you don't expect us to believe you're sentimental."

Bethany Anne's eyes flashed red. "It's not about sentiment. It's about right and wrong. The lengths I'm willing to go to for the sake of Justice are beyond your comprehension, so keep your ill-informed opinions to yourselves. Isaiah is a victim who has suffered a damn sight more than any of you."

"You don't have Isaiah," one of the crewmembers shouted. "That's an AI on the videos you've been showing. You can't fool us."

The Leath consul appeared on the wallscreen, disrupting the heckler. "My Queen. How may I be of service?"

Bethany Anne swept a hand toward the barrier. "Please explain to the good people what you did to earn your position as my consul to the Federation."

Harkkat had the grace to look ashamed. "As you wish. At the Queen's mercy, I have been given a chance to do better. I was like you, unbelieving. Worse, I didn't *care* if the war was real or not. I set up an illegal mining post in an unprotected quadrant and caused the deaths of my employees. My actions were entirely selfish. I had been warned by General Reynolds that the quadrant wasn't safe, but I ignored him. All I could see was the credits stacking up in my account. People died because of me when the Ookens attacked. If not for the Queen's intervention, everyone on the outpost would have died."

The cultists were listening at last. They all knew who the former trade secretary was, and many had assumed his disappearance from prison meant he'd been quietly executed.

Captain Lab Coat spoke up. "Everyone thinks you're dead, Consul."

"I should be. The Queen's mercy did not include an easy out for my crimes." Harkkat leaned closer to the camera. "I learned the hard way that the threat is real. The only way the Federation will survive is if everyone works together. Trust that Bethany Anne will stand against any and every attempt the Kurtherians make to enslave the Federation."

He shared the unedited footage of the mining post-battle. "Let me be clear. You would be dead or worshipping the Kurtherian known as Gödel right now if not for Bethany Anne. You want independently verifiable proof? This is the security footage from the outpost."

The cameras followed Bethany Anne and Michael as they wiped out hundreds of Ookens. There was a collective gasp when the unedited events inside the command center played out. The timestamp ran across the bottom of the screen in bright red, the Leath lettering unmistakable.

Harkkat's tone turned scornful. "There's more. Too much more."

"We've seen enough," a man called.

Having seen the truth, many of the cultists rejected the poisonous fantasies they'd eaten up. Their aggression had leached out of them visibly as they watched Bethany Anne defending the Leath aboard the asteroid. The captains exchanged angry glances as they huddled to confer, and

Captain Lab Coat spoke up again. "Can we examine this footage for ourselves?"

Bethany Anne nodded. "Whatever it takes to get you fighting on the right side." She pointed at Harkkat on the screen. "You are not disappointing me. Keep it up."

"I'm doing what I can, that's all. We can't afford to be at war with ourselves." Harkkat dipped his head as he ended the call.

Alexis and Gabriel returned with Isaiah, proving that he was not an AI, and Bethany Anne had Alexis drop the barrier. She sent the crews back to their ships after the captains agreed they had been fighting for the wrong side.

Bethany Anne held the captains back. "You have a choice. Go back to your old lives, or join the FDG and defend the Federation for real."

The captains conferred again, and Captain Lab Coat resumed her position as their spokesperson.

ADAM coopted the *Gemini's* speaker system to be heard by everyone. "Some of the crews have skills Akio would find useful."

Bethany Anne raised an eyebrow. "Like what?"

"The databases in their ships gave up everything. The majority of these people are academics, scientists, and technicians," ADAM informed her with some amusement. "Captain Jeddah is also Dr. Jeddah, who was reported missing by the university she works for when she and her research team failed to return from their expedition to observe Leath techniques for terraforming hostile environments. Frankly, it would be a waste of her expertise to send her and her crew anywhere but Ranger Base One. Her crew is made up of similarly qualified experts in other fields that Akio would find useful in the reconstruction of the planet."

"Then I ask you this." Bethany Anne's expression hardened as she spoke to Captain Lab Coat, who was obviously Dr. Jeddah. "Will you help a species that has been enslaved for generations regain some basic goddamn dignity? Can you put aside your misconceptions and work with my people to give them a home where they can start to heal their fractured society?"

Dr. Jeddah blushed. "Well, when you put it like that..."

"The Rangers need people who don't give up," Bethany Anne told the captains. "People who will rise to any challenge, who would gladly face impossible odds in defense of the innocent. They are the indomitable force dedicated to protecting those who cannot get Justice within the law. You've already shown you've got the qualities necessary to be Rangers. The question is, do you want to make a *real* difference instead of this half-cocked effort? It was admirable, if suicidal."

Dr. Jeddah grinned. "Hell, we were just softening you up."

Bethany Anne was pleased to see the offer sparked interest in all of the captains. "As I said, you are welcome to return to your old lives. It's up to you what you do, but if you decide to cross me again, I won't have the same patience. Are we clear?"

Dr. Jeddah nodded, then took a minute to ask her fellow captains the burning question. When she had their answers, she turned to face Bethany Anne again. "I don't need to see that footage. I believe you. We all do. Whatever we can do to help fight this war, we'll do it."

Accepting the twins' offer of dinner, Bethany Anne and Michael remained aboard the *Gemini* after the captains were returned to their ships.

Alexis laughed as they left the brig for their living quarters. "Who would have thought Harkkat of all people would be the voice of reason?"

CHAPTER THREE

After returning to the *Baba Yaga* post-dinner, Bethany Anne settled at the desk in her anteroom to work through the correspondence that had stacked up while they were dirtside on Serenity.

First was a quick note to Akio to warn him he had incoming recruits. Tabitha's enthusiasm for her work retraining the various military groups showing up from all over the Federation was infectious.

Bethany Anne was writing her reply to Tabitha when she was distracted by TOM's consciousness hovering around the edge of hers. ***Everything okay?***

I was wondering how to ask you the same question, TOM admitted.

Well, you asked. Bethany Anne resumed typing.

TOM got the hint. He was quiet for a moment, contemplating the outcome for the people headed for the Cosnar system. **You saved a lot of lives today.**

We were here to diffuse the situation. Bethany Anne sighed and gave him access to Lance's report about pockets of anti-Empire protestors popping up at the newly-established outposts. The rioting had fallen off when the Federation Council released a statement assuring the majority of the population that rioting would be suppressed. Nevertheless, the protests were making life difficult for the FDG units stationed in the hotspots.

Gödel can keep trying to divide us. She won't succeed. Bethany Anne attached the video log from the *Gemini's* brig to her reply and sent it to Lance with instructions to run it on every media platform he had access to. ***We fight fire with fire. The tour is going live.***

TOM almost didn't want to ask. **Live?**

Bethany Anne started tapping her nails on the desk as she formulated her plan. ***Yes. The cult is gaining traction by twisting the truth. Let's see how that goes for them when I make my activities public. ADAM, are you there?***

>>**Of course I am,**<< ADAM replied. >>**It doesn't require the ability to read minds to figure out your next move.**<<

Bethany Anne was pleasantly surprised. ***Go on.***

>>**We have a backdoor into the CEREBRO network.**
<<

You're telling me something I already know.

>>**I know you have no patience.**<< ADAM huffed. >>**I foresaw this as one of the solutions when the cult issue first reared its head, so I built some other goodies into the CEREBRO network. From there, I can roll the message out across every screen and speaker, private or public.**<<

Bethany Anne paused for thought. ***I want to make an***

initial address, and I want it to be available separately from the continuous livestream you're going to set up.

Then perhaps a press conference would be more appropriate? TOM suggested.

Bethany Anne lifted a shoulder. ***It would, but I've had enough of being appropriate. The cult sure as fuck isn't stopping to politely announce themselves before they shit on my plans. We're doing it my way.***

>>**What other way is there?**<< ADAM teased. >>**Ready when you are.**<<

"No time like the present." Bethany Anne rolled her shoulders as a camera drone flew out of a compartment in the wall and extended tiny articulated arms holding lighting and a microphone.

>>**I'm playing them a sound bite explaining the interruption to their viewing,**<< ADAM informed her. >>**You're live in five, four, three...**<<

Bethany Anne completed the countdown in her head and offered a grave smile to the camera before speaking. "You may be wondering why I'm talking to you. To *all* of you. I'm here because we are all in danger. There is a sickness spreading through the Federation, one I need your help to cure. Despite my openness about the urgency of our situation, despite providing proof to overturn every false claim the anti-Empire cult has made, people are still being manipulated into working for our enemy."

Give them the footage from the brig in case they missed it the first time around, Bethany Anne instructed. "Today, my ships were attacked by good people led astray. The time for standing back and waiting for you to clean house has passed. I *cannot* continue turning a blind eye to the evil attempting to work its way into the heart of the Federation."

She laced her fingers on the desk, resisting the urge to clench her hands into fists. "The Federation came out of my hope, from my belief...no, my complete certainty that people would do better by one another if they were given the freedom to do so. The Federation is the pinnacle, a society working together to reach true post-scarcity for all. I will say this once and once only. There is no Empire and no reason for us to return to that form of government *because we have evolved beyond it.*

"The Federation swallowed the deficit of every member state, wiping away the debts individual governments had accrued against your future. The Federation provides free education for anyone who seeks it and healthcare that can't be surpassed outside its borders. You are free to pursue whatever path you choose in life without persecution for your species or economic status. Your citizenship guarantees you work, shelter, and protection from those who would do you harm. You live without fear of oppression from the law and without the want of any luxury you are willing to work for. Your children's wealth will eclipse yours, as it should."

Bethany Anne thought back to the heady rush to cement their place on the galactic stage in the first few decades following Exodus Day. She recalled the faces of the first generation of humans to live in space with a surge of pride. "Your grandparents, maybe even your great-grandparents, followed me on my word that this would come. They lived and died in hollowed-out asteroids and shipping containers for the privilege of laying a foundation for the future *on my word* that you would thrive here and now.

"Think about that for a moment."

Bethany Anne's voice hardened as she continued after the moment had passed. "I also vowed I would not rest until the section of Kurtherian society responsible for forcing their religion on lesser-developed worlds were stamped out of existence. My word is as good now as it was then. I keep my promises. I will not stop until Justice prevails. Until we are free from the threat of tyranny."

Her smile returned, projecting the gravity that had accumulated with experience. "For too long, that meant I had to be the bigger tyrant. Who wants to step out of line when the consequence is losing everything? Then people began to see the benefit of trust. The ideal became so much more than the faith of one woman with a short temper and a distaste for fuckery. Peace, maintained by a system of law that works for everyone equally, is not just a human ideal. Not anymore. It is your *inheritance,* the hope your progenitors sweated and bled to make a reality. The desire for cooperation has brought our civilization to the brink of a golden age."

Bethany Anne held her thumb and forefinger slightly apart. "We're *this* close to the dream. This close. All we have to do is reject the evil that is prepared to sink to whatever low it takes to tear us down. I have nothing to hide, but the originators of the cult are dependent on the shadows they've been working from to subvert the utopia that is your right. Whenever the light of truth falls on them, they fail. This is my message to those cowards."

She leaned into the camera and allowed a hint of red

into her eyes. "Come at me. I dare you. I am opening my daily life to everyone so they can see the truth: that I am here to protect them from YOU."

Federation Space, QSD *Baba Yaga* (Two Weeks Later)

Knock-down drag-out fight averted, the tour departed Serenity mostly back on schedule, and Bethany Anne's days returned to the cycle of taking care of the never-ending administration and diplomatic meetings that came with each stop they made—with one exception.

As promised, she live-streamed every minute of her working day to the entire Federation, giving the people an unrestricted view of the day to day operations of the crews aboard the two superdreadnoughts and their respective support ships, as well as access to the way of life on the outer edges of the Federation.

For many, it was eye-opening. Bethany Anne received an avalanche of messages offering support to the colonies on the frontiers from businesses, families, and individuals wishing to extend the benefits of the hand in life they'd been blessed with to the people living with less.

More importantly, the riots and protests stopped. Bethany Anne read through a selection of messages each day, replying to the ones that touched her heart before she switched off the feed at night.

Exile had taken her connection to the people away, a sacrifice she hadn't been aware she was making at the time. Hell, there had been so much going on in the final months of her reign, she'd been lucky to have gotten through it intact.

Bethany Anne dressed in her light armor that morning with a positive outlook on their impending arrival at Dawnseeker University, an experimental society founded around the same time the Federation came about.

Intrigued by her communications with the present committee, Bethany Anne anticipated seeing for herself how the planet was run using a complex voting system developed from pre-WWDE texts by sociologists who masqueraded as science fiction authors.

She tilted her head at her reflection, then had the nano-fabric adjust at the molecular level to give her a pinstripe pantsuit in darkest blue with a three-quarter length jacket. Her boots were already perfect, so she left them as they were and left her dressing room. As she walked, she thought about the almost immediate effect her tactic of openness appeared to have had on the number of people protesting.

Here she was centuries later, in the same position as the men and women who'd looked beyond the ordinary and woven fantastical tales, with the social and political climates of their times as the backdrop. Popular stories digestible by everyone were in part responsible for the shift in attitudes toward the end of the twentieth century. Those sympathetic narratives allowed even the most diehard bigot to experience another point of view.

Bethany Anne was taking back control of her own narrative, thus reducing the power the cult had gained over the misinformed by bringing everyone the uncensored reality of what it took to protect freedom on an intergalactic scale.

She met Michael, the twins, John, and Darryl at the

hangar where the *Gemini* was ready and waiting to take them ahead of the fleet to Dawnseeker.

While John and Darryl were calm about the journey, the twins were enthusiastic about the planet for various reasons. Alexis left the bridge once they'd gotten underway, telling them she had to "prepare."

Gabriel lifted his hands at the pointed look their parents gave him. "Don't look at me. I have no idea what she's planning."

Michael chuckled dryly. "Knowing your sister, we'll likely find out in a spectacular fashion."

Dawnseeker, University of Social Sciences, Mainland Complex

The committee reminded Bethany Anne of the model UN she'd been part of in school. Representative of the Federation's sociological aims, they were a mismatched bunch of sociologists, anthropologists, developmental experts, economists, linguists, and political historians, to name a few of the fields they introduced themselves by before returning to their work.

An elderly Skaine extracted himself from the group as they left and offered a low bow to Bethany Anne, introducing himself as Dr. Scroat, the dean and head of religious studies. "Welcome to Dawnseeker, my Queen. It is our great honor to have you here."

Bethany Anne smiled and shook the hand he offered. "It is mine to be here, Doctor. Thank you for the warm reception. We're a little early, I wasn't expecting the whole faculty to come out to greet us."

The dean chuckled. "Oh, no. That wasn't even half of the faculty."

Alexis repressed her squeal of joy at receiving confirmation the preeminent expert on social modeling was the Skaine from her favorite bedtime story. "I was hoping to meet you, Dean. The story of how you met our Aunt Tabitha was always my choice for her to tell us as children."

Gabriel looked at the modern architecture surrounding the elaborate gardens they were walking through. "This planet is…was Zaphod? This place used to be a monastery, right? What happened to all the temples?"

The dean beamed. "In the age of Empire, yes. We renamed the planet when we joined the Federation and rebuilt it as a center for learning. The temples have been preserved for history, should you wish to visit them." His eyes shone with emotion at the mention of Tabitha. "My father loved Tabitha dearly. They kept in touch until his death, you know."

"Did you know that meeting turned Tabitha's life around?" Alexis asked. "You were the first Skaine she'd met who took care of people."

A tear tracked down the dean's plump cheek. "I remember. My father was the abbot here when Ranger Two uncovered a people-trafficking ring. He died before seeing the Federation come into being, but I know he would approve of what we're doing here."

"What exactly *are* you doing here?" Michael inquired curiously.

Alexis touched Bethany Anne's elbow and leaned in to whisper as the dean elucidated on the various branches of research the university was undertaking on the Federation's behalf. "That station above us used to be a den of iniquity."

Bethany Anne snickered. "Where did you get that phrase?"

Alexis giggled. "I looked it up after the first time Aunt Tabbie told us the story. The reason I'm so interested in speaking to Dr. Scroat is I think Talia has a relative he can help us find."

Bethany Anne's interest was piqued. "Yeah? What does the dean have to do with it?"

"The people-trafficking ring he mentioned Aunt Tabbie breaking up?" Alexis replied. "The person involved was an anonymous Loren. Talia is an orphan, and she's around the same age as the female who was rescued in the Ranger operation."

Bethany Anne saw she was holding onto something else. "And?"

Michael stopped walking. "Talia had a sister."

Bethany Anne wished she'd had more time to spend with the ballsy Loren, whose instinct to protect and survive had saved almost a hundred people when the Ookens had ravaged their colony. "Thank you both for taking care of her. A sister, huh?"

She tilted her head at the dean, who had stopped to listen when Michael did. "What can you tell us about the Loren who was rescued all those years ago?"

Dr. Scroat smiled. "I can do better than tell you. I can take you to her."

"She's here?" Alexis exclaimed.

The dean nodded and consulted a small datapad he pulled from his robe. "Professor Xenia is currently teaching a class in the outdoor auditorium. I'll send her a message and set up a meeting."

Alexis flung her arms around the dean, elated that the hunch she'd had was working out. "I'll go let Talia know."

The cafeteria was moderately busy, with students and professors alike passing through to grab snacks and drinks between lectures.

Talia squirmed in the hard plastic chair and played with her coffee cup on the table while she waited for Xenia to finish giving her lecture. Maybe she should have accepted Alexis' offer to wait with her, but she was too nervous for company, and she was finding it increasingly difficult to be around anyone.

In short, she had been in freefall since her rescue. One moment she was excited, the next she was in tears as loss overwhelmed her. It was worse whenever she was around people, as if their presence amplified her emotions.

Talia was still struggling to deal with losing her home and her life, and Alexis' revelation had her reeling. She'd given up hope of finding Xenia years ago when she'd chosen to settle on Melida. The news that her sister was here had shocked her into leaving the comparative safety of the *Baba Yaga* to venture down to the planet against her better judgment.

She focused on the cup she was holding and the pattern the foam made on the surface of the coffee. The warmth of the ceramic against her skin. Small details she could use to distract herself from the inner turmoil that was building as the pre-lunch crowd grew.

A shadow fell across the table. Talia broke away from her attempts to block her surroundings out and glanced up to see a face that looked so much like hers it hurt.

"Xenia?" Talia jumped to her feet, forgetting to concentrate. Overwhelmed, she almost passed out. She gripped the table and squeezed her eyes closed in an effort to clear her head. "I'm sorry. I should go back to the ship."

Xenia took in Talia's pinched expression and brought all eight of her upper tentacles around to support her. "How long have you been suffering like this? Why aren't you shielding yourself from everyone's emotions?"

Talia looked at Xenia in confusion. "Shielding?"

"Our empathic ability has to be controlled," Xenia told her.

"I don't..." Talia's voice trailed off. "*Our* ability?"

Xenia encouraged Talia to start moving toward the exit. "Let's go to my house. I have active shielding there, so you'll be able to relax."

She guided Talia across the campus to a single-story house set apart from the main buildings by a wooded copse and a large, fenced garden.

Talia followed her sister through the garden gate, admiring the abundance of colorful plant life as they walked to the front door.

"It's not much," Xenia told her as she unlocked the door. "But it's home. Come in."

Talia felt better the moment they stepped inside. "It's perfect. I haven't felt this good since..." Since she went into the Pod-doc, she realized. Maybe the therapy she'd had to repair her injuries had also activated this unasked-for ability.

"You say this is normal for Lorens?" she asked as Xenia led her into the open living area. "That these abilities are the reason our people were enslaved? How do you know this and I didn't?"

Xenia directed Talia to the dining nook while she bustled around the kitchen. She joined Talia a moment later and presented her with a fruit smoothie. "This will replace the energy you burned in the cafeteria. Not all of our people have these abilities. You were young when we were taken, and I don't remember you showing any signs of being gifted."

Talia had a long way to go before she could consider it a gift. "I think a medical procedure I had recently triggered it." She looked around, feeling genuinely comfortable. "What is this shielding?"

"It's from our homeworld," Xenia answered. "I don't know how it works, but it allows me to retreat in peace. Students are emotional as a rule."

"I gathered," Talia agreed with a rueful smile. "I have an idea that the humans will have a solution now I know what the problem is. Tell me about your life. How did you end up here?"

They focused on making the most of their time together until Talia was informed that the tour was preparing to depart. Saying goodbye was hard, but knowing she had Xenia back in her life eased Talia's sadness at being parted from her again after just a few days.

Talia returned to the *Baba Yaga* with more hope than

she'd had when they arrived on Dawnseeker. She had her sister back, and she wasn't slowly losing her mind.

She made her way to her quarters, her thoughts on the best time to approach someone and ask for help. Occupied with practicing what she was going to say and to whom, she didn't notice Michael waiting by the elevator when she left it.

"Talia."

Talia whirled at the sound of her name, throwing her tentacles up in surprise. "I didn't see you there."

Michael gestured for her to continue walking. "I have been informed that you are having issues with newly-developing mental abilities."

Talia bristled, suddenly feeling defensive. "Who told you?"

"I heard your thoughts from deck fourteen." Michael offered no apology.

Talia's irrational anger deflated. "Oh. So you know I was planning to ask for help with whatever the Pod-doc opened up in my brain."

He offered her a small smile. "That is why I am here. I have been working with another person suffering from the effects of mental trauma. After you have been checked over in the Pod-doc to ensure your theory is correct, I'd like to introduce the two of you and see if you can't help each other."

Talia nodded, grateful for the humans' generosity. "Whatever I can do to pay what you've done for me forward."

CHAPTER FOUR

Cosnar System, Ranger Base One, Ops Center

A chime alerted Akio that CEREBRO had picked up an incoming fleet. No flashing lights meant it wasn't another Ooken incursion, which was good since fully a third of the Ranger fleet was currently undergoing repairs for the damage caused in the last one.

Akio had been expecting these ships for the last few days. He was interested in meeting the former cult members and getting a deep read on their intentions. The message from Bethany Anne had assured him of their good intentions at the time of their departure from Serenity. However, weeks had passed since then. Who knew where their allegiances would fall when they were outside of the influence of Bethany Anne's passion for Justice?

CEREBRO held the ships at the edge of the system, far from the fragile planet the base protected. Akio's foresight in calling a meeting of Rangers Two to Twelve to vote on making the system the base's permanent home was vindicated by the need for vigilance. This place was important enough that the Kurtherian who'd choked every living thing on the planet with microcrystals kept returning to test the Rangers' capability to defend it.

They would be back, and Akio would be waiting.

"Hail the lead ship, CEREBRO," Akio instructed, walking over to the wall of monitors. "Put them on the main screen."

A stern-looking woman wearing a lab coat came onscreen. She swept Akio with an appraising gaze. "This is Captain Vivian Jeddah looking for Ranger Base One. To whom am I speaking? Why have our ships been stopped?"

Akio's expression remained dispassionate. "You have reached your destination, Dr. Jeddah. Please give CEREBRO control of your navigation and weapons systems and wait for your escort to arrive."

Dr. Jeddah's eyes narrowed. "I assume you are Ranger One."

"You assume correctly." Akio inclined his head before cutting the call. He reached out to Nickie next.

"'Sup?" Nickie answered, flashing a grin at Akio.

Akio smiled. "I have a job for you."

Nickie's grin faded. "Why are you smiling? What shitty stick are you passing me?"

Akio sent her the fleet's coordinates. "Escort duty for the fleet carrying our latest intake of scientists and recruits."

Nickie rolled her eyes. "Fuck my life, *babysitting*? Sabine isn't around?"

"Sabine is around," Akio replied. "But these particular scientists attempted to attack the *Baba Yaga* less than a month ago. You're going to provide an escort and watch for any duplicity from our newest recruits until I have had the opportunity to ascertain their intentions haven't changed since they departed from our Queen."

Nickie's mouth made a little O of understanding. "The rebels have arrived? Sweet! I wish I could have been there to see Aunt BA's face when she realized she couldn't just kick their asses to the nearest penal world."

Akio sighed, experiencing a pang of nostalgia for the time when Yuko was his right hand. "Dr. Jeddah and her team are much better suited to working on our particular challenge than they are to breaking rocks on a penal colony."

"You mean the unenviable challenge of restarting the planet's climate and building a balanced ecosystem for the Collective from the ground up, plus the added complication of not having access to the Collective's homeworld ecology, meaning it has to be constructed entirely from alien species?" Nickie inquired sweetly. She winked and laughed at the minute twitch of Akio's eyebrow. "You thought I skipped the briefings? Good. I have a reputation to maintain. I have Meredith keeping me up to date on everything to do with the planet. It's boring as shit around here, you know."

Taking Akio's stunned silence for agreement, she clapped and pointed at the screen. "I've got it. We need a bar on the base. Somewhere everyone can take a load off when they're not on duty."

"That's why we have rec rooms, Nickie," Akio told her firmly. "No bar, and please do not give the new arrivals the impression that lawless behavior is the standard around here."

"So, you want me to lie?" Nickie laughed when Akio's spine stiffened. "Relax, they can't be planning to attack us. They got past my aunt and Michael, didn't they?" She made a stern face. "Mr. Kill-first-who-gives-a-shit-about-the-questions wouldn't have sent them out here if they were going to endanger the mission."

"You are a Ranger and should show some respect for your rank," Akio told her, aghast at her flippancy.

Nickie waved a hand. "Yeah, yeah. I'll see you back at the base."

The Penitent Granddaughter, Bridge

Nickie rolled her eyes when Akio finally let her go. "Fuck my life," she repeated, without venom this time. "Maybe Aunt BA really had a change of heart about her scorched earth policy for assholes. Take us out, Meredith."

"As you wish," Meredith replied amicably. "Perhaps you are unhappy because you did not get that chance."

Nickie scowled. "I thought I told you to scrub the therapist subroutine from your code?"

Meredith huffed. "Well, excuse me for trying to help."

Nickie turned at hearing a repressed giggle and spotted the open access panel her bot wrangler and general repair technician was secreted inside. "Get out of there, Durq. Were you listening in the whole time?"

Durq - Image by Eric Quigley

The skinny Skaine crawled out of the duct and clambered gracefully to his feet. He offered his brightest smile, which, no matter how much he practiced in the mirror, would never look anything but creepy to anyone who didn't know him. "Bethany Anne is one of the few people who doesn't scare me," he admitted. "I believe she sees the potential for good in everyone. It's only when they prove her wrong that she gets violent."

Nickie snorted. "You would say that, kiss-ass. She loves you."

"Proves my point," Durq told her. "The Queen knows what she's doing."

"Where would you be today without your sabbatical?" Meredith cut in.

"Exile," Nickie corrected, wondering what her old scene on the frontier looked like these days and finding herself glad she didn't know. "But you're right. I sleep better for accepting who I am."

"You're a wildcard," Durq told her as he dusted off his atmosuit. "And *I'm* wise beyond my years."

Nickie gave him a knowing look. "Yeah, well, you spent your life up until I met you outwitting bigger Skaines who wanted to eat you. I always thought you were the smartest Skaine of all for surviving until we rescued you."

Durq blushed but didn't comment, knowing Nickie would feel obligated to slap his praise down. "What can I do to help with the escort?"

Nickie snorted. "Who says I need help?" She melted under his expectant stare. "Okay, fine. Take a Pod out and watch the fleet from a distance. Meredith will monitor them for any transmissions. You just let me know if any of those ships breaks away once we let them in."

Durq nodded eagerly. "Aye, aye, Captain."

Nickie smiled as he scuttled out through the door. She knew she could trust him not to engage if anything did go down with the ex-rebels. It turned out she was being overly cautious, which was never a bad thing.

Dr. Jeddah had the comm open as she waited for Nickie to arrive. "Tell me everything about the planet we're terraforming," she pressed after introducing herself.

Nickie shook her head, grinning ruefully. "You have an appointment to keep with Ranger One before you're cleared to know about any part of this operation. Feel free to tell me why my aunt decided to send you out here instead of kicking your asses out of the Federation while we head to the base."

Nickie heard the group's story as she led them to

Ranger Base One. Dr. Jeddah trailed off mid-explanation of her team's specialties when the figurative heart of the system came into sight. The base was currently stationed in sight of the planet codenamed "Waterworld" until its new inhabitants arrived and named their home.

"Oh, my," Dr. Jeddah murmured, her severe features softening a touch as the full majesty of the planet came into view. She stared for a moment, transfixed by the sight of tsunamis chasing the horizon. She spotted the familiar climate control modules and wondered why they weren't installed on land, as was usual for that system. "It's an ocean world. I see why the Queen wanted us here."

In a rare moment of restraint, Nickie suppressed her enthusiasm for the injection of fresh ideas their arrival was going to bring. She offered Dr. Jeddah a sympathetic smile. "There's a lot of work to be done. You might be cursing my aunt in a few weeks."

Durq returned to the *Granddaughter* before they entered the lower-level hangar, where Akio was waiting with Hirotoshi, Ryu, and Ricole. Nickie was the only one to leave her ship.

Nickie nodded at the three on guard duty and raised an eyebrow at Akio. "I can't see you'll have any issues with them. The leader is sincere enough. She's pretty fucking angry she got tricked."

Akio lifted his chin a fraction of an inch. "CEREBRO, release Dr. Jeddah and her team."

The ships opened at CEREBRO's command, and the crews debarked and approached Akio and Nickie, with Dr. Jeddah at their head.

Akio held out a hand. "Dr. Jeddah. Welcome to Ranger

Base One." He got a good read on the woman as she shook his hand. She was honest, determined, and as Nickie had told him, angry about being deceived.

"About time we did something for good," Dr. Jeddah blustered, clearly embarrassed by the situation.

Akio nodded. "Past is past, Dr. Jeddah. This is a place where you *can* do good."

"Call me Vivian," Dr. Jeddah told him.

Akio smiled. "Of course." He shook the hands of each of her crew in turn and welcomed them similarly, finding them all to be of the same mind as Vivian.

Nickie winked at Akio as they ended the new residents' tour of the base and left for the common areas attached to the residential wing. She slipped her arm through Vivian's and smiled. "So, what do you guys like to do for fun?"

Vivian was taken aback when she saw Nickie's badge. "You're Ranger Two? I've heard your idea of fun is stealing Skaine ships and running around with royalty."

Nickie laughed. "We all have a past. These days I'm more mature."

Akio snorted.

"What are you implying?" Nickie accused.

Akio gave her a pointed look. "You forget that CEREBRO sees everything. I know you and your crew snuck off to race the housebots last week."

Nickie rolled her eyes. "It was a quiet week! The bots get bored when there's nothing to do." She looked at Ricole, Hirotoshi, and Ryu for support.

Ricole shook her head. "I've got nothing to say. Maybe next time you'll invite me."

Ricole - Image by Eric Quigley

She and Ryu burst into laughter, and even Hirotoshi cracked a smile.

Akio pressed his lips together. "I would like to speak to Dr. Jeddah. Please ensure her people are comfortable in their quarters."

He showed Vivian to his office and gestured at the guest chair before sitting at his desk. "Your expertise is most welcome here, Dr. Jeddah."

"I asked you to call me Vivian," she reminded him. "What do you know about my expertise? I'm not on the news holos every other day."

Akio returned Vivian's smile. "I looked you up when my Queen informed me of your impending arrival. You had an excellent record of producing viable living conditions on harsh planets before you were subverted by the cult."

"I wish I hadn't listened to their lies." Vivian received a ping on her wrist-holo, informing her she had clearance to access the project data. She dived in immediately and was shocked by what she read. "Crystal pollution? I've never heard of that."

"Kurtherian technology," Akio explained. "We have reversed the unnatural disaster that caused total extinction, which has left us with a sterile planet."

"I saw the climate control modules in low orbit," she mentioned. "Is there no way of grounding them?"

Akio shook his head. "No. It took the climatologists weeks to come up with a workable solution to get the ocean currents moving again, but as you saw on your way in, they've succeeded. Our next task is to build a stable ecosystem that will support the kelp forests we are preparing to plant."

Vivian was astounded by the complexity of the operation. "Why are you doing all this? Kelp isn't exactly valuable."

"Oh, but it is," Akio assured her with a smile. "Our goal is to create a home for a species whose planet was much like the model we are working to create before the Kurtherians enslaved them and destroyed it."

Vivian read a list of the people currently working on the project and smiled, seeing a few familiar names. "You already have the A-list working on it. My people will fit in just fine. Who is Eve?"

Akio smiled. "Eve is the expert on the Collective. She is the one who developed the large-scale artificial culturing method we are using to replicate the ecology of their home planet. "

"I can't wait to get started," Vivian enthused.

CHAPTER FIVE

Cosnar System, Ranger Base One, Command Center

Vivian's team had integrated easily. In the weeks since they had arrived, the underwater base had been declared operational, and the seabed was due to be seeded today. More importantly to Akio, tighter security around the system meant there had been no Ooken attacks, although they were still pushing hard to gain access to the Federation in other parts of the quadrant.

While he was grateful for the partial reprieve, he didn't relax for a moment. Neither did the other Ranger leaders.

While Akio kept his eye on the rapid progress of the scientific teams, Nickie and Sabine—with the assistance of Hirotoshi, Ryu, Ricole, Mark, and Jacqueline—had applied their focus to turning out the most highly-trained Ranger squads history had ever seen.

Akio was in the ops center observing the latest session, a laser tag battle Nickie had planned to use localized EMPs for until Ryu pointed out that alternate technology which wouldn't damage the fleet was available.

He recalled his sinking heart when Nickie had announced she would be training the Rangers for open-space encounters, citing the need for them to be prepared for the Ookens to switch tactics once the Collective started arriving. He agreed with her sentiment wholly, if not her approach.

It was a good thing his two closest friends were used to containing fallout caused by headstrong females' shenanigans. Katsu had volunteered to go on the tour and assist with CEREBRO's rollout. Jun and Kouki were on Devon with Tabitha, leaving the two veteran Elites to ensure Nickie didn't accidentally wipe out half the Ranger force in her enthusiasm for coming up with realistic training scenarios that the other women were able and more than willing to set up.

He turned from the viewscreen when CEREBRO announced the arrival of Endaya Clements, the head of the climatology team. "Dr. Clements, what can I do for you?"

The Entarian blinked rapidly as she handed him a datapad. "We had a malfunction on one of the climate control modules. It fritzed somehow, and sector H-9 was experiencing arctic conditions."

Akio handed the datapad back after examining the initial report from the module, his forehead furrowed in concern. "How far does this issue put us back?"

Dr. Clements shook her head. "A few hours at most. We anticipated bugs and built in time to address them. The module that malfunctioned was removed from the network before it had frozen more than ten percent of its sector. My techs are up there right now repairing it, and I got some help from Sabine with removing the ice floes that formed." She smiled. "Don't worry. The seeding is going to happen today, I promise."

"Very well. Report back to me when your team has completed the repairs." Akio dismissed her with a curt nod and left the command center, in search of Dr. Jeddah.

Akio exchanged pleasantries with the people he passed on his way to the transport bay. Rangers, scientists, and engineers alike, everyone in the command center was in high spirits as the shift began and the information that the seeding would be going ahead today trickled out from the labs.

He learned from their unguarded thoughts that the good mood had much to do with their shift winning the pool that had been quietly running in the background as the marine microbiologists grew closer to meeting the quotas of specially selected bacteria, eukaryotes, and archaea that Dr. Jeddah had calculated would be sufficient to kickstart the planet's heartbeat now that the ocean currents had stabilized.

He hopped into a Pod and headed for the skybase.

Skybase, Drone Bay One

Dr. Vivian Jeddah walked between the rows of drones, her eyes on her datapad as she checked that the contents of each drone's payload were secure. There were hundreds of drones prepped and ready to go, each around six feet long and standing waist-high to the scientist.

Inside each drone were hundreds of smaller drones shaped like tiny rockets with drill-bit noses for embedding themselves in the ocean's bedrock. These carried the precious microorganisms and were programmed to release their payloads when they reached the depth and temperature their particular load needed to survive and thrive.

Dr. Jeddah left bay one and made her way to bay two, which the team had lovingly dubbed "Botany Bay." Here they had the makings of the largest marine kelp forest in the known universe.

She made the same checks and found all was well. A brief inquiry to Ranger Base One on the other side of the planet told her that everything was optimal with their share of the drones. Excitement coursed through Vivian as she strolled triumphantly into the command center to prepare for the seeding operation.

It was all coming together.

Vivian had run hundreds of thousands of simulations through CEREBRO before making conclusive choices about the species that would be included in their model.

The planet would provide for the Collective's needs once the microorganisms were established. They would make up seventy percent of the biomass and act to decompose matter. Vivian's carefully designed feeding system would rocket the growth of microbial mats, which in turn would replenish nutrients and speed up the reoxygenation of the water. Marine kelp, engineered to grow rapidly and be compatible with the Collective's digestive systems would fill the clean, clear oceans. Then and only then could the ichthyologists release the millions of fish and other marine life they had in tanks on Ranger Base Two.

It sounded simple if she didn't take into account the effort to source and mass-clone marine species from multiple planets and build a micro-ecology that was beneficial to all of those species from scratch.

While learning on the job, no less.

Vivian had only dreamed of working on an oceanic world before coming here. There wasn't much call for underwater living solutions for beings who required air to live. Her experience was with planets that had once held life, where it could be coaxed back with the right applications of technology and elbow grease.

Technology had progressed to the point where a planet could be systematically stripped and rewilded within three years. Before she'd gone rogue, she'd had a steady clientele of ridiculously wealthy third-and fourth-generation colonists wishing to reverse the industrial damage done by their families' initial settlement.

Many of them had abandoned their depleted planets, which had been stripped of their resources by the first-generation settlers who had been given Eden and only seen the profit they could make on its resources. They weren't to blame, those humans who had fought wars for resources on Earth that were accessible to all in space in abundance. Her clientele, their children's children, had learned the lessons they had failed to grasp.

Vivian admired their dedication. She had little time to work on her personal research into the viability of rewilding planets after heavy industrialization as tourist destinations these days. The Waterworld project took her every waking minute as they got closer to the day the planet would be ready to house the Collective.

She looked up from where she knelt on the floor, surrounded by the calculations she'd been making with a smile when the command center began to fill up. She was pleased to see that one of the arrivals was Akio. "You heard about the iceberg in sector H-9?" she offered in greeting.

Akio approached Vivian with the same anticipation in his expression she suspected was shining from hers. "I was on my way to tell you about it." He toed the edge of the paper walling Vivian in by the command chairs. "You can't use a datapad?"

"There's something about paper that helps me think." She grabbed the stack of papers she'd left in his chair for lack of space. "You're right on time. The ice has been cleared."

Akio checked his internal HUD and saw he had a message from Dr. Clements, confirming the ice had indeed been removed. He closed his HUD and smiled. "What are we waiting for?"

Vivian gathered her papers up and got to her feet. "We were waiting for me to triple-check the calculations for the drone program. Which I have just finished doing." She handed Akio her datapad. "I set everything up. All you have to do is press this button to begin the operation. CEREBRO is recording everything—and I mean everything—and streaming directly to the Queen."

Bethany Anne spoke in the back of Akio's mind. ***Good luck with the seeding. The Federation is watching.***

No pressure, then, Akio replied as he mentally returned the warm feeling that came with Bethany Anne's message. He nodded at Vivian. "Thank you, Dr. Jeddah. CEREBRO, give me a channel to the ops centers on Bases One and Two."

CEREBRO confirmed the channel was open. "Cooperation and respect have brought us together for the most honorable cause there is. When we first encountered this part of space, it was dead, choked with pollution, and incapable of supporting life of any kind. We changed that. We took what was damaged and restored it. We brought back the winds and the rains. We cleaned the water. We risked our lives to build a support base at crushing depths. We invented equipment to do the job when none was available. We fed the people doing those things. *We did it together.* What we have achieved so far is nothing short of a miracle. However, our work is not yet done."

He swept an arm to indicate the technicians bustling around the control room. "Today, we will sow the seeds of new life. Before we embark upon the final steps of this auspicious enterprise, I want to personally thank everyone who has worked to make it a reality. Due to your time and effort, your innovation and determination, the Collective will have a home to return to when Bethany Anne's armada frees them."

Akio pressed the button on the datapad screen, and a dual window popped up to show him the progress of drone deliveries from the skybase and Ranger Base One. "The seeding has commenced," he announced, sharing the data with the control rooms across all three bases.

The belly of the skybase opened and the sky darkened as the drones were disgorged from bay one. The viewscreen was obscured for a full minute, then the drones' Etheric-powered thrusters kicked in. They shot out in all directions, obeying their programming to speed to their targets.

A cheer went up across the command center when

CEREBRO cycled through camera feeds, showing the drones arriving at their target locations. It was followed by strained silence while they waited for the smaller drones to be activated. Another cheer broke out when the viewscreen was displayed the innumerable blue lights of the smaller drones, which immediately began needling the surface of the ocean as planned.

Unrestrained and overwhelmed with relief at their success, some cried without realizing, such was the strength of the emotions rocking them. CEREBRO piped in more wild applause from the two Ranger bases, connecting everyone as they celebrated their parts in returning life to the planet.

Akio took it all in, knowing that the day he could share his sense of wonder with the people this planet was designed for was coming soon.

CHAPTER SIX

Devon, First City, The Hexagon

Harkkat hardly waited for the great glass doors to open before forcing himself through the gap. Ignoring the buttons that were sheared from his tunic in his effort to get inside the building, he sprinted past the ID check, waving his badge and yelling for Tabitha.

The guards were used to the drama surrounding the consul. They stepped aside for the Leath to enter the elevator, their expressions professionally detached until the doors closed.

Harkkat - Image by Eric Quigley

While the elevator guards laughed at his expense, Harkkat bounced from one foot to the other, agitated that it was taking him so long to get to Network Command. Every second that passed stretched out into agonizing eternity.

Harkkat exited the elevator at a sprint and tore along the corridor, then burst into Tabitha's office out of breath. He slammed the printout of Roka's message on her desk, knocking her feet to the floor in the process. "Found her," he gasped as he fell to his knees.

Tabitha vaulted the desk and knelt next to Harkkat. She found his pulse with her fingers as his eyes rolled back in his head. His breathing was shallow and his pulse erratic. "Shit. CEREBRO, call a medic."

"Two minutes," CEREBRO replied a split-second later. "It appears that the consul is having a heart attack. We have warned him numerous times about the dangers of a sedentary lifestyle, advice he chose to ignore."

"Not the time for criticism," Tabitha told the EI group. She slapped Harkkat's face gently, trying to keep him awake. "Dammit, why didn't I choose healing as my ability? Stay with me, Harkkat."

The medics arrived. Tabitha paced anxiously while they worked to stabilize Harkkat.

"He'll be okay," the lead EMT told Tabitha.

Tabitha watched as they attached the relevant medpatches and took Harkkat to the first-floor med bay, leaving her with their assurances that they'd inform her when he was awake.

She picked up the holofile and found a text file and a video message. Saving the text for the moment, Tabitha activated the video message. The grainy, low-res image resolved after a second, and Tabitha had a moment to wonder who the young female Leath was before she spoke in a whisper.

"Uncle, you have to get me out of here. I don't know where we're headed next, and I don't know how much longer it will be safe for me. The captain has been acting strange since we got to Sonmara Station. He's picked up a passenger." She glanced over her shoulder at a noise in the background. When she looked back at the camera, her eyes were wide with fear. "I have to go. I managed to get to the station's Library to send this message, but it's not safe even here."

The text file contained a copy of the ship's log. Tabitha saw that the *Pleiades* was using a fake registration, something Harkkat had suspected when the ship went dark.

Further investigation revealed the fake registration had been logged at Sonmara Station, which belonged to a planet beyond Federation borders.

Tabitha uploaded the video to the CEREBRO network and forwarded it to Bethany Anne with a message asking her to call Network Command.

She dipped into the network while she waited for a response, monitoring Harkkat's condition as the Pod-doc repaired his heart while taking care of numerous small tasks she'd let slide in the last week. Lost in the code, she didn't notice Bethany Anne's presence in her mind until she was pulled out of the network by a sudden shock.

"I hope I'm not interrupting anything important," Bethany Anne stated when Tabitha opened her eyes.

Tabitha blinked at Bethany Anne on the holoscreen. "I was keeping an eye on Harkkat. He had a heart attack, rushing to get that video to me."

Bethany Anne's mouth dropped open. "Shit. He'll be okay, right?"

Tabitha nodded. "Looks like it. You saw the video. His niece is in danger. It sounds like the captain of the *Pleiades* has started drinking the Kool-Aid for real. Harkkat's niece is a smart cookie. She sent the ship's log so we have a record of everywhere they've docked under false credentials."

The Queen smiled. "Fantastic. I'll pass this on to the children. They've been banging their heads against the wall for weeks."

"They're heading into the frontier. Sonmara is pretty far out there. You should have Nickie join them for the op," Tabitha suggested.

"Are you fucking kidding?" Bethany Anne asked incredulously. "Nickie is as likely to turn the op on its head as she is to follow the plan. They can handle whatever they find out there."

Tabitha inclined her head. "That may be, but she has the experience with frontier society the twins are lacking, and unless I'm mistaken, Christina and Kai went back to the Dren Cluster with TH. What's your problem? You can't think she'll be a bad influence on the twins?"

Bethany Anne laughed. "No, they don't *need* her influence for that. Trouble manages to find them every time they're out of my sight. Honestly, I can't see them getting along well." She tapped her lips with a finger. "While I wouldn't describe any of the children as naïve, I will concede that Nickie has an effective if unorthodox way of operating inside the underbelly of society. She has a lot to teach them, especially if the team is going to keep going on undercover operations."

She lost her train of thought when she spotted Tabitha's wicked grin. "Why do I get the impression it didn't matter what I said?"

Tabitha laughed heartily. "It's easier to get forgiveness than ask permission. I already messaged Akio."

Open Space, QSD *Baba Yaga*, Top Deck, Bethany Anne's Ready Room

Bethany Anne reached out to Michael as she left for the family quarters. ***We have an issue.***

We have many issues, Michael replied dryly. *To which are you referring?*

Our agent aboard the* Pleiades *missed her extraction. Bethany Anne shared what Tabitha had told her and sent him the video message from Roka.

Michael's concern came clearly through their mental link. *Picking up the ship is good news. The solution is simple. We send the children to rescue her.*

You read my mind, Bethany Anne told him with amusement. ***Can you pick up Alexis' slack with Isaiah's therapy?***

Of course, Michael assured her. *He is making progress despite the setbacks.*

Setbacks? Bethany Anne asked.

Having your mind rewritten not once but twice is no walk in the park. Michael shared the Vid-doc data from Isaiah's sessions. *The process is brutal. Gödel put in safeguards against her compulsions being undone. I believe Isaiah's inner strength is the only thing getting him through this.*

Maybe the real Isaiah is just that pissed, Bethany Anne commented, her heart constricting when she read how much time Isaiah had spent in the Vid-doc for repairs to his brain. She shook her head in disgust. ***How many brain hemorrhages has he had? Gödel is going to pay for this.***

Yes, she will, Michael agreed.

I'll make time for him as soon as the current shitstorm has been resolved, Bethany Anne promised.

I know he would appreciate that, Michael told her. *Keep me updated on the twins' situation.*

Will do. Bethany Anne closed her link to Michael as she walked into the lounge and found the children watching *Dawn of the Dead.* "Izanami, pause the movie."

She dropped onto the couch and smiled as Alexis,

Gabriel, Trey, and K'aia stared expectantly at her. "Nice to see you taking time for fun."

Alexis folded her arms as she gave her mother a suspicious look. "You have a lead."

Bethany Anne winked and smiled. "Got it in one. The *Pleiades* has shown up."

"Seriously?" K'aia blurted. "We've been searching for that ship *everywhere*, and there's been no sighting of it for months."

Bethany Anne's smile faded. "The undercover agent we had on the crew didn't make her extraction. She managed to get a message to Harkkat with her current location and a request for another extraction attempt."

Alexis sucked in a breath. "Has she been made?"

Bethany Anne lifted her hands. "That I can't say."

"She wouldn't be the first undercover agent to go into Shoken Industries and vanish without a trace," Trey cut in. His statement was met with mumbled agreements from the others. "How long since she reached out?"

"Three days," Bethany Anne told them. She waved a finger and took control of the entertainment system, replacing the zombies onscreen to show them the brief, whispered video message Harkkat had received. "In case you didn't notice the family resemblance, Roka is Harkkat's niece."

She exchanged the video for a map of the Federation, showing markers on five locations scattered around the borders, and one distinctly outside Federation space. "The *Pleiades* docked at Sonmara Station for repairs using a fake registration three weeks ago."

"What are we looking at?" Gabriel asked.

"The places the anti-Empire cult is still holding on," Bethany Anne told him. "Sonmara Station is outside the Federation border. Don't you think it's a little strange the protests have died down everywhere but here?"

Gabriel snorted in disgust. "There are people suffering for real. These people don't know hurt."

Bethany Anne raised an eyebrow. "What brought this on? You're usually the first to forgive people's ignorance."

"Did the Collective get an opportunity to protest when Gödel's people destroyed their planet and enslaved them?" Gabriel sighed in frustration. "I want to have empathy and believe they're vulnerable to the cult's manipulation because they're scared by their status quo shifting. It's just hard to swallow when we've seen so much *real* suffering. Trey's people, the Collective, and the Bl'kheth, as well as the countless number of people killed by Ookens this last few years. Look at Talia! How can I feel sorry for the protesters?"

"You don't have to feel sorry for them," Bethany Anne told him. "As long as you don't take your opinions on duty with you. You represent me, and I will not be seen to work outside the law. I won't give the cult any ammunition."

Gabriel shrugged. "That goes without saying. I'm just frustrated is all. If we were back home, we could just roll up and take the cult out with a well-placed rock."

Bethany Anne snickered internally, seeing herself in Gabriel in that moment. "You understand the MPPS was a reactionary measure. I was so sick of being restricted by the law that I killed the administrative monster before it had a chance to rear its ugly head in the Interdiction."

TOM chuckled. **You admit to being bratty?**

Gabriel groaned.

Not for a minute. Bethany Anne smiled at her son. "I get that it's different from the meritocracy you grew up in on the Interdiction, and I appreciate your restraint. The cult hasn't taken root in the Interdiction for the simple reason the people there have no time for blaming anyone else for their problems. They know I'm only going to intervene if they're up to fuckery. Otherwise, they are the masters of their own fates. The Federation has to serve the needs of, shit, too many cultures to count at this point. Every member state is responsible for itself, as long as they don't break Federation law. The places you see rioters are where people are dissatisfied with their local government."

She paused for a moment. "I don't want you to get the idea that the Federation doesn't work. It works exactly as I planned."

Gabriel raised an eyebrow. "It sounds overly complicated."

Bethany Anne put her hand on Gabriel's. "Politics in a nutshell. You have never been there when the full Federation council is in session. I can't describe what it feels like to know that every species, every planetary state no matter how small is represented. They have democracy without the noose of bureaucracy and an economy that runs on trade, not war."

"Why not take out bad governments?" Gabriel argued. "They're doing their people a disservice."

"For the same reason we're going to arrest the cult leaders and have them tried in the House of Arbitration," Alexis told him. "I know you think we're wasting time, but if we don't do this right, all we'll do is leave a trail of martyrs behind us for the cult to rally around."

"Are you fit for this assignment?" Bethany Anne asked Gabriel without judgment.

Gabriel frowned. "It just doesn't sit well with me, knowing someone is out there making more Isaiahs. I don't want them sitting pretty in a jail cell for the rest of their lives. The suffering they've caused merits suffering in return."

Bethany Anne let him run himself out. "I don't disagree. However, Federation justice is not my Justice."

Alexis waved a hand. "Besides, the whole point of arresting them is so we can make a huge deal out of the trial and prove to everyone who supports them that they're a bunch of low-bellied liars. Can't do that if all we have is their heads. Be practical, not emotional."

"Come on, Gabriel," K'aia interjected. "These aren't new concepts. There's a procedure to follow. I know we haven't always followed orders as a team, but this time it's different. We have to follow Alexis' plan."

"It's a solid one," Trey reasoned. "Sure, we could take them out. What do we do when the leaders slip away? There's no doubt they're going to run as soon as we start rounding up the cell leaders. Where does that get us in the long run? These are the questions we have to ask before we act."

Alexis put her hand on Gabriel's arm to soothe him. "You have to understand who we're getting involved with. I know it sickened you to see how easily people are manipulated when we were embedded with Isaiah's cell."

K'aia cut in. "They might not be suffering, but they *are*

being victimized. The cult preys on people's fear of change, on their insecurities and their ignorance. Bethany Anne is doing everything she can to put an end to ignorance and insecurity."

"I can't just leave the tour to apprehend these merchants of fear," Bethany Anne told them, airing her own frustrations for a moment. "I want to. I can't. As hard as I tried to avoid it, I'm bound by my responsibility to… well, this." She waved a hand to encompass the whole Federation. "You are my hands, the only freedom I have to act until this tour is over and I can drop the politics."

Gabriel scoffed. "There it is again, the P-word."

"You can be crushed by the system, or you can use the system," Trey told him. He shared his datapad screen to the wallscreen. "Check this out. I had Izanami go through the Gate logs for Sonmara Station, and there was a very interesting arrival there around the same time the *Reynolds* got back to High Tortuga. A Larian, would you believe?"

Alexis perked up at that. "Roka mentioned her captain had a new friend."

"That can't be a coincidence, right?" Gabriel enthused, his doubts vanishing in the light of prospective action. "I smell a lead."

Trey lifted an arm and sniffed. "That might be me."

K'aia sighed at his attempt to inject humor into the situation. "Is the Larian still there?" she asked.

Trey shook his head. "I can't say. There's no record other than his entry through port authority Customs. Do you think he's connected to Gödel? Isaiah didn't mention he knew any Larians."

"Did you ask him specifically?" Bethany Anne asked.

"Because that poor man doesn't know whether he's coming or going."

"He didn't react negatively when he met Jiya," Alexis supplied. "We would have noticed if he was afraid. Izanami has been monitoring him around the clock since he had the first seizure."

"He's still having flashbacks." It wasn't a question. Bethany Anne had seen the challenges Isaiah was having with recovering his memory for herself, and she was still angry after finding out how much damage had been done. "Your father explained why traditional treatment isn't an option."

"It's complicated," Alexis admitted. She explained the intricate process, which involved a combination of VR therapy and hers and Michael's careful assistance when they came across one of Gödel's traps. Isaiah was close to reclaiming his memories despite the challenges he faced. "It's two steps forward and one back. Before we can extract his deepest memories, we have to strip away the compulsions that are blocking him from them. Then Isaiah has to work through the cognitive and emotional dissonance in the Vid-doc while the memory…settles, I guess is the easy explanation."

"It sure as hell doesn't look easy," Gabriel stated. "But at least he has the option of Vid-doc therapy."

Bethany Anne thought he would recover given time and their continued care and attention. "I don't think it's a good idea to interrupt the progress you're making with him."

Alexis sighed in relief. "Me either. So, he can come with

us? *Gemini's* got the latest Vid-doc. I can keep working with him while the assignment is quiet."

Bethany Anne shook her head. "Your father will handle his treatment until you get back. I've already spoken to him. He's aware of the situation."

Alexis got to her feet. "I'll go see him now."

"Anything else before we leave?" Gabriel asked.

"Yes. Remember to check in this time," Bethany Anne told them. "Rescue Roka first, then find the mystery Larian."

CHAPTER SEVEN

QSD *Baba Yaga*, Top Deck, Vid-doc Suite

Michael had just finished explaining the idea of helping Isaiah through connecting him with others who had experienced trauma when Talia arrived.

The Loren recognized the former cult leader and hissed, her tentacles moving into defensive positions around her body. "Why is *he* here?"

"For the same reason I asked you to be here," Michael told her. "You have both suffered because of Gödel, and it is important to know you are not alone in your experiences."

Talia bristled but locked her emotions down as she always did in Michael's presence. The Nacht were undoubtedly good, of that there was no doubt, but it was a terrible goodness. Too intense for her emerging empathic ability. If she wasn't careful, she would be burned by it. "I don't know about that. He was the cause of plenty of suffering."

"Under compulsion," Michael explained, making it clear

he wouldn't accept any recriminations on her part. "Against his will."

"I saw video of what happened to your home," Isaiah told Talia quietly. "I'm sorry for what happened to you and your people. I still don't know where I came from. My memory has been altered to make me forget everything I am, so I would be an obedient soldier."

Talia gasped, horrified by the idea of being used as a puppet. "That's...I don't know what to say. I'm so sorry."

Michael indicated the open Vid-docs. "You will remember one day. Today your help is needed to give Talia practice shielding herself from others' emotions. Her anger is affecting her ability to move on from her trauma."

"What do you know about that?" Talia demanded, going back on the offensive. "You're reading me again?"

"You are not the only empath aboard or even the strongest. You're broadcasting your emotions, Talia. Every psychic aboard knows you need help." Michael had a brief fond recollection of the days when people did as he said without question. Of course, his lack of concern for others at the time had made spilling blood to get that obedience much simpler. These times called for empathy and understanding, which apparently meant getting sassed on a regular basis by beings a fraction of his age. "Let me tell you a story about my daughter. As an infant, she discovered she could communicate mentally with anyone, psychic ability or not, before she had the motor function needed to speak."

Talia's tentacles rippled. "You're talking about Alexis? Little Ms. Chatterbox?" Maybe training her ability so she wasn't continually blindsided by revelations about the people she thought she knew wasn't the worst idea. "Just how powerful are they? And you?"

Michael inclined his head, chuckling at the sudden respectful inspection from the Loren. "Let's just say that parenting them came with many unexpected lessons, the most valuable being flexibility when it came to setting boundaries."

"What changed Alexis' mind?" Talia inquired, her curiosity overriding her nervousness.

"My daughter's impatience has always gotten the better of her," Michael told her. "When Gabriel began to speak and the adults praised his progress, she realized she was missing out and caught up rapidly. We grow and heal, or we stagnate. Acceptance is not a weakness. No one thinks less of you because you've been affected by your life being torn away."

"What does that have to do with *him*?" Talia asked, pointing at Isaiah.

"It's my idea," Isaiah told her. "Alexis believes experiencing scenarios that directly contradict the programming in my mind will help me to gain con—" He broke off and reached unsteadily for Michael as his vision blurred and the room shifted beneath his feet. "It's happening again."

Talia stiffened in indecision when Isaiah's eyes rolled back in his head and he collapsed, shaking uncontrollably. The shock caused her to let her mental wall crumble, and she was flooded with fear, confusion, and pain. She lifted a tentacle, reaching for Isaiah.

"I've got him," Michael told her, moving in a blur to catch Isaiah mid-fall.

Knowing she couldn't help, she instinctively backed out

of Michael's way, her three hearts pounding as adrenaline coursed through her.

Michael picked Isaiah up and deposited him gently in the nearest Vid-doc. "Izanami, run Isaiah's program."

Izanami's hard light avatar appeared beside the Vid-doc as it closed. She waved a hand, and the Vid-doc cycled on. "He is sedated. The episode has been halted, and repairs can begin."

The spell holding Talia broke as Isaiah's consciousness ebbed. Realizing she'd frozen to the spot, she forced her tentacles back into action and approached Michael and Izanami at the Vid-doc. "What just happened? Is he going to be okay?"

"He is not in the least bit okay, but he will live," Michael assured her. "It looks much worse than it is."

Talia glanced through the viewing window and saw that Isaiah looked peaceful. "What's wrong with him?"

Michael sighed. "He had a brain hemorrhage."

Talia's already large eyes grew wider still. "You're joking."

Michael shook his head. "I would not make light of the situation. His mind was rearranged, we think by Gödel or someone close to her." He laid a hand on the Vid-doc. "Isaiah has a long and difficult journey ahead of him before he can be whole again. Fortunately, we have the technology to ensure he makes it to that day intact."

"I can't believe a brain hemorrhage isn't considered serious here." Talia had been overwhelmed by the level of technology that was available aboard the Queen's ships from the moment she'd arrived. She was still coming to terms with feeling the emotions of everyone around her, something she'd only had fleeting experiences with before she'd been in the Pod-doc. "Then again, I never expected that knowing when my customers were having a bad day was a normal thing for Lorens."

"Not much was known about Loren physiology until you arrived," Izanami told her. "There are so few of you to begin with, and the majority of the Lorens we know of live extremely private lives."

Talia rubbed the base of her skull to ease the ache seeping in. "I guess I know why. It's not easy living with people when you have to process all of their emotions as well as your own."

"But you aren't working through your emotions, are you?" Michael asked gently. "You haven't allowed yourself an avenue to grieve."

Talia shook her head. She should have departed for Devon already, but she'd been avoiding enlistment, knowing she was too enraged to pass the psychiatric evaluation. "I've been making excuses," she admitted, thinking of her sister at the university. She hadn't replied to her communications, avoiding a relationship because she was afraid to have it taken away.

She sighed. "Maybe I needed to see what was left of my people safe, but I'm just trying to hold it together now that they're taken care of. I want to fight, but I can't do that until I'm not a danger to anyone on my team, or however the FDG arranges their soldiers."

Michael brushed her thoughts and saw she was working to the conclusion that would allow her to move on. The FDG wasn't where he or Bethany Anne saw this free spirit thriving. There was a place for Talia in the Rangers. However, she had to choose it for herself.

Talia wandered over to the Vid-doc beside Isaiah's. "Maybe I'm ready to do more than be angry. What did you have in mind?"

Michael waved Izanami over. "I thought you might get some closure if you saw the good you can do with your expanded ability. Izanami, is the program ready to run?"

Izanami nodded. "The *Waterworld* scenario is complete." She smiled reassuringly at Talia. The feral look her sharp teeth gave her took nothing from the sentiment. "This is your first time in the Vid-doc. Be prepared, this is an immersive experience. Just relax and go with it."

Talia nodded her agreement, afraid to speak in case she backed out. Her rage was still there, beneath the fear of letting go. She was free to reject Michael's help, but where would that get her? Would her anger become a permanent state of fear? Would she be caught in that trap for the rest of her life? She had to show courage, the same courage she'd shown when the Ookens attacked Melida. The only way out was forward.

"Don't worry," Izanami assured her. "Nothing you experience in here will affect you physically. The program settings limit any pain you can feel."

"Thank you, that will be all," Michael told Izanami, ignoring her rolled eyes. He gestured for Talia to get into the Vid-doc.

Talia hesitated after climbing in. "What if all I see is how I could do better?"

"Then I know a good therapist I can recommend," Izanami offered.

Talia laid back on the mat. "Let's get this over with."

Michael glanced at Izanami as the Vid-doc cycled on, putting Talia into the rejuvenation cycle. "Why would an AI need a therapist? Don't you just purge the parts of yourself that aren't working?"

Izanami laughed. "You have read too many stories written before artificial intelligence existed. I would no sooner purge a part of myself than you would hack off your foot."

Michael shrugged. "I can grow my foot back if the only option is amputation."

Izanami raised an eyebrow. "Okay, so that wasn't the best example. Would you offer up a brain sample?"

"God, no," Michael told her with a shiver. "But you have backups, right?"

Izanami smiled and pointed to an empty Vid-doc. "In you go."

Vid-doc Scenario: *Waterworld*

Talia found herself alone in a roamer that was descending into deep, sunlit water filled with thick, lush kelp. She craned to peer outside the roamer's window and was delighted to see shoals of brightly-colored fish darting in and out of the gently undulating kelp. Further inspection of her surroundings revealed coral reefs teeming with all kinds of marine life.

"Put the headset on," Michael instructed.

Talia almost whipped him with her tentacles as she whirled in surprise at his sudden appearance. "What is this place? I can't believe we're not really here."

Michael chuckled at her enthusiasm. "I assure you, we are still onboard the *Baba Yaga*. This is a simulation of a real world, however."

Talia nodded as he spoke, her gaze on the abundant life outside the roamer. She put the headset on and pulled it off again in a hurry when she was blown away by the most beautiful song she had ever heard.

"What is that?" she asked, stunned by the unexpected harmony of many voices singing.

"They are called the Collective," Michael told her. "That is a recording of their group mind communication."

"Their song is so beautiful," Talia whispered. "They lost their home?"

Michael nodded. "They lost everything when the Kurtherians decided to make them into Ookens, along with two other species they enslaved. You've spent time with Trey."

Talia nodded. "He's a good person. Kind."

"He is the heir to one of those peoples," Michael informed her. "We were able to free the Bakas from Kurtherian control. The other is like the Collective, separated and still imprisoned. When we discovered the factories where the Ookens are made, Bethany Anne vowed she wouldn't rest until they have Justice."

"That's why she's so determined to stay on schedule," Talia murmured, more to herself than to Michael. She knew she would feel the same in the Queen's position. These empathic entities who sang beautifully enough to rend her heart deserved so much better than being made into mindless killers.

"The sooner the Federation is protected, the sooner we

can dismantle the Kurtherians' assets and free the innocents they've enslaved," Michael told her. "The Collective has been through a huge ordeal as a species. We freed a few, those you heard on the recording. The rest are still in the factories."

Talia slipped the headset back on and was quiet for the remainder of the descent, lost in the song. On the surface was the pure joy of being connected to each other that had brought tears to her eyes. But there was more. The melody was layers deep, shifting tone and emotions as the voices overlapped to tell her the story of their experiences.

She closed her eyes and her mind began to differentiate between the layers, to see how each refrain was in fact a memory looping eternally. Under the joy was a sense of waiting, of certainty in the future despite the challenges they currently faced. The farther in she went, the more voices she heard. Deeper in time, their song was tainted by grief and separation, the pain of being apart from the whole.

Talia wept as she learned the history of the Collective in their own words. Much like her people, they had been used by others who cared nothing for their sentience. Every Loren remembered what it had been like before the humans came. Those protesting human intervention had much shorter memories, in her opinion.

The Etheric Empire had put an end to the Skaines raiding Loren colonies and selling the inhabitants to the highest bidder. It was only in recent times that the Skaines and many other similarly-minded planetary states had made the necessary adjustments to their societies to get the Federation sanctions on their trade goods lifted. Those who refused? The Queen's Justice cut both ways, and that was just fine with Talia.

Michael touched her shoulder. "We're here."

Talia opened her eyes and saw they were somehow not underwater anymore. She climbed out of the roamer in disbelief, needing to confirm that her eyes weren't lying when they told her brain the ocean was overhead, lit by floodlights on the rooftops of the buildings laid out in neat rows as far as she could see.

Outside the translucent dome, kelp rippled gently. Talia took it all in with a sense of wonder. "We're on the seabed."

Michael nodded. "This is Ranger Base Two. Explore and meet the personnel. Call my name when you're done and we'll discuss the offer Bethany Anne has for you."

Talia nodded, unsure of what offer the Queen could have come up with since they hadn't spoken more than a few words after their initial meeting.

"Bethany Anne has everyone in mind," Michael told her. "Especially those who put others before themselves."

He vanished, leaving Talia twiddling her tentacles as she wondered where to start.

An energetic-looking human approached and introduced herself as Ranger Nine, Jacqueline. "Welcome to Ranger Base Two. Let me show you around."

Four hours later, Talia called for Michael. "What is the Queen's offer?" she asked when he appeared. "Does it get me a place working here?"

Michael smiled, appreciating her straightforward approach. "If you accept, you will join the crew of the *Gemini* for their current operation, the extraction of an embedded asset on an anti-Empire cult ship."

Talia liked the twins a lot, but she had a much bigger rescue mission in mind after everything she'd learned in the past few hours. "I don't see how that gets me here for real. I want to help the Collective. They're… Do you know how many Lorens are left?"

Michael shook his head. "I know it isn't a great number."

"We are scattered among the stars, thanks to the Skaines," Talia stated without malice, thinking of her sister on Dawnseeker. "But that's the past. Even the Skaines changed, thanks to the Rangers. Thanks to the humans denying them the choice of doing anything but evolve or die."

She swept a tentacle to take in the view outside the dome. "This world was dead, polluted beyond being able to support life by the Kurtherians. I'm not going to pretend I understand half of what the scientists told me, but I know a miracle when I see one."

"My wife finds it delightfully amusing to make statements," Michael told her. "There's nothing more demoralizing to the enemy or more heartening to our people than seeing something once used to oppress or destroy turned into a symbol of freedom and hope."

Talia's tentacles rustled in amusement. "She does know how to make a statement. So, what happens if I go with the *Gemini?*"

"Ranger Two will be joining the crew as a consultant for the duration of the operation," Michael informed her. "Your duty will involve assisting her while learning what it takes to be a Ranger. After the operation, you will return to the Cosnar System with her."

Talia did her best to be objective, despite feeling like she'd willingly part with a tentacle for the chance to meet the Collective and be part of the effort to return their basic dignity to them. She clasped all four pairs of her upper tentacles together and gave Michael her most earnest look. "Let's get out of here. I need to pack."

CHAPTER EIGHT

Cosnar System, Ranger Base One

"We are picking up a Gate signature," CEREBRO announced. "It is the *Polaris*."

"Let her pass," Akio instructed, smiling when he sensed the identities of the ship's occupants.

Eve appeared on the main screen, her face glowing with joy. "Hello, old friend."

"Your arrival couldn't have come at a better time," Akio told her warmly. "How are your passengers faring after the long journey?"

"They became more exuberant with every day that passed." Eve laughed, tapping the earpiece she was wearing. "Can you hear the group mind? They are singing."

"I hear them." Akio had no need for a headset, being one of the few whose enhancement granted him strong psychic abilities. He took a moment to immerse himself in the rich chorus filling the mindspace. He, then sent the Collective his feelings of welcome and received an invitation to join the group mind whenever he wished. *You do me great honor,* he told them. *This is a momentous occasion. I welcome you.*

"Meet you there," Eve told him when the Collective returned to their celebration. "I have to see this planet with my own eyes."

Akio continued to smile as he made his way to the base in a Pod, firing off a quick message to Nickie to tell her their VIPs had arrived as he flew. He had spoken the truth; it was his great pleasure to pay forward what had been done for him.

There wasn't a day that went by that he failed to feel gratitude for his freedom, yet as long and dark as his time as a slave had been, it was nothing in comparison to the generations of cruelty inflicted upon the Collective. The trauma they had suffered and that the majority were still suffering at the hands of the Kurtherians disgusted him.

This day had been too long in coming for the passengers of the *Polaris*. He would not be there to see their kin freed when Bethany Anne launched her attack on the factories. When the armada departed, the Rangers had the duty of defending the outer reaches of the Federation. Reclaiming this planet had been his opportunity to be part of the effort to restore a life worth living to the Collective. His contribution was to build a home where they could start to reconstruct their fractured society.

Akio's Pod had him at the underwater base ahead of Eve. The kelp forest parted to reveal a translucent dome with a much larger rectangular enclosure tacked onto the south side. He directed the Pod to the dome covering the sprawling complex of buildings that made up Ranger Base

Two, his gaze drawn by the enclosure filled with gently undulating marine kelp.

CEREBRO admitted Akio's Pod through the airlock. He landed on the roof of the operations center, where he found Dr. Jeddah waiting for him with barely-concealed excitement bubbling under the surface of her professional demeanor.

"Is the acclimation enclosure ready?" Akio asked as they walked inside.

"Of course," Vivian told him. "The last thing we want is to find out the hard way if we got any part of the model wrong."

Akio nodded. This planet was not a controlled environment, it was a fully-functioning biome built from many alien species. The kelp was the only part of the ecosystem the Collective had been exposed to so far. They had to be transferred to the enclosure and introduced to their new environment gradually.

The *Polaris* made its entrance, surrounded by schools of brightly-colored fish and a large group of marine mammals Akio had believed to be dolphins until last week. He had encountered one and been scolded sharply by her for not recognizing that while she shared genetic traits with the Earth *Delphinidae,* she was an Eriba from the planet Eribaum, a world with landlocked oceans and limited room for growth as a species.

A Pod left the ship and made its way to the airlock Akio had used. It landed by Akio's Pod.

"This must be the famous Eve," Vivian commented.

Akio met Eve with open arms when she stepped out of

the Pod. "Welcome to Waterworld. You are a sight for sore eyes."

Eve returned Akio's hug with enthusiasm. "It's been too long."

Akio's smile was tinged with sadness. "War is the cause of many hardships, separation from those we love being one of the most challenging to bear. I'm glad you are here to help the Collective transition to their new lives."

Eve's smile was pure satisfaction. "I wouldn't be anywhere else. I have grown rather attached to them these last few years." She stared at the gently-rippling kelp inside the acclimation enclosure while she examined the water composition data. "The enclosure levels are optimal. I'm going to give the crew the go-ahead to get the Collective settled in."

Akio nodded. "Before we start, meet Dr. Vivian Jeddah. Her input when it came to reviving the planet was invaluable."

Eve shook the hand that was offered. "I have seen your reports, Dr. Jeddah. The results your team has accomplished are impressive, to say the least."

"Vivian, please." She blushed deeply at the praise. "We knew the importance of building a rich ecosystem, of course. While the kelp forests are designed to grow well in the full ranges of temperature and depth the oceans provide, they still require maintenance. Our goal has been to create self-sustaining balance with the macrobiology and microbiology we have introduced."

"The Collective will never go hungry with the bounty science has provided," Akio asserted. "Neither will their souls cry out for nourishment once they are reunited, with such beauty surrounding them."

Vivian chuckled. "You just like spending time on the reef."

Akio shrugged. "Guilty. I did not know psionic fish existed."

Eve laughed lightly as she took Akio's arm and guided him to the viewing platform that looked out over the acclimation enclosure. "The Collective is about to make the transfer."

Vivian placed her hand on the window, observing with fascination as the *Polaris* docked at the specially designed hatch in the roof of the enclosure. There was a flash of light as the docking mechanism engaged and the enclosure's forcefield formed a seal around the corresponding hatch in the belly of the ship.

"It is good to see my design in action," Eve commented as the hatches slid back in unison and the *Polaris'* aquatic decks were joined with the acclimation enclosure. "No more tanks, no more cages," she murmured into her headset.

Eve tilted her head as she connected to the base's systems and activated the speakers. "You need to hear this. Everyone on the base does."

Everyone stopped in their tracks when the Collective's song filled the base. One by one, the nine Collectives flowed gracefully into the enclosure. Everyone listening was overwhelmed by the sudden onrush of visions and emotions they shared as they disappeared into the kelp.

The *Reynolds'* engineering crew downed their tools for a

moment, swept up in the majesty of the Collective's exaltation at seeing their new home for the first time.

Akio put a hand on his chest, allowing himself to be taken by the moment. Almost everyone else on the base was experiencing this as an observer. Immersed in the group mind, he was privileged to feel the Collective's reactions as if they were his own.

He felt the clean water against his skin and wonder at the seemingly unending space. He felt their gratitude, given the tanks they'd lived in since their rescue and the steady patience they'd cultivated, knowing that this day would come. He felt satisfaction, the relief of hopes granted, the longing to share this new paradise with the long-lost.

The Conduit emerged from the kelp and swam to the viewing window. It touched the glass with a tentacle and spoke to Akio. *We cannot express the depth of our gratitude.*

I understand, Akio replied, recognizing the mental signature as belonging to the Conduit. *One day this world will be home to all of the Collective.*

The Conduit broke off and turned to look when the Eriba and their flocks gathered outside the enclosure.

Meet the guardians of the forests, Akio explained, feeling cautious curiosity from all nine Collectives. The Eriba shepherd the creatures who maintain the kelp. I believe your two peoples will be able to live in harmony.

A wave of hope for companionship came from the Conduit. *We can hear them.*

The Eriba sent out a warm welcome as the other Collectives emerged from the kelp.

Eve laid a hand on Akio's arm as the two groups got

acquainted. "I'm recording this," she told him quietly. "Bethany Anne intends to play it into the factory prisons when she attacks, along with messages for the other groups we have had contact with. The Collective will know freedom is waiting for them."

Akio was about to agree when CEREBRO interrupted with an urgent message from Tabitha. He inclined his head to Eve and Vivian. "Please excuse me."

He walked to an empty space and opened the message. There was very little detail besides a request for Nickie to travel on the *Polaris* to the *Baba Yaga* and assist the *Gemini*'s crew with an assignment beyond Federation borders.

Sensing Tabitha's request wasn't entirely aboveboard, he forwarded it to Bethany Anne to get confirmation.

Akio received an almost immediate reply, both confirming the order and adding the information that Nickie was to onboard a Ranger recruit she had aboard the *Baba Yaga*.

He apologized to Eve and Vivian, pleading duty, and went to find Nickie.

Ranger Base One

Nickie decided Durq needed some adventure in his life as she made her way from the ops center to the residential wing. Taking the *Granddaughter* wasn't an option, so she didn't necessarily need any crew with her.

Durq was of the same mind when she found him studying in his quarters.

Nickie waited for him to open the door, then leaned

against the doorframe and folded her arms. "Pack a bag. We're going on a road trip."

Durq remained seated at his desk, all but hugging his study notes. "You don't want me under your feet on an op," he told her. "I just get in the way when you're fighting, and I can't keep a cover story straight to save my life."

"You have to come," Nickie pleaded. "I'm not ordering you to go as your captain. I'm asking you to come as my friend. It's not just an op. I'm supposed to teach the twins what I know about working on the frontier."

"You don't want to take Grim?" Durq asked shyly, forgetting his misgivings at the thought of Nickie choosing him.

Nickie nodded. "Not this time. He has to get Sam Jr. under control before he can go on an op. It's just me and the terrifying twins." She decided to omit that they were picking up a new recruit until they were on their way. "I could use your support."

That part was true.

Durq's look of terror faded. He got to his feet and wrapped Nickie in a tight hug. "Okay, I'll come. Give me an hour to pack and postpone my exam."

"Exam?" Nickie asked.

Durq grinned. "I'm not much of a fighter, but Base Two needs a huge engineering crew. Addie has been helping me brush up on everything I learned working with her, and it turns out I qualify for the fast track program. All I have to do is pass the entrance exam and I've got a job waiting."

Nickie's heart fell. "Then you have to stay and take the exam."

Durq shook his head. "I wouldn't be able to concentrate, knowing I left you hanging. When have you ever asked anything of me? You have the authority to make sure I don't miss out."

Nickie picked Durq up and spun him around before releasing him to totter unsteadily into his bedroom. "I'll speak to...whoever. How soon can you be ready to leave?"

"An hour," Durq promised.

Nickie waved as she headed for the door. "You know I love you. Meet me in the main hangar when you're ready. We're hitching a ride on the *Polaris*."

They met with plenty of time to get settled into their respective quarters on the crew deck before the *Polaris* departed for the *Baba Yaga's* location. Eve greeted Nickie in passing as they boarded, too caught up in taking care of her aquatic travelers to stay and talk.

Nickie dropped her bags on her bed before sitting at the desk by the holowindow to start planning her approach to her assignment. Meredith did what she could to help by procuring records of the twins' previous operations involving the anti-Empire cult from ADAM.

"They've definitely got experience," Nickie murmured to Meredith, noting the professional planning and execution of their undercover operations so far. "What if they're uptight, by-the-book military brats?"

"You're scared?" Meredith inquired via the speaker in Nickie's datapad.

Nickie shrugged. "I don't know about scared. I'm pretty fucking intimidated by the thought of teaching. The last time I saw the twins was before their enhancement. I'm no role model."

Meredith laughed. "That's not true, at least not the way

you're looking at it. Rangers are a different kind of role model. They aren't bound by the same protocols as regular military or law enforcement agencies."

"We're not above the law," Nickie argued.

"No," Meredith agreed. "However, a Ranger is free to interpret the law to fit the extraordinary circumstances they find themselves in on the frontier. If anything, a Ranger's moral compass has to be truer than true. Incorruptible."

Nickie didn't disagree. "I'm not wild about a recruit being there to see me fall flat on my face. Onboarding is more Hirotoshi's and Ryu's thing, or Katsu's if they're tech-minded. They have a shit-ton of experience compared to me."

"You were a Ranger long before you got that badge," Meredith told her, somehow managing to sound like she was chastising Nickie as much as praising her. "I was there when you thought I wasn't. You did right by those who deserved the Queen's Justice even when you were at rock bottom."

Nickie thought about telling Meredith that she hadn't much considered doing good when she'd been taking her frustrations out on the lowest of the low in the process of searching out the next good time on the frontier.

The reminder of her darkest days reinforced to Nickie that Bethany Anne's children had no business operating on the outside without a guide to ensure they didn't get their precious throats cut within a week of leaving the safety of their parents' protection. "I'm not questioning the necessity of my being given this assignment."

"Okay," Meredith conceded. "So, what?"

Nickie shrugged, pushing her datapad away. "Honestly?"

"Well, it would be preferable," Meredith replied coolly. "We'll be at the Dren Cluster in less than thirty hours."

"Fuck you, Mere," Nickie retorted. "Why do you always push my buttons?"

"My core programming compels me to provide you with stimulation," Meredith assured her with a lilt of humor in her tone. "It's not my fault that the thing you find most stimulating is an argument."

Nickie rolled her eyes. "Fuck. My. Life. Meredith, if I tell you, will you leave me the fuck alone?"

"Why don't you try it and find out?" Meredith returned.

"Kill me now," Nickie grumbled. "Okay. Fine. There's an old human saying. '*The past is a different country, and you can't go back there.*'"

"Yet here you are, about to do just that," Meredith sympathized.

Nickie dropped her head on her folded arms. "Yet here I am. I'm not that person anymore, Mere. I've worked my ass off to become someone my family can be proud of."

"Do you think Bethany Anne would have given you this assignment if you weren't?" Meredith asked. "Suck this existential crisis up, Ranger. You have people relying on you."

Nickie snorted. "Thanks, Mere. That's exactly what I needed to hear."

Meredith huffed. "Your sarcasm is not appreciated."

CHAPTER NINE

QSD *Baba Yaga*, Bridge

Morale on the bridge was high, with everyone anticipating a warm welcome from a station that felt like home and the chance to spend a little more time with the Waltons.

"Coordinates received from Spires Shipyard," Izanami announced to the fleet. "We are approaching our destination. Gate activation in five…four…three…two…"

The *Baba Yaga* and the *Reynolds* swept through the Gate Izanami created a thousand kilometers from the shipyard, where they were greeted by an unexpected honor guard in the form of the *War Axe*.

A debate broke out among Gabriel, Trey, K'aia, and Alexis about who was at the helm of the destroyer as Tina and Geroux slipped away to prepare their teams for transfer to the shipyard and station.

"The *War Axe* is hailing us," Izanami told Bethany Anne.

"Onscreen, Izanami." Bethany Anne couldn't contain her smile when the head of the Bad Company's Direct Action

Branch appeared. She had changed this woman's diaper as an infant, but that was ancient history. Bethany Anne had watched from afar as Christina grew from an astute and formidable child into the most capable commander the Bad Company's sledgehammer could ask for now that TH had retired. "I wasn't expecting to see you here, Colonel Lowell."

Christina nodded in acknowledgment of the respect Bethany Anne was showing her in front of the cameras streaming to the Federation. "I didn't want to miss out on welcoming you to the Dren Cluster, my Queen."

Kai bobbed into view, waggling his fingers briefly before vanishing again.

"You two should be on your honeymoon!" Alexis exclaimed in exasperation.

Christina lifted her hands. "What can I say? A working honeymoon is better than none. We've had our manufacturing facilities running around the clock since we got back from Serenity with the specs you gave us. We are ready to join the CEREBRO network."

"That's what I like to hear, Colonel," Bethany Anne praised. "Keeg Station and the Bad Company are shining examples of how strong leadership gets things done."

"We're just a small part of the big picture." Christina glanced at the tiny drones hovering around Bethany Anne and made the decision to speak her mind. "This monumental effort that has occurred across the Federation has taken the cooperation of everyone. Because we *have* come together. We have strived to not only protect but to connect every inhabited planet and space station with the rest. This drive to be together, to be part of the whole, protecting each other, looking out for our neighbors as well as ourselves.

"*That* is what the Bad Company fights to protect. We have a reputation. The rumors are true, I don't deny it. Those we come for lose everything because their crimes against the Federation demand it. We are dedicated. We are ruthless in pursuing Justice. We will fight to the last soldier for the rights of Federation citizens to live without fear. Turning that on the Seven is both an honor and our very great pleasure."

Bethany Anne smiled. "As it is mine. The support of the people makes protecting them that much easier. Keeg Station has been a safe haven for Federation citizens on the frontier for over a decade. By the time the tour moves on, it will be better protected and more heavily defended. Outlying colonies will be able to alert the station immediately in emergencies."

"You have no idea how many lives that's going to save," Christina informed her cheerily. "Dionysus will guide the *Baba Yaga* and the *Reynolds* into their docking spires. Both those babies look as though they could do with some TLC, and we have our reputation as the premier shipyard in the Federation to uphold."

Bethany Anne inclined her head. "Unexpected, but welcome."

"I'll meet you in the transfer lounge." Christina waved and then dropped the link.

Bethany Anne was still smiling when she turned to Izanami after the screen went blank. "You heard the Colonel. Prepare to dock, and inform Tina and Geroux we will be departing from transporter bay one in fifteen minutes. They left too soon."

Izanami's eyes flashed red. "Done. I will join you when I am satisfied with the repairs they intend to make to my ship. According to Dionysus, there are many extras to choose from."

Bethany Anne raised an eyebrow. "Nothing that affects the operational efficiency of the ship. No changes to anything on this deck without my approval."

Izanami feigned indignation. "Credit me with a modicum of self-control. It's not as though you're going to get back and find I exchanged the plasma cannons to get the phase manifold conducers plated with anodized titanium."

"You're not convincing me," Bethany Anne told her, unable to repress her laughter at the AI's idea of a mani-pedi for the Gate drive.

"I am hoping to be shown weapons that compliment my current loadout," Izanami elucidated. "There is a vast array of technology that has been reverse-engineered from the Beniton station called Nadezhda. I am also looking to improve the efficiency of the biomatter processors, and to explore what is possible with the holographic technology used aboard the station."

"What's your budget for all these upgrades?" Bethany Anne asked.

"Reynolds and I have half a million credits each put aside for the improvements," Izanami replied with a smile. "We are meeting Shonna in a few hours to go through her catalogs."

"Sounds like a blast for you both." Bethany Anne transferred five hundred thousand credits to Izanami's account, then the same to Reynolds' with a note explaining what it was for. "Tell Shonna you want something you haven't seen before. Have fun, both of you. You two have earned the right to a little pampering."

"Damn straight, we have." Izanami disappeared in a shower of golden sparks.

"I'll meet you in the transporter bay," Michael told Alexis, Gabriel, K'aia, and Trey before turning back to the viewscreen. "The shipyard has expanded greatly in the last few years, according to Christina. I want to see this wondrous technology she is so enamored of in action."

"Not just Christina." Alexis chuckled fondly at her father's preoccupation with the drama playing out on the viewscreen. She turned to find that Gabriel, K'aia, and Trey had left ahead of her.

"Hey, wait up, guys!" she yelled as she ran after them. "We have to find Talia before we leave!"

Bethany Anne made a side trip to her armory to grab her coat, then made her way to the transporter bay. She arrived in an empty room.

"Izanami?"

No response.

"Transporter systems must remain offline until the docking procedure is completed," a dispassionate male voice told her from the speaker.

"Who the hell are you?" Bethany Anne demanded.

"Dionysus," Dionysus replied. "Transporter systems must remain offline until the docking procedure is completed."

"Well, aren't you just a ray of sunshine?" Bethany Anne

replied, annoyed by being held up. Her patience evaporated, and she stepped into the Etheric without another word.

Michael remained on the bridge, enjoying the spectacle that was Spires Shipyard. The main shipyard was full to capacity, with lanes of ships waiting to dock.

Ships of all sizes were being built or repaired in maintenance docks attached to the many spires that branched off each module of the shipyard's central core. On the opposite side from where the *Baba Yaga* had Gated in, he saw hundreds of sleeping ships awaiting their upgraded crews.

The children could tease him all they liked. What Alexis failed to realize was that her attention to detail came from him. Bethany Anne liked what tech could do. *How* it was done didn't interest her one bit.

This shipyard was a wonder of innovation that he had a special appreciation for. In the fifteen hundred-plus years he had lived, for more than thirteen hundred of those, the most sophisticated form of travel for crossing the sea was a wooden boat sealed with pitch, the only protection the prayers of the brave people sailing it.

Technology had progressed with increasing speed, snowballing from the nineteen hundreds onward with the invention of the combustion engine and the advent of mass production. Advances in computing in the twentieth century had moved almost faster than even he could keep up with, which was how he had ended up employing Carl and his predecessors to keep him ahead of everyone else.

The *Baba Yaga* was large enough to accommodate two hundred thousand people in relative comfort, yet she and the *Reynolds* were dwarfed by the central core of the shipyard. Everywhere Michael looked, there was activity, AIs working in tandem with people to operate the massive robotic repair arms integrated with the maintenance docks. What humanity had achieved when given access to tech created by much older civilizations was nothing short of miraculous. The use of automation here was beyond anything he could have imagined back then. No wonder they were adding as many as six ships a week to the fleet.

Michael's smile shifted when a moment of nostalgia swept over him. Carl would have lost his shit seeing this. He returned his attention to the docking process, examining the unoccupied spire protruding from each side of the station as they came in. He assumed that was their destination.

The AI operating the docks scanned the *Baba Yaga* and the *Reynolds* as they cruised slowly toward the base of the station. Michael lost sight of the *Reynolds* as the ships parted ways, to be received at the two spires.

He received another automated message as the *Baba Yaga* approached the spire, but he barely glanced at it, more interested in watching the marvel occurring outside the ship.

Getting closer, Michael saw that the spire culminated in an octagonal maintenance dock maybe a third the *Baba Yaga's* girth and a third her length. At first, it looked like the *Baba Yaga* was heading for a dock that was far too small to take the city-sized superdreadnought. Michael withheld judgment as the *Baba Yaga* held her position, waiting for permission to dock.

A stream of bots hauling heavy equipment exited the

octagon as it expanded to make a berth wide enough to receive the forward third of the ship. The octagon's angled compartments slid apart, revealing its modular construction. Telescopic scaffolding fixed between the modules unfolded smoothly, keeping the compartments connected as they were configured to line up with the forward airlocks. The bots wasted no time, clustering in the gaps between the modules as soon as the magnetic locks activated to fix the scaffolding in place.

Michael continued to watch the bots' rapid-fire installation for a few minutes, then decided he'd best check the message he'd received as the *Baba Yaga* began creeping forward to enter the dock. It advised that passengers were to remain *in situ* until they had confirmation from Dionysus that the forward airlocks were aligned with the transfer lounge modules, letting him in on the purpose of the modular compartments.

Realizing that Izanami's absence likely had more to do with performing the complex maneuvers needed to move safely through the crowded shipyard than her rush to spend the credits burning a hole in her account, Michael returned to the show on the viewscreen.

The bots were done. The purpose of their equipment became clear when more telescopic scaffolding was deployed from three of the previously empty spaces around the octagon. The scaffolding spiraled out at an angle, forming a triple helix that continued to extend until it wound around the remaining length of the ship. Docking clamps engaged as each section of the support structure moved into place.

The structure continued to expand from the docking

clamp platforms. Gantries sprouted from the junctions to join the three spirals. With the *Baba Yaga* encased in scaffolding, the bots got back to work, swarming the gantries. Some began affixing huge, skeletal arms to the scaffolding. Others hovered over the surface of the hull as they deep-scanned the ship to determine what repairs were needed.

Michael's attention was captured by the elegance of the robotic arms that moved in to begin repairing the wear and tear the ship had racked up in the last few months. He snapped out of his trance when he received a message from Dionysus requesting certain areas be evacuated while the hull was cleaned and repaired.

Michael opened a channel to the AI. "What is the reason for the evacuation?"

"There are a number of places where damage to the hull has been repaired with permacrete foam," Dionysus informed him. "Those plugs need to be removed, and the hull patched. The listed areas are sections of the ship that might experience a loss of atmosphere during the repairs."

Michael thanked Dionysus and cut the call. "Izanami, have all non-essential personnel relocate to Keeg Station. Make sure those who remain are aware of the repairs happening. The affected areas are off-limits."

"Done, and done," Izanami replied from a speaker. "Dionysus has approved transporter use. You are free to leave the ship."

"Where is Bethany Anne?" he asked.

There was the briefest pause before Izanami answered. "She left transporter bay one via the Etheric two minutes and seventeen seconds ago."

Michael strode from the bridge and headed for the transporter bay, amused by his wife's impatience.

Dren Cluster, Spires Shipyard

Bethany Anne exited the Etheric on the other side of the docking spire's transfer lounges. A crowd of station crew milled around, here to meet the teams they would be working with over the next six weeks.

Christina left an elevator and crossed to where Bethany Anne was people-watching, dropping all formality to embrace her when they met. "Good to see you again so soon."

Bethany Anne smiled as she released Christina. "Thank you for the personal sacrifice you and Kai have made. You will get time for yourselves, I promise."

"We could have stayed longer on Serenity. We agreed that duty came before tradition this time. We didn't want to waste any time getting the weapons and transporter tech installed," Christina told Bethany Anne, her eyes shining with glee at the extra destructive power the Bad Company's flagship had been given. "The *War Axe* has all the bells and whistles, including a spanking-new Gate drive, transporter system, weapons upgrades, the latest food-processing units, and sonic showers in quarters. I could go on."

Bethany Anne chuckled at her enthusiasm. "You like the new toys? Have you slept at all since you got back?"

Christina's eyes widened in amused appreciation. "I wasn't kidding when I said we've been busy. Ted, via Plato, has the ship upgrades running with precision, thanks to Shonna acting as an intermediary between him and the workers. Between them, the fabrication and installation crews have delivered all their impossible demands."

Bethany Anne's mouth turned up at the news that Char's suggestion for handling the upgrades of power supplies, Gate drives, and weapons systems without driving their workers insane had been effective. "What does that mean for the armada's status?"

Christina waggled her eyebrows. "It means we're turning out upgraded Federation ships at a rate of six per week. I can't speak for the other shipyards, but we're ahead of schedule. Keeg is almost at capacity with the FDG and the paramilitary outfits from around this quadrant that made the cut as legitimate organizations. Their ships are ready and waiting for them. Those fuckface Kurtherians aren't going to know what hit them when we rock up and blow their shit to space dust."

Bethany Anne snickered. "That's the plan." She glanced at the crowd in the main lounge. "Where's Felicity?"

Christina lifted a shoulder, her brow furrowing. "You know, I don't know. She was supposed to be here. So was Char."

Bethany Anne waved a hand. "Finding them will have to wait. I want to say goodbye to my children before they leave on their next assignment."

Christina wrinkled her nose. "They're getting ready to deploy? Sucks for the bad guys. The twins are relentless. Kai and I had a blast working with them."

Michael, Alexis, and Gabriel transported in with Tina, Marcus, Takal, Geroux, and Reynolds and Izanami in their android bodies. The team leaders Bethany Anne had called in arrived a moment later.

The docking procedure was complete, and the crews of both superdreadnoughts spilled into the transfer lounges. Many had their equipment in tow on antigrav carts of every size, ready to begin the massive overhaul planned for Keeg Station as the central point of defense for that quadrant.

There were a few moments to exchange greetings for those who had been together on Serenity, and introductions for those who had been indisposed by duty and unable to attend Christina's and Kai's wedding. Everyone was delighted to meet Timmons, Shonna, and Merit, werewolves and engineers all.

K'Thrall, a Yollin sergeant major, and Slikira, an Ixtali Bad Company warrior, were taken with K'aia's custom armor, having had trouble acquiring armor suited for the four-legged. The sergeant major's interest was for those under his command, he being two-legged.

Bethany Anne connected to the transfer lounge's speaker system and called for everyone's attention. "Everyone knows what they need to do. Work with your counterparts to get this station connected to the blanket quickly and safely, and there will be a reward of three days' leave aboard Keeg Station. This will be your last leave for the duration of the tour. I am informed that the station is the place to be entertained in this quadrant, should you need motivation."

They did not. There was a brief buzz of conversation while the team leaders took instructions from their respective project managers, then the lounges began to empty as the crews left to catch transfer shuttles with their new workmates.

Bethany Anne lifted a finger to Christina as the civilians debarked. The lounges began to fill up again, this time with family members of the enlisted permanent residents. Delighted children whose energy was boosted by the excitement of being in a new place ran circles around their parents and guardians.

She saw Gabriel and Alexis waiting to speak to her before they left. "One minute."

Christina waved to catch K'Thrall's attention. "Go ahead. I need to find us transport."

Bethany Anne hitched a thumb toward the panoramic window that looked out onto the *Baba Yaga*. "We'll take a roamer. You know where they're kept."

"Don't do the mom thing," Gabriel told Bethany Anne as Christina left.

"What 'mom thing' is that?" Bethany Anne inquired with a wry smile. She turned to look for K'aia and Trey. "Get in here, you two." She held them all for a long moment before stepping back. "Take care, and kick ass like I know you can."

Michael slipped an arm around Bethany Anne's waist as the four of them left to search for Talia, promising to keep in touch. "Young Roka is in the best of hands, whether she knows it or not."

Bethany Anne rested her head in the hollow of his shoulder. "I'm so fucking proud of them. We make excellent children." She laughed when Michael went stiff in her arms and released him with a playful shove. "It wasn't a hint that we should do it again."

Michael held up his hands in surrender. "Good. I don't mind admitting that the first time was experience enough."

Bethany Anne rolled her eyes at him. "I wouldn't bring a child into our life as it is right now. I have enough guilt about Alexis and Gabriel being forced to grow up so fast."

"You didn't start the war," Michael reasoned.

"No, but I'll end it," Bethany Anne vowed. "Then we can all live in peace. I've been thinking about Earth more and more."

"You're homesick," Michael responded softly. "As am I. I believe we left a piece of ourselves behind when we left Earth."

Bethany Anne nodded, relieved she wasn't alone. "I want to go home. Whatever Earth looks like now, however people and society have evolved, it's where we belong." She sighed. "And it's denied to us until we can be sure we're not leading every asshole in the known universe there. Until I can be sure it's safe to bring Earth into the Federation, it stays hidden."

"Then we had better get to work bringing that day around," Michael told her with a smile. "The Bad Company's ranking officers will be the first to be upgraded. They will assist John and Nathan with the rest once they're done, leaving me free to keep working with Isaiah."

He leaned in and pressed a kiss to Bethany Anne's temple. "Good luck with Ted."

Bethany Anne laughed as she tilted her head to catch the kiss with her lips. "Ted's a sweetheart," she told him. "You just have to know how to speak to him. Besides, I have the upper hand. He doesn't know that I know he and Felicity have been to Earth to see their children."

Michael raised an eyebrow. "Is that wise? What if Gödel found out?"

Bethany Anne lifted a shoulder. "*I* only know because Plato slipped up in a conversation with ADAM, and ADAM made him spill. I've assessed the risk. Ted can be trusted not to get caught. With that in mind, I have a feeling that giving him and Felicity dispensation to visit Earth so they can keep in touch with their children will go a long way toward softening his reaction to being diverted from his work."

She glanced at the roamer bumping down the airlock ramp. "I see my ride."

Once Michael had returned to the *Baba Yaga,* Christina and Bethany Anne set off in the roamer.

Christina made a clipped inquiry to Dionysus as to where the manager of Keeg Station was at that moment and the snooty AI referred them to Iracitus, who informed her that Felicity was with Ted in his workshop on Nadezhda Station.

"Dionysus is not my favorite AI," she told Bethany Anne. "He lacks tact and has none of Plato's empathy."

"Plato probably developed empathy in response to Ted's need for it," Bethany Anne guessed. She sent a message to Felicity, asking her to meet them at her office on the main concourse. "I want to lay eyes on this mecca of good taste Char wouldn't stop talking about when we were on Serenity. There's no point in dragging Ted away from his work before we've overseen phase one of the defensive upgrades. If anything comes out of that rift, it's going to be vaporized before it's taken a breath."

"Felicity will leave Ted to his own devices or she won't."

Christina noticed Bethany Anne's stride had purpose. "Where are we going?"

"I messaged Felicity," Bethany Anne told her. "Her office is above the main promenade, right?"

Christina nodded. "Hers, Char's, and Shonna's."

Bethany Anne gave Christina a sideways look as they entered the main promenade. "You didn't want in on their fashion empire?"

Christina shook her head, chuckling. "I have my duty to keep me occupied. That, and a husband with a slim grasp of his mortality."

"He didn't get a full upgrade yet?" Bethany Anne asked.

Christina shook her head. "You wouldn't believe the crazy nanocytes he has. Ted says the reason he had no apparent abilities is conflicting instructions or something."

"He's a lot harder to kill than he was before he went into the Vid-doc," Bethany Anne reasoned. "He should get in touch with Eve. She figured it out when Tabitha's pregnancy was killing her."

"I'll pass that along." Christina smiled as she caught a flash of sequins in the crowd. "Here's Felicity."

Dressed to the nines as always, Felicity stood out among the shoppers in a strapless royal blue gown with silver trim and matching four-inch heels. She carved through the crowds of shoppers on the promenade, waving at Bethany Anne and Christina. "I thought I smelled good shoes," she offered in greeting, eyeing Bethany Anne's feet enviously. "How have you managed to sit on *those* for this long?"

Bethany Anne extended one Louboutin-clad foot and

smiled. "I didn't. They were a gift from a friend who lives outside this universe."

Felicity gave her a skeptical look. "Well, don't you get all the luck. Our humble boutiques aren't anything like as exclusive as Louboutin is in this universe."

Bethany Anne slipped an arm through Felicity's and started walking again. "I've heard nothing but good things about what you've built here. We will definitely have time for shopping before the tour moves on. Right now, we have a station to overhaul and a metric shit-ton of outlying colonies to connect to the CEREBRO network."

Felicity sniffed, somewhat mollified. "Then we'd better get to work. Opening Keeg up to the Gate system attracted a wave of settlers that's still going strong." She smiled, her pride evident. "The Dren Cluster is a hot property, I'll have you know. Turn your back for just a minute, and the frontier has expanded while you weren't looking."

"I'll keep that in mind," Bethany Anne assured her. "We'll start with a walkthrough of the station's current security protocols. ADAM is in contact with the local AIs, and he will inform me when the phase one teams are ready to commence."

After a quick stop at the office, where they found no sign of Char, Bethany Anne, Christina, and Felicity walked side by side through the station, checking off items on their respective schedules as the first-phase engineers began arriving at their destinations around the shipyard.

Bethany Anne remained in contact with Tina, receiving a running commentary on the progress she and Geroux's teams were making in setting up the components of the CEREBRO network.

She was so used to the cameras being on her by now that she periodically had to remind herself to watch her language since parts of the feed were also being shown in schools as part of the "living history" course designed by ADAM and Alexis as part of their effort to ensure no entity like the anti-Empire cult took root in the next generation. There were a lot of things she wanted to teach the children, but fluency in creative cursing wasn't on the list.

"You already have plenty of firepower here," Bethany Anne commented, waving one of her camera drones out of the way when it dipped too close.

Felicity took being broadcast to the entire Federation in her elegant stride. It was no secret that she was fond of any opportunity to dress to impress. The sound of high heels clacking on metal decks filled the corridor as they continued deeper into the station.

"We beefed up the defenses when we were attacked shortly after the shipyard was built," she explained. She smiled when Shonna reported that the first ring of satellites was in place. "Shonna says they're getting ready to start installing the relay beacons. The shipyard will be connected to your security blanket in no time at all, it seems. This is some cooperation. I've never seen anything on this scale."

Christina just nodded, having said her piece already.

"How is Ted handling everything?" Bethany Anne inquired, concerned that the sudden changes were causing him trauma.

Felicity's brow furrowed delicately as she smirked. "Like he finally has the resources he deserves, the tyrant." She smiled. "We had plenty of time to prepare, so he's doing just fine. I'll make sure Plato sends details for the improvements to the network he's going to make."

Bethany Anne smiled, knowing that anything their neurodivergent genius came up with while he was focused on their goal would benefit all of the Federation. "He can have whatever he wants, within reason."

"You may live to regret that statement," Felicity drawled. "Or are you buttering up my husband to make being away from home easier for him?"

Christina looked up from examining Bad Company's upgrade schedule on her datapad. "You and Ted are *so* not going on the factory raid."

Bethany Anne shook her head in agreement. "Good God, no. The armada doesn't need Ted to keep it running. The Federation needs Ted right here, where he can react to any surprises that get thrown at you while I'm gone. Char and TH are staying here too," she told Christina. "I want them keeping an eye on things in this quadrant since you will have the Bad Company to lead."

"Speak of the devil," Christina murmured, pointing out Char walking toward them with a determined stride.

Charumati, queen of the werewolves, lifted an expertly manicured finger as she inserted herself into the conversation. "I'm just *fine* with staying behind. My husband might have something to say about it, but he'll get over it in a couple of years. We are retired. R.E.T.I.R.E.D. If trouble appears on our doorstep, we'll deal with it. Otherwise, we intend to do our part by holding up civilization."

"One bar at a time, right?" Christina teased. "I can see TH's brewery empire growing exponentially. You two don't know *how* to take it easy."

Char shrugged.

Bethany Anne laughed. "I'm sure there will be plenty of action to keep TH busy, even if he has to create some himself."

Char groaned, covering her eyes with a hand. "You heard about the 'sabotage.'"

Char ignored Bethany Anne and Felicity's continued teasing. "You can laugh, but you all live with men. You know what stubborn asses they can be if you don't humor them occasionally."

"I don't know," Christina contended. "Can't say I have that problem. Kai's—"

"A stubborn ass like his grandfather," Char told her.

Christina shrugged. "I'm a Lowell. They don't come any more stubborn than us."

The women laughed as K'Thrall approached with another soldier wearing a dress uniform Bethany Anne didn't recognize. She admired the alien's effort with his hair, although she didn't think the rainbow coif would hold up for long in a battle situation.

Christina permitted the soldiers to approach. "K'Thrall, Paithoon, what can I do for you?"

The two-legged Yollin glanced nervously at his Belzonian companion before handing Christina his datapad. "The Trans-Pacific Task Force has, um, cultural issues with the upgrade."

"The who, now?" Bethany Anne asked, confused since she hadn't heard of them.

Paithoon shoved K'Thrall aside and tossed his hair back before bowing to Bethany Anne. "Belzonians, Your Majesty. My people."

K'Thrall rolled his eyes. "See what I have to put up with?" he asked Christina gruffly. "Why you couldn't have had Marcie send Monsoon, I don't know."

Paithoon spluttered. "Because Monsoon has no finesse when it comes to the subtleties of politics!"

"Exactly," K'Thrall grumbled.

Bethany Anne gave Christina a pointed look. "Care to explain…well, this?" she asked, indicating the bristling officers.

"Long story." Christina separated the officers and explained who the Belzonians were and why a loss of sensation would impact their species negatively. "What is the issue, Paithoon?" she asked.

Paithoon flicked his impressive plume of rainbow hair back and gave Christina the look of the perpetually offended. "You can't take away our orgies!" he exclaimed. "It's un-Belzonian!"

"The last thing the Queen needs is for people to bring her problems that don't exist," Christina thundered. "Sergeant Major, please return Protocol Officer Paithoon to his station before I lose my temper."

"Colonel, please!" Paithoon insisted. "I have a right to be concerned that our way of life is going to be altered by the upgrade."

Christina pinned him with her patented give-me-no-bistok-shit look. "Have any of the troops actually made a complaint or decided not to take the opportunity?"

Paithoon had the grace to blush. "Well, not exactly."

Bethany Anne scanned the schedule. "You're down to be upgraded in group fourteen. That's three weeks away. What is your issue?"

"I'm concerned for morale," Paithoon pleaded. "How do I keep morale up if nobody can *feel*? It's intrinsic to who we are."

"Did you miss the part where the upgrade is reversible?" Bethany Anne pointed out. "You're the officer in charge of morale for your people. I suggest you help your people make the most of their time before the upgrade."

Christina whispered to Bethany Anne what that meant.

Bethany Anne shrugged. "Keep it out of public areas, but if your warriors need a three-week orgy to prepare, who am I to argue?"

Paithoon bowed at the waist. "I, well, thank you, most esteemed Majesty," he stammered. "I wish to express how indebted I am to your generosity, but words fail me."

Bethany Anne smiled. "Don't you have some sex swings to hang or something?"

Christina instructed K'Thrall to keep his eye on the celebration to make sure it didn't get out of hand as Paithoon hurried away, mumbling to himself about arrangements.

Bethany Anne watched them go with amusement. "Those Belzonians must be incomparable on the battlefield."

"They're the best ground-pounders outside the FDG," Christina told her, feeling pride on behalf of Marcie's and Kae's efforts to get their army operating to the highest Federation standards. "They went into their first operation with very little training. The op went tits-up, but they still came out of it on top. Marcie has had time to complete their training since then. They are a valuable asset."

Bethany Anne had another asset in mind. "I want to see the rift on Benitus Seven."

Char waved a hand. "No problem. We'll take a shuttle out there in a few days, after you have everything set up to run without you."

Bethany Anne cleared an afternoon three days ahead and sent the appointment to Plato. "It's better to give Ted time to adjust to the idea."

Felicity threw her arms around Bethany Anne and squeezed tightly.

Bethany Anne accepted the hug, wondering what had brought on Felicity's sudden surge of emotion.

Felicity let go and dabbed at her mascara with a tissue she produced as if by magic. "Thank you for how you treat him. Not getting mad."

Bethany Anne shook her head. "Never. I can't get mad at someone for being who they are. I can't say I've ever spent much time with him, but I can see it takes him a lot of effort to break away from the world in his head."

"Ted's way of thinking has been saving lives ever since TH freed the pack from Marcus' control," Char murmured. "He sees what's possible, not what's stopping him. It makes him hard to protect sometimes."

CHAPTER TEN

Dren Cluster, Spires Shipyard

Talia entered the transfer lounge of the docking spire Dionysus had directed her to and found an out of the way place while she awaited the *Polaris*.

Having found her, the team had made an inquiry and discovered the ship hadn't yet arrived. Alexis, Gabriel, K'aia, and Trey had returned to the *Gemini* to dock the ship separately from the *Baba Yaga* in preparation for their departure, while Talia went to meet Nickie Grimes.

Talia used the time to work through the nervousness she felt at meeting Ranger Two. She wanted badly to make a good impression.

She didn't have long to wait. Per the information she'd gotten from Dionysus, the *Polaris* arrived a few minutes later.

The ship glided into the shipyard and docked at the direction of the steward AI.

Talia spotted the Ranger the moment the tall blonde human woman entered the transfer lounge. Were all the enhanced so perfect-looking? She smoothed her tentacles and hurried to meet the Ranger, swallowing to do something about the desert that suddenly took up residence in her mouth.

Nickie couldn't help but grin in relief when she saw the nervous recruit.

She's intimidated, Meredith supplied.

You don't say. Nickie muted Meredith and strode over to meet her trainee. She offered the nervous Loren a hand to break the ice, accepting the tentacle she was offered without reservation. "You must be Talia. I'm Ranger Two. You can call me Nickie."

Protocol! Meredith reminded her sharply.

Dammit, I muted you! Nickie growled.

You can keep trying, Meredith replied sweetly.

Talia recognized the momentary glazed eyes of a human talking to their onboard… "AI or EI?" she inquired, tilting her head in curiosity.

Nickie rolled her eyes. "My pain-in-the-ass EI, who is reminding me I should be enforcing my rank or some such shit. My actions speak for themselves, so I have no need to walk into a situation swinging my dick."

Talia's eyes widened and confusion covered her face. "I don't…"

Nickie waved Talia's reaction off and slipped her arm around the Loren's shoulders. "Consider this lesson one in how the universe really works. I'm not your boss, I'm your instructor. Chain of command is important, but there's no need to be an asshole about it."

Talia drew an involuntary breath, wondering what she'd gotten herself into when she saw a Skaine in a

Ranger uniform enter the lounge. She forced her involuntary reaction down when the Skaine flinched at the sight of her as if *she* was the scary one. Admittedly, he was the scrawniest Skaine she'd ever seen.

Nickie folded her arms and fixed the Skaine with a knowing look. "What kept you?"

"Missy called," he mumbled, abashed.

Nickie laughed. "Fair enough."

Talia looked at Nickie and the Skaine, who was blushing furiously. "So, um, I'm supposed to take you straight to the ship."

Nickie rolled her eyes. "Typical Aunt BA."

Talia shook her head. "It wasn't the Queen who gave me the order to meet you. I mean, it was, but we're headed to the *Gemini*. This assignment is an emergency extraction. One of our agents is in a sticky situation. The agent in question is the niece of Devon's Federation Consul."

"Fuck my life, not Roka?" Nickie cursed some more when Talia nodded and then pushed her hair back with a hand. "She's still with the merc ship, right?"

Talia nodded again. "As far as we know."

Nickie narrowed her eyes, concern and anger for her friend welling. "This isn't adding up. The request didn't say anything about a rescue."

"There was a need for secrecy," Talia answered. "The Queen is live-streaming her days to the Federation."

"I'd forgotten about that. Roka's cover would be blown for sure if my aunt got involved." Nickie didn't want to contemplate the increase in danger to Roka if her identity was broadcast to the entire Federation.

"That's why the twins are taking point," Talia told her

amiably as they left the elevator at the *Gemini's* dock. "It's their...jam, I think I heard Trey say. I'm still getting my tentacles around the way he and the others talk. I used to live on a Yollin colony, and there weren't too many humans there."

Talia filled Nickie in on the rest of what she knew while they made their way to the ship, ignoring the way the Ranger used the word "fuck" like it was the only adjective in her vocabulary as she peppered Talia with questions.

She was surprised by the sensitivity of Durq's contributions to the conversation. He wasn't like any Skaine she'd met. Even the good ones had a certain roughness to their thinking, a selfish streak she'd believed to be genetic until now. Durq was kind, thoughtful, and empathetic, not qualities someone could fake.

She paused before reaching for the door to the situation room. "May I speak freely?"

Nickie nodded. "Knock yourself out."

Talia tilted her head. "Why would I do that?"

"It means, go ahead," Durq clarified with a wry grin. "You weren't joking about not being around humans much, huh?"

"I knew a few," Talia replied, repressing memories of Chief's mustache drooping into his beer. She changed the subject as her anger welled. "I hope my lack of military experience won't count against me when you make your report to Ranger One. I'm able and willing to fight to the death for the Collective. It might be too late for my people, but *they* have a chance, thanks to the work the Rangers are doing."

Nickie looked from Talia to Durq and back. "We're not gonna have a problem, are we?"

Talia smiled warmly at Durq. "No. He's not to blame for what his people did to mine. I know a good heart when I see one." Her tentacles dropped to her sides. "I want to be accepted into the Rangers more than anything I've wanted in my life. Too many good people have died already in this war. If I have to live by Ranger rules to prevent the Kurtherians from getting what they want, then there's no question. I have to do it."

"You don't have to worry," Nickie assured her. "The Rangers train hard and work harder, but we're not the FDG with all their rules and regulations spewing out of our asses. We're the only Justice the frontier has, and we have to be flexible, personable, and decisive."

Durq agreed enthusiastically. "Look at this assignment as practical experience, the kind you can't get in the classroom. You'll appreciate the perspective when you start Akio's ethics class."

Talia was comforted by their efforts to make her feel comfortable. Maybe the twins had been exaggerating with their stories about Nickie being the wild-child scourge of the Skaines. "Thanks. I guess we should get inside."

Activity ground to a halt when they entered the situation room. Talia smiled at Nickie and Durq before walking over to where K'aia and Gabriel were working.

Alexis put down her datapad and came over to greet Nickie and Durq. "I'm so glad you're here!" she told Nickie, embracing her without warning. She laughed as Nickie returned the hug awkwardly. "It's a shock at first. You'll get used to it."

"You're a fucking supermodel, kiddo. Last time I saw you, you still wore your hair in braids." Nickie held Alexis at arm's length and studied her face. "I thought I was prepared for this. Shows what the fuck I know."

She recognized K'aia and realized the man Talia was talking to was Gabriel. The Chewbacca doppelgänger must be the scrawny Baka who'd delighted in pranking the adults at the gala. "I'm not gonna lie, this is pretty fucking surreal. Trey, you filled out pretty well, you magnificent furball."

Trey flexed his arms, flashing a grin. "All the females seem to think so."

Gabriel laughed, picking up the amazement Nickie was feeling. "You should try it from our perspective. We went away for years, and nothing had changed when we got back."

Nickie nodded, her expression serious. "I had a trip go that way once. My sympathies."

The four of them looked at her in disbelief before dissolving into laughter. Nickie lifted her hands. "What do you want me to say? I'm here because you guys have lived sheltered lives. There's no shelter where we're going. You think fast and shoot faster or you die."

Alexis opened her mouth to ask a question but was cut off by Gabriel.

"You can't ask her about her exile!" he hissed.

"She literally just told us that's why she's here, Gabriel," Alexis retorted.

"It *was* an exile, right? Call something what it is, and it sure as shit wasn't a vacation." Nickie's defenses evaporated. She grabbed a chair and turned it around before taking a seat at the table. For once, she didn't feel judged by her past in the presence of family. "You kids are all right."

Alexis took the seat across from her, and the others settled around the table. "You were younger than us when Mom sent you away. I think you got a raw deal."

Nickie didn't see it that way anymore. "I used to think so too, but I learned on the frontier that sometimes Justice is rough. I'm the Grimes I am today because Bethany Anne stripped me of my privilege and forced me to grow the fuck up."

"What made you decide the exile was a good thing?" Gabriel asked, his curiosity getting the better of his manners. "Don't get me wrong, your adventures are legendary in our generation, but it had to be hard being out there alone."

Nickie waved a hand. "I was never really alone, and when I realized that, I also realized I was grateful for what your mom did for me. I was such a whiny little bitch back then, never taking responsibility for my actions. I know exactly who I'd be without her intervention, and prison cells and early graves aren't my style. Neither is standing by uselessly when everyone else is doing their part."

"I wouldn't say you were useless," Trey countered with a grin. "You made a great example of what happens to kids who mess up."

Alexis nodded vigorously. "I don't know how many times you were brought up as a cautionary tale when I was being willful."

Gabriel nudged her in the ribs with his elbow. "Worked, though, right?"

Alexis snickered. "No."

Nickie couldn't resist their infectious laughter. "Do any of you know Roka personally?" she asked when the moment had passed.

Everyone replied that they didn't. Nickie nodded. "Well, I do, and she's as tough as boiled bistok skin. This will be a rescue, not a recovery. I don't want to waste any more time. The sooner we're on the trail, the sooner Roka is home safe."

"We can launch the operation as soon as you're read in," Alexis told her.

"Send everything to Meredith," Nickie requested. "I have to get myself a ship."

Keeg Station, All Guns Blazing, TH's Office

John sipped the dark beer appreciatively. "That's an improvement on the last batch."

Terry Henry's face darkened. "We do not speak of that batch."

"No," Nathan bitched. "Because then you'd have to admit that Floyd's *gifts* are not always welcome."

It turned out Wombat poop did nothing to improve the taste of beer, a literal nugget of information Terry and Nathan had stumbled upon when testing the offending batch of Terry's famous dark beer on their return from Serenity. After a considerable amount of indignity on the part of both men when their stomachs objected to the additional ingredient, Terry Henry had suffered a four-day break in production while maintenance bots sterilized the affected vat and all its connecting pipes.

"Without video evidence, no one can say how it got into

the vat," Terry Henry countered. "By all accounts, Floyd was with Rivka the whole time she was on board the station. I suspect—"

"Sabotage," Nathan finished for him. "I've heard, and I find it unlikely I wouldn't have found out before it happened. Sometimes, those hoofbeats are horses."

"Blaming Floyd is unfair," Terry Henry insisted. "That sweet creature would never ruin something as important as good beer. Unlike my competitors. I fucking hate saboteurs. Something ought to be done before they strike again."

Nathan sighed. "TH, for the last time, the Bad Company cannot be deployed to take out your rival breweries."

Terry turned to John for support. "What do you think is more likely? Big Beer getting their panties in a twist they're having to share the market in this sector, or the innocent wombat I rescued ruining the thing that's most precious to me?"

Nathan raised an eyebrow. "I wouldn't let Char hear you talk that way."

"Aren't you still in the doghouse with your wife?" Terry replied acidly.

John watched the exchange with amusement, savoring the fact that all that was required of him at the moment was to enjoy his beer. He regretted tempting fate when his senses tingled. "Dammit, here comes trouble," he grumbled to himself, reluctantly relinquishing his glass to the table.

Nathan's nose twitched a moment before there was a knock on the door, immediately followed by the door opening and Nickie sauntering in without waiting for an invitation.

"Captain Grimes. Please, come in. To what do I owe the unexpected pleasure?" Nathan asked, giving her a stern look.

"I'm not here to see you," Nickie told Nathan. She made a beeline for John's chair and deposited herself unceremoniously on the arm. "I need to borrow the *Sayomi*."

"Why do you need my ship?" John asked, knowing better than to fall for her butter-wouldn't-melt act. "What's wrong with the *Penitent Granddaughter*?"

"I made her too famous, kicking all that Skaine ass back in the day of course," Nickie told him sweetly. "I'm headed outside the Federation with the twins. If I rock up in my ship, the bad guys will run for the hills, and I've got a recruit to onboard. First impressions count, you know."

"Would that recruit be Talia by any chance?" Nathan inquired. He smiled when Nickie confirmed it. "I'm glad for her. She hasn't got the temperament for the FDG, but I can see her doing well with the Rangers."

Nickie gave John big eyes. "Please? You know I hate to be cramped."

The *Gemini* was hardly a tin can. However, John relented in favor of peace and quiet to finish his beer before Bethany Anne noticed he wasn't busy. "You bring her back without a scratch, you hear me? And be careful the *Sayomi* doesn't end up more famous than the *Penitent Granddaughter*. She's hardly a stealth ship if everyone knows about her."

"I know you meant 'infamous.'" Nickie flung her arms around his neck and planted a kiss on his cheek. "I knew I could count on you."

She swept out of the office as quickly as she'd arrived,

leaving John to shrug at the accusing stares of the other two men. "What?" he asked. "Nickie asking permission is an improvement. You do realize she would have taken the ship whether I allowed it or not, right? Sayomi likes her too much to stop her."

TH lifted his glass. "Here's to pretending we're the ones in control."

John laughed. "That's what you think. I have one of the new scout fighters, like all the Bitches. I keep the *Sayomi* around because I like to see my granddaughter every once in a while."

Nathan gave him a knowing look and tapped his glass against Terry's. "To pretending, and an easy life."

John changed the subject. "The Bad Company is about done with their enhancement. Should have the last of them released from the recovery suite by end of day tomorrow."

TH smiled. "Good. I've been meaning to catch up with Kai, but he's been working the whole time we've been here."

"I haven't seen much of Christina either." Nathan shrugged. "Guess I'm used to her living her own life, but I won't be here long. We should make time to get together before the tour moves on. Family time, you know?"

"I'll drink to that." Terry Henry sighed contentedly. "To family, and to retirement. Christina has been handling everything just fine without Char and me looking over her shoulder. Kae and Marcie have made the Trans-Pac untouchable on the battlefield. My only remaining fight is to produce the best damned beer the Federation has ever seen." He lifted his glass.

"When your family business is war, retirement is

wishful thinking, TH," Nathan told him. "If I were you and Char, I wouldn't relax until our beloved Queen has left the station."

John snickered at the look TH gave him in response. "I hear *that*."

CHAPTER ELEVEN

Beyond Federation Borders, Aboard the *Pleiades*

Their so-far-nameless passenger had his claws well and truly into the captain, that there was no disputing.

Roka was certain the captain's mind had been altered in some way. She had dined with Captain Janko on a few occasions. He had always made it clear that his only loyalty was to the profit they made running contraband. She would have bet the asteroid field on him absconding the moment the cult got serious.

Against her expectation, the captain had given the alien a private audience when he had boarded at Sonmara, and he had stepped out of the meeting with a completely different mindset. Since then, the bridge crew had been banished from their stations, forced to work from substations around the ship while Captain Janko gave orders over the ship's speakers. The crew had no idea where they were heading, and the officers were as much in the dark as the rest of them.

It was the alien's doing, she was sure. He came from no

world Roka was familiar with. Who was to say what mental capabilities his species had?

Roka was determined to find out what power the alien had over the captain, but she'd had no choice but to keep her head down after the effort of persuading Captain Janko she had to visit the station Library.

The captain had permitted Roka to go, sending Hafnar, the Shrillexian security chief, to "protect" her. At the time, she had supposed the extra scrutiny was because of her move to Engineering, which had been unexpected, even though she had listed engineering expertise when applying to join the ship's crew.

She'd believed that right up until the point when she'd gotten to the Library and Hafnar had planted himself behind her in full view of her holoscreen with an apologetic smile.

Distracting him wasn't a challenge. Hafnar was as mystified as Roka about the changes that were happening aboard the ship, and he didn't suspect her, despite the odd order he'd been given. Before he'd returned with the Coke she'd persuaded him she couldn't live without, Roka had sent the message to her uncle and hidden the interface before returning her monitor to the manifold specs she'd told Captain Janko she needed to study as an excuse to leave the ship while they were docked at the station.

As an experienced undercover agent, Roka had expected all would become clear in the days after their departure from Sonmara.

However, the mystery continued to deepen.

She noticed a change in the human crew members as the days passed. Those whose anti-Empire sentiment had already been strong became more assertive in their beliefs, and tensions were rising as a consequence. Humans were an emotional species at the best of times, prone to reaction and generally unmoving in their convictions.

The last thing any group of people whose survival depended on being able to work together and maintain their environment needed was conflict. Space was already trying to kill them in a million and one ways. They didn't need to help it any.

Half the mercenary ship's crew were understandably concerned by their captain's sudden change of philosophy. The other half defended the captain's actions with increasing vehemence. In a way, she understood that their attitudes came from a place of fear. The stability in their lives came from the captain, and he wasn't looking so reliable right now. Outside of the cult, they celebrated their mortality, using their time to shine brighter than many of the long-lived. Without a place to belong, the unenhanced human was a fragile being.

Roka's fascination with humanity's impact on an intergalactic scale was the reason she had chosen to become an agent for the Federation. It saddened her to see that the cult was succeeding in teaching that the differences between the guardians of humanity and the general population were something to be feared and rejected.

Take her current situation. Her crewmates were generally decent people. They were technically criminals, but day to day life aboard the ship ran much as it did on every other successful freighter. People were friendly, and they socialized between shifts.

It was only when Roka had been there for a while and

started getting past the exteriors of her crewmates that she began to find maintaining the façade of agreeing with some of them increasingly exhausting. Under the veneer of civility, there existed a faction who held some disturbing deep-seated beliefs about human superiority. She would be doing herself no favors if she pointed out that the superiority the anti-Empire faction boasted belonged only to the enhanced they were so against.

Living apart wasn't an option if she wanted to maintain the trust she'd worked to build with them, so she did what she could to ride the fence while the ship's community fractured. Roka had to use everything she knew about human nature to keep her cover intact while playing both sides.

She didn't relax for a moment, not even with Hafnar, the one person on the crew she was certain she could trust to have her back.

Captain Janko had jokingly referred to the Shrillexian as his moral compass on many occasions. Hafnar didn't subscribe to any form of government and he had nothing against the Federation or the Queen, and now he had vanished.

A grown-ass Shrillexian didn't just disappear without a trace, not even on a ship as large as the *Pleiades*. Hafnar had been kind to Roka from the start, which was why she had spent all her off-duty time since it had happened surreptitiously searching the ship for him.

Using the maintenance ducts and borrowing the ship's general-purpose bots without signing for them, she had combed every inch of the upper decks in the last week. Her search had not only failed to turn up the missing security chief, but it had also uncovered the information that he wasn't the only one who had vanished since their departure from Sonmara. The junior cook was also missing. Roka had found nothing on the habitable decks, leaving her no option but to suit up and head down to the cargo bays.

Grumbling internally about her atmosuit chafing, Roka deactivated her comm as she left the access corridor and stepped into the cage elevator going down to the upper cargo deck. There were two more depressurized decks below that one, but the upper deck had a remote command station where Roka could access the ship's systems without anyone asking what she was doing.

The elevator rocked slightly as it descended, giving Roka a chill as she imagined getting stuck down here. She was relieved when it reached the cargo deck without breaking down. She double-checked that her air reserves were at full capacity before opening the safety of the pressurized elevator car. Satisfied she was good for the next six hours, she stepped out into the deafening silence of the empty cargo deck.

The deck was split into sixteen bays. Roka made her way to bay twelve, where the cabin containing the command station was situated, and keyed in the access code she'd created for herself. Hydraulics hissed loudly as the doors slid apart.

Roka walked inside, stopping in her tracks when she saw the bay was empty. That in itself was unnerving, even without all the other strange shit that had been going on. In all the time she'd been embedded in Captain Janko's crew, they had never left port without a new cargo to deliver.

The bots followed Roka obediently, waiting for instructions. She sent them to search for organic matter and began her own investigation of the area. Further exploration revealed the adjacent bays were also bare. She checked every bay on that deck, finding all but one empty. Roka searched out the manifest and found they were carrying tons of food, body armor, and weapons. There were twelve shipping containers that had no information on their contents listed.

Roka hunted one of the containers down and opened it. Inside, she found weapons crates. Wondering what the need for secrecy was when there were at least another hundred shipping containers stuffed with all kinds of guns and projectile launchers, she pried the lid from one of the crates to get a closer look.

Inside the crate, nestled on a bed of foam, were six pistols. Roka picked one up to get a closer look, failing to see where the ammunition went.

"Would you look at that?" she murmured, deeply impressed by the high technology she was holding. Where she'd expect to insert a cartridge, there was a red jewel the size of an egg.

Further examination of the pistol increased Roka's lack of understanding. The jewel was obviously the power source. Roka had seen similar technology on Devon. It was not removable, nor was there a charging port. She'd never seen an energy weapon with a built-in, self-sustaining power source, not even on Leath, where her family's wealth and political position meant nothing was denied.

This was the Queen's technology. There was no other explanation.

Roka was tempted to test the weapon to confirm it used Etheric energy, but common sense told her that discharging it might bring attention to the fact she was down here. She leaned against a crate to think through the implications of her discovery. It hurt her to think someone close to the Queen might have betrayed them. It was also unlikely, since only those who passed rigorous mental checks worked with her proprietary technology.

Or at least, Roka figured it was that way.

Where then had the weapons come from? It occurred to Roka that the Queen had a habit of turning her enemy's technology against them. What if the Kurtherians did the same? Had *they* sent the weapons?

A chill passed through Roka's body. How close was she to the truth? An alien with possible mind-control powers, the captain's sudden pod-person personality. Was the *Pleiades* headed for a hidden Kurtherian base? Would she be the one to get confirmation that the anti-Empire cult was controlled by the Seven? If so, she had to stay alive long enough to get that proof to the Federation.

The bots returned a positive identification, distracting Roka for the moment. Having only instructed them to distinguish between organic and inorganic matter, she wasn't sure what she would find until she rounded a corner and found the bots clustered around a bloody knife.

The bots backed up at her arrival, beeping their happy little asses off at their success. Roka covered her mouth with a hand when she recognized the knife as the one Hafnar wore on his belt, the one passed down from his father, and his father's father before that. He would die before leaving it behind.

Roka had no way to determine whose blood was on the blade, but she could guess. She backed away, murderous rage rising to swamp her normal professional detachment. Horrified and angry that anyone would intentionally hurt Hafnar, she dashed for the door, still holding the energy pistol, determined to avenge his death.

Fortunately, her training kicked in as she passed the shipping container she'd left open. With logic returning, Roka told herself that tearing the head off the alien wouldn't solve the larger problem. She got a grip on her urge to act and diverted back to the container, where she secreted the other five pistols from the crate in her bag and returned everything else to the way it had been when she arrived.

She couldn't blow her cover until she knew who the weapons were meant for. Roka returned to bay twelve, formulating a plan as she walked. Her first task was to hack the security system and check the cameras. Next would be to find out where the hell they were going with all those weapons, and who they were meeting. There was no point in breaking cover to get a message to the Federation if she didn't have all the information.

Roka opened the control room door slowly, half-convinced she would be ambushed by the alien interloper. When that didn't happen, she took a seat at the console and got to work. She logged in using the admin privileges she'd given herself when she'd joined the crew. Whoever had attacked Hafnar had been smart enough to disable the cameras.

She exited the security logs and opened the navigation interface. Finding the coordinates for their destination, she searched the location in the navigation database. Roka's heart beat a little bit faster when the database returned the result.

This assignment was driving her crazy. The result made no sense. That part of space was listed as impassable, empty but for an asteroid field feeding a smallish black hole that had formed when the system's star went supernova. Why the hells were they going there and not to one of the habitable star systems surrounding it?

There was only one way to find out. She combed the servers with the same diligence she'd applied to searching the ship, rooting out every communication and personal log entry made in the last six weeks.

Hours passed as Roka immersed herself in the personal lives of the crew, their daily successes and struggles, and their growing fears about the situation aboard the ship. She absorbed it all with detachment, A crewman concerned about getting home to his wife and children wasn't plotting to abandon his family to fight for a cause he didn't believe in. After ascertaining that the main body of the crew wasn't involved, she moved onto the officers' logs, starting with Hafnar's.

She hoped he would forgive her the intrusion.

A quick scan of Hafnar's personal log confirmed Roka's assumption that he had stumbled upon the alien's agenda. Although she didn't have time to do more than scan the lengthy text entries, Roka thought it was likely Hafnar had left a clue to the identity of his murderer in there somewhere. She copied his logs for further study once she was in her quarters with more than ninety minutes' air and moved onto the captain's personal log.

It was no surprise to find that Captain Janko had been in contact with the alien, whose name appeared to be Phraim-'Eh—after the Kurtherians who had manipulated her people into warring against the Karillians? Again, *why*? —but it was a revelation to discover that their communications were one-sided.

Phraim-'Eh's initial order was met with belligerence on Captain Janko's part. The captain made it clear his crew didn't work for free and sent him a list of captains who were invested in the cause. It was a haggling tactic, of course. Roka knew none of those captains were as good as Janko. Anyone who hired the *Pleiades* did so knowing they were paying for the best, and pay they did—including Phraim-'Eh, it appeared.

Roka copied the entire exchange, studying the increasingly indignant tone of Phraim-'Eh's messages as the conversation progressed. Finally, the alien had relented and offered a price Captain Janko found acceptable.

If only he'd known he was selling his autonomy.

Roka ascertained that the conspiracy was contained to the captain and Phraim-'Eh before removing all traces of her activity from the system. She gathered the bots and herded them into the elevator, her mind turning over the new information.

On returning to her quarters, Roka had the food processing unit make her a mug of hot tea. She settled onto her bunk and opened her e-reader to read Hafnar's logs in detail.

Before Sonmara his entries read simply, documenting

his daily routine. Who he'd spoken to that day, what his duties had entailed. Normal things. Roka smiled when she came upon his recounting of her visiting his personal quarters and insisting he show her the holo images he kept of his six children. Gods, she missed his gentle dry humor already.

Roka was torn. She wanted more than anything to be able to tell his wives what had happened to him. That wouldn't happen if she made a mistake because she was angry for six children who had just lost their financial stability. She put her emotions aside and continued to read, filling in the subtext of each entry.

She scoured the entry for the day Phraim-Eh arrived, hoping to find some clue that would tell her what had happened to the captain.

She was bitterly disappointed.

Hafnar barely mentioned the alien, which Roka found odd in the extreme. When she'd arrived, he had presented her with a thick file of information about her life—her cover life, that was. His office contained a similar file on every crew member save the captain. Why the lack of interest in Phraim-'Eh? If that was even his real name. She doubted it.

Roka scrutinized the words, *The captain's guest is exactly what I expected,* trying to glean any extra meaning behind the casual comment. Without context, she could only guess.

Hafnar didn't mention Phraim-'Eh again. The following week's entries were guarded, all levity gone as he expressed his concerns about the changes to how the ship was run. Roka sighed, reading her name again. Hafnar had been worried about her wellbeing after their Library visit. Worried. For her.

This was the part of undercover work Roka had to work hard to justify—lying to genuine people she would be proud to call friends in her real life. Good people who, for whatever reason, didn't fit into society and found themselves marginalized, vulnerable to the underbelly of society. Criminals didn't care if a being didn't conform. Employment was employment when you had mouths to feed. It made for an unjust universe, whatever your species.

With that in mind, Roka made a point of singling out the people who were in a situation life had forced upon them in her reports, recommending they be given a chance to do better.

There would be no recommendation for Hafnar.

Worse, he appeared to have known his time was short. Shortly after the entry detailing their trip to the Library, he had ceased reporting his day and began recounting tales from his life.

Roka was disheartened. She skimmed the next few entries without really reading them, her dismay growing. While she understood it was important for a Shrillexian to share their battle deeds with the next generation, she needed information about the enemy's intent that she couldn't get from Hafnar's past. She focused only on the subject of each entry as she continued to skim to the end of the logs, feeling she'd already intruded into Hafnar's private life enough.

However, the title of one of the entries she'd skipped past caught her attention. She scrolled back to double-check, alarm bells going off in her head when she saw she hadn't misread. Hafnar had told her the story of how he came to leave the Empire, and it had happened on Shrillex, not on the *Meredith Reynolds*.

Roka's eyes widened as she read the entry in full and realized it had been made for her benefit. Why, she couldn't fathom. Whatever Hafnar was trying to tell her was too well disguised in the altered narrative.

She reconciled herself to a night without sleep as she lay back on her bunk with her datapad and returned to the beginning.

Twenty minutes before her shift began, Roka finally figured out how to read the hidden message. She counted carefully, writing down the letters that matched the cypher. Her heart rate surged when she made out the complete sentence.

ONLY THE QUEEN CAN SAVE US NOW.

Roka dropped her stylus. *Shit.*

CHAPTER TWELVE

Open Space, QGE *Gemini*, Bridge (Two Days Later)

"Prepare Gate sixty-four." Sayomi's gravelly voice caused feedback over the speakers.

They were crossing the Federation almost a third faster than either ship had the ability to travel under its own power, thus increasing the margin for error. The two AIs had communicated continuously as the two ships passed through one Gate after another, stopping only to make course corrections. Alexis took her share of the calculations that kept their trajectory true since it had been her idea to remotely connect the *Sayomi*'s Gate drive to the *Gemini*'s in order to give them a boost in power.

"Navigation is green," Alexis called.

"Activating Gate drive," Gemini announced.

"How long until the next Gate?" Nickie asked over comms.

"Six hours," Alexis told her with a grin as she got to her feet. "Come on over. We can have the ops meeting before breakfast, then get some training in."

Nickie kept up a running commentary over breakfast. She entertained them all with some of the lighter-hearted tales from her time on the frontier, tales that nevertheless informed the team what it took to get in and out of a non-Federation location with your possessions and body intact.

Talia ate slowly, content to listen while Nickie regaled them with an only slightly embellished retelling of the time she'd been stiffed at poker and spent three months tracking the asshole who'd ripped her off. Said asshole had fled through the territory of a notorious warlord who had put a ten-thousand-credit bounty on Nickie's head for refusing to join his harem.

Gabriel soaked up the information, building a mental image of a lawless sub-society where immorality ran rife and the only guarantee most had of any stability in life was the "protection" of whatever criminal enterprise they swore allegiance to.

"He was a slippery fucker," Nickie continued. "I chased him clear across the quadrant, always a day late and still fifty thousand credits short. I'm not gonna lie, my overheads were pretty high back then."

Not just your overheads, Meredith cut in dryly.

Mere, I swear to fucking God, I'll rip you out of my skull and have a party over your broken chip. "That snake knew damn well I was a target, and he slithered right to the source of my problem."

"So, you let him go?" Trey asked, his printed bacon and eggs forgotten for the moment.

"Like fuck I did!" Nickie laughed, waving her fork to emphasize her words. "I slipped into his room and planted evidence that landed him in hot water with Ylehen and his band of mercs. There's nothing like a public hanging to get the blood fired up. Ylehen and I came to an agreement; we split the fifty thousand, and I went on my merry way with my head still attached to my body."

"He was executed?" Talia exclaimed. "That's...barbaric!"

"That's the frontier," Nickie told her without apology. "When it's his life or mine, it's never going to be mine. You kids are about to get a taste of what life was like before Bethany Anne left Earth. I'd say it's a zoo, but that's giving animals a bad name."

"I grew up on pre-Bethany Anne Devon," Trey told Nickie. "So did K'aia."

"My and Alexis' experience is limited to the gameworld, but we have a good idea of what to expect," Gabriel added.

Nickie shook her head. "Expectations are going to get you killed. You need to be on your guard, all of you."

"Well, we're going to see for ourselves," Alexis cut in, looking up from the interface her wrist-holo was projecting. "We'll be leaving Federation space in twenty minutes."

Nickie got up from the table and dumped her meal packaging in the recycling unit. "I suggest you spend the time after training finding out how much weaponry you can hide from scanners. Your Jean Dukes are a dead giveaway, so leave them behind unless you want to spend your time fighting off idiots."

Trey and K'aia exchanged looks before high-fiving, thrilled by the prospect of action that didn't involve Ookens.

Alexis grinned as she manifested a plume of Etheric energy over her hand. "I *am* the weapon."

The twins locked eyes, amused that they were thinking

the same thing. "This isn't our first rodeo," Gabriel told Nickie.

Nickie snorted, knowing they were thinking their VR experience was enough to prepare them for the reality of people who gave no fucks about anything but their own sorry selves. "No, but it's the first one where you can't flick a switch and get a redo. You might be mostly bulletproof, but if we fuck this up, we lose Roka." She smiled to soften the blow of her words. "Look, we're going to get her back. We just have to be smart about it."

Trey rubbed his hands together. "That we can do."

Nickie grinned. "I didn't doubt it for a second. Smart means sneaky."

"As long as it's by the book sneaky," Alexis interjected. "I don't want any of those bastards getting off on a technicality when we bring them in."

"What's with that?" Nickie asked. "The Bethany Anne I know would be mass-producing coffins by now. What's the law going to do that you can't accomplish with your Jean Dukes Specials?"

"It's going to force them to pay for their crimes for the rest of their long and miserable lives," Alexis told her. "It's going to prove to the people who have been suckered into believing those liars that we aren't merciless killers, and we don't place ourselves above the rules they have to follow. We hold up the Federation's ideals, and the Federation will see it."

"I was in favor of the JDS option," Gabriel commented. "Still might be if it comes to a choice between putting a hole between their eyes or letting them go. Until then, we work to bring them in."

"We need to find them first," Talia stated, pushing away her tray. "Maybe they docked at the station because they have people here. I can pretend I'm looking for work and check out the bars. You'd be surprised what people will say around the help. It's like we don't exist."

"That's a good point," K'aia agreed. "I'll join you."

Trey nodded, his expression thoughtful. "Yeah, and after that, we should dig around the permanent residents. See what we can turn up."

"I want to know everything that happened on and around the *Pleiades* while it was docked there," Alexis stated. "Who debarked, who went aboard, who they did business with, what supplies they picked up, and what they paid for them."

"We should compare those to the prices paid by other customers," Gabriel suggested. "Odds are if they got a good deal, it's because they knew the vendor."

Nickie did some mental math as the twins went back and forth, building a solid plan for information acquisition. "You think the cult has a foothold out here."

"I think we should do our research before jumping to conclusions," Alexis told them all. "Assignments. Trey, K'aia, Durq, and Talia, you're going to do a sweep of the bars and merchants to see what you can find out."

She smiled at Talia. "Listen to your gut, but don't let yourself get overwhelmed by what you're sensing."

Talia nodded. "I've been working on filtering what I pick up."

Alexis nodded. "We need credentials."

"I will take care of that," Gemini announced from the speaker.

Alexis was last to dispose of her breakfast tray. "Okay, then. Who's up for a little light exercise?"

"Sounds good to me," Nickie agreed. "What are you thinking? Sparring?"

Alexis gave Nickie a smile that reminded her far too much of the young woman's mother's. "Full armor and melee weapons, everyone. Reconvene in the APA, I'll have Gemini fire up the droids."

Beyond Federation Borders, Aboard the *Pleiades*

Roka wished Hafnar was here to help her. The Kurtherians had been bold enough to send an agent bearing the name of one of their clans, and she was stuck aboard the ship until they reached their destination.

She had everything she needed to send an emergency transmission. However, doing so was signing her death warrant. Even if that wasn't a consideration, would Phraim-'Eh still go through with the meet if he knew the Federation was on to him?

There was no way of knowing, and her shift was about to begin. Roka checked the duty roster and decided to mull it over while she worked. Purging the intake manifolds was scutwork, but the bots weren't sophisticated enough to do the job without damaging the tubes. With any luck, Dex would leave her to work alone, and she would have time to come up with a plan to get a message out.

Roka gathered her tools, left her quarters, and headed to the mess hall to grab a bite to eat before she went to Engineering to meet her supervisor. She entered the mess hall and joined the line for the food processing units. She nodded to those who acknowledged her, sensing the tension was higher than ever. That was good. If everyone was exhibiting signs of stress, she wouldn't look out of place.

The woman in front turned and took in Roka's apprehensive inspection of the mess hall with a sympathetic smile. "Things are grim, right?"

Roka nodded, chastising herself for not realizing her supervisor was standing right next to her. "Sure are, Commander," she murmured.

Roka assessed the situation. Clay and his supporters were sitting on one side of the room, pointedly ignoring the smaller group on the other side. The smaller group, consisting mostly of non-commissioned officers, was the same group pushing their anti-Empire beliefs on the rest of the crew.

"You think there's going to be trouble?" Dex asked. "Clay's boys're pretty riled up."

"They're not happy the captain took a run with no profit for them." Roka had done undercover work in prisons with less crushing atmospheres. She breathed a sigh of relief when the NCOs left without aggravating anyone.

"Who is?" Dex turned back to input her order into the food processing unit. "At least you and me have the intake manifold to take our frustrations out on. That baby's going to shine by the time we're done with it. Those guys have to sit around with their thumbs up their asses without a cargo. It's gotta be adding to the problem."

Roka chuckled despite herself. "You said it. Good thing we're all the way out of this."

When her turn came, Roka ordered a veggie burrito and then took a seat with Dex. She casually observed the dissatisfied faction while they ate and discussed the repairs they had to make, sensing an opportunity. This wasn't the place to start a riot, but maybe it was a good place to plant the seeds for one. The question was, how close was Clay's group to mutiny?

The chances of getting a message out without being caught would be much improved if she could light the fuse. Weighing her options, Roka decided the risk was acceptable when the alternative was letting whoever her uncle had sent from the Federation be unprepared for what they found when they caught up with the *Pleiades*.

As the mess hall emptied out in preparation for the start of the next shift, Roka and Dex walked out just ahead of Clay and his group. The corridor traffic was heavy, giving them little room to maneuver. Whatever they said would be heard by him.

Roka was considering the best way to drop her verbal incendiary when Dex helped her out by turning the subject to the vacation she was going to take after their next run. "I don't know about you, but I'm going to need some serious pampering by the time we get back to the Federation."

Roka gave her a concerned look. "I don't know. I heard the captain is working for the anti-Empire movement now. It could be a while before we see another payday."

Clay moved past them in the narrow corridor, knocking Roka's tool bag off her shoulder in his haste to get by. It clattered as it landed on the floor and spilled its contents.

"Excuse me, ladies," Clay apologized without looking

back. He didn't feel the translucent tracker patch Roka pressed to his shirt sleeve.

Dex threw up her arms in indignation when Clay's entourage followed suit, charging around her and Roka to push through the crowded corridor after their leader.

Roka bent to pick up her tools, masking her satisfaction with indignation. "I wonder why they're in such a hurry?" She held up her broken multimeter with a sigh. "Dammit, my spare is in my quarters."

Dex waved at the thinning crowd "Go get it. I'll make sure you don't get a reprimand."

Roka fastened her tool bag and slung it over her back as she got to her feet. She felt bad about manipulating Dex's kind nature, but she needed to act fast if her plan was going to succeed. "Thank you. I'll be quick."

She almost ran to the elevator, looking for another moment of opportunity.

It arrived in the form of security officer Ensign Porter, who was a vocal supporter of the captain's new policies. He nodded at Roka as the elevator doors closed. "Crewman."

"There's a reason I'm not at my post, Sir," Roka blurted, informing the ensign of the circumstances as she waved the device to show him the damage. "I have to get a spare from my quarters. Commander Dex sent me. I don't see Clay coughing up for a replacement, either. He's pissed about the captain not paying out on this run."

Roka covered her mouth with a hand, feigning embarrassment. "I'm so sorry, sir. I didn't mean to speak out of turn."

As she'd hoped, Porter became alert at the mention of

dissent. "Where did you say they were headed?" he inquired brusquely.

"I didn't," Roka replied. "I left the mess hall access corridor and came straight here."

She smiled when the elevator came to a stop. "This is me. Thank you, sir."

Roka exited the elevator and hurried to her quarters, where she locked the door, wondering how long it would take Porter to get some backup and track Clay's faction down. She had a few minutes at least before she had to move.

The tracker showed Clay was in the engine room, which she had to pass to get to the maintenance ducts for that deck. If everything had gone to plan, she would be walking into a brawl.

Retrieving what the humans would call her Hail Mary from a compartment in the large trunk she kept stored under her bunk, Roka planned her next steps. The device was a one-time transmitter that would send its contents through the Etheric to a preprogrammed destination and then disintegrate, leaving no trace. The pulse of Etheric energy it gave off when used was the only giveaway. It was meant to be a last resort, untraceable.

However, Roka didn't know if Phraim-'Eh had Etheric ability. She activated the device and transferred every bit of information she'd gathered, gambling on the chaos of a mutiny being enough to cast doubt on the origin of the message if he somehow knew one had been sent.

Roka slipped the replacement multimeter into her hip pocket and left her quarters. A klaxon sounded as the elevator was taking her down to Engineering. She held onto her composure as the elevator came to a stop.

The door opened, revealing two men rolling around on the floor and punching the crap out of each other. Roka's mouth twitched.

So far, so good.

She stepped over the fighting men and looked around to get an idea of what she was walking into before making her way slowly toward the engine room. She heard more fighting up ahead but didn't see the flash of weapons discharging. Getting through the corridor was going to be difficult enough without those.

The narrow space was clogged with men and women arguing, or trading blows in some cases. Clay's group was all there, as were the junior officers led by Ensign Porter.

As a crewman, she wasn't permitted to carry a weapon, but her trusty dogs made a decent club. She grabbed the adjustable wrench from her tool bag and hefted it in one hand, ready to take care of anyone who rushed her.

A few of them stopped fighting and eyed her.

Roka pointed the wrench at them, maintaining a sour expression. "You can fight all you want. I have an intake manifold to purge if any of you want to live to see the next port."

She nodded when a path opened for her.

With a firm grip on the wrench and her other hand on the device in her pocket, Roka took a deep breath and walked into the corridor, activating the transceiver when she was in the middle of the crowd. She felt the device crumble to atoms, leaving her fingers coated with fine dust.

She reached the access hatch without an issue and turned as the fight broke out again. "As you were," she muttered, climbing into the maintenance duct.

Dex was already at work when Roka found her. She backed out of the tube she was preparing for the purge and flashed her wry grin at Roka. "Took you a minute."

Roka began unpacking her tools. "Yeah, there was trouble in the engine room. I had to threaten to beat some sense into them with my dogs if they didn't let me past."

Dex snickered. "I see you made it through unscathed."

"Not quite," the captain stated coldly.

Roka and Dex turned in shock to see Captain Janko and the alien responsible for everything going wrong on the ship standing at the base of the access ladder.

The captain had one of the energy weapons pointed at Roka. "Traitor."

"What's going on, sir?" Dex asked, stepping in front of Roka as though her wiry spacer frame was enough to shield Roka's bulk. "Roka isn't a traitor. Captain, you're not thinking clearly..." Her voice trailed off, and her eyes darted to Phraim-'Eh.

Roka slipped around Dex and pushed her back gently. "It's okay. I'll go with them."

The captain waved the pistol barrel to indicate that Roka should ascend the ladder. "Answer my questions and I might not space you for betraying me."

Hours later, Roka was dragged bleeding and barely conscious out of the captain's quarters. Squinting through blurred vision, she did what she could to get her bearings as she was carried along a corridor she didn't recognize.

Bright lights overhead stung her eyes, and the thuds of her jailers' boots was too loud in her pounding head. She registered a door being opened and being taken inside and deposited on cold metal.

The door slammed shut, setting off another bolt of pain in her head.

Roka curled up on the metal slab, doing what she could to ride the wave instead of being obliterated by it. She had no nanocytes, nothing but her body's ability to heal itself.

She fought to remain conscious, sensing she was not alone.

The sound of shuffling metal—chains?—forced her to open her eyes a crack. The harsh light was gone, replaced by a softer glow that nevertheless made her want to screw her eyes shut again. Her vision still blurred, she saw only the outline of someone leaning over her.

Roka protested weakly against this addition to her suffering, raising a hand to swipe at the looming figure.

Her hands were captured and placed firmly at her sides.

Roka moaned as gentle fingers probed her dislocated jaw. She passed out when it was pushed back into place.

She came to again, feeling the orbital fracture Phraim-'Eh had given her. Her broken ribs felt like they'd been bound, and a cold cloth was pressed gently to her jaw, soothing the swelling.

Someone spoke, their voice coming to her distorted as if she was underwater. Roka's mind registered the owner of the voice as friend, not foe. She relaxed, drifting back into the fog that promised to give her relief from the pain. She wanted the release of sleep.

Moisture touched her cracked lips, stinging the cuts and bringing her back to consciousness. She blinked to clear her vision and finally recognized the person helping her.

"Hafnar," Roka croaked. "I got a message out."

"You need water," he told her.

"You're alive," Roka mumbled, the effort to talk excruciating.

"For now," Hafnar agreed as he pressed the water bottle to her lips. "Now, drink."

Roka wept with relief and kept sipping until she passed out again.

CHAPTER THIRTEEN

Beyond Federation Borders, Sonmara Station

They docked the *Gemini* and the *Sayomi* at one of the port authority shipyards attached to the three-ring station and took the provided shuttles to the outer ring. Getting through Customs using their forged identities went without a hitch and they entered the public concourse, ready to find their next lead on the *Pleiades*.

Nickie pointed out a motel advertising suites for group arrivals as they walked away from the Customs barriers. "One of those will do."

"For what?" Talia asked.

"A base," Nickie informed her, choosing the one with the least garish signage. "If we get split up, the motel is where we meet."

Durq trotted after Nickie, hauling a heavy case.

Talia fell into step beside him and glanced at the case curiously. "Is she always this decisive?"

Durq shook his head. "This is Nickie in relaxed mode."

Talia's mouth fell open.

They paid a week in advance for a suite on the third floor of the chosen motel, then checked out the bedrooms surrounding the living area.

Trey examined the food processing unit's menu with dismay. "Alexis, you have to make this do better."

"All you think about is your stomach," Alexis chided with a chuckle. "I'll take a look after I've come to grips with the station's mainframe."

"Let me see what I can do," Durq offered. "You live on the *Penitent Granddaughter* awhile, you learn how to feed yourself."

"What's wrong with Grim's cooking?" Nickie protested.

"Nothing," Durq replied. "But Grim's not always there, and the only damn thing you stock the galley with is chili in a can."

"Don't forget the canned beans," Nickie reminded him, her voice rising in indignation.

"Oh, yeah," Durq snarked as he eased the front panel off the food processing unit. "Who could forget the beans?"

Ignoring Durq's grousing, Nickie instigated a sweep for bugs.

Talia dropped two devices into a glass of water on the table. "That second camera was in the bathroom. Gross."

The others agreed.

They continued the search while Alexis worked on hacking her way to the information they needed, tossing their findings into the glass to disable them. Everyone but Nickie was surprised by how many different listening devices and micro-cameras they'd found secreted around the suite.

Nickie dropped the glass into the trash chute, dooming

the bugs to whatever matter reclamation process the station used. "We'll have to do this every time we come back to the suite. While we've got to get rid of the bugs because we have something to hide, well..."

"It makes us look like we've got something to hide," Gabriel finished.

Talia went to the window. "We just let every petty criminal who had eyes and ears on the suite know we're worth looking at. Are we going to be in danger? What about the AIs?"

"Don't sweat it," Nickie assured her. "It's a dog eat dog world out here. Chances are, most of these go to dead drops that won't get checked until after we've left the station."

"Sayomi knows how to defend her ship from hacking attempts," Durq chipped in. "And Gemini isn't a pushover."

"You're telling me," Alexis cut in, looking up from her holoscreen. "This might be more challenging than we originally thought."

Twenty minutes later, Durq declared dinner was ready. He'd laid the table with a number of dishes, having persuaded the food processor to accept the recipe list he'd had Achronyx look up before leaving Ranger Base One.

"*Sahn Shui*!" Talia cried, her tentacles rippling in surprise when she saw and smelled foods she hadn't tasted since leaving her home planet. "Tiny bites," she translated at the blank looks from the others. "It's always been my favorite."

"In honor of you joining the team," Durq replied, making a little bow at the waist as he pulled a chair out for her. "The rest of you will find it similar to Chinese dim sum. I added a few human dishes to the selection."

"Well, aren't you a sweetheart?" Talia declared as she took her seat, making Durq blush. "Thank you for making me feel welcome."

"That's my Durq," Nickie agreed, rubbing his head affectionately before sitting next to Talia and helping herself to a plate with dark purple noodles. "This is good, not even for printed food."

"You will eat whatever you didn't have to cook for yourself." Durq sat down and picked up a bowl containing mixed pulses in a tarry-looking sauce.

Nickie lifted a shoulder. "True. It's still good, though."

"Are those crab rangoons?" Gabriel asked, snagging one of the fried pastry parcels. He dipped it in the accompanying sweet and sour sauce and closed his eyes as he bit into it.

Alexis continued working as they ate, snatching bites between frenzied bursts of typing.

"Dammit!" she hissed after reading that her inquiry wasn't recognized one more time than she had the patience to bear. "How can there be no way to hack the administration database? All this network will give me is restaurant recommendations and discounts for escort services. I can get to the accounts behind the businesses, but that's it."

"You can't find a way through to the other side?" K'aia asked.

"There *is* no other side," Alexis told her, closing the interface with a frustrated slap. "The administrative network must be separate from the public access network." She caught herself tapping the table with her fingers the way her mother did and clenched her hand. "Closed networks. Heavily guarded servers. I can't find them."

Nickie rolled a shoulder. "It's common to find low-tech solutions out here where you can't spit without hitting a pirate. Saves on expensive technology to prevent your data from being stolen. Our next step should be finding someone to bribe who knows where the administration servers are hidden."

"We need to split into two teams," K'aia declared decisively. "One to backtrack the movements of the *Pleiades'* crew while they were here, one to work the Larian angle."

Trey chewed rapidly to make room to speak. "We can take care of the crew. Getting access to hidden servers sounds like a job for you three." He pointed at the twins and Nickie. "If you think you can find them."

"We'll find them," Nickie vowed. "Roka is counting on it."

"They aren't running this place from the Stone Age." Alexis started typing again. "I can work out where the *Pleiades'* crew spent credits, which will give you guys a head start. They have to have computers in the port authority offices, even if they're on a closed network. The Larian's information will be stored there."

"There's nowhere that's inaccessible for us," Gabriel reasoned. "All we need is the location of the hidden servers, which means we need to know who will be the most motivated by the application of a little pressure."

"I like your thinking," Nickie enthused. "There's not much else we can do until morning."

"We could sleep," Durq suggested.

"In shifts," Nickie agreed. "Split the records between us.

We'll get through them in a fraction of the time."

Alexis sent everyone a portion of records to scour, and they settled in for a long night of gathering the information they needed to get in order to gain access to the *other* information they needed.

With Roka's life hanging in the balance, the nastiness of the flea pit they were working in soon faded into the background.

Alexis collated the information Trey, Talia, and Durq uncovered by digging deep into the financial records of merchant vendors and other independent business owners to identify the places that had done business with the *Pleiades* crew.

Gabriel focused his search on the captain. They had Janko's name from Roka's previous reports, so it was easy to find the upscale massage parlor he'd visited three times while the ship had been docked.

Nickie found the surveillance recording of Roka's Library visit and got the name of the Shrillexian who had logged in with her. That name led them to several others they hadn't had names for. She found arrest records for three of them, which she traced back to a barfight on the central ring.

The other place the crew had been noticed was a fight club on the other side of the outer ring. K'aia claimed that assignment before anyone could object.

"I can take the bar," Talia offered at the same time Trey called dibs.

Trey held up his hands. "Go ahead, I'll take the..." His face dropped. "Massage parlor."

Talia looked him over and laughed to ease the embarrassment rolling off him in waves. "I'll take it. I can see you blushing under your fur."

Trey mumbled his thanks and went to help Durq with dessert.

The next day, K'aia, Trey, and Talia took Etheric comms and split off to get jobs in their assigned businesses, promising to break radio silence if they got any leads. Gabriel, Nickie, and Durq remained in the suite with Alexis, continuing to work on coaxing the information they were looking for out of the station's heavily restricted public access network.

Almost a week passed before they made any progress. Before midday station time on the sixth day came around, Alexis reached the end of her patience with searching through endless directories for connections to the people of interest Talia, Trey, and K'aia reported on each day. "I vote we go get lunch, then go to the port authority offices and see what we can find out there about the Larian."

"I'll stay here," Durq offered, opening his case to reveal a chunky matter disruptor rifle. "The base can't be compromised if it's occupied. I have my comm and my blaster if anything goes down."

Alexis, Gabriel, and Nickie made their way out of the motel and crossed the concourse, looking like any other group of visitors out to take advantage of the station's amenities. They ate in an open café before looking up the address of the port authority office and hailing one of the many available electric taxicarts.

"Where to?" the driver asked, turning in his seat to look at Nickie. "If you're looking for entertainment, I know all the best spots."

Nickie glared at him. "Central ring. I'll tell you when we're there."

The driver read Nickie's "talk to me and die" vibe perfectly and activated the privacy barrier before setting off.

Nickie was reminded of her childhood home aboard the *Meredith Reynolds* as they made their way into the middle ring. In contrast to the free-for-all consumerfest of the outer ring, the majority of the middle ring was made up of residential areas that branched off wide corridors.

Alexis stirred in her seat to get a better look at a number of small businesses clustered around the six-way intersection they came to. At first glance, it looked familiar to her. The first floor of the habitation units had been turned over to open-fronted stores selling everything from clothing and footwear to electronics. Others advertised bot repair, military surplus goods, or personal services behind barred windows. Fast food outlets interspaced with bodegas selling foods from residents' homeworlds broke up the vendors hawking goods. Others operated from food carts dotted around the sidewalks.

I swear I just saw a Panda Express, Gabriel exclaimed over the Etheric comm, pointing behind them.

It doesn't seem so different from the Federation, Alexis commented. *Or the world Eve built for us.*

Take a closer look, Nickie invited as the taxi slowed for the turn. *See the parts of society that can't be filtered out.*

They did as she asked, their gazes landing on a shadowy niche between two stores where two men were making an exchange. Another store had a display of banned weapons and other destructive technology filling the window.

Gabriel was astounded to see high explosives available without restriction. *Anyone could walk out of there with everything they need to blow the station up.*

Rule number one of doing dirty business, Nickie told him. *Don't shit on your own doorstep.*

Keep amazing us with these pearls of wisdom, Alexis grumbled.

That one was more of a turd, Gabriel added. *This is dangerous. Nobody should have fragmentation grenades on a space station.*

A pearl is just a polished turd, its value is in the eye of the beholder, Nickie chastised, thinking that her grandfather would be belly-laughing if he could see the difficulty she was having with their boisterous naiveté. *It's like this. The station is a neutral zone, used by everyone in the surrounding area. No one wants to cut off their suppliers, so the station is safe as long as they continue to provide discreet, no-questions-asked services for visitors.*

Alexis noticed that many of the people on the sidewalks looked like they could do with a good meal and a new pair of shoes. *There's poverty here? Why?*

No laws preventing it, Nickie informed them with regret. *The Library here has a paywall. There's no such thing as universal healthcare outside the Federation. Injustice prevails. Anyone who wants to protect what they have has to make choices. Doesn't make everyone here a bad guy, it just means they're approaching life with different motivators.*

So, follow the money, Alexis reasoned.

Bingo, Nickie replied.

They traveled the rest of the way in silence. Nickie opened a comm link and gave the twins space to work through their culture shock while keeping up with the investigation.

Mere, baby, are you ready to shine? Nickie asked as she accessed the public directory. *Alexis was right about everything being compartmentalized here. Property and banking services are located in this ring. I need to find properties registered to port authority workers and any available data on the additional residents registered at each dwelling.*

You want to know who works there and has a family? Gabriel inquired. *I'll check out the security protocols for the port authority office.*

We want to break down their lives to see who will be most receptive to giving us information about the Larian. Nickie's brain crawled as Meredith accessed its processing power. She closed her eyes, waiting for Meredith to be done. *This is annoying as shit.*

You can get an upgrade for that, Gabriel mentioned offhand, sensing her discomfort.

Nickie's mouth quirked. *Don't tell Meredith, but I don't want to risk her personality getting damaged by the move. I've gotten used to her cranky-ass guerilla therapy.*

Aw, you do care, Meredith simpered. *I have the names of the workers most likely to conform to a new way of thinking.*

How can you know that? Alexis asked incredulously.

The parameters of my personality matrix were designed by ADAM, Meredith answered.

That's hardly an answer, Alexis pointed out.

Meredith sniffed audibly over the comm. *It's the only answer you're getting.*

Suit yourself. I was only showing an interest in your heuristics programming. Alexis sat back and opened her internal

HUD to cross-reference the names on the list with the financial records they'd uncovered the day before. Eliminating those with run-of-the-mill expenditures narrowed the pool further, and it shrank considerably more when she accessed the accounts of those remaining and added that information to the picture she was building of their lives. *We have a few who are living above their means, and two who don't seem to have enough to stay on top of their spending no matter how much money they make.*

One of those is our guy, Nickie told her with a wink.

Here. Alexis shared the profiles she'd made with Gabriel and Meredith. *These four are obviously taking bribes for allowing cargo to pass through the station without a trace, and the other two have something they're hiding sucking up their income. One of our corrupt officials covered the Larian's tracks.*

Which one? Gabriel pondered.

We'll burn that bridge when we come to it, Nickie assured them. *I think we're almost there.*

The corridor they were in fed into the open center of the ring, which was enclosed by a translucent dome. The driver turned onto a tree-lined avenue flanked on both sides by sidewalks filled with people walking briskly. Many had their attention on their wrist-holos, regulating the flow of foot traffic with their pace. Families and couples ate together on benches between the trees. After being in the confines of the middle ring, the open space and the bright light from the local star were uplifting.

Conversation dropped off until Nickie tapped the privacy barrier when their destination came into sight. "Here is fine."

The driver pulled in at the next opportunity and

thanked them for the tip when they paid before driving away.

Nickie gestured for the twins to pull the hoods of their cloaks up to hide their faces as they headed for one of the empty benches. Discussing the tourist map Gabriel had snagged from the back of the taxi as a cover, they got their first look at the port authority office.

The simple three-story building was dwarfed by skyscrapers belonging to the various financial institutions and security companies that dominated the central avenue under the dome. The tired aura of the building made a statement among the lavish architecture of the other buildings. This place didn't have to care what it looked like. A visit to the port authority was inevitable for everyone wishing to trade with or sell from the station.

What did you get on building security? Nickie asked Gabriel.

Gabriel drew their attention to the guard station recessed into the barrier across the entrance. *No one who doesn't work there gets in without an appointment. There are more guards inside, two teams of four on each floor. There are face-rec cameras in every corridor. Every office has a silent alarm that connects to station security.*

Alexis' expression made her opinion of the obstacles clear. *I get that they're paranoid out here. Fighting our way in isn't an option.*

Nickie sighed. *Then I guess we do this the hard way.*

The twins gave her identical inquiring looks.

We can't wait for an appointment, Nickie told them. *We're going to have to create one.*

It can't be that hard to get what we want without dangling someone out an airlock and getting ourselves arrested in the process. Alexis opened her HUD and got to work hacking a remote access path one of the appointments clerks had foolishly left on their workstation. *Let's try the soft approach before we start a war Grandpa Lance will have to deal with.*

Or we could just... Nickie flourished her hands.

Alexis shook her head. *Not unless you want to get naked when we have to escape from every guard on the station. We can't move your armor through the Etheric.*

Nickie tilted her head. *What, and you can move yours?*

Gabriel nodded.

Alexis sighed. *I can't get us in without being noticed. Okay, plan B.*

Which is? Nickie pressed.

Breaking my rules, Alexis admitted. *I can get us in, I can divert the cameras, and I can make it so no one sees us.*

What's the issue? Nickie asked, seeing the discomfort Alexis felt.

She doesn't like messing with people's minds, Gabriel explained when Alexis hesitated to answer.

Altering someone's perception is more complicated than a simple mind-read, Alexis told Nickie. *It requires an exchange. Unless I'm willing to hurt them, which I'm not, I'll feel everything they're going through and be immersed in their thoughts and memories. There's a risk of getting stuck there.*

Nickie couldn't keep the distaste off her face. *Shit, kiddo. No wonder it's the last resort.*

Roka's life is depending on us, Alexis whispered, steeling herself for the mental assault from the guards. *Just get me through it, Gabriel.*

I've got you, he promised.

CHAPTER FOURTEEN

They decided to work from the top of the building to the bottom, starting with Officer Badoon Marsten, who worked on the third floor according to the directory and was person of interest number four on their list.

The twins walked just behind Nickie, leaving her to speak to the guards while Alexis worked her manipulation and Gabriel held her psyche steady.

Nickie felt a surge of Etheric energy from Alexis as they approached the barrier. She flashed a smile as the guards moved to allow them through the turnstile without a word.

"Damn, girl," Nickie whispered when they were out of earshot. "Remind me never to piss you off."

I would never force anyone to do something against their will unless there was no other option, Alexis replied, resisting the instinctive urge to look back at the guards whose hopes and fears she now knew as intimately as her own. She shook it off. *There was no other way to get through without causing a scene.*

She took hold of the atrium guards' minds as they

passed, masking their presence from all but the pair at the elevator bank beyond the clerks' cubicles, where people with appointments were arranged into lines guided by winding ribbon dividers.

Gabriel was quiet as they progressed to the elevators, his focus on monitoring Alexis' mind as she made the elevator guards let them pass unquestioned. They entered the third-floor corridor they were aiming for and were relieved to find it empty beyond the four guards stationed by the elevators.

Alexis made certain the guards paid them no attention as they walked away. She didn't relax, however, since she still had the facial recognition cameras to deal with.

Nickie spotted Marsten's name on a door and waved the twins over. *You want me to handle this?* she asked, seeing the toll their entrance had taken on Alexis.

Alexis nodded. *Sure. I can't say I've got much experience with corrupt officials besides seeing Mom remove them from power.*

Me either, Gabriel added with a small grin. *Go ahead. We want to watch the master at work.*

Fair enough. How are you at playing the muscle? Nickie grinned when the twins dropped the cloaks they were wearing over their armor and activated their helmets to conceal their identities.

You should thank your lucky stars Alexis and Gabriel weren't around when you were younger, Meredith commented acidly. *There might have been three of you in exile.*

Nah, Nickie told her. *Aunt BA would have killed me for corrupting her precious babies long before it came to that.* She opened the door and smiled brightly at the saggy-looking bureaucrat behind the desk when he looked up in surprise.

"Who are you?" Marsten demanded in a harried tone.

"A friend," Nickie told him as the twins walked in behind her.

"A friend?" Marsten repeated dimly, his attention on Alexis and Gabriel.

His mind has been tampered with, Alexis informed the others. He has safeguards against his memories being read. I've deactivated the silent alarm. He can't call for help.

Marsten paled when Gabriel closed the blinds on the door.

There's more than one way to skin a cat. Nickie took a seat in the guest chair and placed a credit chip on the desk. "Someone who helps you when you need it. For instance, I have ten thousand credits I have no need for, but I am in sore need of information. See how we might come to an arrangement?"

Marsten narrowed his eyes in speculation. His suspicious look was replaced by a sly smile when greed won out. He rubbed his hands together before reaching for the credit chip. "I do see. What do you want to know?"

"There was a ship docked here a week ago under a false registration." Nickie gave him the details of the *Pleiades*. "I want to know where that ship went, and everything you know about the alien who left with it."

Marsten drew his hand back without picking up the credit chip, the shutters dropping on his previously amenable expression. "I don't know anything about a Larian," he blustered. He scrunched his eyes closed when he realized he'd given himself away. "I can't tell you anything. You need to leave before I call Security."

"Security won't be coming." Nickie got to her feet, her regretful expression entirely fake. "I hoped it wouldn't come to this." She crooked a finger at the twins, who stepped around the desk to take hold of Marsten.

Marsten scraped his chair back and clumsily attempted to avoid the twins. They grasped one arm each and lifted him off the floor to carry him after Nickie.

We're not going to actually hurt him, Alexis stated over the comm.

He doesn't need to know that, Nickie replied.

Just clarifying, Alexis told her. *Otherwise, I wouldn't be comfortable doing this.*

Nickie stood back to admire the approach the twins were taking when Alexis dragged Marsten to the nearest airlock and slammed a palm on the button to open it. The guards did nothing, still under Alexis' compulsion to ignore the team.

They then escorted him to the waste management room beyond, which had a sign by the door instructing users to be sure they were outside the eight-by-eight foot room before the airlock was activated.

Nickie smiled, amused by the stick-figure illustration that showed anyone inside when the airlock was activated would be incinerated before their ashes were scattered to the solar winds. "You should have taken the money," she told Marsten. "I will have that information, whatever it takes. You aren't the only person with access."

"You can't do this to me! I'm an officer of the port authority!" Marsten argued weakly as Gabriel shoved him into the room without ceremony. "I demand you let me out before I have you banned from this station for life!"

"You have to survive this first," Nickie told him coldly.

He banged his bloodied hands fruitlessly on the airlock door as Alexis watched with a blank expression and folded arms, glancing casually at the release mechanism.

Alexis deactivated her helmet, letting him see her face.

Marsten's protests ceased as he squinted through the viewing port. "What? You're...

"I am not the Queen," Alexis snapped. "You wouldn't still be in the airlock if my mother was here. Start talking before I decide we're wasting our time."

The bureaucrat's mouth opened and closed in shock.

"You should have taken the bribe," Gabriel told him sincerely. "I could spend the day listing the reasons you should cooperate, but that would imply we have a day to waste on persuading you to do the right thing."

Nickie stepped in before Marsten figured out the twins possessed simple human decency. "Look here, asshat," she growled, letting her eyes flash red. "There's a cult trying to destabilize the Federation, and we want to know what you know about the Larian who was here. You can help us, or you can die, and we'll get what we need from your replacement. I have no other options for you, so consider your answer carefully."

Marsten appeared not to grasp the seriousness of his predicament. "The Federation has no authority this far from its borders."

"Fuck authority," Nickie told him flatly, reaching for the airlock's release mechanism. "Are you going to give us the information we want, or do I pull this lever and move on to the next scumbag?"

Marsten read the resolve in her eyes and saw the light. "Okay, okay. I'll talk. Just get me out of here."

Nickie stepped back and nodded for Alexis to open the door. She blocked Marsten's exit by standing in the doorway. "Start with telling us where the building's servers are."

At *V-I-Please,* Talia had been in hot demand since joining the massage parlor's staff. The other employees had made her feel welcome, and she'd settled into her cover role easily. Word had quickly spread that there was a Loren working there, and within a few hours of starting her first shift, she had her pick of the station's who's who filling her client list.

All "exotic alien" stereotypes aside, Talia's physiology was ideal for manipulating even the most stubborn knots and kinks in patrons' bodies. An hour on her table guaranteed relief from the everyday aches and pains that built up in a sedentary worker's body. With her clients in a relaxed state, she was able to get clear readings of their emotions even before employing her empathic ability.

It was a strange thing to have a deep yet fleeting understanding of a person without any context about their life. She focused on their worries, getting snatches of thoughts as the clients released them for the moment. Many of the port authority workers who visited her were honest, stressed-out people doing their best to keep tabs on the millions of tons of cargo that passed through the port each galactic year. Others, not so much.

Still, while she had identified several people operating outside the lines, she'd discerned nothing so far that would help the team figure out where the *Pleiades* had been headed, nor had she come across anyone who had knowledge of a Larian.

Talia removed her apron at the end of her shift and balled it up before throwing it into the laundry hamper. She left her room and headed for the employee kitchen, where she ordered a Coke and a sandwich from the food dispenser.

She took a seat at one of the three tables and checked her messages as she flexed her tentacles, working out the stiffness in each muscle group. Nothing from the others. It was time to take direct action, but how?

"Drinking on the job?"

Talia looked up in surprise to see the Yollin station security officer who was assigned to the business leaning against the doorframe. "What?"

"Your Coke." Tare'gen pointed at Talia's glass. "Must have been a hell of a day if you're hitting the hard stuff."

Talia chuckled to hide her initial shock. "Sugar and caffeine don't affect me that way. You see me sitting here with a bottle of AGB premium rum, then you should be concerned."

"Bring a bottle of AGB rum, and I'll check it out with you," Tare'gen told her with a laugh. She ordered a bitterroot tea and came to sit at the table with Talia. "Seriously, if you're having any problems with your clients, we're here to make sure it doesn't happen. This is a safe place to work."

Talia buried her face in her tentacles, activating her Etheric comm surreptitiously. This could be her chance. Tare'gen might be the way to get the lead she was looking for. "My clients were all perfect gentle-beings. If I'm honest, I'm mooning over a guy I met in the Daolagen System."

"You?" Tare'gen looked at her skeptically. "I don't see it. Any male would be lucky to get your attention."

"This one got away," Talia told her, thinking fast as she wove a tale of star-crossed lovers separated by war. At the same time, she focused on reversing her ability to empathize. If Bethany Anne could make her enemies feel fear, maybe she could compel Tare'gen to help her. "The timing wasn't right; there was fighting, and we got separated. We arranged to meet here. I was hoping he made it out of the Federation before they closed the borders."

"Maybe he did," Tare'gen consoled her. "It's a big station, and there are hundreds of people arriving every day."

Talia threw up her tentacles in dismay, willing tears to form in her large eyes. "It's hopeless, I'll never find him. He can't find me because he has no idea I was brought here by the humans who saved me. All I have is this photo of his sister that he asked me to keep safe until we were reunited." She pulled up a photo of Jiya on her holo and showed it to Tare'gen.

Tare'gen scrutinized the photo, recognition in her eyes. "That red skin looks familiar." She hesitated, clearly torn between her duty to her badge and the desire to help Talia. "Daolagen, you said?"

Talia nodded fervently, giving her a hopeful look. She

had no idea if her attempt to use her ability was working, but she felt close to getting whatever information the security officer had. "Do you know of any ships that came in from there?"

Tare'gen shook her head. "No, but I know about the ship he left on."

"He left? Without me?" Talia, who was already aware of that, burst into sobs.

Tare'gen put an arm around her shoulders. "I shouldn't be telling you this, but you're a sweet person, and I'd hate to see you get hurt."

"I swear," Talia promised, "no one will know you told me anything. Please help me find him."

"That's the thing," Tare'gen told her hesitantly. "I don't think this guy is someone you should be getting upset over."

Talia pulled away, feigning ignorance. "What do you mean?"

Again, Tare'gen hesitated. "We intercepted a transmission from a Federation agent aboard the ship. The male you are seeking is part of the anti-Empire rebellion. He probably caused the fighting on Daolagen."

A series of clicks sounded over the comm as Alexis, Gabriel, and Nickie joined their audio to the channel.

Excellent work, Ranger, Nickie told her.

What Nickie said, Gabriel enthused. *We're in the port authority server room right now.*

I have the transmission, Alexis confirmed. *It's from Roka.*

Talia continued to sob, playing the part of the misled lover. "I thought we were meant to be. I had no idea he was part of the rebellion. I feel so used!"

Tare'gen comforted her. "You deserve a male who will make you his world, and there will be plenty of those lining up for you. Do you want me to take you home?"

Talia shook her head as she got to her feet. "I'm still staying in a motel in the outer ring. I guess I have some decisions to make. I'm swearing off relationships until I get my asshole radar back in alignment, that much is for sure."

She smiled at the officer, regretting that they wouldn't get the chance to be friends. Still, she wanted to leave the compassionate Yollin with the knowledge that she'd helped, even if Talia couldn't reveal that she'd broken the case open for them. "Thank you. You're a lifesaver; you have no idea."

Tare'gen waved as Talia left the room. "See you around. Good luck."

CHAPTER FIFTEEN

Benitus Seven, Nadezhda Station, Ted's Workshop

Bethany Anne was impressed by the Benitons' application of holotechnology to replace fixed workstations. "You are drawing the station's power directly from the rift on the planet below?" she asked, not bothering Ted with small talk.

Ted nodded without looking at her.

Bethany Anne raised an eyebrow. "The same rift the Skrima came through."

Ted declined to respond.

>>**Plato is asking permission to connect to your HUD,**<< ADAM told her.

"Permission granted," Bethany Anne replied aloud. "What's got Ted so distracted he can't answer me about his pet project?"

He and Ankh are close to being able to safely mass-replicate that technology for Federation use, Plato explained.

Bethany Anne frowned. "Meaning they're thinking of tearing millions of holes in the fabric of reality?"

>>**Incredibly tiny, completely controlled holes. We will have the technology to harness rift energy,**<< ADAM enthused. He dived in and assimilated the rift data Ted had compiled in the two years since the Bad Company's Direct Action Branch had dealt with an infestation of the Etheric-enabled aliens called Skrima.

Bethany Anne tapped her foot as ADAM worked. "That doesn't answer my question about the Skrima."

"You didn't ask a question," Ted commented absent-mindedly.

"Okay. What are the odds of another Skrima invasion?" she clarified, sighing internally.

>>**Pretty low, actually.**<< ADAM gave her the Cliffs-Notes version of the rift's history, starting with the first Skrima incursion and finishing with how Ted's equipment had closed the rift, cutting off the Skrima's access to this dimension.

Bethany Anne was less than pleased to learn that the Skrima's attacks grew in sophistication each time they came back. "Pretend I want to shut the jammer down and take a look at what's on the other side of the rift."

Ted's head whipped around. "You can't." He returned to his interface without another word.

"I can if you build me a device to open and close the rift from the other side," Bethany Anne told him.

Ted didn't react.

Should I call Felicity? Plato inquired.

No, I can handle Ted. Bethany Anne walked around the interface and stuck her face into Ted's calculations, scattering the symbols. "Ted, I need you here. Please. I need to know whether the Skrima are going to try and come through here again or attack somewhere else. You have no equipment on the other side, which means I have to look for myself."

Ted mashed his hand on the button to terminate the interface. "If I do this, will you let me work in peace?"

Bethany Anne smiled. "If you can do what I'm asking, I'll go you one better and give you permission to visit your children on Earth again."

Ted engaged fully at last. "That would make Felicity happy. I'm listening."

Bethany Anne explained what she wanted.

"Give me a few hours to put something together," Ted told her. "If you encounter any Skrima, you have to prevent them from phasing."

"If I encounter any Skrima, they're going to regret it when I kill them," Bethany Anne replied with a cold smile.

Almost four hours later, Bethany Anne walked toward the rift on the planet's surface, fully armored and prepared to repel a horde of Skrima if one should appear when the jammer was deactivated to allow her to cross.

Deactivating jammer, Plato intoned in her ear. *I am informed there will be a search party sent for you should you fail to return within two hours.*

"Got it. Back in two hours or less," Bethany Anne murmured, glancing at the camera drones circling above her.

A crack appeared, suspended in the air. Bethany Anne drew her katanas as it widened, spilling out bewitching light and tendrils of Etheric energy. She decided not to be disappointed when no horde came rushing out. Revenge for the Benitons would have been sweet, but she was there to make sure the threat was gone. If she didn't have to spend time separating Skrima from their body parts to make it happen, all the better.

Bethany Anne walked into the rift, feeling a momentary increase in weight as her katanas reacted to being inside the Etheric. The sensation passed in a heartbeat as she was pulled through to the other side, and then she was standing on a barren, dusty world.

The camera drones, fabricated entirely from silicates, had made it through the rift unscathed. They resumed their positions above Bethany Anne's head as the rift snapped shut behind her.

The area around the rift was clear, the dust repelled by lingering Etheric energy. Outside of the affected area, it was a different matter. The air was choked with dust whipped up by hot winds. A quick check of the scan data scrolling in her internal HUD confirmed Bethany Anne's initial assessment that the ambient Etheric energy beyond the rift site was lower than it should be for a planet supposedly holding hundreds of thousands of Etheric-reliant beings.

Bethany Anne shielded her eyes with her hand as she looked around. She couldn't see more than a few feet into the storm, much less whether there was a Skrima encampment nearby. She switched to sensor view in her HUD as she examined her surroundings, then sent an instruction for her drones to do the same.

After checking that the wristband jammer Ted had

given her was still in ready mode against the unlikely eventuality that her senses and the technology were wrong, she instructed her armor to integrate it to protect it from the dust.

Bethany Anne remained where she was while she sent the camera drones into the lower atmosphere to take more readings. She cursed inwardly as her HUD fed her the results. Outward from the rift, there was nothing but the thick regolith and a dust storm as far as the drone sensors could read.

The dust storm covering the planet also obscured any evidence of the Skrimas' occupation. There was nothing to say a multitude of living beings had inhabited this empty space at one point, although the raging storm gave Bethany Anne an idea that anything anyone built here would be scoured down to the foundations if it wasn't continuously maintained.

Pulling her hood low over her eyes and activating her faceplate, Bethany Anne angled into the wind and started walking, determined to find any clues the Skrima had left behind. She couldn't see the calm spot where the tear in reality lay waiting to be reopened, but she could feel it like eyes on her, creeping.

Keeping the rift site at her back, Bethany Anne widened her circle, moving farther from the central point. The word "barren" didn't do this planet justice. How it had ever supported life was beyond her, adding to the mystery of where the Skrima came from. Had they been transported here? By whom?

That answer at least was easy to guess. Etheric-powered aliens attacking Federation citizens going about their lives peacefully? The Benitons had been insular to the point of being considered antisocial by those who didn't know their culture.

It practically stank of Gödel.

Bethany Anne registered a slight ridge beneath her feet and paused to investigate. A shining white bone protruded from the divot she made with the toe of her boot. Another nudge uncovered more bones. Her HUD flashed a radiation warning, which she ignored.

She decided the risk of attracting an ambush of Skrima was nonexistent and drew on the Etheric to remove the dust ten feet around her. She lifted it in one layer, revealing the macabre evidence of someone's scorched earth policy.

She widened the circle to twenty feet, then forty, uncovering more evidence of genocide. She continued to remove the dust, ending up standing at the center of a carpet of irradiated bones a hundred feet in diameter.

Bethany Anne couldn't even guess how many Skrim skeletons she had uncovered. They were packed in together. She could tell from the way they had fallen haphazardly against each other that they had died together instantaneously. Worse, now that she knew what was beneath the dust, she could sense that the field of bones went on far beyond the boundary of the crater she'd made.

What value did this planet have to Gödel besides easy access to Federation territory? Value that was lost when Ted slammed the door in her face. Was this massacre Gödel's punishment for the Skrimas' failure to conquer Benitus Seven and gain control of the Benitons' advanced technology?

If that was Gödel's goal, why send a technologically immature species to capture it?

Bethany Anne looked up at the drones and pointed at the mass grave beneath her boots. "If you doubted it before, now you can see for yourself. This is what Kurtherians do," she told the billions watching her discover the atrocity in real-time. "They come and they take *everything*."

With too many questions to begin forming answers, Bethany Anne filled the crater back in out of respect for the dead. If her instinct was on the money, and she knew deep down that it was, these were yet another people whose fate had been diverted by Gödel's evil.

Whether they'd joined Gödel's cause willingly or by force, it looked like the Skrima were out of the game. With only a few minutes of her two-hour deadline to go, Bethany Anne returned to the rift, locking down her heavy heart behind an imperceptible mask.

Michael was waiting on the other side of the rift when it opened. Bethany Anne's self-control wavered for a split second at the sight of him.

Michael saw the slip in Bethany Anne's carefully composed expression and deactivated her camera drones. Without a word, he wrapped his arms around her and took them both into the Etheric, away from all eyes.

The Etheric reacted to Bethany Anne's presence, the energy drawn to her body's demand for her pent-up emotions to be released. Tactically speaking, Gödel was helping them by mass-murdering her own forces. However, Michael knew his wife, and stating the obvious wasn't going to assuage her guilt any.

Bethany Anne leaned into Michael's strength for a long

moment before speaking. "It still counts as saying it if you're not shielding your thoughts," she muttered, her words muffled by his shirt.

"I didn't think platitudes would make you feel any better," Michael told her without reproach. "Otherwise, I'd tell you that it's going to be okay and you can't save everyone."

"It's really fucking far from okay," Bethany Anne retorted, pulling away. She clenched her fists as she stared into the rapidly coalescing mists. "It's not okay for the Skrima. Assholes or not, they deserved the chance to fail on their own terms. They had that right."

The regret she felt for every living being who had died in Gödel's quest for ultimate power went beyond anger, beyond grief. It churned up the pit of rage that had resided, repressed inside her from the moment her mother had died. It was the same furious determination that had driven her to pursue Justice, no matter the personal cost, throughout her life.

"I have to stop Gödel." Her voice was ice, her eyes blazing red light as she clamped down on the energy her excess emotions were churning up around them. "Everywhere we go, every first contact we make, we have to tear out the roots of the evil the Seven have laid. The first genocide she committed was one too many. The species we've saved don't balance the scales."

The mists sparked, breaking into a squall as Bethany Anne's voice broke in anger. "It's never *enough*."

Michael took Bethany Anne's shoulders and turned her to face him. "Your anger is rooted in a perceived failure to protect the weak. I would have walked into that massacre without feeling a shred of pity for the enemy."

Bethany Anne held him and raged wordlessly, her emotions bleeding into the mists.

Michael held her to him, wishing he could share her load. She lacked the heedless arrogance of hubris Gödel protected herself with. The injustice of others' suffering was a slow-burning pain she carried that was capable of flaring and swallowing her whole in the conflagration. He knew that Bethany Anne would rise from the ashes of her pain with her determination strengthened, as she always did. Deep down, he knew the parts of her personality that caused her pain were the same parts that had made him choose her all those years ago. He'd had no idea what he was asking of her at the time. However, her empathy, twinned with her resolution to see Justice done and the stubborn will to see it through, had brought them to the inevitable point where she was all that stood between all sentient life and the will of the Ascension cult.

"It is enough," Michael swore as flashes of lightning preceded a prolonged crash of thunder. "I know you believe Gödel will ultimately lose."

Bethany Anne's eyes returned to their unfathomable black and the storm dissipated in an instant. "Gödel's days are numbered. I have zero doubt about that." She opened the Etheric back to the *Baba Yaga*. "I'm done indulging my feelings. I want this tour finished. I want the armada ready to launch. She isn't getting her hands on one more species if I can help it."

. . .

Spires Shipyard, QDS *Baba Yaga*, Top Deck, Primary Bridge

Izanami's hard light avatar appeared beside the transfer area on the mezzanine level when Bethany Anne and Michael exited the Etheric there. "You're back. Akio urgently requests you contact him."

"Put me through to him," Bethany Anne instructed as she and Michael descended the staircase to the lower level. They waited for the call to connect after taking their seats. However, the viewscreen remained blank.

"Where's the problem?" Bethany Anne asked Izanami. "Our end or Akio's?"

"Akio's." Izanami tilted her head. "I'm having some difficulty establishing a connection to Ranger Base One."

"More than usual?" Michael inquired.

Akio appeared on the viewscreen before Izanami had a chance to reply. "Bethany Anne. Michael. I apologize for the difficulty you had getting through. Our comms have been down for the last few hours. Our technicians are still reestablishing the grid."

Bethany Anne leaned forward in her chair. "What happened?"

"Part of the satellite network we set up in preparation for your arrival was vandalized by two cultists posing as technicians," Akio explained, his anger made clear by his clipped tone. "The cultists destroyed several relays before CEREBRO were able to raise the alarm."

"They knew what they were doing, then," Bethany Anne ground out.

Akio nodded in affirmation. "They had high-yield explosives planted all around the planetary satellites. We were lucky not to lose any of the CEREBRO EIs. As you are aware, while we were equipped to get the communications aspect of the blanket up and running, CEREBRO has limited offensive capability until the tour reaches us. The EIs did what they could to defend themselves from the attack until Sabine and I got out there, by which time the perpetrators had fled down to the planet. They were headed there to destroy Ranger Base Two when the Collective discerned their intent and apprehended their Pod."

"Were any of the Collective injured?" Bethany Anne asked with concern.

Akio shook his head. "No. The cultists chose to surrender themselves."

"When a two-ton cephalopod tells you to stop, you don't argue," Izanami commented before deactivating her avatar in a shower of golden sparkles.

Bethany Anne kept her attention on Akio. "Where are the cultists now?"

"In the brig here at Ranger Base One, waiting to be interrogated," Akio informed her, his concern evident. "They are not from Dr. Jeddah's former cell. I was able to discern that much from their thoughts without setting off the safeguards that have been placed upon their minds."

"Safeguards?" Michael echoed, his interest piqued.

"I've never seen anything like it," Akio admitted. "I had them confined and reached out to you immediately, assuming there might be a Kurtherian connection."

Bethany Anne exchanged glances with Michael. "Sounds to me like Isaiah wasn't the only victim of Gödel's agent."

Akio's face fell when Michael nodded his agreement. "Then it is as I feared."

Michael held onto his growing anger at the situation for the moment. "Do not begin the interrogation just yet," he told Akio. "I need to be there. Can you keep the prisoners separated until we arrive?"

Akio nodded. "*Hai*. They are in separate cells and can remain there indefinitely. However, I believe this attempt to cut our communications might only be the preliminary to a larger attack. We might not have much time to delay questioning them."

"If they've been screwed the same way Isaiah was, they'll die before you get anything useful from them," Bethany Anne predicted. "You need Michael there."

"You won't have to keep them indefinitely," Michael assured Akio. "We're due to arrive in the Cosnar System in a few weeks—"

"Six," Bethany Anne supplied. "Which I'm planning to cut down to three, four at the outside. Alexis should be there to help you with the interrogation."

"That would mean recalling her from her current assignment," Michael pointed out. "Akio has the necessary skills to assist me with undoing Gödel's mental traps once I show him how it is done. If Akio is right, and I trust his judgment as much as my own, there will be an attack on Waterworld. We must be ready to repel it."

"Agreed. I want you to ensure Gödel understands that the Collective is off-limits." Bethany Anne returned her attention to Akio. "What do you need?"

"I believe prudence calls for immediate action," Akio maintained, his solemn expression enhancing the seriousness of his recommendation. "The Ookens have withdrawn from the surrounding systems, which my experience tells me is the calm before the storm. Any intelligence we can get from the prisoners would be an advantage."

Bethany Anne nodded. "This is revenge for closing off the Federation, cutting off her access to the Bakas and preparing to do the same with the Collective." She began to pace, her thoughts turning on Gödel's likely plan of action. "I haven't hidden what we're working to achieve out there. It wouldn't surprise me to find out she intends to have us arrive to find a smoldering ruin."

"That gives us time to prepare," Michael reasoned. "I can take a ship and be at Ranger Base One in just under two weeks."

"John won't be going anywhere, so take his scout ship," Bethany Anne decided. "The *Reynolds* will follow, just as soon as I've spoken to Reynolds to update his orders."

"We can have the Bad Company divert to the Cosnar System instead of heading straight for Devon," Michael suggested.

Bethany Anne nodded. "I like it. Christina said she'd prepared a special welcome for the first Kurtherians they met. No time like the present. Akio, are the Rangers ready to hold off a major incursion until we get there?"

"I have the Rangers at battle stations around the clock," Akio remarked dryly. "Of course, that means I have to catnap between shift changes, but who needs sleep?"

"Not us either, apparently," Michael returned with a wry smile. "I'll be with you in twelve days."

Akio inclined his head. "I look forward to your arrival, my friend. Farewell, my Queen."

"See if anyone aboard the *Gemini* is answering the comm," Bethany Anne asked Michael when the viewscreen returned to showing the docking spire. "They might be closer to finding Roka than we think, and Nickie needs to be informed of the situation in the Cosnar System."

"I'll pass along Reynolds' and Christina's orders while I do," Michael replied.

Bethany Anne pinged John on the comm. "I'm changing your duties," she told him when he opened the channel.

"Hello to you too, boss," John replied. "What's going on?"

"My presence is required at Ranger Base One," Michael informed him. "You will have to take over the upgrade schedule in my place."

"Which needs to be moved up." Bethany Anne filled him in briefly on the situation Akio was facing.

"Shit," was all John said when she was done.

"We'll get it figured out," Bethany Anne told him. "Right now, Michael needs the access codes for your scout ship so he can get to the Cosnar System ahead of us. I'm aware that Nickie has the *Sayomi*, and you will be too busy with the upgrades to need a ship."

John sent the codes. "I've gotta agree with Akio. Whatever the Kurtherians are doing, it looks like they're gearing up for a major attack. BA, are you sure you don't want me to go with Michael? Gabrielle and the guys can handle the upgrades."

"That's not the worst idea," Michael agreed in response to Bethany Anne's questioning look.

She waved a hand. "Done."

The viewscreen activated again as someone aboard the *Gemini* picked up.

"Got to go," Bethany Anne told John. "The children are calling."

"I'll find you when we're done talking to them," Michael added as K'aia appeared onscreen.

K'aia's expression showed concern. "Has something happened?"

"Not yet," Bethany Anne assured her, wrinkling her nose at the drab hotel room K'aia was calling from. She broke down the situation for her like she had for John. "I'd feel better knowing you were making progress finding Harkkat's niece."

K'aia's mandibles parted in a grin. "Then you'll be happy to know we've got her location. I'm waiting for the others to get back here, then we're good to go."

She turned to reply to Durq. "Wait, this is probably them getting back."

Bethany Anne raised an eyebrow. "Probably?"

"I ordered pizza," Trey interjected, leaning in to wave at Bethany Anne and Michael. "But it's them."

"Don't look too disappointed," Gabriel called, walking in ahead of the women with a stack of pizza boxes.

Talia had four more pizza boxes balanced on her tentacles. "We ran into the delivery bot outside," she explained after a grateful sniff of the uppermost box.

Bethany Anne smiled and blew her son a kiss before settling in as Alexis nudged K'aia out of her seat. "I'll brief Mom and Dad. Don't eat all the damned pizza."

Nickie, Trey, and Gabriel made a show of being offended before laughing and stuffing their faces. Even

Michael chuckled, earning himself a thorough teasing from everyone in the hotel room except Durq, whose eyes widened at the cheerful chaos erupting.

"It's nice to see you all feeling good," Bethany Anne told Alexis. "You should let your hair down after we're done. You made a breakthrough, right?"

Alexis nodded slowly. "I suppose everyone is in a great mood because we broke the case."

"But not you?" Michael asked. "What deeper thread did you uncover?"

Now Alexis smiled, although there was no humor in it. "Dad, you know me too well. This is serious. The captain of the *Pleiades* has been brainwashed by the Larian, it seems. They're headed for an empty part of space with everything they need to equip an army, including what she thinks are Etheric-powered weapons."

Alexis paused. "The rest of the message doesn't make complete sense. Roka says the Larian is called Phraim-'Eh. You killed that whole clan, right?"

"All but one," Bethany Anne informed her. "And that Kurtherian was in no shape to body-jump into a Larian. Send me the transmission and get back on the trail. The sooner you can get back to the *Baba Yaga,* the better. Gödel is preparing to launch an attack on the Collective's world."

"She's doing *what*?" Gabriel exclaimed, abandoning his pizza in his shock. "What are we doing sitting around eating? We can take this to the ships. We've got to get moving."

Bethany Anne held up a hand to calm his flurry of activity. "You have time to eat. Call me when you have the *Pleiades* in your sights."

CHAPTER SIXTEEN

Beyond Federation Borders

Roka opened her eyes. She had no idea what part of the ship she was in until she spotted the porthole. That told her she was still in the captain's domain, or rather, Phraim-'Eh's.

She recalled the torture she'd endured at the alien's hands, and the pain of him attempting to break into her mind.

Somehow, Phraim-'Eh had failed, and she was still alive. Incredibly, so was Hafnar. Maybe. Or maybe she'd hallucinated that part in the grip of concussion.

"You're awake," Hafnar exclaimed.

He loomed into Roka's eye line a moment later, accompanied by the same sound of metal shuffling against metal she remembered from her fugue state.

"You're not a hallucination, then." Roka groaned as she forced herself into a sitting position on the metal slab. It hurt her to see him in chains. "How long was I out?"

"Fortunately for you, I'm real," Hafnar replied with an

amused chuckle. "Three days, maybe four. It's hard to keep track of time in here. Your mind may be intact, but they worked your body over pretty thoroughly. I set your jaw while you were out. Bound your hands and ribs."

Roka looked around. They were in a large-ish cabin that had been stripped of all comforts except the rare window into space. "Where are we? How are you here? Last I remember, that bastard Phraim-'Eh was trying to beat answers out of me in Captain Janko's living quarters."

Hafnar eased himself onto the chair next to the bare bed and offered Roka a water bottle. "This used to be his sleeping quarters. The captain and his new master are just outside the door, so keep your voice down."

Roka accepted the bottle gratefully and took a few deep gulps before passing it back. "Do you know who we're headed to meet?" she whispered.

Hafnar shook his head, refusing to take the bottle. "Only that Phraim-'Eh's ability to bend others to his will is limited to humans. I wondered if that was the case when he wasn't able to force me to accept his control like the captain. You're proof I was right."

"But why keep us alive?" Roka asked. Her head throbbed, making it difficult to think. She sipped more water, waiting for the pain to recede.

"You said you got a message out," Hafnar mentioned, a note of hope in his voice. "To the Federation? I heard them questioning you about an Etheric energy signature."

Roka hesitated to tell the truth. As much as she wanted to trust Hafnar, keeping the information to herself protected them both. "When we get out of this, I'll come clean about everything."

Hafnar's shoulders slumped. "But you're not going to tell me anything now."

Roka shook her head, regretting the movement when another spike of pain drove itself through her skull. "It's safer for you that way."

A thought struck her. "How are you not raging without the serum your people take?"

Hafnar tapped his bicep. "Implant."

Roka got off the bed slowly, forcing herself to move one leg at a time.

"Careful," Hafnar cautioned. "You'll make it worse."

Roka held her ribs, doing what she could to suppress her groans as she shuffled over to the window. "I should be grateful that prick didn't break my knees," she growled, leaning against the window's deep sill for support.

"The captain has the best view on the whole ship." She looked out at the stars, hoping her message had reached the Federation, and that whoever the corps had sent to retrieve her was prepared for this.

Hafnar indicated the bed. "You need to rest."

Roka shook her head. "I can't just sit here." Lacking answers, she stared out the window, the restriction of confinement getting to her. While she had been trained for being captured by the Guardian Marines, this was the first time she'd actually been caught. Commander Nikolayev had told her class that they couldn't prepare for the psychological impact of being a prisoner.

Hafnar, much older and wiser, nodded in understanding. "Then tell me about yourself. They already know you're a Federation agent, and I'm guessing you're here because you found the message in my personal log."

"When did you figure it out?" Roka asked, settling gingerly onto the bed.

Hafnar winked. "I know everything about everyone aboard this ship." His amusement faded. "If the Federation saw fit to put an agent aboard the ship, there was a reason. I wish I'd taken your arrival more seriously. Instead, all I did was watch you and wait."

"My...bosses have been monitoring the anti-Empire cult for a while," Roka told him. "My assignment was to report on the captain's cargo runs, who he was supplying inside the cult." She sighed. "This is a shitshow. No one expected Phraim-'Eh."

"No," Hafnar agreed. "So tell me, how does the niece of a high-ranking Leath end up being a Federation spy?"

Roka's thoughts drifted, taking her back to the start of her career as an operative specializing in deep undercover work. "My parents were killed when I was an infant and I was raised by my uncle. He treated me like his daughter, took me everywhere with him. I learned all the tricks he used to conceal his criminal activity so he didn't lose status with the Representatives or the Federation Council."

"That must have been confusing for you," Hafnar sympathized.

Roka shrugged. "It was normal since I had no other example. It wasn't like he didn't care about me, but I knew what he was doing was wrong. I figured out that living a double life wasn't how normal people live when I left Leath for school." What she didn't tell Hafnar was that she had grown up watching her uncle profit from trickery and lies and hated him more with every year. "I took the Etheric Academy entrance exam without his permission when he told me it was time to get more involved in the family business."

"How old were you?" Hafnar asked.

"Twelve," Roka replied. "I knew if I stayed, I would end up being a criminal just like my uncle. I didn't want that, so I ran away to get an education in how to be better." She chuckled. "I didn't exactly fit in, but they didn't reject me. I was diverted to another school, and here I am."

"Spy school?" Hafnar asked.

Roka gave him a stern look. "There's no such thing as a spy school. I'm talking about the Diplomatic Institute. The undercover work came after I graduated." She laid back and closed her eyes as tiredness added itself to the pain that permeated her body. "You're right. I should rest."

Hafnar withdrew to his side of the room while Roka attempted to switch off her mind and get some sleep. Overriding her need to rest and heal was the concern that Phraim-'Eh had deeper plans for her and Hafnar. Why else would they still be alive?

The day passed slowly, with no relief for her pain.

Roka got up again, restless and feeling the urge to do something—anything that gave her the illusion of taking back *some* control of her situation.

Hafnar said nothing to deter Roka as she worked her way around the room, looking for a weapon or some way to escape.

She examined the food processing unit, but it was restricted. She wasn't able to get it to give her a simple glass of water, never mind reprogram it to print weapons. She gave up, exasperated.

Frustrated, she banged on the door. "You can't just keep us in here with no food or water!" she yelled.

The captain opened it, his pistol trained on Roka. "Step back," he ordered. When Roka obeyed, he pushed a box into the room with his foot and closed the door again without a word.

Hafnar collected the box and opened it. "Rations."

Roka shrugged, accepting the self-heating packet he handed her. "Better than nothing."

They ate in silence, Roka with a growing dismay that Phraim-'Eh had a purpose for them. Her training told her to conserve her energy and watch for any opportunity to escape. As much as she hated being a damsel in distress, it looked like the only option she and Hafnar had was to hope her extraction team had gotten her message.

Roka and Hafnar fell into a routine over the next few days, eating between periods of exercise—gentle exercise in Roka's case—and sleep. Sometimes they shared stories from their lives. The captain delivered more food on the third day, telling them it would be the last they got before they docked.

"What happened to you, Captain?" Hafnar asked sadly. "We were friends. The man I knew would never treat his crew this way."

Captain Janko turned in the doorway and pinned Hafnar with a hard stare. "Bethany Anne is Death," he stated. "She has to be stopped before she enslaves us all. You wouldn't take sides, so here you stay until I figure out what to do with you." He shifted his gaze to Roka, his eyes brimming with hate. "*You* are a traitor, and an example will be made of you soon enough."

Hafnar spun to face Roka as the captain slammed the door shut. “That’s not good.”

Conversely, Roka felt a weight had been lifted with the revelation, as bad as it was.

She walked over to the window. “What will be will be.” The extraction team had to be getting close by now. Either they would intervene before whatever public display the captain and Phraim-‘Eh had planned for her, or she would commit suicide-by-guard before it happened.

A blank spot in the distance caught her eye. “Hey, come look at this.”

Hafnar joined her at the window, and she pointed out the anomalous break in the stars. “See?”

“What is it?” Hafnar pondered.

Roka pointed out a slowly-swirling mass in the far distance, the asteroid field marking the location of the black hole she’d read about in the navigation data. The anomaly was much closer than the asteroid field that filled most of their view. “It’s too big to be a space station. Why isn’t it being pulled into the accretion disc?”

Hafnar shook his head, nonplussed. “I don’t know. Maybe it’s a rogue asteroid? It must have some mass to break free of the black hole.

Roka had a sinking feeling in the pit of her stomach. “We’re going to find out pretty soon. Look at the stars; we’ve altered course.”

They remained at the window, watching as the ship drew closer to the anomaly. Both their theories proved wrong when the object was close enough for them to see that its rounded surface was covered by a desert broken up with bands of forested mountains.

Hafnar put his hands on the window. "It's a planet. A small one."

Roka frowned. "What's it doing here? The maps say this part of space is empty."

With nothing better to do, they continued to observe as the *Pleiades* entered the thin atmosphere and came in to hover above a settlement in the mountains at the equator. They were able to make out people bustling below but were too high up to identify individuals. Transport shuttles left the ship, delivering the supplies Roka had discovered to the army on the ground.

After a couple of hours, they were startled by the door opening suddenly. Roka and Hafnar turned away from the window to see Phraim-'Eh and four armed guards.

Phraim-'Eh glared at them. "Come, traitors."

Roka spat at him. "You're the traitor. When the Queen catches up with you, you're going to wish for death."

One of the guards smashed the butt of his rifle into her face, dislocating her jaw all over again. "What, the truth not good enough for you scumbags?" she slurred, using the pain to keep her mind sharp. Her time might be growing short, but she'd be damned if she faced her end with anything other than dignity and honor. She would not be broken. "Fuck yourselves. You're already dead."

Hafnar ducked in to block the guard's rebuttal to Roka's insult. The rifle didn't do much damage to him and the guard stepped back, confusion blossoming on his face.

"Try that again and you'll find out why I was the chief of security aboard this ship," Hafnar warned in a low growl.

"Get them out of there!" Phraim-'Eh demanded shrilly.

"Just do as they say," Roka told Hafnar when the guards hesitated to act.

Two of the guards bound their hands with strips of cargo webbing and forced them to start walking.

Roka complied with their instructions without argument, looking for any opportunity to palm a weapon. Her opportunity came when they left the captain's quarters and she was shoved roughly ahead of Hafnar. She spotted the card table the guards had been using and stumbled purposefully into it, knocking everything over.

"Watch it!" she yelled.

One of the guards in front turned back and kicked her. "Get up, traitor."

The guards behind Hafnar shoved past him and dragged Roka to her feet, cursing her clumsiness. One of them struck her, ignoring Hafnar's protest.

Roka fell onto the guard, grasping his vest with one hand while she stole the knife from his belt with the other.

"Keep moving!" Phraim-'Eh ordered.

Maybe later she'd get a chance to bury the blade in his eye. For now, she secreted it in her clothing and got moving as ordered, not needing to put much effort into exaggerating her injuries to slow their progress. She wanted to buy every second she could. She hadn't given up on the extraction team.

Asteroid Field

The *Gemini* and the *Sayomi* lay in wait, holding position some twenty thousand kilometers from the rogue planet. Cloaked side by side and anchored against the pull of the black hole the asteroid field surrounded, everyone aboard both ships was quiet, waiting for the AIs to determine the purpose of the energy field holding the asteroids back from the event horizon.

Alexis paced while Gemini built a 3-D model of the enemy stronghold, the AI translating the sensor data she was gathering from cloaked probes they'd dropped around the planet as they came in to hide in the asteroid field. "We need to tell Mom and Dad what we've found."

"What *have* we found?" Gabriel asked as the model began to make sense. "This looks like a staging post."

"Some of the components in the satellites producing the field around the black hole have similarities to Gate drive components," Gemini informed them. "I have no comparable technology in my database. Perhaps Plato would have better information. I have forwarded the specifications to ADAM."

"Mom will appreciate a new toy," Gabriel commented. "We can assume the components mean Gödel has some way to use the black hole's energy to power a long-distance Gate connection."

"Which they're planning to use to attack the Federation," Alexis stated.

The AIs voiced their agreement.

"But *where* in the Federation?" Alexis murmured, sitting down and opening her chair's holointerface. "Route any active communications to my station," she requested, typing a list of keywords to search on the audio feeds into her analysis tool.

"There are more than two hundred ships hidden in numerous caves beneath the planet's surface," Sayomi snarled. "We should drop a few motherpuckers on the caves and crush them."

"Rein it in, my friend," Nickie ordered. "This isn't a situation we can shoot our way out of."

"You're turning into a killjoy," Sayomi grumbled. "Where did fun Nickie go? If all we're going to do is hide, you might as well have left me in the hangar bay."

"Fun Nickie checks out the second her batshit crazy AI suggests a suicide mission," Nickie shot back. "Trust me, the second we're in a position to fight, we will."

"I've got Roka's location," Alexis announced without removing her headset. "She's being held under guard at a compound in the mountains just south of the equator."

"Anything about their target?" Nickie asked.

Alexis skimmed the search results, selecting a video that had been played on almost every ship. "This could be something. It looks like a welcome message."

She watched for a few seconds before sending it to the viewscreens on both bridges, giving everyone their first look at Phraim-'Eh.

The Larian's smile was warm and genuine, his aura of power coming across loud and clear on the video. "Welcome, warriors for truth," he began. "You have answered my call to arms. Ours is a hard path. We alone know the truth about the Nacht—that their quest for power won't be complete until they have control of every part of the Federation."

Talia forgot the headache that was beginning to form behind her eyes, gasping in shock when the video showed a montage of scenes, one of which was the smoking ruins of

Melida. She smiled at Nickie when the Ranger touched her arm in sympathy.

Phraim-'Eh returned to the screen. "We know that the 'proof' the false Queen has shown us of these Ookens is staged. She created the monsters to attack innocent Federation citizens, and she must be sto—"

"I can't listen to this!" Talia exclaimed, covering her face with her tentacles when the headache's intensity suddenly bloomed. "It *hurts*!"

Nickie glanced at Durq, whose glazed eyes were fixed on the screen. She poked him with a finger, but he didn't react. "Stop the video. He's laid in some kind of compulsion."

"Anyone else feeling it?" Alexis asked.

K'aia lifted a hand. "It's not bothering me. I live with you two, so mental shields are kind of essential."

"Yeah," Trey agreed.

Talia shepherded Durq to the door. "I'm going to take him to the Pod-doc. Watch without me. I don't need the headache."

K'aia and Trey remained on the bridge of the *Gemini* since they were aware of the compulsion but unaffected by it. Alexis rewound the video to the start and played it to the end.

"We have found the planet where the Ookens are made, and we are going to destroy it," Phraim-'Eh concluded. "Report to Base Command to receive your orders."

"They're going after Waterworld," Nickie stated with certainty. "It's the last place Bethany Anne hasn't closed off. They've been pushing us for months with Ooken attacks, but they started tailing off just before I left Ranger Base One."

"You sure we can't shoot our way out of this?" Talia asked, returning from the medical bay with Durq. "We could probably break her out of the compound without being seen."

Alexis shook her head. "If we had transporters and a sample of Roka's DNA, this would be a cinch. She's underground."

"We can't do anything until we've called home for orders," K'aia reminded them.

"Not until we've got a clear view of the situation," Alexis insisted. "We know they're planning to attack the Cosnar System. We need to know when."

"Agreed," Gabriel, Trey, and Nickie chorused.

Nickie put her hand on Durq's shoulder when he curled up in his chair with his arms around his legs. "You okay, buddy?"

"This is *bad*," Durq fretted, trembling as he looked up at her.

"All hail the king of understatement," Trey snarked without malice. "But we've been in worse situations and come out with all our body parts in approximately the same places. Your specialty is operating outside the lines, right? Ours is infiltrating and dismantling asshole oppressive organizations like this cult."

K'aia agreed. "This is what we do."

Nickie spread her hands wide and offered them an only slightly sarcastic curtsy. "I defer to your experience."

"You're giving in, just like that?" Talia inquired.

Nickie shook her head. "I'm not giving in. Alexis is the

mission commander. We have to follow her lead, but I don't have to agree with her."

"It wouldn't hurt our chances if you tried," Alexis commented.

"I should be writing these down," Talia murmured.

Alexis left her search to run and got up to pace while she contemplated possible solutions to the problem. Taking out the emotional factors left her with variables, and those she could work with.

Nickie, lacking Alexis' objective outlook, sighed. "Fuck. My. Life."

Alexis glanced at the Ranger's scowling face, which filled one side of the split viewscreen. "All of our lives," she agreed gravely. "Roka's too if we can't figure this out."

"I'm not saying we can't figure it out," Nickie replied. "Just saying we should recognize that the situation has the potential to devolve into… I don't know. What's worse than a clusterfuck?"

There were no takers. Her scowl deepened. "Any plan we make has to take into consideration that Bethany Anne and Michael will lay waste to this entire region of space if their precious children are killed."

She pointed at Trey and K'aia. "You two as well."

Alexis, K'aia, and Trey objected loudly to Nickie's advice.

"And there we have the real reason Fun Nickie declined to join us on the mission," Sayomi supplied unnecessarily.

Nickie bent to comfort Durq, who was shaking uncontrollably. "Will you just shut up for one minute?" she yelled at the AI. "All of you! You're scaring Durq!"

Everyone stopped shouting.

"Sorry, Durq," Alexis apologized. "It's okay. No one's really mad."

Gabriel held up his hands as he looked at Nickie. "We appreciate you being the voice of caution, but that's between our parents and us. They know there's always a risk we won't come back from an assignment. They gave us every advantage they could to make sure that won't happen. We have an obligation to Roka and to the Federation, and we're not going to turn tail and run like a bunch of untrained kids the first chance we get to fuck with one of Gödel's plans."

Nickie lifted a shoulder, seeing the twins weren't going to be moved. "Fine. Ignore your consultant, and we'll all die making a hopeless stand. Why the fuck is your generation so reckless? You do *know* you're not indestructible, right?"

"You assume we're going to attack," Alexis countered. "This is exactly the kind of operation we've trained for. Yeah, it's dangerous, but we can get in, trick the fleet into going willingly to their doom, and save Roka in the process."

Nickie narrowed her eyes, her interest sparked despite her doubts about taking on a fleet of that size without serious backup. "What are you thinking?"

Alexis folded her arms when everyone else turned their attention to her. "That we steal Roka out from under their noses and activate their Gate as an escape route. The fight can't be avoided, but there's no reason to allow the cult to choose the terms. One call to Mom and the Rangers, the *Reynolds*, and the Bad Company will be ready and waiting for them on the other side of that Gate."

K'aia laughed when she caught on to Alexis' plan. "Those dumbass cultists have no clue how much trouble they're flying into."

Alexis smiled. "All we have to do is get Mom to agree to what we're planning, figure out how to activate that Gate tech, and get the cult to follow us through it. Once we've rescued Roka, that is."

Everyone on both bridges started talking at the same time.

"Leading them through that Gate into an ambush is a good plan…if we can make it happen," Gabriel stated.

Nickie gripped Durq's chair with both hands, her knuckles turning white. "*If* we can do it without getting killed, I'm in."

"Two ships against two hundred is bad odds whichever way you look at it," Talia contended. "Maybe we should wait for backup."

"What backup?" Trey scoffed. "It would take weeks for anyone to reach us."

Alexis knew the others would bring Nickie's team around. She returned to her seat and the holointerface to check on her analysis of the communications being shared around the planet. The translation software was still working on the subtleties of the new languages she heard, but she didn't need assistance with any of the Federation languages being spoken.

Her analysis tool singled out a shortwave frequency being used in the compound where Roka was being kept. Alexis tapped it, fumbling for a moment with the headset when it caught on her hair. Her concern spiked when she heard two laughing males talking in Torcellan about a

Federation spy who was going to be executed in two days. That had to be Roka.

She waved to get the others' attention and sent the audio to the speakers.

Everyone held their breath while they listened to the two guards at opposite ends of the compound talk about their plans for after the execution and the rumors Phraim-'Eh was going to speak.

Gabriel felt the surge of satisfaction from his sister. "That's a start, right? Two days isn't nothing."

Alexis gave everyone access to her analysis tool. "We're going to get Roka back and turn the attack the cult is planning back on them. We need to dig down on Phraim-'Eh's plan so we can hijack it. I want us to have a solid proposal to present."

They spent the next few hours intercepting communications on the rogue planet. Using the conversations and messages, they built a picture of the cult's command structure that led them to Phraim-'Eh's inner circle.

Eventually, Alexis announced they had enough to take to Bethany Anne. She got up from her chair. "Gemini, call Mom."

CHAPTER SEVENTEEN

Open Space, QSD *Baba Yaga*, Top Deck, APA

Bethany Anne had shown ADAM and TOM the metaphorical door and put up a mental and physical Do Not Disturb barrier around the APA. She wanted to be alone while she worked out in an effort to release the tension that was causing her to snap at everyone.

Michael had arrived at Ranger Base One a week ago, too late to get any information from the cultists. Both had killed themselves rather than betray their leaders. His terse message had informed her that the Rangers, the SD *Reynolds,* and the Bad Company fleet were preparing to defend the planet from the attack, whenever it should come.

She had Izanami pushing the *Baba Yaga's* Gate drive to its limit in her urgency to reach the Cosnar System before the Collective was attacked by Gödel's forces. The children had been radio-silent since their last call, adding to her stress. She had to accept their choice to live their lives on a knife's edge, but it didn't assuage the voice of paranoia telling her to go out into the field, but they might have found themselves in over their heads this time.

Knowing they had Nickie there to back them up made her feel better. So did punching the head clean off the axe-wielding Lotaran warrior who came at her. The hard-light avatar winked out in a shower of sparkles as the warrior's head hit the mat ahead of her body. Bethany Anne dispatched the next one with a spinning kick and increased the program's pace. She drew her katanas, dropping into a back stance in preparation for the next group of opponents.

If she had been in a lighter mood, Bethany Anne might have been running the program that generated random opponents from pre-twenty-first century arcade games. Since her temper was threatening to spill over, she'd set the program to give her approximations of the species they might expect to counter on the raid and Ookens whose difficulty setting exceeded the real thing.

Sixteen more opponents materialized, thirteen horned, scaly bipeds armed with curved two-handed blades and three Ookens. Ookens being Ookens, they attacked every biped in the room with equal ferocity, unable to distinguish between Bethany Anne and the computer-generated avatars.

Bethany Anne dropped and swept the feet from beneath one of the bipeds, throwing an elbow into his temple as he fell for good measure. With the brave one out for the count and the others faring badly in the face of three maddened mutant Ookens, Bethany Anne turned her attention to taking out the tentacled monstrosities.

Too bad one of them was already paying attention to

her. Bethany Anne had the air knocked out of her when she was slammed into the floor. She pushed a pulse of Etheric energy outward when the owner of the tentacle pinning her down landed on her chest and started doing its best to chew through her armor.

The Ooken's face contorted with surprise and rage as it shot up and collided with the ceiling. It fell to the floor in a flaccid heap, down for the moment but not out.

"I'll deal with you in a minute." Bethany Anne told it as she narrowly avoided the next attack, throwing herself back as one of the other two Ookens attempted to snap a tentacle around her waist. A flick of her blade severed the other tentacles snaking toward her, drawing an enraged screech from the Ooken.

"You're uglier than the real thing," Bethany Anne muttered, hammering the mutant Ooken with a lightning strike to distract it while she moved in to sever its head with a double-handed slice.

The Ooken Bethany Anne had put down for an unscheduled nap pulled itself up off the floor. Bethany Anne slipped through the light shower left by the Ooken she'd just decapitated and turned, releasing a wall of flames to keep the remaining two back. The nanocyte-infused polymer coating the walls nullified the burning Etheric energy that lapped the room as Bethany Anne bathed the Ookens in fire.

Emerging from the flames unscathed, she darted away from the writhing mass and finished off the single bipedal alien who hadn't been mortally injured by the Ookens or the fire. She glanced around, seeing only shimmering light where the others had been. "This program needs some work."

Fire alone was not enough to stop the Ookens, so bitching about her opponents taking each other out would have to wait. Bethany Anne ducked a lashing tentacle, slicing it in two lengthways before stepping into the Etheric and coming out behind the Ookens.

They reacted in a split second, turning on the spot and resuming their rush.

Bethany Anne drew her arms back and hurled her katanas through the eye sockets of the closest. The Ooken exploded into golden light as she grabbed the tentacles of the other to tear it in two.

The Ooken suddenly dissipated in her hands and Izanami appeared.

Bethany Anne growled. "This better be important, or you will be replacing the computer-generated avatars for the remainder of my workout."

Izanami inclined her head. "If you wish to spar, all you have to do is say so," she replied. "I interrupted to tell you that the children are calling."

"Meet me in my ready room." Bethany Anne deactivated her camera drones' live feed and vanished into the Etheric.

Izanami got there just ahead of Bethany Anne and connected the incoming call to the wallscreen.

"Great news," the twins announced in unison when they saw their mother.

Bethany Anne raised an eyebrow. "You found the *Pleiades*, you rescued Roka, and you're on your way to meet the *Baba Yaga* in the Cosnar System?"

"That *would* be great news," Alexis agreed.

"But no," Gabriel continued. "We found a staging post belonging to the cult."

"The Larian is Gödel's agent," Trey broke in. "We found out they've got over two hundred ships here, and they're planning to attack the Cosnar System."

Nickie joined the twins onscreen. "Can you pass on a heads-up to Akio?"

Bethany Anne waited for K'aia to say something. "Nothing to add?"

The stoic Yollin looked up from her holointerface and slid her headset back. "It's a shitty situation, I'm not going to lie. But with your help, we can deal with it."

Bethany Anne was intrigued. "My help? What exactly have you gotten yourselves into?" She listened while Alexis briefed her on the situation. "Okay, so get the agent and get out of there. What's the problem?"

The camera view shifted back to the *Sayomi's* bridge as Nickie took the lead. "We're balls-deep in their communications. Phraim-'Eh is running the show. He has been from the start."

"Again, what does this have to do with the agent you were sent to extract?" Bethany Anne pressed.

"He's planning to publicly execute Roka in two days, right before he launches the attack," Alexis informed her. She glanced over her shoulder at the others. "We're going to save Roka before that happens, but we're going to need backup once the cult realizes we're here. We've identified some kind of Gate technology set up around the local black hole. It gives them a door right to the Cosnar System."

Bethany Anne's lips drew back in a snarl.

Alexis continued before her mother had a chance to lose her temper. "We're going to hijack the Gate and use it to escape with Roka. Can the Rangers be ready to spring a reverse trap if we get the cult to chase us through the Gate?"

Bethany Anne raised an eyebrow as Alexis began outlining the plan in detail. "Wait while I get hold of Michael and Akio. They need to hear this."

"What's going on out there?" Nickie asked.

Bethany Anne filled them in on the developments that had taken Michael to Ranger Base One ahead of the *Baba Yaga* while they waited for the connection to go through. "The *Reynolds* arrived last week. The *Baba Yaga* is still…" She consulted her HUD. "Sixty hours out at our current speed."

The viewscreen changed its configuration when Akio answered. Another window was added when Michael joined them a moment later.

Ranger One took in the group on his screen. "What fresh hell are we being served?"

"We will be the ones serving hell," Bethany Anne assured him. "We know how many and where Gödel's forces are, and when they are planning to attack. Are you ready to defend your position?"

Michael's mouth curled. "We are. One moment." He leaned over, and yet another window appeared on Bethany Anne's wallscreen when he added Christina to the conversation.

"Is that everyone?" Bethany Anne checked.

"It is now," Reynolds announced his presence over the speaker.

"Not sure why we all need to be here but go ahead," Christina commented amiably.

Bethany Anne laced her hands on the desk. "Just so we're all clear on what is happening, I'll run through it once, and then everyone can get to taking care of their part. The anti-Empire cult is currently holed up on a rogue planet somewhere in Buttfuck, Nowhere, where they're getting ready to launch an attack on your location."

"You found those squirrely bastards?" Christina exclaimed. "Nice!"

"You wouldn't be saying that if you were on this side of the Gate," Nickie retorted. "They've got more than two hundred heavily armed warships of every kind."

"Anything as big as my ship?" Reynolds inquired.

Bethany Anne waved down Christina's response. "We'll review that next. The Bad Company will continue to operate separately from the Rangers. Your job is to make sure the *Gemini* and the *Sayomi* get through that Gate in one piece."

"Just make sure everyone knows ours will be the first two ships out of the Gate when it opens," Gabriel requested. "I'd hate for us to go to all this trouble to save Roka, just to have her taken out at the finish line by an itchy trigger finger."

Bethany Anne shook her head. "Not funny, Gabriel."

"I wasn't kidding," Gabriel replied. "We could be in bad shape by the time we've led the cult through the Gate."

"I'll be waiting with the *War Axe*," Christina asserted.

"The second you get through the Gate, I'll be there to cover you guys."

"Did the Collective name the planet yet?" Bethany Anne asked Akio.

He shook his head. "They simply refer to it as 'the new world.' We are sticking with the codename until they decide."

"Waterworld it is, then," Bethany Anne responded with a grin. It was amazing what a little room to maneuver did for her mood. "I've had ADAM and TOM look over the specs you sent. They agree the setup you found at the black hole is Gate technology. How certain are you that the target is Waterworld?"

"It's all over their comm chatter," Alexis confirmed. "Can you give us any hints about how we activate the black hole Gate?"

Bethany Anne consulted ADAM and TOM before answering. "I'll have to get back to you on that."

Alexis nodded, her expression severe. "Tell them we have two days before Phraim-'Eh's sick version of a pep rally."

"Will you get here in time?" Michael asked.

"Even if I have to feed Etheric energy into the Gate drive myself," Bethany Anne vowed. She held up a finger before Alexis could speak. "I know it doesn't work that way. Izanami is working to get maximum efficiency out of the drive. We'll be there, I promise."

Michael remained on the call after everyone else had left to take care of their parts. "Cutting twelve hours off your journey would be ideal, but it's not necessary to put the ship under such pressure."

"Izanami has sacrificed enough," Bethany Anne told him. "I won't allow her to push the ship so hard it damages her."

Her shoulders softened as she allowed herself the luxury of savoring the relief she felt for a moment. "This could have been a disaster. Thanks to the children, we can take out the cult from the moral high ground."

Michael nodded. "There's no better place to be shooting from."

Bethany Anne smiled. "Every ship that comes through the Gate will be disabled and the crew will face trial. My dad is next on the list to call. We need Red Rock in the Cosnar System to deal with the aftermath."

"It might take some time for the penal world to place thousands of new inmates," Michael pointed out. "It could delay our departure."

Bethany Anne raised an eyebrow. "I don't particularly want to burden the Federation with the responsibility of providing the security of free food and accommodation to thousands of people who hate everything it stands for." She pressed her lips together while she thought it over. "In fact, not only do I not want them being given a free ride, I want them working to repay their debts to society. To make things right for the crime of fucking over everyone in the Federation."

Michael tilted his head. "How so?"

"It's not safe to expand at the rate we have been." Bethany Anne drew her thoughts out slowly. "The need for new worlds isn't going to drop. Planets inside Federation borders will have to be made livable. New stations built. I'm considering the consequences of asking that the

Council sentence cultists who respond to deprogramming therapy to be retrained for the workforce."

"The consequences being getting pulled into politics again," Michael commented.

Bethany Anne shook her head. "Never going to happen. But I will speak for the people who were tricked by the cult's lies. The people who believed the Federation was in danger and stood up to do something about it, however misguided. Gödel might see people as resources to be spent, but I see people torn from their lives and their families. People who deserve a chance to redeem themselves, fuckdammit."

She snorted softly. "Guess my good mood wasn't ever going to last long. The minute the battle is over, I'm handing the whole thing over to the House of Arbitration with my recommendation and pointing the *Baba Yaga* at Devon."

"Give my regards to Lance," Michael replied. He gave her a long look before dropping the connection.

Bethany Anne checked the time on Red Rock before calling her dad. It was early morning station time, according to the CEREBRO network.

She got herself a Coke and removed her boots before putting the connection request through to his personal quarters, knowing her father would already be awake.

He answered in his pajamas, his expression somewhere between happiness at seeing Bethany Anne and concern that she was making an unexpected call.

Bethany Anne smiled. "Hey, Dad."

"I wasn't expecting to hear from you until the next

logistics briefing." Lance leaned into the camera, reading her mood in a glance. "What's wrong?"

Bethany Anne's smile faded at her father's knowing tone. "We've got a situation about to break out that's going to need the House to clean up."

She told him about the battle being set up in the Cosnar System and explained her request that the House rule mercifully where possible.

"You have a right to blow the shit out of those people," Lance countered. "I don't see why they shouldn't spend the rest of their lives under lock and key."

"Because then Gödel has robbed us of thousands of people who would fight to their last breath to see the Federation safe." Bethany Anne wondered if she was going crazy from having the same conversation with everyone she spoke to. She rubbed her tired eyes with the heels of her hands and sighed. "They will face Justice."

Lance nodded. "What do you need?"

"How soon can Red Rock get out to the Cosnar System?" Bethany Anne asked in return. "It's the only place large enough to hold the cultists while they're processed for trial."

"I can clear our route through the Gate system to eliminate waiting time," Lance informed her, leaning over to do the calculations on his datapad. "One week, maybe eight days."

Bethany Anne made a note to explore temporary brig solutions on the *Baba Yaga*. "We'll figure something out until you get there. I need you to get with your logistics people and divert the final groups of soldiers to be upgraded to Devon. If they don't make it in time, the armada will leave without them."

Lance's forehead creased in concern. "I know you know better than to be goaded into a reaction."

Bethany Anne arched an eyebrow. "Hardly. This isn't an emotional decision, Dad. Gödel is making her move on the Federation. She's committed over two hundred ships to this attack. Launching our counter-attack while she's reeling from that loss is a sound tactical decision."

Lance chuckled. "Just checking. Consider it done. I guess I'll see you in a week."

Bethany Anne remained at her desk after Lance said his goodbyes. She folded her arms on the desk and rested her head on them. She needed to focus on her next move.

You need to sleep, TOM told her.

>>**This can wait for a few hours,**<< ADAM agreed.

"I will," Bethany Anne mumbled without moving. "Just as soon as I've figured out how this is going to affect my plans to deliver a 'fuck you' to Gödel."

Bethany Anne lifted her head. "You're right. What am I doing?" She drew on the Etheric to replenish her energy, breathing slow and deep to center her racing thoughts. "ADAM, I want you working with Izanami to increase the engine efficiency as well as the Gate drive's range."

>>**We're already working on it,**<< ADAM assured her.

"Good." Bethany Anne yawned as she opened the holointerface on her desk. "I need to speak to Tabitha, and *then* I can sleep."

CHAPTER EIGHTEEN

Devon, First City, The Hexagon, Network Command

Tabitha cleared the empty Coke cans on her desk into the wastepaper basket with a sweep of her arm as the morning shift began filtering in with entirely too much energy. There was seriously something wrong with people who woke up at the crack of dawn full of joy for the day.

Bethany Anne's updated orders were going to cause chaos if she wasn't careful.

The former Ranger left Network Command and headed for home. She worked in her HUD as she walked, making changes to crew assignments to have the area cleared for the groups arriving ahead of schedule. Devon was already surrounded by over two and a half thousand ships of all classes. Travel in this part of the Interdiction was restricted to ship lanes monitored by CEREBRO.

Where was she going to put another two or three hundred ships?

Tabitha wished Achronyx was here to offer some snark to push her in the right direction. She decided to put them on the far side of the system, where the superdreadnoughts were lined up to receive the assigned fleets for their section. The *Baba Yaga* and the *Reynolds* were battle-ready, so there was no problem with having the maintenance docks dismantled to make room—besides Jean being pissed at her for taking people from her teams to get it done.

When the armada departed, this system would look bare but for the satellites. The people of Devon would take care of themselves without them around, but she would miss them and this planet. Tabitha shook the thought off and focused on solving her problem.

The arriving military groups would need to be upgraded and put through training for Ooken combat. Peter and Tim would have to come up with a way to make sure the incoming soldiers got the training they needed before they were deployed. She could help by cannibalizing Eve's Vid-doc program to take care of the time issue. They would have a week at least when the tour returned, while Bethany Anne orchestrated their departure.

Tabitha returned to the penthouse apartment feeling she had everything under control. She headed for the kitchen and started Peter's morning coffee, making a start on the adjustments to Eve's program as she ground the beans.

Peter joined her in the kitchen a few minutes later, drawn by the aroma percolating through the apartment. "How did it go with BA?"

She passed him a cup and relayed the news that the final groups were heading to Devon instead of the Cosnar

System. "Things are about to get crazy," she finished with a sigh. "The only thing I can't reschedule is Todd's surprise."

"What's the timeframe on the unexpected arrivals?" Peter asked. "I can meet with Tim and get the ball rolling on the logistics. You should catch a nap and have your time with Todd."

"We have a few days." Tabitha sandwiched Peter's face between her hands and kissed him thoroughly. "Have I told you lately how lucky I am to have snagged the perfect man?"

"You must have forgotten," Peter told her, grinning as he slipped his arms around her waist. "You've been a little busy recently. Maybe you should remind me."

"Poor baby, not getting enough attention." Tabitha went up on her tiptoes and wrapped her arms around Peter's neck to catch his earlobe in her teeth. "We've got a couple of hours before Todd wakes up. Maybe you can persuade me to take that nap."

"Yes, ma'am," Peter replied with a grin. He scooped Tabitha up and made for their bedroom, muffling her giggles with his lips.

Tabitha woke up refreshed when the alarm Peter had set for her before leaving for the QBBS *Guardian* went off.

She dressed quickly in her leathers and walked into the kitchen to find Todd watching a video on his VR glasses while he demolished his breakfast. His school bag was discarded half-packed on the breakfast bar. "How's my favorite son?"

Todd looked at Tabitha over the rim of his VR glasses. "I'm your only son," he told her with an eye roll worthy of… well, her. "You're not wearing your uniform. What gives?"

Tabitha let his pre-teen snark slide off without comment. "Well, I'm kinda missing my only and favorite son. I arranged some time off and got you out of school."

Todd's mouth dropped open. "For real? Why? What about my classes?"

"I spoke to your principal when the chance for this trip came up." Tabitha ruffled his hair as she walked past to get to the food processing unit. "We're going to the Kaan'Trii System. Apparently, the binary stars there are nearing supernova."

Todd slid off his stool, excitement coursing through him. "You've got to be kidding!" He'd been researching binary systems comprised of white dwarf stars since the start of the school year, and the name was familiar to him from reading about the long-term research project in the system. "You know I've been working on this supernova project for months."

He stared at Tabitha in amazement. "That would mean..."

"I've been planning this for a while, yes," Tabitha told him with a smile. "Go pack for a thirty-six hour trip. I borrowed William's ship, the one he uses as a runaround between here and High Tortuga. He told me it has a butt-load of sensor capabilities. We won't miss a thing."

Todd snickered as he left the kitchen. "A whole butt-load, huh?"

"That's the official scientific measurement," Tabitha

called after him, her attention on selecting the ingredients for her breakfast taco. "Time's a-wasting, kiddo."

Todd returned ten minutes later with a backpack containing his clothing and other necessities, as well as a box of hastily packed instruments.

Tabitha wolfed down the last bite of her breakfast, amused by the similarities to her packing method. "Please tell me you have spare underwear this time?"

Todd rolled his eyes. "I forgot my underwear *one* time. Will you let it go already?"

Tabitha grinned. "Just checking. I've got a Pod waiting in the Plaza to take us to the ship."

Todd raced to claim one of the two sleeping cabins and unpack when they boarded the *Kathy's Dream,* a modest cargo transport that nevertheless had all the comforts one would expect to find on a ship belonging to one of the Federation's premier engineers.

Tabitha shook her head in amusement and left him to explore while she got them underway to the Kaan'Trii System.

A quick examination of the bridge familiarized Tabitha with the ship's systems. She made a note to thank William for his generosity when she investigated the sophisticated sensor equipment and found a note explaining the extras he'd installed for Todd's project.

Todd joined his mother on the bridge about an hour into their journey. "William has the best biomatter printers I've ever seen," he told her as he dropped into the chair beside her. "If I'd forgotten my underwear, I could just print some."

Tabitha laughed. "I thought you wanted to forget about that?"

Todd grinned, folding his arms behind his head as he leaned back in his chair. "Worth it. How long until we get to Kaan'Trii?"

"Another hour," Tabitha replied. "This ship doesn't have a Gate drive."

Todd waved the datapad he'd brought with him. "No worries. We can work on the sensor array to make sure it's calibrated to track oscillations in the EM field."

Tabitha grinned. "I think you'll find the calibrations are done. William modified the sensors to record a full spectral analysis. Whatever emissions the event produces, you'll know about them."

Todd's eyes widened as he looked for himself and saw the modifications were every bit as sophisticated as the ones he'd found on the biomatter printer in his quarters. "Seriously? William is a genius. This presentation and the predictive software I'm building makes up, like, sixty percent of my grade for the class. I can't *not* get an A with this equipment. Thanks for doing this, Mom. I know you're busy with taking care of everyone on Devon until Aunt Bethany Anne gets back."

Tabitha was warmed by her son's enthusiasm for learning. Granted, Todd's experience was far removed from hers when it came to being a student, but she was nevertheless grateful astronomy had a stronger grip on his imagination than the military.

She gave him a one-armed squeeze. "There's nothing I wouldn't do for you."

For once, he returned the hug without complaint,

although there was no escaping the snark that was built into his age group. "You gonna let me go into the Pod-doc and get my nanocytes activated?"

Tabitha narrowed her eyes. "Don't push it."

Todd laughed. "You're too easy, Mom. Where are we watching the supernova from?"

"I spoke to the astrophysicists who have been studying this region for the last few decades," Tabitha told him as she adjusted their heading. "They asked that we share our data and invited us to visit their research station."

"Do we have time?" Todd asked. "Dad said Aunt BA is coming home sooner than planned. It sounded like you were going to be busier than ever."

"True, so I'm making time," Tabitha replied. "The research team expects the event to begin within a few hours of our arrival. We're going to meet with them before we leave so you can talk through your findings. Professor Hackett told me you will be credited for anything they use from your research."

"This is incredible," Todd breathed. "This project could be enough to make Professor Bai Hu take me seriously."

Tabitha tilted her head. "Why is that name familiar?"

"He's the head of astrophysics at the Etheric Academy," Todd replied, glancing at her. "I'm thinking I should take the entrance exam and go there next semester."

Tabitha choked back her initial reaction to Todd's announcement. "I guess you're starting to think about what you're going to do with your life, huh? You're definitely Academy material. Have you told your dad you want to go?"

"I wanted to see how you felt about it first," Todd

admitted. "It's not just for my education. You and Dad can take care of your duty better if you know I'm safe on the *Meredith Reynolds* while you're with Aunt Bethany Anne."

"Oh, Todd." Tabitha sighed, smiling. "You're breaking my heart."

"I can stay and study remotely," Todd interjected quickly, the color draining from his cheeks.

Tabitha turned in her seat to face him. "That's not what I meant. If the Academy is where you want to go, we'll support you every step of the way. You remind me so much of the man you were named for sometimes is all."

"Todd Jenkins?" he asked. "I've been watching old videos of him and Dad. He was a total badass. Dad doesn't talk about him much, and even less since the *Jenkins Phoenix* got here from QT2."

"His death hit everyone hard," Tabitha explained. "Your dad most of all. I think seeing a superdreadnought named for him has brought it all back. They were best friends, more like brothers. Your dad lost part of his heart that day. You were the gift that helped him heal."

Todd was quiet for a moment, thinking about the close relationship he had with his father. How Peter was always there when he needed him. "You said I reminded you of the other Todd. How?"

Tabitha smiled, her eyes shining with pride. "Let me tell you about Todd. That man was Batman without the emotional baggage. He held his own against the Guardians and trained his men to do the same at a time when most humans were still getting used to the idea that vampires and Weres were part of everyday life."

She wiped away the tears that formed as countless

memories of Todd's many kindnesses flooded back. "He wasn't super-enhanced like the rest of us. He earned his rank as Marine Commander with his determination to do right and his good heart. He didn't perceive everyone else's advantages as obstacles to his goals. He followed his conscience, and he believed in *people*. You could speak to anyone under his command, and they would tell you that he always had time for them. He never lost his empathy, not even after a century of fighting the Leath."

Todd listened raptly. "He was a hero."

"In every sense of the word," Tabitha agreed. "But he wasn't just a great soldier or a great leader. He was a great friend, devoted to his family. He never turned away from anyone who needed his help. His light touched the lives of everyone he knew. Just like you."

"I wish I could have known him," Todd told her.

"One day, I'll take you to meet his family," Tabitha replied without thinking.

Todd frowned. "He had a family? Why haven't I met them already?"

Tabitha cursed her carelessness. Her mouth quirked to the left as she decided how much she could tell him about Phina without sharing sensitive information. He would find out for himself once he got to the *Meredith Reynolds* and spent some time with Maxim's family. "It's complicated, and I don't know all of it. There's the family you're born into, and the family you choose. Todd had both. Like I said, one day. Maybe soon if you move to the *Meredith Reynolds*. They live in the Federation."

Todd nodded. "Who knows what the future will bring, right?" He flashed an easy grin.

Tabitha ruffled his hair. "Scientific discoveries, according to you."

"For the next few years, at least," Todd replied. "Astrophysics gives me options the military doesn't. I could get a posting on an expedition ship after graduation, discover new worlds, and meet new people. Experience their culture firsthand."

His eyes shone as he spoke.

Tabitha smiled. "You were always an adventurer."

They spent the remainder of the journey talking about everything that would need to be done to make his Academy plan a reality.

The Kaan'Trii System came into sensor range shortly before they were able to distinguish the binary stars from the others pinpointing the backdrop of space.

"Take us in as close as you can," Todd pleaded as the colliding stars became distinct on the viewscreen. He jumped out of his chair in excitement when Tabitha indulged his request.

Tabitha chuckled as they got to work setting up the sensor arrays and external cameras, Todd continuing to chatter enthusiastically about his project. "I'm glad I arranged this," she commented as she worked on reconfiguring the viewscreen.

"Do you know how lucky we are to see this?" Todd asked. "This type of event has only been recorded a few dozen times; it's really rare."

Tabitha tilted her head. "Oh, yeah? I thought stars went supernova all the time?"

"Well, yeah," Todd answered. "But different stars or star combinations produce different types of supernovae. The circumstances that created this event were stupid-complex."

He grinned when Tabitha gave him a pointed look. "That's the scientific term. The Kaan'Trii System was created when two other binary star systems collided millennia ago. The other two stars were ejected, leaving the white dwarfs Kaan and Trii to be pulled into each other's orbit. For thousands of years, Kaan has been, just, sucking matter from Trii."

He paused when the viewscreen came to life, displaying the ship's external cameras' view of the binary stars on one side and a real-time graphic of the spectral analysis being done on the stars' emissions on the other.

"White dwarf stars have no way to regulate their temperature," Todd continued to explain. "So for the last few centuries, Kaan has been simmering, the accretion gradually building until today. The mass will exceed the Chandrasekhar limit, and..." He cast his arms wide and made the sound of an explosion. "Goodbye, white dwarf stars. Hello, neutron star."

"Just like that?" Tabitha's eyes crinkled with amusement.

"Unless the remnant has enough mass to collapse into a black hole," Todd replied. "The mass of the white dwarf only has to exceed the limit for a few seconds. The temperature soars, setting off the chain reaction that ends in a neutron star being formed."

Tabitha spent a moment appreciating the beauty of the stars and her son's fascination with them before heading over to the food processing unit. "How much better would this go with popcorn?"

Todd grinned. "How about soft pretzels?"

Tabitha turned to look over her shoulder at Todd. "You are your father's son, with his poor taste in snacks. Three bites and your pretzel is gone."

"Not if you have one the size of your head," Todd contended.

They turned to look at the viewscreen when the sensor array alerted them to a surge in EM activity in the star.

"It's starting!" Todd exclaimed. "The envelope is collapsing."

Tabitha returned to her chair with the snacks as the outer envelope of Kaan ceased its infall and was flung outward in a burst of light.

Todd jumped up and punched the air triumphantly. "We have neutrinos!"

He darted to the console. "I'm calculating the mass of the remnant…one-point-oh-nine solar masses."

"So, no black hole?" Tabitha commented.

Todd shared the scan data to the viewscreen. "No, look. The star is stabilizing at just over forty thousand revolutions per minute. Help me with the readings?"

They got to work processing the sensor readings Todd needed for his project, chatting as he typed the variables into the predictive software he was building.

Tabitha coordinated with the research station, sharing the scan data they were gathering and feeding the researchers' data to Todd. "I'm impressed with this," she told her son as his model began to take shape.

"I still can't believe this happened in my lifetime," Todd admitted. "When I chose this type of supernova for my project, I thought I would have to rely on second- and third-hand sources for data. Being here to witness the event in person means I can publish my findings through the Library and add to our collective knowledge."

Tabitha snorted softly. "That's my boy."

Todd's reply was cut off when the ship suddenly lurched. He banged his head on the console as he was thrown roughly to the floor.

Tabitha twisted, splitting her attention between Todd and the need to defend them from the Ooken destroyer that had just Gated in and opened fire on them. "You okay?"

Todd got to his feet, the gash on his forehead healing as he spoke. "I'm good. What hit us? An asteroid?"

Tabitha shook her head, turning back to the flight controls. "Weapons fire. We've got Ookens on our ass. Strap yourself in and give me a minute, kiddo."

The ship rocked again as the destroyer took a shot at the engines. Tabitha sent an SOS to the QBBS *Guardian* and dived mind-first into the ship's to take control of its defenses. The shields were holding for now, but it wouldn't be long before the continual assault depleted them. She found they had a net of proximity-sensitive mines and released them to surround the *Kathy's Dream,* following it up with a spread of exploding pucks to discourage the destroyer from coming any closer.

Tabitha was thrown back when the Ookens scored a direct hit to the rear thrusters. The flight control panel exploded in a shower of sparks when the resulting explosion fused the Etheric energy injection relays.

She heard an all-too-familiar tearing sound behind her as the ship ground to a halt, leaving them dead in the water without any chance to get the propulsion systems back online. She jumped to her feet, her heart sinking when she came face to face with a six-foot Pricolici standing in a pile of shredded clothing. "Todd, do you know where you are?"

Todd's lips drew back in a snarl as adrenaline flooded his body.

"*Kathy's Dream,* come in," Tim Kinley yelled through the speaker. "We're sending help, so hold on."

Todd's head snapped toward the console, his eyes and nostrils flaring with aggression.

Tabitha put her hands on her hips and stared her son down as the ship shook around them. "If you start smashing up the ship, I'll have no choice but to sedate you. I need you to remember how to control yourself. Can you do that for me?"

The rage overwhelming Todd abated, replaced by confusion as the instinct to obey his mother overtook his sudden need to do...*something*. He tried to speak, but his mouth was the wrong shape. He lifted a hand to rub his eyes and jerked it away when he saw the thick fur and deadly-looking claws.

He looked at Tabitha in distress, a soft whine escaping his reformed throat.

"The stress activated your nanocytes," Tabitha explained gently, taking his arm to lead him to his chair. "It's your first time shifting, so it will be over soon. I just need you to sit tight while I take care of these Ookens, okay?"

Todd nodded as she fastened the chair's harness buckles and strapped him in.

Grateful he didn't have any telepathic ability, Tabitha's

internal dialogue ran wild as she fought to keep the ship intact. The mini-ESD was useless without the power to run it. She had a limited number of pucks and no power to gather the material to make more.

Tabitha maintained her mental connection to the ship, diverting power to life support and shields from the non-essential systems to give them a few more minutes before they failed, leaving her and Todd vulnerable.

She glanced at Todd when they were hit again. He'd returned to his human form and was slumped in his chair, having fallen asleep after the massive exergy expenditure of shifting for the first time and skipping straight to his ultimate form.

Tabitha tightened his harness, hoping help would hurry the hell up so she wouldn't be forced into the last resort of taking them both into the Etheric.

The destroyer was too far away for her to use her hacking ability. She tried anyway, reaching out with her mind and looking for a way to connect so she could send the destroyer hurtling into the newly-formed star before the *Kathy's Dream*'s shields gave out. She could "see" the destroyer's systems, but she couldn't reach them mentally. She clenched her jaw in determination as she pulled Etheric energy into her skeleton's superstructure in an attempt to expand her range and connect.

Still, the destroyer remained infuriatingly out of reach, and the integrity of the hull was failing further with each impact the shields deflected. There was no way to know where they would be hit next, so Tabitha had no choice but to divide the scant remaining power they had to the ship's critical areas.

The speaker crackled, then exploded in a spray of sparks and melted plastic. Tabitha unbuckled Todd and balanced his sleeping body over her shoulders. They were out of options.

Just as Tabitha was about to drag Todd into the Etheric, knowing full well that they could be stranded there until someone with the ability to get them out could get to them, the attack ceased.

The bridge was plunged into silence as the power cut out completely, leaving Tabitha and a still-unconscious Todd alone with only the light of the dozen or so electrical fires to light the bridge.

The ship lurched as docking clamps were engaged on the airlock outside the bridge. Tabitha spat a few choice words and hid Todd in a locker before drawing her Jean Dukes Specials and heading for the airlock with a cold smile.

Let the Ookens board them. She would kill them, then thank their corpses for the use of their ship.

The Ookens appeared to be having trouble with the airlock. Tabitha got impatient after waiting for them to break through for two minutes. She dialed one of her JD Specials down to two and shot the airlock mechanism, releasing the seal in a shower of metal and plastic.

Before the airlock door was pushed open, she had both pistols set to level eleven and was preparing herself for the pain of firing them when a human hand holding a white t-shirt poked through the door.

"Don't shoot!" Tim Kinley called.

Tabitha lowered her weapons and sighed with relief.

"Fuck me! Tim? You're the last thing I expected to see coming through that door."

"Sorry to disappoint you with my lack of tentacles," Tim joked as he pushed the door all the way open. "Those Ookens won't be bothering anyone again. What say we get you and the kid outta here?"

Tabitha hooked a thumb over her shoulder at the bridge. "We kinda have another situation going on. Todd's flat out in a storage locker right now. He shifted when the Ookens attacked."

Tim ran a hand over his hair. "Well, shit. Peter's gonna be mad he missed that."

"He'll get over it when he hears how it went down," Tabitha assured him. "We need to increase the patrols around the Devon System. Preventing Gödel from getting eyes on the armada might just turn into a full-time occupation before Bethany Anne gets back."

CHAPTER NINETEEN

Beyond Federation Borders, Rogue Planet, Cult Stronghold

Roka woke Hafnar early on the morning of their execution. Sleep had evaded her. The limited time they had was too precious to waste resting. There was nothing they could do from their prison cell, but she'd be damned if she didn't do her best to create an opportunity before they ended up swinging by the neck for the sake of public entertainment.

Hafnar had taken the news that he was going to be executed alongside Roka badly. He'd stopped speaking, spending his time since they had been moved to the first-floor cell last night staring through the narrow bars of the slit window at the open square where the gallows had been built on a wide, high stage.

Roka had tried to talk to him without success. She'd given him as much space as their cell allowed and spent the night telling him everything she'd held back. He'd withdrawn completely, so she didn't know if he had even heard her.

So, she resorted to passing the early hours by testing her body's capacity for movement in preparation for what was to come. Her ribs still gave a twinge of pain if she moved sharply, but she could suck up a little pain for the sake of her preemptive strike in the name of Saint Payback.

People began to arrive shortly after the arc lights came on in the open square, the signal that morning had come. Strains of conversation filtered into the cell as the cultists passed the window. There were notes of worry and regret among the general atmosphere of anticipation.

Roka wondered if living under the inadequate artificial light had contributed to the cultists' mixed moods. Or maybe the reality that attacking the Queen amounted to a suicide mission was setting in now that Phraim-'Eh had arrived and preparations to depart were underway.

She laid on her bunk and closed her eyes to think through how she would react if presented with an opportunity. She had the knife, and she expected that Phraim-'Eh would be front and center at their execution. While there had been no confirmation from Phraim-'Eh's lieutenants, she figured he planned to use their execution as a rallying point to fire the cultists up for the attack.

The morning crawled by. Nobody brought them any breakfast. Why feed the condemned? The crowd in the square grew steadily as midday approached. The smell of cooking meat teased them mercilessly as people in the square enjoyed food and drink in the carnival atmosphere.

Hafnar eventually emerged from his semi-catatonic state. He turned from the window and picked up the water bottle Roka had left beside him. He stared at it, incomprehension on his face.

"Drink it," Roka urged, opening her eyes at the sound of his movement.

Hafnar scoffed. "I'd rather not add pissing myself to the indignity of dying at the end of a rope, thanks."

"Did you listen to a word I said?" Roka chided, showing him the knife. "We're not done for just yet."

Hafnar rolled his eyes. "That's not going to do much."

Roka pointed to the small lump in Hafnar's arm. "No, but an angry, unmedicated Shrillexian could do a hell of a lot of damage in a crowd, and a sneaky Leath could slit a Larian bastard's throat while said Shrillexian was going down in a blaze of glory."

She lifted a shoulder. "We're going to die, so we might as well do it right."

Hafnar held out his arm, strength returning to his posture as Roka presented him with the chance to dictate the terms of his death. "What are you waiting for? Cut out the implant."

Roka made a slit in his bicep with the tip of the knife and worked out the implant that kept Hafnar dosed with the anti-aggression serum.

Hafnar bore the pain stoically. "I have maybe an hour before I start wanting to smash my way out of here. Just..." He paused. "I don't know how I will react without the serum. If I get reckless, don't let me be the cause of your death."

Roka cut off a strip of his shirt and tied it around his wound to stem the bleeding. "I don't think that will be a problem." She glanced at the window when the people in the square cheered. "We should see what's going on out there."

They squeezed in at the window, Hafnar on his tiptoes to see over Roka's head.

Hafnar spat a Shrillexian word that didn't translate for Roka and pointed out Phraim-'Eh leaving the building opposite their prison, surrounded by guards. "Look, it's Captain Janko."

Roka scanned the crowd around the stage as it parted for the procession. "Not just Janko. I think they're Phraim-'Eh's lieutenants. Look at their weapons. That's Etheric technology. Get hold of one of those, and you might even make it out of here. My extraction team will get here eventually. You can tell them what happened to me."

Hafnar growled laughter. "You don't get to keep all the glory to yourself." He squinted to make out the energy weapons, calculating how much damage he'd be able to do. "If we both get our hands on those weapons, maybe we can kill Phraim-'Eh and shoot our way out of the compound. We could hide in the mountains, give your team time to get here."

Roka's eyes widened. "You don't think I'm wishing on air?"

Hafnar shook his head. "The Queen doesn't leave her people behind. Someone will come. The only question is how long it will take them to track you here."

Further discussion was interrupted when the crowd became silent and feedback whine from a speaker system filled the square. Roka and Hafnar resumed their observation through the small window.

Phraim-'Eh climbed onto the stage at the head of his entourage, imposing in steel-blue armor that complimented his crimson skin. His hair was pulled back in a tight topknot, revealing his severe expression.

Roka wondered why no one had come for her and Hafnar yet. It looked like Phraim-'Eh was planning to make a speech. She could feel the crowd's anticipation, and he obviously knew exactly how to work it to his advantage.

Phraim-'Eh handed the helmet he carried to one of his men and walked to the front of the stage to address the cult with the gallows as his backdrop.

Roka felt a wave compulsion wash over the square as he began to speak.

"Let me tell you about the galaxy I came from," Phraim-'Eh proclaimed. "I was born on a world where three nations existed, each sovereign over its own land. We lived in relative peace until the false Queen sent her agents to take my planet. The crew of the Superdreadnought *Reynolds* overthrew not just my government, not just the other two governments on my planet, but every government in the Chain Galaxy."

Phraim-'Eh's voice rose and fell as he drew the crowd into his narrative. "They came with the same claims we hear from the Nacht. Kurtherians." He raised his arms above his head. "Where are these Kurtherians? Has anybody here ever seen one?"

The crowd responded in the negative on cue.

"With my people brainwashed into believing the Federation was an ally, and given everything I lost in the upheaval, I decided I would confront the Queen and find out the truth." Phraim-'Eh's voice dropped into the tone of someone confiding a secret. "But when I arrived in the Federation, I found that the people were enslaved by the same lie."

He began to pace as he spoke, his eyes on the stage and his hands clasped at the small of his back. "As a stranger in a hostile land, I was fortunate to encounter others who saw the truth. As I traveled, I met more and more people who were afraid the Federation was being dragged into a war that didn't concern them. People like you, people who were ready to fight for the Federation they believed in."

That raised cheers.

Roka felt sick to her stomach as Phraim-'Eh described a hidden facility on an ocean world that sounded an awful lot like the Ranger base.

"The false Queen would have everyone believe this world is a refuge," he thundered, confirming Roka's suspicions. Righteous anger spilled from him, infecting the crowd. "A sanctuary for a forgotten species. Those are *lies,* fabricated to hide the *true* purpose of the facility. We have twice as many ships as the Rangers. We will destroy the facility and *expose the Nacht*. The Federation will be free!"

The crowd erupted into wild applause.

Phraim-'Eh waved down their vociferous approval. "But first, we have to take care of the trouble on our own doorstep. As you are aware, a Federation spy found her way onto one of our crews and enlisted the help of a traitor."

He turned to the guards standing by the gallows behind him as the crowd booed and hissed, many shouting for Roka's death. "We have only one reward for spies and traitors. Bring the prisoners."

The thread of hope Roka had held of getting out of this alive vanished. As a highly trained agent, she was prepared to encounter the rhetoric manipulators used to control people, but she had never expected to witness the horror of mass compulsion. Phraim-'Eh had entrenched his hate in their minds. A few words from him and everyone in the square would do their level best to tear her and Hafnar to shreds without a care for their own safety.

Hafnar stepped back from the window and held out his hand. "It's been an honor."

Roka took his hand, looking into his eyes and seeing her urge to fight reflected. "Same. Your children will be proud of your legacy."

Their heads turned as one when the door was unlocked from the outside.

"Here goes nothing," Roka murmured.

Two armored humans entered the cell, a dark-haired woman with more than a passing resemblance to the Queen and a blonde woman Roka recognized immediately.

Roka's mind was thrown, unable to process the dissonance. "Nickie? Where are the guards?"

"Taking a nap," Nickie told her. "Let's go."

"You too," the other woman told Hafnar as she handed them each one of the guards' pistols. "We have maybe thirty seconds before someone comes to look for them."

"What about Phraim-'Eh?" Roka urged as they ran along the corridor. "He's planning on attacking the Ranger base."

"Bases," Nickie corrected, taking out a stray cultist who had the misfortune to exit the room at the far end of the corridor. "We know. We're kinda on a tight schedule here, so just run. We'll tell you everything when we're not in the middle of a fucking cult lair."

Nickie paused as they came to a double door in the middle of the corridor. "Alexis, which way?"

Alexis closed her eyes for half a second, then pointed to the stairs. "Gabriel will have the Pod waiting on the roof."

They barged through the doors and started up the three flights of stairs to the roof with Alexis in the lead. They made it to the third floor before anyone attempted to stop them.

"Get down!" Alexis yelled from the landing just ahead of them as a hail of bullets and Etheric energy beams tore into the place she was standing.

Hafnar made to dart onto the landing, but Nickie stopped him with an outstretched arm.

"Stay behind me," she told them both in a tone that left no room for protest. "Alexis is fine."

Roka put a hand on Hafnar's arm to calm him as Nickie stood guard on the landing. She peered through the cloud of plaster and brick dust but Alexis' body wasn't there to retrieve, confirming what Nickie had told them.

A series of muzzle flashes on the landing above lit the falling dust, and one, two, then three bodies fell past them.

Roka stepped back to avoid being hit when the third body hit the railing and bounced off the banisters as it fell instead of plummeting through the open stairwell like the others.

"We're good," Alexis called down a moment later.

Nickie lowered the Jean Dukes Special she had trained on the stairs. "You two good?" She gestured for Roka and

Hafnar to follow her up the stairs after ascertaining they hadn't been injured.

Mystified, they did as she asked. Everyone reached the roof without any more incidents and boarded the waiting Pod in a hurry. Gabriel introduced himself to Roka and Hafnar as they took off.

Roka's adrenaline began to abate as the Pod broke the atmosphere. She closed her eyes as the pain in her face and ribs reasserted itself now the imminent danger had passed.

"Let me take care of your injuries," Alexis told Roka.

Roka nodded, too exhausted to argue that she was fine. She sucked in a breath as Alexis applied med patches to her obvious injuries. Where are we headed?" she asked.

"Now!" Nickie announced.

Roka glanced at the Ranger leaning over Gabriel's chair. "What just happened?"

"We dropped an explosive on the compound," Alexis replied without concern.

"What?" Roka exclaimed. "They've got a couple hundred ships down there!"

"We know," Alexis told her as she applied a one-time-use regeneration patch to Roka's jaw. "We wanted them to know we rescued you. We need them to follow us through the Gate."

She smiled. "Don't worry, we've got everything under control. Our ships are hidden in the asteroid belt."

"And our parents are waiting on the other side of the Gate," Gabriel added as if that explained everything.

Nickie snorted. "They haven't figured it out yet. These are Bethany Anne's children," she told Roka and Hafnar.

"When they say they have it under control, you can believe them."

Roka winced as Alexis applied another patch to her orbital fracture.

"There, your eye should be fine once the swelling goes down," Alexis told her. "You'll need a Pod-doc for the rest. You took a lot of punishment."

Roka smiled, which made her wince. "It comes with the territory sometimes. Glad you and Nickie were there to pull us out."

"What am I, chopped liver?" Gabriel called from the pilot's seat. "Nobody ever gives the getaway pilot credit."

Roka looked across the Pod at Hafnar and saw that he was putting everything into keeping his reactions under control. "Concentrate on breathing. We'll get you back on your serum as soon as we're inside the Federation."

Alexis twisted her upper body and scrutinized the Shrillexian. "Can you hold on for a few more minutes?"

Hafnar nodded without speaking, clenching his fists.

"Gabriel," Alexis called.

"I heard," Gabriel returned in the same tone. "I've asked Gemini to synthesize a batch of the serum. Talia will meet us in the hangar to get him to the med bay."

Roka had no time to wonder who Talia was.

"We've got company," Gabriel announced as a flash of weapons fire on the viewscreen cast the shadows on the bridge into stark relief. "They missed."

"Those are Kurtherian ships!" Trey exclaimed. "We're screwed!"

He put the stern's external cameras up on the

viewscreen and cursed when they saw the battleships eating up the distance between them.

"Dammit, we only needed another minute!" Alexis dropped into the copilot's seat and took control of the Pod's weapons. "How far are we from the asteroid field?"

"Close enough that they can provide some fucking *cover*!" Nickie snarled, annoyed at being unable to act. She connected her comm to her ship and screamed into the link, "*SAYOMI! YOU WANTED TO BLOW SHIT UP. NOW'S YOUR CHANCE!*"

Sayomi's guttural voice came over the Pod's speaker. "As you wish."

The Pod rocked as the ship on their tail exploded in a fireball. Two more ships came flying out of the debris, followed by another six.

Sayomi went on the attack, her nails-on-a-chalkboard voice sending chills down the spine of everyone who heard her whoop every time she scored a direct hit on one of the ships trying to shoot the Pod down.

Gabriel wrestled the Pod controls, fighting to keep the resulting shockwaves from Sayomi's successes from knocking them off course. A barrage of pucks came screaming out of the asteroid field and impacted the lead ships as the Pod slipped into the *Gemini*'s hangar and vanished behind her cloaking.

CHAPTER TWENTY

Cosnar System, Ranger Base One

Akio was monitoring the CEREBRO network from the ops center when the alert sounded. He flowed to his feet, a large part of him relieved the wait was finally over. "CEREBRO, report," he yelled over the alarms.

"We are picking up an anomalous incoming Gate signature thirty thousand kilometers from the planet," the EI group responded. "Sector Three-Nine-Delta. Activating satellite defenses."

Akio left his quarters and raced for the hangar, thankful the *Reynolds'* arrival had given the EI-controlled satellites the weapons upgrade they so desperately needed.

The ramp of the QBS *Achronyx* dropped as Akio crossed the hangar. He boarded and made his way to the bridge as the ship lifted off. "Achronyx, connect me to all Ranger bases, the *War Axe*, the *Baba Yaga*, and the *Reynolds*."

"Done," Achronyx replied. "The *War Axe* has responded to the alert. Colonel Lowell promises to give the cultists your regards should the Gate open before we arrive."

"Tell her we're going to make it." Akio slid into his captain's chair and prepared to give the intruders a blistering Ranger-style unwelcome as he spoke to the bases. "All hands to battle stations. This is not a drill."

The viewscreen split into multiple windows, showing Akio the ops centers on all three bases, the bridges of the senior Rangers' ships, Christina on the *War Axe,* and Reynolds and his first officer.

"Colonel Lowell, Captain Reynolds, report your positions in relation to sector Three-Nine-Delta," Akio began without preamble.

"We are standing by in sector Three-Nine-Echo," Christina confirmed. "The second the *Gemini* and the *Sayomi* are through, we'll be there to cover them and get them to the *Reynolds.*"

"Holding position at Two-One-Beta," Reynolds confirmed. "Those fuckwits will have to get through me to reach the planet."

"And if they do," Eve added, "I will be waiting."

"As will we," Hirotoshi seconded. "Ranger units are in place around the planet. All our ships are equipped with Nickie's targeted EMP emitters."

Akio's face hardened. "Good. While I do not expect anyone to lay down their lives for the sake of saving the cultists, we have a duty to ensure they face Justice."

The screen adjusted to add another window as Bethany Anne joined them.

Bethany Anne looked around and pressed her lips together. "Fucksticks. It's starting without me."

"I'm afraid so," Akio informed her regretfully. "We will make sure the children are safe."

Bethany Anne nodded. "Good luck, all of you. I'll be there as soon as I can."

Eve remained on the viewscreen after everyone else had signed off. "Everything is going as expected. Dr. Lawless reports that all of our medical facilities are ready to receive the cultists for deprogramming once they have been apprehended. They deserve to die for trying to take this home from the Collective."

Akio nodded. "Some will. Remember, these people were compelled. It is no easy thing to put aside personal grudges, even if it is the honorable thing to do."

Eve's smooth face gave no hint of her feelings. "There is no honor in Gödel or the Seven."

Akio inclined his head. "I agree. True honor resides between empathy and logic. The pursuit of honor without one or the other leads to a hollow existence, and Gödel has neither at her command."

"Okay, so we free them from the compulsion and send them to the House of Arbitration." Eve's wicked grin lit her face. "But first, they will get a taste of what it feels like to be helpless."

The screen cut out before Akio could caution Eve against her clear desire for vengeance. He considered calling her back but decided against it.

If any of the cultists got as far as the planet, they were resourceful enough that Eve's measures would likely be necessary to protect the base and the Collective.

Beyond Federation Borders, QGE *Gemini*, Bridge

"Increase power to the inertial dampers!" K'aia yelled as she was almost thrown from her chair.

"I can't," Trey responded, hanging onto his console while the ship was rocked by another nearby impact on the asteroid field, which was disintegrating around them under fire from the cultists' ships. "We need the power for cloaking and shields."

Nickie returned from the med bay, where she'd left Roka and Hafnar with Talia and Durq. "Alexis, how long?" she asked. "Sayomi's taking a beating keeping the cult off our asses."

"*Pew-pew*!" Sayomi cackled over the speaker as she spiraled to avoid a missile. "I'm having *all* the fun."

"Why are you venting plasma?" Nickie demanded. "Have you taken a serious hit?"

"Trust me," Sayomi assured her. "You're going to get a kick out of this."

Nickie cursed. "Don't take stupid risks just because you're out there on your own. I don't want my grandfather to disown me a second time."

Alexis and Gabriel ignored everyone for the moment, fighting for access to the satellites ringing the black hole. They'd convinced the network firewall they belonged there and were getting close to locating the Gate activation protocols.

Damn Kurtherian code! Gabriel hissed into the mind-space as they were halted by yet another firewall. He doubled down on supporting Alexis as she worked to prevent them from being thrown out of the network.

It was never your favorite, Alexis murmured in consolation, the majority of her brain's processing ability dedicated to simultaneously working around all the host-based firewalls in the satellites. *We're almost there. Gemini, are you ready to activate the Gate?*

Just get me in there, the AI assured them.

Alexis found the Gate protocols at last and forwarded them to Gemini. "Heads up," she called. "We're in. Sayomi, get out of there. We need to get into position."

"Heading for the event horizon," Sayomi confirmed as she dropped a single remote-detonated mine at the end of the intricate plasma trail she'd laid. "Give me thirty seconds."

"Decloak on my mark and make sure they don't miss us," Alexis ordered when both ships were in position. "Gemini, activate the Gate in three...two... *Mark*!"

The satellites activated and began pulling energy from the black hole. The Gate shimmered open across the event horizon, spilling dark, heavy-looking light as opposed to the shimmering green-white-gold spectrum Gate portals usually emitted.

"The Gate is holding steady," Gemini announced as the cultists' ships ceased firing on the asteroid field. "There are no incoming signals from the other side."

"Send a probe through," Alexis ordered. "Let them know we're coming."

"Why isn't anyone shooting at us?" Trey pondered.

"Phraim-'Eh's ships are not picking us up on their scanners," Gabriel replied with frustration. "The Gate's energy is masking our presence."

Sayomi detonated the mine she'd left at the end of the plasma trail. "That should get their attention," she crowed triumphantly as the trail ignited in the shape of a human hand giving Phraim-'Eh's fleet the finger.

Nickie howled with laughter as the fleet came around to face them. "Yeah, that worked."

The *Gemini* was hit three times in quick succession as the lead ships opened fire. The viewscreen flickered and went out, dropping the bridge into momentary darkness.

"Let's go!" Alexis commanded.

The *Sayomi* led the way as they hurtled through the black hole Gate into the Cosnar System—and right into CEREBRO's defense network. Sayomi flipped her ship and continued firing, darting behind the satellites to evade the return fire from the emerging battleships.

The *Gemini* barely avoided crashing into a satellite that was firing on the ships swarming through the Gate behind them.

"Cloaking is down," Trey announced as the emergency lighting kicked in.

"Get us out of this, Gemini!" Gabriel yelled over the blaring alarms.

"Perhaps we should not have gotten into this," Gemini admonished as she redirected the ship's thrusters to get them out of range of the Gate.

K'aia held onto her chair as they plummeted out of the line of fire. "Perhaps you could save asserting your personality for when we're safely aboard the *Reynolds*. Where are my damned railguns?"

"They were supposed to know we were coming!" Alexis yelled. "Where is the *War Axe*?"

Christina's flushed face appeared on the viewscreen

when it came back on suddenly. "Somebody order a rescue?"

Alexis raised an eyebrow. "A little help would be appreciated."

"Quit chatting and get us moving!" K'aia snapped without letting up on the railguns. "I'm running low on ammunition, and those bastards have us trapped where we can't collect any more material."

"Follow us," Christina told them. "We have—"

The connection was lost when the *Reynolds* discharged its main ESD into the Gate. The Gate collapsed behind the final few ships, cutting off the cult's escape.

Alexis glanced at everyone in turn. "We can't stay here."

"We can't exactly move," Gemini stated. "I've lost external sensors."

"Targeting systems are down too," K'aia informed them with regret. "We're out of this fight."

"Can you get the *War Axe* back?" Alexis asked.

"I'm attempting to do so," Gemini confirmed.

"Screw this!" Nickie exclaimed, heading for the door. "Gemini, fire up the Pod. I'll guide you in myself."

SD *Reynolds*, Bridge

Reynolds jumped to his feet. "Tactical alert!"

"I am alert," Tactical shot back. "We are surrounded by Kurtherian vessels. They're charging weapons."

"Then charge ours!" Reynolds thundered.

His apoplectic spluttering ceased when the viewscreen lit up with multiple explosions.

"You talk too much," Tactical told him as he released another complement of Etheric-capable missiles. They used the extra dimension as a way past the enemy's shields, where they drilled into the hull before detonating their payload.

Reynolds turned to Jiya's station. "Did the *Gemini* make it into the hangar?"

"Safe and sound, Captain," Jiya replied. "Alexis and Gabriel are on their way to the bridge now with Ranger Two."

"Very good, Number One," Reynolds told her as the twins stepped out of the Etheric with a nauseated-looking Nickie.

"Next time, remind me to pack a barf bag," Nickie groaned, holding her stomach.

"Do you need medical attention?" Doc asked from a speaker.

"I'm good, thanks." Nickie looked for the source of the voice, taking in the heavy *Star Trek* vibe of the *Reynolds'* bridge.

"Is this…" She looked at Reynolds. "Did you do this on purpose?"

"Damn straight. Welcome aboard," Reynolds greeted her, indicating the empty stations his splinter personalities currently occupied. "Now get to work."

He turned around in his chair and closed his eyes.

"He's picking up the slack around the ship," Jiya explained. "We're a little shorthanded with a third of the crew on the *Baba Yaga*."

"Our teams went to give the repair crews a hand," Gabriel told her, including Nickie with a nod. "Durq is a great engineer. Any news on when the *Baba Yaga* is going to get here?"

"The Queen has remained in contact. We expect her in the next thirty minutes." Jiya shook her head. "I'm glad you're here. I could use a hand."

Alexis hugged Reynolds in passing as she made her way to Navigation's seat. "What's the play?" she asked the AI as she integrated her HUD with the station.

"To stay between the flagship and the planet," Navigation replied.

"While coordinating the transfer of prisoners from the damaged ships to the temporary brig on deck three," Comms added.

While Alexis got acquainted with Navigation and Comms and Gabriel assisted Jiya with keeping the repair crews on top of the damage the superdreadnought was taking in the battle, Nickie took a seat at the tactical station and scrutinized the weapons console.

"What do we have here?" she murmured, activating the holointerface. She grasped the control sticks that manifested on the chair's arms, and the ship's weapons systems came up in her internal HUD. She spied the ESD options immediately. "Hello, gorgeous!"

"It's polite to at least buy someone dinner before you handle their joystick," Tactical told Nickie.

"Let me play with your little ESD, and I'll buy you all the steak on Devon when this is over," Nickie purred, grinning when she saw that the targeted EMP emitters she'd designed for the Ranger fleet had been rolled out to other ships.

"It's a *mini*-ESD!" Tactical spluttered incomprehensibly

as Nickie fired on three Kurtherian ships targeting her Rangers.

Jiya laughed. "Looks like Tactical has met his match."

"Are you going to talk all the way through this battle?" Reynolds asked pointedly. "*Work,* Tactical!"

Ranger Base Two

Heavy bombardment began pounding the surface immediately after the first Kurtherian ships Gated in. The forcefields held, deflecting the barrage by channeling the force of each impact into the ocean floor.

The Collective broadcast their distress and anger across the base.

I'm coming, Eve promised.

She accessed the base's shielding and searched out the forcefield controls for the acclimation enclosure. Finding they could only be accessed from inside the enclosure, she ran for the roamer dock. The non-military personnel she passed were clearly anxious at being under attack, but everyone appeared to know their role in this event. In any case, no one stopped her to ask for help.

She climbed into her personal roamer and drove at speed to the acclimation enclosure. The Conduit was on the other side of the enclosure's airlock, waiting for her.

The Conduit - Image by Eric Quigley

Release us, the Conduit requested.

That's my intention, just as soon as I can get in there with you. Eve cursed her inability to walk the Etheric while she waited for the airlock to cycle open.

You need to go far from here, she told the Collective once she was through to the other side. Just until the enemy has been subdued. *I'm going to open the enclosure.*

The Conduit surged out of the mass, its wise old eyes fixed on the light filtering down from explosions occurring above the surface. *We will fight to protect what is ours.*

If that is your wish, Eve told them. *Please be aware that the people piloting the enemy ships are under compulsion to do so. The Queen asks that we avoid killing them if possible.*

The Conduit observed Eve for a long moment. *We will respect the Queen's wishes.*

Eve smiled. *Let's get you out of here.*

The Collective moved carefully so as not to crush the

roamer as Eve passed through the loops of their tentacles, heading for the substation where the enclosure could be deactivated with a code only she and Akio had.

Eve deactivated the forcefield, and the Collective surged toward the surface. She followed in her roamer, breaking the surface in time to see one of the Collective snatch a Kurtherian battleship out of the sky.

The *Achronyx* flew low overhead, and a thick cable descended from the open drop doors and clamped onto the roamer.

Akio's voice came over the roamer's speaker. "Are you ready to join the battle up here?"

"Wouldn't miss it for the world," Eve replied.

CHAPTER TWENTY-ONE

Open Space, QSD *Baba Yaga*, Bridge

Bethany Anne was monitoring the comm feeds coming in from the Cosnar System as the *Baba Yaga* rushed to join the battle. She accessed the camera in the cockpit of Michael's borrowed scout fighter and saw through the transparent canopy that he was engaged in a dogfight with a similar-sized fighter ship.

"Trust you to get all the fun," Bethany Anne told him with a rueful twist of her mouth. "Where is Phraim-'Eh's ship?"

"He is playing mouse, with the *Reynolds* as the cat," Michael informed her as he corkscrewed to evade enemy fire, his lip curling in distaste. "Every time Reynolds makes a move, he counters. The coward currently has a number of his ships surrounding his flagship. We are working to prevent any more from joining the blockade."

"Let him play," Bethany Anne stated, not bothering to hide her own distaste. "I'm twelve minutes out from the edge of the system. Then it's game over for the cult."

Comm chatter continued in the background as they spoke. Bethany Anne listened in on the activity occurring closer to the planet while Michael's attention was diverted by his next target.

"There is good news," Michael commented as he exchanged fire with the Kurtherian ship and took out their propulsion systems. "The ships Gödel provided the cult do not appear to have the ability to cross into the Etheric."

"She can't be concerned about the Bl'kheth," Bethany Anne told him, considering the only reason Gödel would be holding back. "She's saving her resources for another attack."

"It is too late for her to attack the Federation directly without significant losses." Michael's gaze snapped to the left as a flash of light illuminated the cockpit. "One moment. Ricole is pinned down."

Bethany Anne waved a hand. "Help her. I have a few things to take care of before we arrive." She transferred the comm to her internal HUD and headed for her ready room, where Izanami was waiting for her.

"Has the crew finished preparing for the battle?" Bethany Anne asked as she walked over to the hidden weapons locker in the wall behind her desk.

"The modifications to deck eleven are complete," Izanami assured her. Her avatar's aura swam with dark red, giving her armor the appearance of being blood-washed. "The transporter has been modified to transfer the prisoners directly into the cabins the crew has prepared to hold them until Red Rock gets here."

Bethany Anne nodded as the wall panel slid back in

response to her touch. "Make sure everyone who worked through two or more shifts gets some rest."

Izanami laughed. "You'll have to take that up with Captain Jameson. We have an agreement to stay out of each other's wheelhouse, and it makes for a happy ship."

"Noted." Bethany Anne smiled as she withdrew her Jean Dukes Specials and holstered them at her hips before taking her katanas from their stand. "What about the modifications to the forward baffles?"

"We'll know if we can convert the Etheric pulse to EM once we get there," Izanami replied. "We can't test it while we're traveling at this speed, obviously."

Bethany Anne wasn't anxious to test the *Baba Yaga's* shields against the debris the baffles cleared from their path. "Pass the modifications on to Reynolds."

Izanami nodded. "Done. He will have them completed by the time we arrive."

"Good. It will make getting past the blockade without destroying the ships that much easier." Bethany Anne sheathed her katanas in her back harness and moved on to attaching pouches filled with various gadgets and small explosives to the webbing on her armor.

Izanami watched Bethany Anne's preparations with longing. "I am impatient for an opportunity to test my new armaments. The sooner we deal with this pissant and his followers, the sooner the real fight can begin."

Bethany Anne's mouth turned up at the corner. "My sentiments exactly. Red Rock will be here in four days. I expect us to be en route to Devon in five."

"Then we should hope the gods of best laid plans are

looking down upon us favorably," Izanami commented dryly.

Bethany Anne raised an eyebrow as she closed the weapons locker. "What's one more obstacle to be flattened if they aren't?"

Izanami grinned. "We will be Gating into the Cosnar System in two minutes. I have informed CEREBRO of our approach."

Bethany Anne left her ready room and returned to the bridge. She gripped the back of her chair, watching the viewscreen in anticipation as she waited for the *Baba Yaga* to exit into normal space.

"I have our exit coordinates," Izanami announced. "Activating Gate in five…four…three…"

Bethany Anne's eyes flicked from one side of the viewscreen to the other, assessing the status of the battle as the *Baba Yaga* emerged from the Gate Izanami created.

The planet caught Bethany Anne's gaze, a majestic, swirling blue and white marble. It was accompanied by Ranger Base One, an asteroid a tenth of its size that looked like an orbiting moon. Most of the fighting was clustered on the same side of the planet as the Ranger base. In the distance, the blockade of Kurtherian ships clustered thickly around Phraim-'Eh's flagship. The *Reynolds* held position between the two, preventing any more cultist ships from joining the blockade.

Bethany Anne saw at a glance that the majority of the Kurtherian ships had been disabled. They floated aimlessly in the space between the *Reynolds* and the planet, providing cover for the few ships still in the fight.

Reynolds appeared on the viewscreen. "My Queen, you

arrived just in time. My engineers have made the adjustments to our deflector array."

"Your *what?*" Bethany Anne's eyebrows rose in confusion. "The modification is for your Etheric baffles."

"Same thing. Just go with it," Izanami informed Bethany Anne, rolling her eyes.

"Are we ready to put those ships out of commission or not?" Bethany Anne asked as Michael arrived on the bridge.

"Yes," the twins chorused from offscreen.

Michael walked over to stand beside her. "Do we have a problem?"

Bethany Anne shook her head at Michael, then waved her hands to dismiss the subject. "That's all I needed to hear. Reynolds' alternative naming system for the parts of his ship needs to be added to the translation software."

"Or you could watch a few episodes of *Star Trek,* my Queen," Reynolds grumbled.

Bethany Anne decided not to hear that. "Have you returned John's ship?" she asked Michael.

"John has his ship," Michael confirmed. "Gabrielle is waiting for the green light to take the Bitches into the fight. There's no way to get to Phraim-'Eh's ship with the localized emitters. The ships surrounding his have some kind of EM shielding."

"It's being generated by the flagship," Reynolds supplied.

"That's why we're going to hit them with all the power two superdreadnoughts can generate." Bethany Anne opened a secure channel to the *War Axe* and the *Achronyx.*

"Akio, Christina, pull your people back to the planet. We're about to unleash a huge-ass EMP."

"The *War Axe* is in position to provide cover for the Rangers as they fall back," Christina responded as Akio passed the order to the Ranger fleet. "I'll report back when we're out of range."

"I'm sending you some support," Bethany Anne told them. She reached out mentally to Gabrielle and gave her the go-ahead.

Six sleek black scout fighters exited the *Baba Yaga,* looking like stingrays with the Queen's Bitch insignia emblazoned in white and crimson on their hulls. They fanned out to cover the space between the *Reynolds* and the planet as the few dozen Kurtherian ships still in the fight renewed their attacks, using the disabled vessels as cover while they fired on the Rangers.

Bethany Anne followed the strategic retreat on her viewscreen with only half her attention. Her main focus was on tracking the activity around the blockade, while Michael coordinated with Izanami and Reynolds to position the superdreadnoughts to keep the planet and each other out of the line of fire.

She opened a private channel to Christina when the *War Axe* plowed into the side of a Kurtherian battleship, removing a stubborn group of small but heavily-armed fighter ships that were shrugging off the targeted EMP. "Snag one of those fighter ships intact, and Bad Company gets first dibs on their shielding tech after Jean's figured it out."

"Deal," Christina agreed. "One moment. Get a grappler on that ship!" she yelled.

Bethany Anne saw the *War Axe* alter course slightly before continuing on its way.

"Those were the last three outside of the blockade," Christina informed her. "We're heading back to the planet."

"Something is happening at the blockade," Reynolds informed them.

"Define 'something,'" Michael requested.

Bethany Anne wasn't going to wait to find out. "Are the EMP emitters ready?"

Reynolds and Izanami confirmed they were.

"Then prepare to transport the cultists and fire," Bethany Anne commanded. "Alexis, Gabriel, get over here. We need you on Phraim-Eh's ship."

The forward baffles of the *Baba Yaga* and the *Reynolds* flashed as the AIs released a narrow-beam pulse. The wave was unspectacular, invisible to everyone watching on viewscreens across the two superdreadnoughts. The result was not.

The shield around the blockade flared when the pulses hit, a blink of incandescence that was over in a flash. The shielding generated by Phraim-'Eh's ship winked out and was followed by a wave of small explosions rippling across the Kurtherian ships as the EMP burned through every circuit, overloading their systems.

"I'm reading numerous casualties," Izanami reported.

"Are the cultists contained?" Michael asked.

"They're trapped without power," Izanami replied.

"Start the transporters," Bethany Anne told the AIs. "Prioritize the injured and those with minimal life support."

Alexis and Gabriel arrived on the bridge as Bethany Anne and Michael prepared to leave for Phraim-'Eh's ship.

"We had to stop by the armory and switch our loadout," Gabriel explained.

Bethany Anne opened the Etheric. "Phraim-Eh isn't going to arrest himself. Let's go."

Phraim-Eh's Ship

Bethany Anne exited the Etheric ahead of Michael and the twins. The ship was dead. There was no emergency lighting, and the air was already growing stale with the CO_2 scrubbers offline. Every circuit in the ship had been fried by the EMP. Even with their enhanced vision, none of them could see a thing, although they heard the crew flailing around in the darkness below.

"Switch your HUD view to IR," Bethany Anne murmured so only Michael and the twins could hear. She had the camera drones shine red light, revealing their position between an elevator and the bridge door on a suspended walkway above the engine core.

When no one below started shooting, Bethany Anne released the camera drones from their tight circle above her head and gestured for the twins to move to secure the elevator at the far end of the walkway.

They heard two thuds in quick succession. The twins returned to the center of the walkway a few seconds later.

"Two guards," Gabriel confirmed.

"They're sleeping," Alexis added.

Michael turned his attention to the bridge and listened

in on the minds within. "There are ten people in there. Nine of them are being controlled."

Bethany Anne's lip curled. "No prize for guessing who Asshole Number Ten is."

Screams from below, accompanied by a pale glow, drew their attention. The mesh walkway floor gave them a view of the engine deck, where the crew was panicking as individuals were transported out by either Reynolds or Izanami.

Alexis looked over the rail. "At least they're all down there and not up here shooting at us."

"They will have time to cool down before Red Rock gets here." Bethany Anne drew her Jean Dukes Specials and double-checked the setting was correct for the night-night rounds they were loaded with. She returned them to their holsters and extracted a handful of coin-sized discs from one of the pouches on her armor.

"Explosives?" Alexis inquired.

Bethany Anne shook her head. "You'll see. Prepare to breach."

Michael, Alexis, and Gabriel drew their Jean Dukes Specials, which were also loaded with night-night rounds, and took their stances while Bethany Anne placed the adhesive discs around the door casement.

Bethany Anne stepped back and retrieved the detonator from another pouch. "Izanami, stand by to activate transporters on my command."

"Standing by," Izanami confirmed in her ear.

Bethany Anne activated the detonator, and the casement turned to dust as the nanocytes in the discs ate through the metal. She strode through the hole after the bridge door fell inward with a clang. Michael and the twins were at her back, their weapons trained on Phraim-'Eh and his lieutenants.

The bridge was lit by emergency chemical lanterns hanging from cords over the consoles. Phraim-Eh was clearly expecting Bethany Anne. He stood by the captain's chair, surrounded by his human lieutenants.

Phraim-Eh Image by Eric Quigley

Every one of the humans was holding a knife to his or her throat. They shook with fear, aware of their precarious situation but unable to disobey their master.

"Move a muscle and they die," Phraim-'Eh threatened, his hateful glare wavering as he looked down the barrels of Bethany Anne's Jean Dukes Specials.

Michael lifted a shoulder without altering his aim. "What makes you think we care?"

Phraim-Eh grinned and pointed at Bethany Anne. "You might not care, but *she* does."

Bethany Anne noted the bulging eyes of the lieutenants before settling her gaze on Phraim-Eh. "You're right. I do. Izanami, nine to transport. Leave the Larian."

The bridge glowed as the nine lieutenants were broken down to their constituent atoms and beamed over to the cells waiting for them aboard the *Baba Yaga*.

"Cut your throats!" Phraim-'Eh screamed, but they were gone before he uttered the second syllable.

"The prisoners are under a compulsion to cut," Michael informed Izanami over the comm, "Make sure they are disarmed and put into stasis immediately."

Phraim-'Eh covered his fear with anger. Clenching his jaw, he attempted to push a compulsion on Michael and the twins.

Alexis laughed.

"That's not going to work on us," Gabriel told him.

Michael's expression contained no hint of humor. "You will cease your pathetic attempt to gain mental control of my children, or by God, you will not make it to trial." His eyes flashed red as he spoke, reminding Phraim-Eh that he was in the presence of real power.

"Trial?" Phraim-Eh scoffed.

Bethany Anne holstered her Jean Dukes Specials. "It's over. Everyone you have compelled will be freed. The people who fell for your lies will be enlightened. The Federal House of Arbitration will be arriving soon to deal with your followers."

"He doesn't care," Alexis cut in. "I can hear his thoughts. He intends to start over at the first opportunity."

True, TOM agreed. **I have looked into his mind. He is programmed to propagate Gödel's lies and twist everything you do into a tale of evil intent. His knowledge of her appears to be blocked.**

Worse, Michael added.

For the cameras, Bethany Anne reminded him.

"His personality is still intact under the compulsion to sow dissent," Michael continued aloud. "He is a true believer in the Ascension path."

Phraim-'Eh's eyes widened in reaction to Michael's statement.

Alexis pulled Gabriel in to check that what she was interpreting from Phraim-'Eh's mind was correct.

Gabriel frowned. "He thinks he will be Ascended for his work here."

"That's what I thought," Alexis told him grimly, drawing back from Phraim-'Eh's mind. She felt like she needed to sterilize her brain to get the ick off. She turned on Phraim-'Eh with a snarl. "Mental abilities are a gift, not a weapon. You disgust me."

Bethany Anne lifted a hand to stay her daughter's anger. "He will face Justice."

"How?" Gabriel asked quietly, his brow furrowed in thought. "He'll wreak havoc on any prison he's sent to."

"If he even makes it to prison," Alexis agreed. "What's going to stop him from compelling the court to free him? Or if they manage to get him there, from taking control of the penal world?"

"Kill him where he stands," Michael advised. "He's too dangerous to be allowed off this ship."

Bethany Anne saw the idea take root in Phraim-'Eh's

mind. Her family was right. Putting him through the same process as his followers put the entire Federation at risk. "Are those your orders? To get in front of the Federation Council, and what? Have them open the Gates for Gödel?"

Phraim-'Eh clutched his head. "What are you doing to me?"

"I haven't done anything yet," Bethany Anne told him coldly. She knew what the solution had to be, and it wasn't what she'd wanted. She glanced at Michael and Alexis. "Can you remove his ability to compel others?"

"I was born for this power," Phraim-'Eh spat, regaining his composure. "You will have to kill me before I give it up!"

"He believes what he's saying," Gabriel insisted. "He's under the same compulsion as the rest of them."

Without doing a deep dive into Phraim-'Eh's mind—definitely *not* on her to-do list for the day—Bethany Anne got much the same impression.

"It's not the same compulsion," Michael informed them. He glanced at Alexis, who nodded to confirm his assessment. "The changes are similar to those made to Isaiah, although there is less damage in the areas that have been altered. I believe this is Gödel's work, and he welcomed it."

"There is no Gödel!" Phraim-'Eh screamed. "No Kurtherians!"

Bethany Anne tuned out his outburst. "Can we undo the compulsions on him the same way we did with Isaiah?" she asked Michael.

"Not without killing him," Michael answered.

Phraim-'Eh fell silent.

Bethany Anne made her decision. "Then Gödel has

given me no choice by making him too powerful to be contained. This will be his trial, witnessed by the entire Federation. Phraim-'Eh. You have committed mass mental coercion, subverted Federation citizens, created a terrorist organization, incited treason, and attacked multiple locations across the Federation. You are responsible for the murder of every Federation citizen who died fighting for or against your fabricated cause and the attempted destruction of the planet known as 'Waterworld.' The penalty for these crimes is death."

"What happened to the due process you humans are so proud of?" Phraim-'Eh sneered. "Where is the representation your laws state I am entitled to?"

Bethany Anne shook her head slowly. "You were misinformed. You are not in the Federation. This is an Interdiction location. The only law this star system is subject to is mine, and I have no taste for incarceration. Your followers being tried under Federation law is down to my mercy. You are a different matter entirely. I cannot in good conscience hand you a planet filled with dangerous criminals to build another army."

Phraim-'Eh glared at Bethany Anne for a long moment. "Then this is my end."

Bethany Anne nodded. "It is. How you meet it is up to you. Show some remorse for the lives you have destroyed. Confess. Tell me your orders, and I'll kill you outright instead of leaving you here to suffocate. That's the only mercy I am prepared to offer you."

The air pressure shifted as Phraim-'Eh momentarily pulsed with Etheric energy.

He's throwing off the barriers Gödel placed on his mind, TOM warned.

Phraim-'Eh's expression shifted as thin rivulets of blood began to leak from his eyes, ears, and nose. He jutted his chin and sneered at Bethany Anne with new knowledge in his expression. "I have no regrets about the fate of nonbelievers. You haven't won."

"It wasn't a competition," Michael informed him dispassionately. "You are not a Federation citizen. You are wanted for the same crimes in your own galaxy that you have committed here. Gödel cannot protect you from the Queen's Justice."

Alexis snorted. "He doesn't even understand that Mom is protecting him from *your* justice. We're wasting our time and giving him a platform to continue spreading hate."

Bethany Anne silenced Alexis with a look before turning her stare on Phraim-Eh. "What are your orders? Hmm? What were you supposed to do if by some miracle you won?"

Phraim-Eh said nothing for a long moment. The blood running from his eyes left oily black tracks down his face. "Death will die, and the goddess will prevail. That's all that matters."

Bethany Anne wasn't done. "Do you really believe Gödel gives a shit about you? That she would allow anyone who isn't a pureblooded Kurtherian to ascend? You're nothing but a tool to her, something to be used and discarded the moment you outlive your usefulness."

"That's not true!" Phraim-Eh exclaimed, lunging at Bethany Anne with his hands outstretched.

She lifted her foot and kicked Phraim-Eh in the chest,

and he landed heavily in the captain's chair. "So, you admit you serve Gödel."

"I admit nothing," Phraim-Eh whined.

"What are your orders?" Bethany Anne repeated calmly. "I calculated this cabin had maybe an hour of air remaining when I took the power out."

"There are nineteen minutes remaining," Alexis supplied.

Bethany Anne's mouth curled up at the corner. "We're leaving in eighteen, max." She returned her attention to Phraim-Eh. "You're running out of time."

Phraim-Eh shook his head vigorously. "No."

"Yes," Michael told him. "Take the honorable way out."

Phraim-Eh hunched into the chair and clutched his head, his eyes rolling as his back arched. "I have been granted mercy already. Death…Death took my honor."

His wild gaze snapped to Bethany Anne and he shrank back against the chair, scrambling to get away from her. "You won't get anything from me. The goddess granted me a reprieve for my failure."

"What's he talking about?" Bethany Anne asked. "Why am I getting the feeling Gödel made sure this would end badly however it turned out?"

"His mind is fracturing," Michael answered simply. "He triggered the failsafe Gödel implanted. He's dying."

Bethany Anne's eyes flashed red. "Not before we find out where he was supposed to go if he won the battle here."

"You're too late!" Phraim-Eh declared. "The Federation will fall. All will know the glory of Ascension." Blood poured from his eyes and nose, running into his mouth as he spoke.

His words began to lose their cohesiveness. He got to his feet unsteadily and grabbed for the console to steady himself. "Gödel wields the power of Ascension. Her rule stretches across the known universe. She is going to crush the Federation like the insignificant bug it is."

Bethany Anne slowly and deliberately drew one of her katanas. "Michael, take what we need. He does not get to dictate the method of his execution."

"I have a location," Michael confirmed.

Bethany Anne's katana flashed as she removed Phraim-Eh's head with a practiced flick of her wrist. "The anti-Empire movement is over."

CHAPTER TWENTY-TWO

Devon, QSD *Baba Yaga*, Bethany Anne's Ready Room

Bethany Anne noted Alexis' tension as her daughter entered the room.

Alexis glanced around.

"I made an announcement earlier today," Bethany Anne told her. "The live feed has to be switched off for the trial and will remain off for security reasons."

Alexis snorted. "Handy."

Bethany Anne just smiled. While she didn't give a shit if Gödel knew she was coming for her, she wanted to keep the details of how the Kurtherian was going to get her ass kicked a surprise. "Why so serious?"

"I completed work on the virus," Alexis responded heavily. "Can you drop the lights? I made a slideshow to break down how it works."

Bethany Anne raised an eyebrow as she lowered the lights. "How do you know it works without a live test?"

"I don't need a live test. Gödel's paranoia gave us a way to hurt her badly." Alexis connected to the holoprojector in the desk and loaded her simulations. "The attack phase of the virus triggers the backdoor she built into every soldier in her army. Then the worm can get in undetected and attach itself to the failsafes written into the enhancements she has given them."

Bethany Anne straightened in her chair when Alexis paused the simulation.

Alexis eyed her, eyebrows narrowed. "What happens next is *extreme,* Mom."

"What happens next?" Bethany Anne asked.

"That depends on what you want to happen." Alexis resumed the simulation. "There are two options at this juncture. Both are pretty nasty."

Bethany Anne resigned herself to the necessity of extreme measures and put aside her discomfort to look at the situation with her head and not her heart. "So is picking up the pieces after every atrocity committed in Gödel's name. Mass-murdering soldiers who chose to fight for evil doesn't look so bad after you lose count of the number of lives you've failed to save."

"I'm just making sure I understand your motivation in having me create something this, well, *bad,*" Alexis admitted. "The Kurtherians have no defense against it. Those we infect will die. Ethically, this is a weapon of genocide."

"I know, my love." Bethany Anne came around the desk and embraced her daughter as she wept for her creation. "I know."

Alexis fought to regain her composure. "They keep forcing us into taking the conflict to the next level. It hurts my heart. I love science and technology because they can help people. I don't want to take lives."

She lowered her eyes, the strength of her convictions continuing to bring tears to her eyes. "This virus makes me into what they say you are—a murderer. I feel a terrible weight." She wiped her tears away, her expression fluctuating between resolution and horror. "*Nobody* should have this much power."

"You won't be taking anyone's life," Bethany Anne assured her, stroking her hair. "We should not have this much power, you're right. Using this virus *is* crossing a line, but understand that I will be the one using it, not you. Although the Seven are a plague on this universe, I will live the rest of my life regretting that I had to kill an entire species to ensure peace for the rest. I don't want that for you. Not ever."

Alexis squeezed her mother tightly. "I appreciate you saying that, but you didn't create the virus. I did. Don't you think Oppenheimer felt the same about every nuclear weapon deployed in his lifetime?"

"I think it was a good thing he had no clue about WWDE," Bethany Anne told her gently. "But not one of those incidents was his responsibility. They were the responsibility of the people who chose to wield his discovery as a weapon, knowing the consequences. Remember that Gödel and the Seven clans before her have twisted ethics and morality to place themselves above everyone else. They've wielded their power without empathy or compassion. All I can do is hope it doesn't take crossing a line I can't come back from to put an end to it, but I have to be ready to cross it if the day comes when there's no other choice."

Alexis had nothing but an idea of her mother's burden.

She held on that bit tighter and said nothing.

The silence allowed both to grieve in their own way, separately, together.

"The price of freedom is the parts of ourselves we give up to win it. You're my hero, Mom. You know that, right?" Alexis released Bethany Anne and walked back to the holo-projector. "We should get back to work. Option one."

The simulation showed the virus replicate almost faster than Bethany Anne's enhancements allowed her to track. As it propagated throughout the sim host's system, it tweaked Gödel's code to give Bethany Anne full control of the host's mind and body without removing the enhancements.

Bethany Anne shook her head vehemently. "Puppet slaves? Fuck. *That.*"

Alexis nodded. "I understand the icky feeling. This version gives us the option of turning Gödel's allies on each other, but you're going to get a lot of background noise from their repressed minds."

Bethany Anne's face expressed her distaste clearly. "If it's a choice between that and innocent lives, maybe. The other option. Tell me it's less drawn out and doesn't involve immersing myself in a mental cesspit."

Alexis ran the simulation. "I used what we learned from Roka about the compound that killed Paul Jacobsen to build this version. It wipes the existing nanocyte code and replaces it with the instruction to replicate without restriction. The host body is essentially broken down from the inside out. The nanocytes convert the mass into fissionable material, and within the space of a minute, the host body is transformed into a series of interconnected chain reactions. When the nanocytes detect multiple critical masses, they self-destruct. It's almost immediate."

They watched the simulation run to its conclusion in silence.

Bethany Anne eyed the end result. "Please tell me we can make sure she can't back-trace this or reverse-engineer it to target *our* nanocytes?"

"No." Alexis shook her head. "It was one of the first concerns I had when I started developing this. The inert virus is harmless. It's *only* activated when it comes into contact with Gödel's backdoor, which we don't have because you wouldn't do something like that to your people."

"I've got more important things to do to waste my time playing Big Brother," Bethany Anne told her with a smile. "There's a benefit to not being an evil overlord. Everyone I've enhanced has my trust." She paused when she realized that wasn't strictly true anymore. "Wait, the upgraded troops. Are they safe?"

"The upgraded troops won't be affected," Alexis promised, pulling up details for the nanocyte program that had been given to millions of soldiers during the course of the tour. "The program has built-in protections against tampering. We figured out how to mess with the Ookens, and you can bet Gödel has people working on turning the tables. We're not taking any chances. Troop nanos are designed to cease functioning and break themselves down if their code is altered in any way. Watch. That's how we're planning to undo the upgrade. Uninstalling enhancements isn't possible, right? Well, now it is."

Bethany Anne let her amazement show. "This all happens without any negative effects?"

Alexis nodded. "ADAM and TOM have both confirmed it. The upgraded troops can safely deploy the virus to take care of Ookens with no ill-effects. They just need to make sure they take precautions not to infect themselves."

Bethany Anne turned the lights up and got herself a Coke after Alexis had gone. She sipped her drink while she contemplated the upcoming trial of Phraim-Eh's people.

The virus was both a turning point and a last resort.

One she prayed she would never have to use against a sentient species.

Cosnar System, Red Rock, Federal House of Arbitration (Four Days Later)

Bethany Anne watched her father conduct the opening procedures for the mass trial of Phraim-'Eh's followers on the anteroom's wallscreen while she waited to be called to the stand.

She sipped her Coke and relaxed on a comfortable sofa, savoring the alone time. While the majority of the cultists were resigned to their fate, the last three days aboard the *Baba Yaga* had been close to unbearable.

The *Reynolds* wasn't equipped to handle more than five thousand prisoners, so the only logical decision was to have them transferred to the *Baba Yaga* and have the Reynolds crew come over with them to assist Captain Jameson with putting the ones who insisted on belligerence into stasis.

Everyone with the ability to undo Phraim-'Eh's

compulsion had worked nonstop to free the prisoners from his mental control. However, there were still thousands in need of deprogramming, and many were doing their best to make life difficult for their jailers.

Bethany Anne suspected the moment the last cultist was transferred to Red Rock, Paul would have the crew prime the engines and point the *Baba Yaga* toward Devon, ready for Izanami to get them the hell out of there as soon as she returned from giving evidence.

An aide knocked on the door before entering. She offered Bethany Anne a serious smile as she held the door open. "It's time, Your Highness."

Bethany Anne put her glass on the table without a word and followed the aide into the corridor. She'd had time to draw up her proposal. Whether the council took her recommendation or not, she intended to make her position clear.

The aide led Bethany Anne down a polished stone corridor hung with landscape paintings of scenes from Federation planets and through a shining brass-plated door into the arbitration room, where she handed Bethany Anne off to the two bailiffs waiting to escort her to the stand.

Bethany Anne's appearance caused a stir among those who had been present when she'd brought an Ooken to chambers to prove her point. The civilians, civil servants, and media representatives in the galleries murmured animatedly as the bailiffs walked ahead of Bethany Anne to the stand before returning to their positions by the door. She ignored the speculation, nodding politely at her father and the assembled council delegates sitting behind him after taking her seat.

A scuffle broke out in the central gallery as Bethany Anne was sworn in. She restrained her urge to remove the brawlers from the room with a well-placed boot to their argumentative asses and a healthy dose of fear to underline her opinion of their manners. While tweaking those pompous assholes would have been fun, she wasn't there to play games.

Bethany Anne spotted a familiar face among the bailiffs who filed out of the gallery entrance to remove the troublemakers and smiled. Of course the Diplomat Emeritus would find a way to be here.

Lance banged his gavel and called for order. "The House will hear Queen Bethany Anne." He banged his gavel again when the muttering from the galleries continued. "I said, *order*! We will hear the Queen. Anyone who wants to find themselves in contempt of the House should continue arguing. We have the fate of over twenty thousand people to decide, and it's going to happen in an orderly fashion if I have to have the bailiffs empty this room to make it so. Am I making myself clear?"

Order was restored. The holoprojector was switched on at Lance's command, and over the next few hours, the delegates questioned Bethany Anne in detail about her efforts to counter the cult over the last eighteen months.

Bethany Anne presented her evidence, talking the House through Harkkat's initial concerns about Shoken Industries and Roka's undercover mission to uncover cult ties to the company. She shared information about Paul Jacobsen's suicide that she'd held back and laid out the steps of the twins' investigation, culminating with a scaled-down 3D analysis of the attack on the Cosnar System and the video from the bridge of Phraim-'Eh's ship.

The delegates broke into an uproar when they saw Phraim-Eh's execution.

Bethany Anne got to her feet and turned to face the council. "I am not the one on trial. We are living in unprecedented times. The Federation has been under attack from within, our people turned against one another. The Larian who called himself Phraim-'Eh was served Justice. We are here today because there are over twenty thousand people in cells who also need to face Justice."

"We are well aware of Your Majesty's particular brand of justice," the Kezzin delegate proclaimed.

Bethany Anne singled him out with a hard stare. "Is that right?"

"There will be no mass graves on our conscience," the delegate stated.

Bethany Anne smiled. "We would have a serious problem if mass execution was the House's ruling. I don't wish to see these people locked away with no avenue to redeem themselves. This cult grew and gained popularity because of Phraim-Eh's manipulation. The majority of the people facing these charges are in this position because they were tricked into believing the Federation was in danger from me.

"Do you get it? They mobilized against *me*, knowing that they had no chance. Wherever I have encountered the cult, I have found intelligent, courageous people who were willing to die for the sake of protecting the ideals this Federation is built upon. People who, when presented with the real evidence, turned their backs on the cult and did everything in their power to make up for it. The planet we are orbiting was lifeless. Our ability to restore it was moving slowly until I encountered Dr. Vivian Jeddah."

"We will be hearing her testimony later in the day," Lance interjected.

Bethany Anne returned to her seat. "I'm here to advocate for a better solution than incarceration for the majority of the accused. The Federation is not a closed system. Expansion is still possible. However, it will be extremely difficult to keep new colonies established outside of the Security Blanket connected to the CEREBRO network.

"Pending deprogramming and successful rehabilitation, I recommend that expansion within Federation borders be made possible by sentencing these people to serve their time working for Dr. Jeddah, who I would like to see on the board of the expansion committee."

"We don't have an expansion committee," Txeina pointed out.

"You're going to need one," Bethany Anne told the council. "The Federation will be forced to close its borders for the duration of the war. People need homes, and they cannot be left undefended."

"This is hardly the time to suggest new infrastructure!" the Noel-ni delegate proclaimed.

Bethany Anne raised an eyebrow. "Isn't it? So you're good with burdening the penal system with over twenty thousand people and denying the Federation twenty thousand assets? Perhaps you need to be replaced by someone who doesn't let personal grudges get in the way of what's best for their people."

"Objection!" the delegate yelled.

Lance banged his gavel repeatedly to calm the uproar Bethany Anne's statement caused. "Order! Please restrict your comments to the matter at hand, Your Highness."

Bethany Anne inclined her head minutely, repressing a smile. "I apologize. This has been a challenging time for us all. Honestly, I don't want to be here. However, it is necessary to get my point across. We are one people with one goal: to live in peace no matter what planet we come from and strive for a future where our children don't know war. Ask yourselves, what do we gain from depriving the Federation of people who would die to see it secure?"

She turned to look at the galleries before continuing, "I have done all I can to prepare the Federation for the war that is coming.

"Gödel has done everything she can to divide us. Will you allow her to win?"

Temple of the Ascension Path

The court was empty of all save Gödel and her Chosen servants.

She had recalled her generals and ordered them to return to their posts around her Empire on learning that Death had killed Phraim-'Eh and dismantled his following. Her wrath at losing yet another asset had cleared out the supplicants and hangers-on.

Only the most faithful were devoted enough to remain in the temple to tend her needs, and even they were circumspect, keeping their eyes on the floor and their responses prompt lest they offend her.

Gödel seethed on her throne, her inner voice frantic in its insistence that the optimal outcomes were dwindling to nothing. Meditation did nothing for her state of mind. Neither did medication.

Her hours were filled by endless visions tumbling one over the other. Visions of human supremacy. Democracy for even the lowliest, most barbaric species. Laws preventing contact with pre-space civilizations. The Kurtherian species hunted to extinction. Some part of her that was still sane recognized the fallacy of her belief since the majority of their species was very much alive, if altered physically by the nature of being Ascended.

Gödel refused to validate any thought that cast her as the villain. It was her destiny to return the universe to the Path and undo the damage humanity had caused to the fabric of society.

For millennia untold, the Kurtherians had presided over the Path in order to guide lesser species to greatness and advance their knowledge of science and the Etheric dimension. It was her right and her duty to impose structure on the universe, to prevent the unworthy from rising and elevate those she saw as acceptable to the advancement of Kurtherian interests.

After Death had been dealt with and the humans destroyed utterly, order would be restored. Gödel seethed as she concentrated on considering actions that would lead to victories.

Laughter-Brings-Meaning-to-Life approached the throne with her eyes on the floor. She was taking a huge risk. While she would never admit that her breakthroughs in recent centuries were mainly due to the work of her old friend Peace-Through-Superior-Genetics, she didn't hide the fact in her mind, knowing her goddess would punish her for keeping secrets more than the contents of them.

Staying alive in Gödel's proximity was akin to walking a razor wire. One misstep and you bled for it as you fell. How much you suffered depended on which aspect of her personality the goddess chose to manifest, and she'd been stuck on "homicidal maniac" since the defeat of Phraim-'Eh.

Laughter kept her thoughts clear as she bowed low and waited for Gödel to give her permission to rise.

Gödel turned her head to acknowledge the geneticist. "Hope for your sake that I find what you have to say worthy of my time, Laughter," she stated dispassionately.

Laughter bowed again, knowing Gödel's lack of visible emotion meant nothing. "My goddess, I have made a breakthrough with the Skrima."

Gödel shifted on the throne. "What have you accomplished beyond teaching those beasts to bear weapons and die at the hands of humans?"

Laughter hastily explained the weapons had been a mistake and she'd gone a different route altogether with the Skrima. "I wanted to make up for the loss of the Bakas, and instead, I have created something much deadlier."

"How so?" Gödel asked, her schemes forgotten at the prospect of a real distraction from her visions.

Laughter's stomach unclenched as the tension Gödel was pushing suddenly abated. She took it as a sign she wasn't going to lose her head in the next few minutes and briefly described her results. "Using genetic manipulation techniques you perfected in the creation of the Ookens was the right way to go. My mistake was making the original modifications too sophisticated," she admitted hesitantly.

Gödel waved for her to continue.

"The level of intelligence required to operate complex weaponry came with a decrease in the ability to control the subjects," Laughter continued, heartened and relieved that Gödel had snapped out of her murderous funk.

"We must see that with Our own eyes," Gödel declared. She rose from the throne and descended the dais, holding out her hand for Laughter to take.

Gödel opened the Etheric and took them to Laughter's experimental facility, a series of interconnecting caverns cut deep into the planet's crust a short distance from the center of the temple. "Where are your monsters?" she asked as Laughter recovered from the unexpected journey.

"Forgive me, my Goddess," Laughter begged, crouching on the floor and holding her pitching stomach as she fought for control of her thoughts. "I am unused to that method of travel without the assistance of technology. Your magnificence overwhelms me."

Gödel's aura of power pulsed, bathing the reception area in warmth and dull red light. "Do you feel better?"

Laughter got to her feet, nodding as the nausea passed. "Your generosity is great, my Goddess. If you will come with me, I would be honored to present to you the creatures I have created for your glory."

Gödel gestured for Laughter to lead the way to the pit. As they got closer, Gödel felt the ambient Etheric energy drop. "What is this?" she demanded, snatching Laughter's arm.

"It is necessary technology," Laughter assured her. "It is no danger to you, my Goddess. I swear on the Path. All will become clear when you see the Skrima."

Gödel accepted the truth Laughter spoke. "Very well. Proceed."

They passed through the final cavern, the largest yet. Brightly lit, the vaulted workspace contained rows of benches populated by busy Kurtherians wearing protective gear.

The workers dropped to their knees as Gödel's aura of fear proceeded her into the cavern. Gödel paid no attention to them. She sensed the Skrima ahead.

Laughter fell behind as Gödel swept toward the pit entrance. Being careful not to think about anything except the desire to please the goddess, she palmed the device her loyal assistant had slid across the workbench toward her and pocketed it without acknowledging the look he gave her.

She quickened her step to catch up with Gödel, and they walked down the short corridor to the thick steel door barring the pit entrance.

Gödel didn't bother to wait for Laughter to open the door. In truth, she barely remembered her servant was there. All she heard was the Skrima raging, and it intrigued her immensely. She exited the Etheric on a jutting spit of polished rock that stretched ten feet over the pit before ending abruptly in a waist-high wall.

Laughter entered the pit cavern as Gödel approached the wall, her fingers brushing the pocket containing the device. It was now or never, and if she died for her efforts, she would die knowing she had erred in the pursuit of faith.

Drawn to the chaos in the pit, Gödel was unaware of Laughter's lapse in mental diligence. Unable to resist connecting with the Skrimas' energy, she stood at the edge, staring down at the horned beasts. Frozen between this dimension and the Etheric, their bodies appeared translucent. They writhed in anger and pain, caught between states.

She imagined them set loose on the humans. The pleasure was immense as imaginary screams echoed around her. Lost in her fantasy, Gödel dimly registered Laughter falling to her knees beside her.

"Forgive me, my Goddess," Laughter began, looking at Gödel's feet in shame.

Gödel let the screams slip away and focused on her favored servant. "Why would you ask Our forgiveness?" she asked, sweeping her hand to indicate the pit. "This pleases Us immensely."

Laughter extracted the device and offered it to Gödel. "I need forgiveness, for I have committed a great heresy. I stole this technology from the humans at Benitus Seven and altered it to serve Your purpose." She closed her eyes and waited for the pain of punishment. When none came, she cracked an eyelid and looked up. She gasped to see the face of the goddess unveiled.

"We are not pilots, bound by scripture and blind to the advantages we can wrest from the hands of the unworthy," Gödel told Laughter, waving for her to get up after taking the device to examine it. "What does this device do?"

"Two things," Laughter responded, encouraged that she was still breathing and more importantly, still on the Ascension Path. "As we already know, it closes rifts. It also disrupts the ability of the Skrima to pass between the dimensions. However, humans do not have the technology to target a specific species. That has been the focus of my work these two years, and as you can tell, I have succeeded."

"How did you acquire this?" Gödel asked, turning the device over in her hands. "We are impressed with your devotion."

Laughter haltingly explained how the first encounter with the humans had come by surprise during her attempt to take the Benitons' technology for the glory of Gödel. "The humans made the error of reopening the rift, my Goddess. When they returned, I was ready. I launched an attack, sacrificing almost half a million Skrima in order to get aboard the space station and acquire the jamming technology."

She shivered, recalling the close shave she'd had when her personal guard had been killed distracting the humans as she fumbled with her wrist-holo to open the Etheric. "I narrowly escaped with my life. The humans believe they won, but they did not know the attack was a diversion."

Gödel handed the device back to Laughter with a smile. "You have done well. What is your plan?"

Laughter dipped her head. "With your permission, I will return to Hyrrheim and continue to work on harnessing the Skrimas' energy to control them."

Gödel nodded, glancing at the pit as she considered how she would reward the clearly ambitious geneticist.

Ambition in her servants was useful right up until it began to whisper in their ears about the attractiveness of the throne. Bestowing power on such people was high-risk. However, after Phraim-'Eh's failure, the temptation to take a sneaky shot at Death without her knowing was too great to resist.

She continued to smile at Laughter. "Come. We wish to give you a gift. Your devotion to your calling deserves to be rewarded."

Laughter followed in a daze. She had fully expected to be executed for her actions. Her goddess didn't speak again as they made their way through a network of torchlit passages Laughter hadn't known existed.

Gödel connected to the Pod-doc in her private quarters as she walked. She selected the prewritten program she wanted and had the Pod-doc compose the nanocyte infusion, making sure she had multiple backdoors into the programming in the event it turned out she had been unwise to grant Laughter the ability to sow terror on Earth.

Laughter stopped in her tracks when a section of the wall opened, seemingly of its own volition.

"This way," Gödel instructed as she entered the chamber beyond. She gestured for Laughter to get into the open Pod-doc in the center of the spartan steel chamber.

Laughter didn't dare refuse. She climbed in and laid back as the lid closed, hoping the gift wouldn't be an unwelcome one.

Gödel set the Pod-doc to cycle on the program she'd selected and left the chamber to go to her library, humming along with the screams when she began hearing them again. Laughter's choice to step outside the lines had created an opportunity they would both benefit from. Laughter would have a fertile testing ground for her battle monsters, and Gödel would have the satisfaction of knowing defenseless humans on Earth would suffer in her name.

Her satisfied expression faded as she entered her library.

Gödel walked through the stacks of crystal memory banks that lined two-thirds of the library. Each stood twelve feet tall and four feet wide and cast soft blue light over the space, illuminating her path. There were no doors, no windows, and no outside connections. It should have been impregnable, but it was not. Not when Death could walk the Etheric with the same ease she did.

She used to feel at peace in the cradle of her knowledge. She thought longingly of the time before Death had discovered her cache on Qu'Baka, a time when she had lived in certainty that no being on this plane of existence could enter her hallowed space.

It was impossible not to debate the wisdom of keeping the library intact when she was wracked with visions of Death getting her filthy human hands on the wealth of information she had amassed. However, the loss of just a few petabytes of information had drastically changed the shape of her crusade already. Gödel had no choice but to keep it all here in the temple.

It was enough to change her association of the space. She rarely came to her former sanctuary these days unless she needed to extract information from the crystals.

Today the gnawing sense of impending loss chose not

to surface. Gödel walked with purpose to the center of the library, where light pooled around a single console. She activated the console and began inputting instructions to retrieve her data on Earth. Death might have believed the Sol System was hidden, but she had records of every experiment the Seven had done on the planet. It would not stay hidden for long.

Gödel copied what she needed onto a memory crystal and left to make arrangements for Laughter and her workers. She could have had her Chosen perform these menial tasks, but she found she felt a certain amount of satisfaction in moving the pieces on the board herself.

Her next stop was the acolytes' shared living accommodations, where she chose ten adepts with the ability to channel their power into others and ordered them to the ship she'd assigned Laughter before vanishing in a swirl of robes to return to the facility where the Skrima were kept.

She instructed Laughter's workers to pack up their equipment and prepare to transfer the Skrima to the ship for transport to the planet Hyrrheim, then returned to her Pod-doc chamber to await the completion of Laughter's transformation.

CHAPTER TWENTY-THREE

QSD *Baba Yaga*, (One Week Later)

Bethany Anne was in her ready room going through her correspondence. She was surrounded by the cards and gifts the crews of the fleet had sent to celebrate the news that the trial was over and the Federation Council had ruled in favor of accepting her recommendation.

They'd all needed some downtime to make up for the stress of taking care of Phraim-'Eh's followers before their transfer to Red Rock. With that in mind, Bethany Anne had encouraged everyone to make the most of her ship's amenities before the next phase of the war began.

Reynolds and Christina had been happy to dock their ships on either side of the *Baba Yaga* and allow their crews a few days' leave aboard the Queen's superdreadnought. Negotiating a compromise between Izanami and Paul Jameson with the aim of freeing up the majority of the crew had been as simple as telling the two of them to figure it out.

The party was still raging on deck four, mostly thanks to the Belzonian officers traveling with the *War Axe,* when Izanami came to inform Bethany Anne that they were twelve hours out from Devon.

Bethany Anne sent the reply she'd composed to a school choir on the *Meredith Reynolds* whose teacher had sent her a video of the children performing a medley of seasonal songs from around the Federation. "Is it almost holiday season already?"

Izanami chuckled. "It generally comes around once a year. Of course, we will have departed long before Exodus day."

"Then we'll have to make sure the fireworks in Gödel's territories are spectacular." Bethany Anne stretched and yawned as she got up from her desk. "It's a shame everyone in the Federation will only see them on video. Tell everyone who isn't currently on shift that the party's over. I want everyone rested and fit for duty in ten hours."

"Including you?" Izanami inquired.

"Including me." Bethany Anne opened a path through the Etheric to her quarters. "And you. Watch a movie with ADAM and Reynolds, or whatever it is you three do with your downtime."

"Mostly we comment on the strange habits of organics," Izanami confessed with a throaty chuckle.

Bethany Anne rolled her eyes and stepped into the Etheric.

Michael was reading on the couch when she appeared in their living area. He looked up from his datapad and smiled. "Izanami told you we are almost to Devon?"

Bethany Anne nodded and perched on the edge of the couch to take her boots off. "Mm-hmm. I ordered the crews to rest before returning to their posts." She laid back with a yawn and put her feet up on the couch. "You have no idea how good this feels. You're still going over the raid logistics?"

Michael put his datapad down and patted his lap to indicate Bethany Anne put her feet there. "Gabriel made a comment earlier that got me thinking."

Bethany Anne closed her eyes as his thumbs worked the tension out of her left foot. "Don't you just love it when our children do that? What was his comment?"

"That by taking out Gödel's infrastructure, we are removing what stability these civilizations have," Michael answered with a frown. "I hadn't considered our responsibility to provide relief to the disenfranchised. Do we fold these civilizations into the Federation? Do we give them a choice?"

Bethany Anne opened an eye, feeling positive about his exploration of the complex moral challenge the operation posed. "Damn straight, we give them a choice. I forgot to tell you I saw Anna Elizabeth while I was at Red Rock." She chuckled at Michael's blank expression. "I guess you two never met. She's the Diplomat Emeritus for the Federation. She's been in semi-retirement for a while."

Michael shook his head in amusement. "You already have this covered."

Bethany Anne flexed her foot in his hands. "Don't stop." She closed her eyes again when Michael continued massaging. "The short answer is yes. Anna Elizabeth went back to Yoll to pick up her team. They'll meet us on Devon in a couple of days."

"That's a lot of ground to cover in a couple of days," Michael commented.

"She's traveling with the QBS *Stark*," Bethany Anne told Michael, wriggling her toes when he went over the sensitive spot on her arch. "I know you know Link. It's his ship."

Michael was pleased to hear that name. "He was a potential candidate for being made part of the family. I had him monitored in the event he ever met the mortality requirement. Why am I not surprised he ended up working for you?"

Bethany Anne just smiled. "I don't know what we're going to come across out there. Gödel's allies aside, experience tells me we're going to meet people who welcome our intervention a lot less often than we find places where the people are ignorant of the Kurtherian influence on their society. In any case, we need a major diplomatic effort as part of our offensive. Allowing entire civilizations to collapse into chaos is not an option, and neither is hesitating to move on after we've taken out the factories. The Diplomatic Corps will follow us and help the people move on from Gödel's rule, whether that means assisting them with their application to join the Federation or instituting measures to help them learn how to thrive as independents."

"It would be better to have a dry run," Michael told her. He dropped her foot. "Not possible, I know."

"What are you thinking?" Bethany Anne sat up, seeing he was working toward something good.

Michael's expression shifted as he considered his

thoughts. "That tyranny is inordinately simpler to create than a utopia."

"Nothing good comes easy," Bethany Anne told him with a smile. "It stands to reason that we have a battle ahead of us. I've had almost two years to build my armada. If there's a factor I *haven't* overthought, then I sure as hell want to consider it before I launch the raid. Tell me what you were getting at."

Michael picked up his datapad and opened the galaxy map. "I've been researching the intel the Spy Corps agents have fed you on the neutral zone while things have been relatively quiet. I believe I have discovered an abandoned factory site in a populated star system on the far side of the zone."

Bethany Anne scooted over to sit next to him. "Show me."

Michael lifted his arm to make room for her and showed her the information he and ADAM had collated on the two planets in the system. "It appears the people held on after Gödel abandoned them, although I wasn't able to discern to what degree from the data we have."

"You're thinking they might serve as an example for those who are afraid of what will happen without Gödel's rule." She saw the sense in investigating the factory. "We'll make it our first stop after leaving Devon."

Bethany Anne leaned into her husband. "Seems like the minute we set foot on land, it's time to leave again. Only this time, it's to scatter across the universe. This has to be the largest-scale invasion since the Seven fractured from Kurtherian society."

Michael returned her embrace. "You have the benefit of

experience this time around," he reminded her. "This won't be the Leath War repeated."

"Oh, I know," Bethany Anne agreed. "We're going into this with contingencies for our contingencies. Whatever Gödel decides to throw at us, we'll be ready."

She yawned again as she got to her feet. "But first, sleep. The crew might have been living the life of Riley for the last week, but a Queen's work is never done."

Michael dropped his datapad as he got up from the couch to capture Bethany Anne in his arms. "The Queen's work is done for the next eight hours." He picked her up, enjoying the half-hearted protest she made as he carried her to the bedroom.

Izanami woke them with a soft chime an hour out from Devon. She was waiting outside their quarters to brief Bethany Anne when they emerged, Bethany Anne cradling the large Coke she'd gotten from the food processing unit to keep her going until breakfast.

Alexis, Gabriel, K'aia, and Trey were already at their stations when they arrived on the bridge.

Bethany Anne looked at the information scrolling on the viewscreen and noted that they were still half a million kilometers from Devon. "This isn't exactly *there*."

"We are as close to the planet as we are going to get," Izanami replied. "You've got to see this to understand the scale."

Bethany Anne's heart swelled when she took in the external view. The planet was barely visible through the masses of ships arranged to form shipping lanes around it. The QBBS *Guardian* had moved to the opposite side of the behemoth shipyard to the superdreadnoughts, placed to defend the main entrance to the shipping lanes. She leaned against Alexis' chair and drank it in. "Well, damn. I knew what this was going to look like in theory, but the real thing is beyond impressive."

"Tabitha is calling," Izanami announced.

Bethany Anne dragged her gaze from the armada. "Put her onscreen."

Tabitha appeared on the viewscreen. "It's about time you guys got here. Welcome back."

Bethany Anne returned her warm smile. "It's good to be here and to see the results of everyone's hard work coming together. Do we have a secure location to hold the logistics briefing?"

Tabitha nodded. "Everything you asked for is in place. Transport for the crews is on its way. I assumed you wouldn't want to wait to get started."

"You assumed right. We'll be there in a few minutes." Bethany Anne waved before dropping the link. She glanced around the bridge. "Why is everyone still here? Let's move!"

Alexis, Gabriel, Trey, and K'aia grabbed their belongings and gathered around Bethany Anne and Michael.

Trey bounced from one foot to the other. "I can't wait to see my parents."

The others agreed, enthusiastic about being back on the planet they thought of as home.

"You'll have a few hours before the briefing. Say hi to Mahi' for me." Bethany Anne opened the Etheric. "Hold tight. This is going to be a bumpy ride."

. . .

Devon, The Hexagon, Indoor Arena #1

Bethany Anne met Tabitha outside the arena after Michael and the children had scattered to take care of their various errands. "Thank you," she told Tabitha, giving her a heartfelt hug. "I couldn't have assembled the armada without you, Peter, and Tim organizing everything here."

Tabitha laughed as she returned the embrace. "Don't get any ideas about leaving me behind again any time soon, okay? I need my bestie around to save me from insanity." She flourished her hands. "I need to soak up some female energy. It's been a total nutfest around here since Eve went to join Akio."

Bethany Anne chuckled. "Is that so?"

Tabitha's eyes widened. "Like you wouldn't believe. The Vid-docs are tied up with upgrades, meaning less availability for the amped troops to burn off excess energy. Keeping the 'friendly rivalries' friendly came down to funneling the energy into healthy competition."

"Define 'healthy.'" Bethany Anne raised an eyebrow. "Testing the limits of their upgrades is a good idea, but I don't want to hear that resources are being wasted on repairing injuries caused by reckless behavior."

Tabitha slipped her arm through Bethany Anne's and guided her into the arena. "Joel got the ground units together and organized fight clubs. It does mean you can't walk five feet in the city without being hit up by a bookie, but the people are loving it."

Bethany Anne had a moment to wonder how long it would take the twins to get distracted by the fights. She was thinking about putting on a disguise and getting distracted by them herself—*after* she made sure preparations for departure were underway. "It must be nostalgia for the old days of street fights on every corner."

Tabitha snickered. "Yeah, that must be it." She sighed when she received a message. "Dammit. There's been an accident in the EI core room. I have to go."

"What happened?" Bethany Anne asked with concern. "I know we don't have any more Bl'kheth running loose down there."

Tabitha shook her head. "One of the power relays shorted. We're stretched pretty thin, but I can reroute it for now. The fix should hold until a maintenance crew can get down there. I won't be back in time for the briefing. I'll get dinner together for everyone."

"Are you cooking?" Bethany Anne asked skeptically.

"If by cooking you mean calling Totto's and begging Leonardo to cater for his favorite customers, sure," Tabitha called over her shoulder, pointing at the table in the center of the stage. "Operating the holoprojector is easy. It's ready to connect with your HUD. Just have ADAM manage the data transfer."

"I'll figure it out." Bethany Anne made her way to the stage as Tabitha left to take care of the power relay.

The places at the table in the center of the stage were marked with name cards. Bethany Anne took her seat and examined the interface for the holoprojector embedded in the table. She had twenty minutes or so before she was due to start the briefing, but the "early is on time, on time is late" crowd were already arriving to claim their places on the tiered seats facing the stage.

The commanders of the military units and the senior diplomats sat apart. New arrivals gravitated to their colleagues, forming a clear divide between military and nonmilitary personnel. The two groups were separated by a buffer of senior engineers, tactical officers, medical personnel, and the journalists handpicked to accompany each unit who sat in the central stand.

All three stands hummed with speculation as to why almost the entire DipCorps leadership was there. The Spy Corps agents scattered among the crowd, including Phina and Roka, knew exactly what was coming as far as it pertained to their part of gathering the intelligence for this operation.

Bethany Anne ignored the chatter, her focus on getting the projector set up with her battle plans. Since the moment the factory raid had become a set event in her mind, she had been moving pieces to make it happen.

She had monitored the shipyards as they had turned out every type of warship from superdreadnoughts to short-range attack vessels like the scout fighters, and an ancillary fleet including but not limited to aquatic transport vessels, scout ships, and troop transports. While the tour was underway, Bethany Anne had been matching ship production to the upgrades of the numerous military and qualifying militia groups, designating their assignments to the superdreadnoughts based on their skillsets and willingness to work with others and planning their routes through Gödel's territory accordingly.

>>I have the galaxy map uploaded to the projector,<< ADAM informed her.

Bethany Anne got to her feet and stepped back from the

table to give herself some perspective. "Put up the modified version in the space between the stage and the stands. Show me every known star system and its status in the war."

>>**Your wish is my command,**<< ADAM replied.

The projector spindles in the rigging above the arena floor whirred, and a cloud of light shot out of the ends. The light hovered in the air as it began to resolve into infinitely complex swirling patterns. The galaxy map emerged from the light as the image resolved, showing everyone the vast emptiness of space, interrupted only by pinpoints of different-colored light marking the locations Bethany Anne had asked for.

Green markers clustered within Federation borders, forming a solid sphere with Yoll at its center. The Interdiction stood out. Devon was marked clearly near the border, with Gödel's territory marked in red and the neutral zone shaded in gray.

Bethany Anne smiled to herself, awed by how small the Federation looked in the larger picture and how scattered Gödel's holdings were in the vastness of space. *This* was combat chess.

"You look like the cat that got the cream," Jean remarked, drawing Bethany Anne's attention from the projection.

"Why not?" Bethany Anne responded with a smile. "You're a sight for sore eyes. How long have you been here?"

"Couple of weeks," Jean told her, eyeing the door where John stood guard. "The *Sigrún* was the last superdreadnought to be built. My team finished construction, and we closed up the shipyard and hitched a ride here on her with the Admiral."

Bethany Anne was distracted by the arrival she'd been waiting for. Looking at the arena entrance, she spotted Anna Elizabeth Hauser and the Federation's current Diplomat Spy, Seraphina Waters-Jenkins. "Dammit. Can you give me a minute?"

Jean followed her gaze and nodded at Anna Elizabeth. "We can catch up later. I want to save a seat for John."

Bethany Anne waved the two women over as Jean left the stage. "Today is turning me into a hugger," she told them with a laugh as she briefly embraced first Anna Elizabeth, then Phina. "It's good to see you both. You especially, Phina. It's been a long time."

Phina dipped her head without showing a hint of emotion. "I've been focused on the mission. It's good to see you too, Bethany Anne. It's been lonely in the neutral zone. We don't have too many friends out there."

>>**Hey, what about me?**<< ADAM protested loudly.

You are the one who got me through it, Phina told him, sending a mental hug.

Wow. Such devotion, a distinctly feline voice chastised in the mindspace. *Where is the praise for my companionship? For the operas I performed to entertain you in the long nights?*

Bethany Anne gave Phina a sympathetic look, recalling the personality quirks of the younger woman's bonded Previdian. "Sundancer is his usual delightful self, I see."

"He's not happy about being persuaded to stay on the ship with Chris," Phina explained, chuckling. "I heard there were lions roaming free on this planet."

"One lion. Demon is friendly enough if you bring

snacks," Bethany Anne assured her. "Your contribution to this operation has been vital. Without the intelligence you brought back, we would have missed the opportunity to explore an abandoned Kurtherian factory."

She waved her hand in front of Phina's face when she didn't reply. "You in there?"

Phina smiled, her eyes refocusing as she left the mind-space. "I guess I missed having a good connection to ADAM. What were you saying?"

"The abandoned factory you found in the neutral zone," Bethany Anne repeated.

"Oh, yeah. I got out of there as soon as I saw it." Phina's eyes widened when she spotted someone she hadn't expected in the center stand. "Jace is here? I'll leave you two to catch up. It's good to be back."

Bethany Anne nodded. "I'm not the only one who's glad to have you come in from the cold."

Anna Elizabeth put her hand on Bethany Anne's arm as Phina left to take her seat with the other diplomats. "You said to go big. I've brought everything but the kitchen sink. Link even decided to come out of retirement to lead the delegation accompanying the *Baba Yaga*."

Bethany Anne's mouth curled up at the corner. "Good. We're going to need every trick in the book to pull this off without it turning into a house of cards for the people under Gödel's rule."

Anna Elizabeth offered her a knowing look. "You pretend I don't know you. Don't blame yourself for the social trauma undoing Gödel's damage will cause. This is what you founded the Diplomatic Corps for. We will ensure that the people are taken care of."

Bethany Anne nodded. "I appreciate it, but I'm not tearing myself up over it. Your and Link's people are my safety net for those whose lives I'm about to interrupt. This is not the Leath War again, Anna. Gödel wasn't smart enough to stay hidden forever. The next phase of this war will be the last. I don't intend to leave that sociopath so much as a transport Pod she can use against the Federation."

Anna Elizabeth turned when she heard her name and waved, seeing Link scowling arrogantly at her. "Oh, *fabulous*. He's come as Greyson Wells. I'd better go sit down before he causes a scene."

Bethany Anne snickered, knowing Link would cheerfully embarrass himself to get one over on Anna Elizabeth. "I'll see the three of you aboard the *Baba Yaga* for family dinner tonight."

She had a moment to reflect on the past while the final stragglers trickled into the arena, her thoughts landing on how Phina's hidden role in the Leath War had helped them get to this point. Everything came full circle in the end, but this time, *she* had the upper hand.

>>**Everyone is here,**<< ADAM told Bethany Anne. >>**I'm going to seal the arena and activate the shielding.**<<

John double-checked the arena doors before taking the seat next to Jean.

Bethany Anne was heartened to see them reunited now that there was no reason for Jean to remain at the QT2 shipyard. She brought the arena lights down, leaving only the stage illuminated, and turned on the microphone. "Admiral Thomas, Colonel Lowell, Colonel Walton,

Diplomat Emeritus Hauser, and Guardian Commander Nikolayevich, please join me on the stage."

She waited until they were seated at the table before addressing the assembly. "I heard many of you wondering why the diplomatic arm is so large for this operation. Let me clear that up right away. As you are all aware, we are planning to wage war on the Kurtherians. What we are *not* aiming to do is further destroy the lives of the people they have oppressed. Our military effort will be restricted to the factories where the Ookens are made and any support structures Gödel has assigned them. ADAM, next set of images."

Bethany Anne laced her hands on the table while cycling images of the civilizations living in the shadows of the factories collected by Spy Corps agents replaced the galaxy map. "This operation is codenamed 'Emancipation.' Our primary objective is freeing the Collective and every other person the Kurtherians have enslaved for the purpose of creating more Ookens. The Diplomatic Corps, combined with the Guardian Marines, will be our front and rear guards, working to minimize the damage to local civilizations after the Kurtherian influence has been removed from their governments."

ADAM switched to the next set of images without needing a cue. Bethany Anne talked the assembly through the information they had on the standard layout for the factories while they watched the footage she'd held back from the public, emphasizing the need to wait for the extraction teams to free the prisoners held on the lower levels of the crystalline structures before destroying them.

"Your communications officers must be protected at all

costs," Bethany Anne emphasized. "Without them, you will be unable to persuade any Bl'kheths to leave with you, and you will be unable to follow the procedure for establishing trust with the Collective. ADAM, release the superdreadnought unit assignments."

Bethany Anne got to her feet. "Everyone, get up. Find the other section commanders in your unit." She gave the assembly a few minutes to rearrange themselves before she pointed out Trey, who was sitting with his father and his uncle Li'Orin. "Get to know the Baka warriors assigned to your unit. They have recent experience with Kurtherian rule and the different mindsets you will encounter."

Diplomats and military commanders alike turned to look at the relative newcomers. Almost every species in the gathering had been affected by Kurtherian meddling to one degree or another at some point in their history. For the Yollins and the Leath, the memory was still fresh enough to hurt.

Bethany Anne gave them another minute to start forming the bonds that would hold them together through the battles to come while she returned to the projection of the galaxy map and highlighted the routes the superdreadnoughts would follow. "We are about to scatter far and wide. Make allies where you can because there's no backup but the people to the left and right of you right now. Remember, an informed decision is a decision that saves lives. Rely on each other. Work closely with the other section commanders in your unit to get the right result for each target location. Does anyone have any questions?"

She took questions for the next hour, then ended the

briefing by thanking everyone who had stepped up to be there.

Waving down the applause, Bethany Anne walked to the front of the stage. "Pass that gratitude down to the people under your command, and light a fire under their asses. The final group being upgraded will complete their training in six days. We depart in seven."

CHAPTER TWENTY-FOUR

The Hexagon, Penthouse Apartment, Terrace

"Leonardo needs a knighthood for his services to food," Tabitha remarked. She put her hand on her sandwich to steady it before the stack of sliced brisket stuffed between two pieces of Leonardo's fresh-baked bread escaped onto her plate.

Bethany Anne laughed. "If I was going to start knighting people, Leonardo would be at the head of the line."

Devon's favorite restauranteur had pulled out all the stops, bringing his catering staff to the apartment to cook and serve the impromptu barbecue. The terrace had been set with tables laid with checkered cloths. Leonardo himself presided over the grill, cheerfully fending off the crowd of hungry males gathered around him.

They made their way along the line, avoiding the children underfoot as they filled their plates with meats and sides.

"This is amazing," Bethany Anne told Leonardo as they edged in to where he was tending numerous racks of ribs.

"Feeding the enhanced is my great joy," Leonardo enthused as he added to the growing piles on their plates.

"You'll never hear a complaint about the calorie count from a Were." Bethany Anne thanked him again for his effort and followed Tabitha to a shaded spot under the vines.

Bethany Anne looked around as they sat down to eat. "Where's Todd? I haven't seen him to give him his gift."

Tabitha groaned. "He's been following Phina and Link around since Maxim and Peter shut him out of the study. I made the mistake of mentioning her when we were studying the stars collapsing in the Kaan'Trii system. Saint Payback answered my mom's prayers that I have a child just like me. Kid's got radar for things he shouldn't know."

"Just like his mother, then." Bethany Anne chuckled. "I heard he had two once-in-a-lifetime experiences on the same day out there."

"Pete was sad to miss his first shift," Tabitha told her with a rueful twist of her lips. "Todd got into the Etheric Academy. He's heading back to the Federation with Maxim and Alina. Chris has moved out to join Phina's team, so they have a spare room for him."

Bethany Anne heard the note of sadness behind the pride in Tabitha's voice. "It's not easy when they're ready to spread their wings. Maxim and Alina are good people, and they'll take care of him."

"I'm just glad his curiosity won out over his urge to join the Guardians," Tabitha admitted.

"This isn't his generation's fight," Bethany Anne replied.

"Although, tell my children that and they'll deny it to their last breath. ADAM showed me the journal Todd's paper was published in. He's a smart kid."

She caught sight of the twins sitting at another table with their father, Peter, Todd, Maxim, Phina, Alina, and Drk-vaen. "It's so good to see them back together. I've asked a hell of a lot from Phina in the last few decades. It's about time she got to be with her family."

Tabitha followed her gaze and broke into a smile. "Sure is. Sis-tael must be around somewhere." She spotted the female Yollin deep in conversation with Jean, Admiral Thomas, Izanami, and Reynolds at the bar. She ducked as William walked by, engrossed in conversation with Kathy. "Crap, he's still pissed about his ship."

"With you?" Bethany Anne asked, surprised.

Tabitha shook her head as she gathered her plate and glass. "No, with the Ookens, but I don't want to hear about it tonight."

Bethany Anne laughed and walked over to join the twins at their table. She took a seat next to Gabriel and continued eating as talk centered on Todd's acceptance to the Academy. Alexis pumped Alina for fashion tips as Maxim and Chris regaled Todd with hacks for Academy life.

"I visited the White House Fashions boutique on Keeg Station," Bethany Anne told Alina. "It was just like being at the original store."

Alina laughed. "I had a call from the store manager that day. She couldn't believe the Queen came to shop there."

Bethany Anne smiled. "You and Mal have grown a business I'm happy to support."

Alina flicked her hair back as she returned Bethany Anne's smile. "You made that clear to the whole Federation when you bought half the items Tiffany was stocking at the time. Of course, we always had the royal seal of approval, but it was good of you to remind everyone of that. We have been approached by a number of people asking us to expand to their location since your visit."

Phina had her arm around her best friend, pride shining on her face. "Even before Mal made you a partner, you were the most sought-after designer in the company. There's no limit to what you can achieve with your creativity."

Alina somehow managed to make a snort look ladylike. "I have to have something to occupy me while you're off on secret missions for years at a time."

Maxim put a hand to his chest, feigning a fatal wound. "I give her my life, my home, and my heart, and she gives me nothing."

"Where have you been?" Todd asked Phina as Alina slapped Maxim playfully.

Phina glanced at Bethany Anne, who nodded. "I've been inside the neutral zone for the last few years, searching out potential allies and mapping the safe routes into Kurtherian territory."

"I knew it!" Todd exclaimed. "You're a spy!"

"She's *the* spy," Link cut in, smiling fondly at Todd as he approached the table with a loaded plate in each hand.

"Look who's feeling gracious all of a sudden," Anna Elizabeth teased, leaning over from the next table.

Link squeezed between John and Alexis and reached for

the hot sauce. "Let's just say that after years of holding everyone at arm's length, it's good to be with family."

John clapped him on the back. "Well said."

"I'll drink to that," Peter declared, getting to his feet. "To family, and to building a world worth living in." He lifted his glass and was met with hearty agreements from everyone on the terrace.

The conversation around the tables resumed after the toast. Bethany Anne moved around as the meal went on, making sure she got some time with everyone there as the gathering continued into the night.

She ended the evening sitting under the pergola with Alexis after the majority of the guests had left the penthouse to find their beds. They sat side by side, watching lights twinkle across the city in companionable silence while Alexis rested her head on Bethany Anne's shoulder.

Alexis sighed. "Truth, I'm glad the cult is gone. It will be good to stay close to you and Dad for a while."

Bethany Anne stroked Alexis' curls absentmindedly, feeling full and content. "I wondered why you hadn't asked what your assignment during the raid is yet."

"I figured you'd tell us when it was time, but now that you mentioned it, I have to know." Alexis sat up straight and turned to pin Bethany Anne with an expectant stare. "Please don't say bridge duty. I'll be the only one on the raid to die of boredom."

"I guarantee you won't get bored," Bethany Anne told her with a smile. "Roka will be joining your team. You will be liaising with Link on the forward offensive."

Alexis jumped to her feet and punched the air. "I knew you wouldn't let us down! I have to go find the others."

Bethany Anne had all of five minutes to herself before Mahi' joined her.

The Baka queen eased herself onto the bench beside Bethany Anne and rubbed her leg with a sigh. "The launch cannot come soon enough."

Bethany Anne had spoken to Li'Orin earlier and gotten much the same sentiment from him. "Your brothers driving you crazy?"

Mahi' laughed. "How wise you are, my Queen. Fortunately, my husband and uncle have been keeping them occupied with drills since our superdreadnought arrived."

"How are you finding the *Addix*?" Bethany Anne inquired.

Mahi' grinned. "My ship is large enough that I don't see Da'Mahin unless I summon him. What more could I ask for?" She turned serious for a moment. "Waiting to get vengeance for Addix's death and right the dishonor Gödel has committed against my people has been difficult."

"Your agreement to station a group of warriors on every superdreadnought looks to me like you're in a prime position to spread that vengeance far and wide," Bethany Anne told her. "I can't imagine that was easy to accomplish."

Mahi' gave Bethany Anne a knowing look. "You imagine correctly. It was a tactical decision to avoid infighting among the houses. My warriors will be no use to anyone in the brig."

"Just getting them to agree to this must have been a headache." Bethany Anne understood her position all too well. Baka society was comprised of hundreds of families with history going back centuries. The recent twisting of their culture had left the houses fractured and mistrustful of one another. Despite all sides being in agreement about the war being their first priority as a people, bad blood between the families made getting a consensus on the smallest issue challenging. "I thought you and Fi'Eireie were resolving the feuding between the houses?"

"We made a lot of progress while you were gone," Mahi' replied. "I simply presented it to the houses as you saw it, and made it clear that every warrior has equal opportunity to gain honor by obeying their unit commander, no matter their species. Xenophobia is a thing of the past; only by working together will we prevail over the Kurtherians. We still have a long way to go as a society before the hurts of the past are healed, but we are working toward the day when all our people are one."

Bethany Anne sat back and resumed watching the city. "Aren't we all? It will come, I swear it."

QSD *Baba Yaga*, Bridge

Sitting apart from the rest of the armada as they were, everyone aboard the *Baba Yaga* and the *Reynolds* had a clear view of the staging area where the ranks of superdreadnoughts waited to be called to war.

Bethany Anne looked at the staging area on the viewscreen, where one hundred and seventy-five superdreadnoughts and the fleets assigned to them waited to be called to the area that had been cleared for Gating, and saw one hundred and seventy-five unstoppable forces, one for each factory on the galaxy map.

Her heart constricted as she scanned the ships in the

staging area while she waited for confirmation from Admiral Thomas that the first fifteen sections were ready to depart. She was unable to miss how many of the superdreadnoughts were named to honor those who had made the ultimate sacrifice over the centuries. She saw the names of fallen warriors and infamous battlegrounds, names that meant something to the people aboard emblazoned on the hulls for all to see.

"Here we go," Bethany Anne murmured under her breath.

Michael touched her mind, anticipation overriding his usual calm presence. "This, I believe, is the clearest statement you could make."

"It sends a message," Bethany Anne agreed.

"It says, 'Don't fuck with us.'" Michael lifted a shoulder when she turned to raise an eyebrow at him. "How many galactic powers have the resources to produce a fleet this size? How many of those would use their power to remove the cancer from the fabric of society without tearing it asunder? It's an undeniable show of force."

Bethany Anne wasn't blind to the fact that the civilizations they encountered would see the armada as an invading force. "We have the means to suppress any resistance we come across with minimal loss of life, and to make sure the people can take care of themselves after we leave. I'm not out to replace one form of oppression with another."

She turned back to the viewscreen. "We don't know what Gödel has promised them in exchange for their loyalty, but I know I would feel the need to fight if a fleet of alien ships showed up to take out the Federation Council."

"Time will prove that the invasion is only happening to the Kurtherians," Michael reasoned. "We have seen the intelligence from the neutral zone. What little we were able to learn about the societies beyond was enough to tell us they are unaware of what it means to be the masters of their own destiny."

"Not for much longer," Bethany Anne vowed as Admiral Thomas called in from the bridge of the SD *Colorado*. "Admiral, what is our status?"

"We're green across the board," he reported. "Group One is ready to move into position on your command."

Bethany Anne opened a video channel to every ship in the armada, her resolve stronger than she thought it possible to bear. This was it, the moment she had been inexorably drawn toward since the day she'd woken up in TOM's ship back on Earth and learned about the existence of aliens who wanted to enslave humanity. The beginning of the end for the Seven.

Michael felt the focused emotions inside her as clearly as his own. *Are you ready?*

Yes. Yes, I am. Bethany Anne smiled. Etheric energy surged around her as her adrenaline rose, agitating the air. "Superdreadnoughts *Aeternus, Addix, Brennan, Jenkins Phoenix, K.O. O'Donnell, Merrek, Morrigan, Nacht, Nightingale, Okami, Paper Moon, Salvation, Sergeant T. Coles, Sigrún,* and *Rameses' Vengeance*. Move into position and prepare to Gate on my order."

Fifteen superdreadnoughts extracted themselves from the ranks in the staging area and slowly approached the Gating area. The accompanying battle cruisers and destroyers moved into formation around them, each section positioned to cross their Gate battle-ready.

Bethany Anne's hair whipped around her face, her eyes glowing red as she addressed the armada. "I have one final reminder. The Collective, the Bl'kheth, and everyone else imprisoned inside the factories are relying on us to refrain from getting drawn into combat with the local species. Stay focused, stay on target, and do not lose hope. You are heading into hostile territory. That does not make it enemy territory. Today, you face strangers in a strange land. One day, the people you meet will be part of our society. History has shown us that adversity can be overcome with empathy and a mutual desire to trust. Let's do what we can to make our introduction painless. Admiral, you may commence the launch."

CHAPTER TWENTY-FIVE

Neutral Zone, Ilion Nebula

Izanami brought the *Baba Yaga* out inside the gas cloud half a million kilometers from the outlying planet, where they could remain hidden until Bethany Anne was ready to reveal their presence.

Bethany Anne got out of her chair as Reynolds reported his ship's arrival. "Scan that star system. I want to know if there's any traffic between the planets and the factory."

Izanami looked at Bethany Anne in confusion. "The scanners are only showing the two planets. I'm not picking up any signals that would indicate the presence of a factory."

"Has it been destroyed?" Michael asked.

"There's no trace of microcrystal debris in the system," Izanami answered.

Bethany Anne frowned. "Then where the fuck is the factory? Hold your position, and put me through to the *Gemini*."

Gabriel appeared onscreen, his brow furrowed in bemusement. "What's going on out there? Gemini is saying there's no factory."

"That's what I want to find out," Bethany Anne told him. "Come back to the *Baba Yaga*. Izanami, get us out of this cloud. Reynolds, stay close by. I want to know what kind of fuckery this is."

Bethany Anne was hit with a momentary overload of Etheric energy when the crystalline structure came into sight around the curvature of the inner planet. Her nanocytes compensated immediately, decreasing their continual draw from the Etheric to stem the surge in the ambient energy levels in the other dimension.

Michael reached for the Etheric instinctively as he experienced the same surge. He got to his feet, sensing a void in the energy where the factory lay in the distance. "What the..."

The crystal structure shimmered with unnatural energy as the superdreadnoughts approached to within two thousand kilometers.

Bethany Anne felt Phina's presence at the edge of her consciousness. "Hold our positions," she told Izanami and Reynolds. She let Phina into the mindspace. ***Do you have any idea what's going on here?***

There's something funky going on, Phina replied. *Can you sense that disturbance in the Etheric?*

Wait, everyone needs to weigh in on this. Bethany Anne opened a video link to the QBS *Stark*, adding Phina to the conversation onscreen.

Alexis and Phina waved at each other, smiling.

"Any takers on what's causing that void in the Etheric?" Bethany Anne asked, including ADAM and TOM in the question.

"All I can sense is an...absence," Phina answered uncertainly. "I haven't come across anything like it before."

"It wasn't like this when you found it?" Bethany Anne inquired.

"It wasn't like this or I would have noticed, but I also didn't get this close since we were being chased," Phina admitted. "The people around here don't like visitors. I saw the factory as I was passing through, noted it in my logs, and left the system before my ship was attacked."

"It's some kind of shielding," ADAM ventured over the speaker. "The light you can see is space dust being vaporized. I don't recommend approaching it."

"No shit, Captain Vague," Bethany Anne retorted. "What's generating it?"

"I don't know," ADAM admitted. "The source is inside the factory, and I can only see what Izanami and Reynolds see."

"The Etheric is blocked," Alexis exclaimed. "How?"

"That's what we need to figure out," Bethany Anne replied. "Whatever species made this technology, I want to know their intentions."

"I've never encountered shielding like this," TOM commented, his tone filled with confusion. "I can't actually *see* the factory."

Bethany Anne narrowed her eyes. "What do you mean, you can't see it?"

"I mean, I can't see the factory," TOM repeated. "I can

see there's something hidden now that we are close, but before that, I didn't even register the void created by the shielding."

"You're looking out of my eyes," Bethany Anne stated. "Are you telling me that we are seeing different things?"

"I'm saying I'm back to not trusting my perception," TOM replied with growing agitation. "My mind is telling me there's nothing there, even though I can see that you are seeing it."

"No, I get what he's saying," Phina interjected. "It looks kind of fuzzy to me too, like it's stuck in phase. I think if I wasn't looking directly at it, it would vanish. This couldn't have been here before. I wouldn't have seen the factory."

"Perhaps the purpose of the shielding is to hide the factory from Gödel's people," Michael hazarded. "We might find that the prisoners are the ones responsible."

"Maybe." Bethany Anne narrowed her eyes, considering the low probability of Gödel leaving any prisoners alive when she withdrew from this area. "But where would they get technology that can fool Kurtherians? Speculation isn't going to get us anywhere. Alexis, Gabriel? What are you both getting?"

"Looks solid enough to me," Gabriel confirmed. "I can sense the shielding, though."

"Same. We should go in there and investigate," Alexis suggested hopefully.

Bethany Anne shook her head. "No. Your father and I will go."

Reynolds appeared onscreen. "I'm picking up activity from the second planet. It looks like they've sent out the welcome wagon."

"Some welcome," Izanami retorted. "I've seen bigger bath toys than those cruisers."

Alexis moved to Bethany Anne's chair and activated the holo HUD. "We'll take care of this."

"You know what to do," Bethany Anne told Izanami and Reynolds. "Alexis, work with Greyson and Phina to deescalate the situation. Gabriel, have the breach teams prepare for deployment to the factory on my order. Michael and I are going to examine the shielding up close before anyone gets near it."

"Pod or Etheric?" Michael asked.

"Etheric," Bethany Anne decided. "I want to see what effect the shielding is having there."

"At the very least, we should find it easier to get into the factory from that side," Michael reasoned. He flourished a hand, bowing. "After you."

Bethany Anne laughed as she opened the Etheric. "Who said chivalry was dead?"

They stepped into the Etheric and were hit by high winds the moment they set foot into the mists. Beyond agitated, the mists were dark and thick with concentrated Etheric energy.

Bethany Anne pulled the hood of her coat up and activated her faceplate. "This is a hell of a storm!" she yelled over the thunder breaking all around them. "How much do you want to bet it's being caused by the shielding?"

"It is not a natural occurrence," Michael agreed, activating his helmet seal as he formed a barrier around them to deflect the lighting splintering unrestrained in the mists. "It's static, for one thing."

Bethany Anne searched for the edge of the storm wall

as she oriented herself. “Gödel wouldn't risk entering a storm of this magnitude.”

“What does that say about us?” Michael commented dryly.

“That we aren't afraid of a little Etheric weather,” Bethany Anne shot back with a smile. “That isn't my point.”

“You're coming around to the idea that we might find allies in the factory?” Michael inquired.

“Someone went to a lot of effort to make sure this place is unattractive to Kurtherians. It's not exactly a paradise for us, either.” Bethany Anne set off into the mists. “The shielding is this way.”

Steadying one another, they fought to keep moving. The mists grew denser the farther into the maelstrom they went, the increasing pressure pushing back against them as they pushed into the wind, heading for the eye of the storm.

A few kilometers more and their armor started to struggle with the pressure. Bethany Anne turned off the annoying alarms in her HUD and gripped Michael's arm, forcing herself to continue putting one foot in front of the other against the rising pressure coagulating the mists, turning them to a turgid soup.

They sensed the abrupt drop in pressure in the eye of the storm a few minutes before they saw a bright glow ahead. Michael slowed as the light became stronger, forming a dome that lit the mists so brightly the lightning faded into obscurity. “Can you feel that? Whatever is at the center is drawing energy from around us.”

>>**Wait, I've seen this before,**<< ADAM exclaimed.

>>Or something similar to it. The technology was outlawed after what happened on Lyriasha.<<

Bethany Anne narrowed her eyes, remembering the close call the planet's inhabitants had with a device that had sucked the life force from the planet. "It's been modified to draw from the Etheric instead."

>>Looks that way,<< ADAM replied. **>>Be careful. It's going to affect you.<<**

"How so?" Michael asked.

>>Once you are inside the shield, you should be fine, but getting through it while it's draining you isn't going to be a picnic,<< ADAM told them.

It seems our speculation was correct, TOM added. **Whoever built this has figured out how to protect the factory from both inside and outside the Etheric. I'll do what I can to protect you while you are passing through the shield, but there's nothing I can do to shield Michael from the energy.**

Bethany Anne frowned. "Well, fuck."

"I have survived worse," Michael stated, tilting his head back to try to figure out the height of the dome. "If we'd had this technology, we wouldn't have had any problems keeping Gödel out of the Federation."

"At what cost?" Bethany Anne countered. "Unleashing a storm of this size at every location in the Federation could have consequences for the Etheric we can't imagine. Right now, I just want to know that whoever created this technology isn't going to intercede in Gödel's favor."

Bethany Anne locked herself down as they emerged into the eye of the storm, compensating for the sudden drop in resistance. Her momentum carried her a few steps toward the dome of light in the middle of the eye.

She turned to look at Michael. "Ready?"

He nodded, and they approached the dome together. Closer inspection revealed the dome's light was generated by an inestimable number of micro-storms producing energy in the form of tiny sparks of Etheric lighting.

When Michael pushed his hand into the dome, the compressed energy felt like a hot, dry membrane even through his nanocyte-infused armor. "It's going to be tough, but we can get through."

Bethany Anne shivered as ambient energy ran through her in the split second before she made contact with the shield. She was hit with the worst Etheric drain she'd ever experienced as the light swallowed her hands. "Sonofa*bitch,* that stings!"

Michael pulled his hand out and watched his nanocyte-infused glove repairing the scorched metal. "Let's go before the twins decide we need help."

Bethany Anne exchanged a glance with Michael as they entered the light.

The energy burned, setting their armor ablaze. Bethany Anne lost track of Michael almost immediately. She pushed through the resistance while the device behind the shield drained energy from her almost as fast as she could replace it.

Her armor resumed its complaints about being unable to keep up with repairs, cut off from the Etheric and drained by the shield. Bethany Anne cursed internally, sucking in a breath just before the seal on her helmet lost integrity.

She smelled burning hair and felt her skin crisping as her armor was breached, exposing her to the energy. Her lungs burned from the inside as her body was cooked from the outside. Bethany Anne knew with certainty that she was fully mortal for the first time in a long time.

Still, she pushed on. There was nothing to do but keep moving. She blocked out her fear, her pain, everything but the need to get to the other side.

Bethany Anne became vaguely aware of Michael again just as her lungs refused to hold the used air any longer. His mind grasped hers, and she returned the sense of determination and love he was broadcasting through his agony.

It was enough to keep them holding on for a few seconds longer.

Just as Bethany Anne felt her consciousness slipping, the heat vanished without warning, replaced by a tsunami of Etheric energy. Barely conscious, she pitched forward and tumbled out of the Etheric as she broke the inner edge of the shield and landed roughly in the shadow of the factory.

She forced herself into a roll to break the fall despite the pain in her cracked and bleeding skin. Her body refused to complete the maneuver, and she ended up lying flat on her back with a dislocated shoulder, looking up at the ash-covered factory. Low light came from the building, its baleful yellow tone different from the obscene fleshy glow she'd encountered at other factories.

Bethany Anne gasped for breath, disoriented by the flood of energy her nanocytes so desperately needed to keep her alive. Whoever had brought this place back to life wasn't around to take advantage of her moment of weakness. Bethany Anne gritted her teeth and dialed down the pain while her nanocytes raced to repair the dislocation and the burns covering most of her body.

Michael fell out of the Etheric and landed beside her with a pained grunt. He was wracked with coughs as his nanocytes worked to replace the toasted alveoli in his lungs. He savored the reduction in difficulty with each new breath he drew.

Bethany Anne turned her head to look at him, ignoring the pain of the movement. "You okay?"

Michael gingerly lifted a hand to check that his hair was still there. "Dammit, no." He felt his scalp prickle as his nanocytes worked to replace what had been burned off. "Maybe. Yes. You?"

"I make a bad barbecue," Bethany Anne told him, wincing as her smile cracked her blistered lips. Already, her hair had grown back, and the damage to her internal organs was repaired. Her skin was healing rapidly, and green lights were scrolling in her HUD as her armor reversed the damage done to it while it was cut off from the Etheric. "As soon as we don't look like a couple of strips of overdone bacon, we should move."

Michael murmured his agreement as Bethany Anne pulled herself to a sitting position. He blinked a couple of times, then frowned, regretting the movement immediately when every muscle in his face screamed its disapproval of the action. "My neural chip isn't connecting to my armor."

Bethany Anne checked hers. "Mine's good."

I was able to protect it, TOM told her. **The tempera-**

tures you just experienced should have killed you both. I am surprised Michael didn't suffer extreme brain damage.

Bethany Anne laughed. "It would need a lot more than that to take him out."

Michael ran a hand through his hair, his shoulders losing their tension when he realized it was back to normal. "I tried dying once. Didn't care for it all that much."

"Your thick head probably insulated your brain," Bethany Anne told Michael with a grin. "Who knew stubbornness would save your life one day?"

Michael sat up slowly, his burns still healing. "Very amusing. Shall we go, or would you like to stay here and make jokes until whoever is in charge of this factory realizes we are here?"

Bethany Anne got to her feet and ran her hands over her armor. Finding it was mostly intact, she stretched experimentally while Michael checked himself over. "I'm good to go. Let's find a way in. Our armor still needs a few minutes."

They made their way around the west side of the factory, staying close to the wall. Neither of them sensed any living beings. The factory wall ran for a couple of miles before they came to a recess containing a ramp that led to a reinforced roller door.

"Looks like a loading dock," Michael commented, walking up the ramp to examine the door.

Bethany Anne didn't see an opening mechanism. She reached for the roller door, intending to force it up.

>>**Wait,**<< ADAM told them. >>**It's a trap. I'm picking up multiple dormant EI signatures behind that door.**<<

Bethany Anne dropped her hand. "How many?"

>>**Hundreds. All in android bodies.**<<

"Can you make sure they stay dormant?" Bethany Anne asked.

>>**That depends. Do you want to announce our presence?**<<

"No," Bethany Anne told him. "We'll do this the old-fashioned way."

"The large digital presence is yet more proof this facility is not under Gödel's control," Michael stated.

"Not necessarily," Bethany Anne replied, drawing her Jean Dukes Specials. "For all we know, this is just another of her tactics. I want to see who or what we're dealing with before I make a decision about this place. I don't know how I feel about an army of potentially sentient androids, and I fucking *hate* mysteries."

Michael drew his weapons as well. "Agreed."

Bethany Anne aimed one pistol at the top of the roller door and fired.

The mechanism disintegrated, dropping the roller door with a clang.

>>**Ummm...**<<

Whatever ADAM had been about to say was cut off as a hail of Etheric energy bolts lanced at them from inside the factory.

Bethany Anne and Michael dived in opposite directions to avoid getting hit, returning fire as androids began pouring out of the loading dock with their weapons hot.

They worked their way back to each other, obliterating

the androids that zeroed in on them. Reluctant to use her abilities before being certain of Gödel's absence, Bethany Anne emptied her Jean Dukes Specials into the androids around her. This close, the EI-controlled army abandoned their weapons and grasped at Bethany Anne and Michael in a concerted attempt to tear them to pieces.

Bethany Anne dipped and dodged as she fought off the attacks, figuring out quickly that the androids were concentrating their fire on the spaces she and Michael were creating with downed bodies. "They're trying not to damage each other," she called.

"Duck!" Michael yelled.

Bethany Anne sidestepped and dropped her center of gravity as an android came flying through the space her head had just occupied and smashed into the group coming out of the building. She felt Michael at her back as she opened fire on yet more androids pouring out of the loading dock. "How many of these fucking things are there? We need to make some room and draw them out."

"I have grenades," Michael told her. Without slowing his rate of fire, he smashed his elbow into the face of an android with a satisfying crunch.

"I have one of Tabitha's nanoswarms." Bethany Anne pointed at an outbuilding a few hundred meters away from the wall with the barrel of her Jean Dukes Special. "We need the high ground. Make a hole. I'll cover us."

Michael grinned. "My pleasure." He continued shooting with one hand while he freed two grenades from his belt with the other, then pulled the pins with his teeth and tossed them into the mass of androids without hesitation.

Android parts spewed in all directions, giving Bethany

Anne and Michael the space they needed to escape the crush. They made a break for the outbuilding, keeping the path Michael had made clear with their Jean Dukes Specials.

Bethany Anne's boots crunched on the mangled android bodies piling up beneath their feet as they ran through falling debris and flames. She took out eight androids in quick succession while Michael kept the ones rushing to backfill their path off their backs.

Michael leapt onto the roof of the low building and covered Bethany Anne while she made her jump. "Those nanobots are programmed to leave us alone, right?"

Bethany Anne nodded as she extracted the capsule containing ten thousand nanobots from a pouch on her webbing. "I had ADAM program them while we were shooting our way through."

The androids were piling up at the foot of the building, but Michael continued to hold them back. Despite his efforts, they were gaining ground, climbing the bodies of the fallen to get to the roof.

"Whatever you're doing, do it quickly," Michael called, risking a glance over his shoulder at Bethany Anne. He saw the android before she did. "Behind you!"

Bethany Anne threw the capsule to Michael as she turned and grabbed the android around its neck. She plunged her free hand into its chest cavity and pulled out the power source—a mechanical heart.

Her eyes blazing with anger, she drew her arm back to launch the defunct android into the masses gathering at the edges of the roof.

"Release the nanoswarm!" she yelled as the androids closed in on all sides.

Actually, I'd prefer it if you didn't keep damaging my workers, a harassed voice exclaimed in the mindspace.

The androids stopped their advance, and their eyes lit up.

Michael hesitated with his fingers on the capsule's activation button when he saw the look on his wife's face. "Bethany Anne? You look like you've just seen a ghost."

Bethany Anne's face was ashen. "It can't be."

She pushed through the androids and leapt lightly to the ground, then made her way back to the loading dock.

Michael moved behind and to the right of Bethany Anne, his Jean Dukes Specials trained on the doorway. He tensed when he felt a presence in the shadows. "Who is it?" he murmured, knowing Bethany Anne would hear.

"I don't care who it is," Bethany Anne ground out, the air around her becoming agitated as she drew on the Etheric. "Using a dead girl to tweak me was their *last* mistake."

The glow from Bethany Anne's eyes cast the silhouette in the doorway into relief. "Show yourself," she commanded. She didn't believe her eyes when Anne stepped forward. "You should have chosen someone else to imitate. Someone who didn't die right in front of me."

"Why is Father's human so angry?" Jinx whined, moving to stand in front of Anne.

Anne's smile faded as she bent to wrap an arm around the German Shepherd. "It's okay, Jinx. Go tell Dio and Matrix that Bethany Anne is here. It looks like we're finally going home."

Bethany Anne lowered her weapons. "*How?* How are you here?"

Jinx looked at Bethany Anne. "You're scarier than I remember." She turned and trotted back into the factory with her tail in the air, leaving the three humans to continue staring at each other in silence.

Anne folded her arms. "Really, if you could just hold off on shooting me for a few minutes, we need to get a message to the outside before a fight breaks out. The Ilions are not the friendliest species."

"It's all right," Bethany Anne told Michael as she lowered her weapons. Confusion overwhelmed her. She should have had Michael examine Anne's mind, but deep down, she knew the woman standing in front of her wasn't a fake. "Your ship blew up. You died."

"I didn't die," Anne told her. "The jump drive malfunctioned and spat us out in the middle of Kurtherian territory. We'd been working our way back home for the longest time when we came across this facility."

Anne's eyes widened. "There's no time for this now. The Ilions are the type of people who will destroy themselves to answer what they see as an insult. Their problem is, they see *everything* as an insult, and they respect only themselves."

"We are prepared for nonlethal combat," Michael told Anne. "Our people will suppress any attack from these Ilions."

Bethany Anne couldn't process the reversal of loss. She put her emotions aside for the time being and focused on the need for action. "Can you take the shielding down?"

Anne shook her head. "Not without alerting the Kurtherians that this place wasn't destroyed, and I know you won't want to risk the people who live here. Follow me. The only place we can get a signal out of here is my lab."

CHAPTER TWENTY-SIX

Factory, Residential Level

Bethany Anne and Michael followed Anne along descending Echeresque walkways while she elaborated on the events that had culminated in her decision to remain at the factory.

What had been the cell levels was now home to a vibrant community for the air-breathing residents. Anne had taught the former prisoners how to build the basics. They had stripped the factory floor bare in their quest to provide power, heat, water, and most importantly, create a sense of home.

Bethany Anne enjoyed not being the center of attention for once. The people gathered around Anne everywhere she stopped to talk. They listened to her calm instructions and began dismantling their lives quickly and efficiently. Evacuation had always been a possibility, and they were prepared.

"Why didn't you send a message?" Bethany Anne asked.

"I knew you'd find me eventually, and the Collective

would have died without my help." Anne took the turn to her lab. "I had to persuade the Kurtherian controller to abandon their post. By then, I knew that protecting the Collective meant cutting myself off as well. I opened a little rift to kickstart the shield, and that did the trick. Since then, I've been helping everyone here get on their feet."

A Bl'kheth materialized on Anne's shoulder and grimaced fiercely at Bethany Anne and Michael. "Are you sure they're not spies?" she asked Anne, caressing her tiny sword menacingly. "Maybe we should stick them a few times to make sure they're not a danger to us."

Anne shook the Bl'kheth off and pointed a finger at her. "Bellaflora, didn't you hear a word I said? You will not attack the Empress."

Bellaflora pivoted gracefully in midair to look at Bethany Anne in wonder. "My bad."

Anne giggled when Bethany Anne raised an eyebrow at her. "What? You taught Yollins to shrug. Why can't my friends learn Earth slang?"

Bethany Anne extended a hand for Bellaflora to land. "I have my most loyal companions searching for your home planet. It was my hope they would return with an army of your people to help free you from these factories, but they didn't make it in time to leave with us."

"Perhaps they await your return, as Anne has," Bellaflora answered. "Are you truly the Empress?"

"I was," Bethany Anne replied, smiling warmly. "I'm just a Queen these days. A lot has changed since Anne was lost."

"Like what?" Anne asked eagerly. "I can't wait to get back to Yoll. I've missed the *C3PO* so much."

Bethany Anne gave her a sympathetic look. "Like I said, we have a lot to catch up on."

"Then we need to hurry," Anne announced, resuming her fast walk. "You trashed pretty much all of Seshat's bodies, so I don't have too much stuff to take."

QSD *Baba Yaga*, Bridge

The Ilions didn't seem to care that they were massively outgunned.

Alexis monitored the status of the six battle cruisers edging toward their position with their weapons locked on the *Baba Yaga.* The Ilion ships had retreated after the superdreadnoughts responded to the initial attack by arming their main ESDs.

Gabriel reported no casualties from the two troop transports waiting for the all-clear to move on the factory. "Everyone is edgy, frustrated they can't react to being attacked."

"Understandable," Alexis reasoned. "You guys are okay out there, right?"

"We're fine," John called without appearing on the camera. "Everyone will hold tight until we hear from Bethany Anne."

"Open a link to whoever is giving those ships their orders," Alexis told Izanami. "I don't care what you have to do to get it, just do it before I run out of options."

Izanami hijacked the bridge communications on the lead ship and followed the connection back to the satellite network orbiting the planet, which in turn led her to a facility on the moon. "And if they get over their outbreak of common sense?"

"If they come at us again, take out their weapons and propulsion systems," Alexis instructed.

"I have the office of the First Minister," Izanami informed Alexis.

"Onscreen." Alexis maintained a polite expression as the pale green alien on the screen accused them of violating their space, his antennae waving wildly in his shock of white hair. "I assure you, Minister—"

"Assure me nothing!" the Ilion First Minister spat. "Turn your ships around immediately, or we will destroy them!"

Izanami laughed. "You can try."

Alexis silenced her with a stern look. "My parents are inside the Kurtherian facility. We are not leaving without them," she told the minister. "Withdraw, or I will have no choice but to disable your ships."

"Your parents are dead," the minister scorned. "Leave now, before you join them."

The viewscreen shifted, and Bethany Anne and Michael appeared. "You would not be the first to assume my early demise," Bethany Anne told the minister acidly.

The First Minister gaped. "The Empress!"

"Queen," Bethany Anne corrected sharply. "Izanami, Reynolds, retarget your ESDs. I want them pointing at the planet at…" She looked at someone off-camera, then listed a longitude and latitude that made the minister's antennae shrink back against his skull.

"That's…that's our seat of government!" he spluttered.

"I'm not going to punish your entire planet for one

asshole. If you had been stupid enough to offend the Kurtherians, your entire species would already be dead." Bethany Anne fixed the minister with a scathing look and held up a finger to cut off whatever he was about to say. "I am informed that your culture places value on respect. You have disrespected my daughter, and by extension, me. This insult cannot go unanswered. I'm giving you one chance to retreat, and then I'm going to run out of patience."

The minister's demeanor changed completely as his advisor approached and whispered in his ear, informing him of the ESDs' capability.

Bethany Anne gave him a long moment to contemplate the situation his arrogance had gotten his people into. "I have more important things to deal with than the petty complaints of a planet I have no intention of setting foot on. I suggest you count yourself lucky and recall your ships before I destroy them as penance."

She booted the minister off the call and turned her attention to Alexis. "Your father and I had a little bit of a surprise. Anne, come and say hi to my daughter."

A dark-haired woman joined Bethany Anne onscreen and smiled shyly at Alexis. "Hey."

Alexis' mouth dropped open. "No. Freaking. *Way*. Wait until everyone finds out you're alive!"

"Not the concern at this minute," Bethany Anne told her. "When Anne disables her shielding, Gödel is going to find out her factory didn't get destroyed in a rift accident. We have to get the people living here transferred to the *Baba Yaga* and destroy the factory before anyone comes to investigate. Relay my updated orders to your brother, and have Captain Jameson deploy the aquatic transport modules. We have forty-seven Collectives awaiting transfer."

Alexis blinked when the viewscreen went blank. "That's huge," she told Izanami.

Izanami gave her a knowing look. "You're telling me. I have passed on Bethany Anne's request to Captain Jameson."

Alexis reached out to Gabriel. "Change of plans, bro."

Factory

In the three hours since the Ilion fleet had gone back to their planet with their tails tucked between their legs, Bethany Anne had reluctantly agreed that the *Reynolds* had to go ahead and complete the mission without them so she could take care of the fallout from Anne's bombshell.

The task of moving forty-seven Collective was only the beginning. While they were transferred to the *Polaris,* there were also almost sixty thousand people of varying species and ages living in the factory, thanks to Anne's intervention. Michael had rolled his sleeves up to help Seshat organize their transfer to the *Baba Yaga,* freeing Bethany Anne and Anne to make their way back to the lab on what had been the production floor.

Bethany Anne followed Anne through the maze of passages created by defunct machinery, the route familiar from her time in the other factory. Anne led her through the control room to the adjacent rooms where she had her lab set up.

"The first thing I did was shut down production of the nanocyte-stem cell base they were using to force-grow those tentacled nightmares," Anne told her as they entered her small office through a sliding door.

"We call them Ookens," Bethany Anne supplied. She lifted a shoulder at Anne's look of confusion. "Because they look like orangutans crossed with krakens," she clarified.

"I'm still processing the idea that you found Michael, and you two have adult children," Anne confessed. She picked up a datapad from a pile of them scattered across her desk. "I wish we weren't in such a hurry. I've missed my life back home. I have so much catching up to do."

Bethany Anne saw tears in Anne's eyes and drew her into a hug. "We'll have all the time in the world once your people are safely returned to their real homes. You've been so brave holding on out here. It's not easy being a leader."

Anne squeezed Bethany Anne tightly before letting go. "I just kept asking myself, what would Bethany Anne want me to do?"

"I want you to come home," Bethany Anne told Anne, holding her at arm's length. "To see Stevie and Ronnie and everyone else who never gave up hope that you'd return one day."

Anne lowered the hand holding her datapad, a frown etching her delicate features. "Once I do this, there's no going back."

Bethany Anne comforted her with a smile. "It's okay. I'm here now. The second you drop that shield, our people will be here to help everyone get through it."

"What if the Kurtherians come before everyone is aboard your ship?" Anne asked.

"If they do, they won't live to regret it," Bethany Anne promised. "But they won't. You and I are going to go out there and open a rift to destroy this place for real. Then we're going to take these people to safety and a stable home."

Anne nodded, her mind made up. "Okay, then. Here goes nothing."

The shield dropped.

Open Space, QSD *Baba Yaga*

Bethany Anne was in her ready room, updating the galaxy map with reports from the armada while they were en route to rejoin the SD *Reynolds*.

Given the spread of green markers on the map, the reports from the first sections to arrive at their target locations were largely positive. However, until the data the breach teams had recovered was decrypted, she had nothing to go on to indicate where the next wave of attacks should be launched.

Bethany Anne looked up when Anne entered the room. "How is everyone adjusting? I made it to the *Polaris* to visit with the Collective before they left for Waterworld, but duty called before I made it to deck seven."

"The little ones are finding it tough, but mostly, everyone is doing fine." Anne's gaze was drawn to the galaxy map. She lifted a finger and pointed out the location the SD *Colorado* was headed for. "What is this? You're attacking the Kurtherians?"

"Every one of those locations has a factory," Bethany Anne explained.

Anne turned to frown at her. "What about the other factories?"

Bethany Anne straightened in her chair. "We have to find them first."

She explained how she'd gotten the galaxy map and her suspicion that it only contained information about a portion of Gödel's assets. "You have an idea about where to find other locations?"

"Here, for one." Anne pointed out an unmarked area of space, her brow knitted in thought. "This was where the jump drive took us. There's a factory in this star system. Maybe not just a factory. I was captured by pirates after the jump drive accident and taken to a floating city to be sold. They called it 'the temple.' That's what I came to talk to you about. There were Kurtherians there. A *lot* of Kurtherians."

"You'd better tell me what happened after you vanished." Bethany Anne frowned. "I don't think it can wait any longer."

Anne waved her hands as she described her narrow escape from becoming a slave. "The pirates weren't too smart. Luckily for me, they didn't know what a human looked like. They thought I was Torcellan."

"Did you go inside the temple?" Bethany Anne asked.

Anne shook her head. "I don't think I'd be here today if Gödel had known I was there." She shuddered as she considered what she'd learned about the Kurtherian ruler from ADAM in the last few hours. "It took everything to get back to Seshat and the dogs. Bethany Anne? If there's one location you didn't know about…"

"There are more," Bethany Anne finished when Anne's voice trailed off. "I know. What I don't know is where they are, but we're working on that. This helps, you don't know how much. Does ADAM have your ship logs from the accident?"

Anne nodded. "I had Seshat share everything with him. Why?"

Bethany Anne started sending messages to the armada's section commanders. "Because the next place we're headed is the temple."

The *Reynolds* was slightly bruised but nowhere near broken when Izanami brought the *Baba Yaga* out in the wreckage of the factory.

Reynolds gave Jiya the bridge and made his way to the *Baba Yaga*.

Izanami greeted him as he stepped off the transporter pad. "We are somewhat short on roamers. Do you mind sharing?"

"Not at all," Reynolds assured her as she brought Link and Phina aboard.

Izanami directed them to a roamer programmed to take them to the situation room on the top deck. "Bethany Anne is waiting for you."

Phina couldn't help speculating as the roamer traversed the corridors. "One hundred and seventy-five is too neat," she announced, breaking the silence.

"So, we're in condition SUSFU." Reynolds folded his arms and leaned back with his eyes closed, monitoring the progress of the cleanup operation his crew was running to remove the crystal debris from the system.

"SUSFU?" Phina asked.

"Situation unchanged, still fucked up," Reynolds replied without opening his eyes. "In other words, it's above my pay grade."

"Not ours," Link told him quietly. "Phina, how is ADAM doing with the decryption?"

Phina's gaze turned blank for a second while she checked in with ADAM. Her eyes widened when he replied. "Fudge. Can we make this roamer go any faster?"

"What is it?" Link asked.

"Anne told Bethany Anne she was taken to a temple. A *Kurtherian* temple." Phina's expression hardened as she relayed the information. "I thought I'd lost the trail forever."

Link put a hand on her arm. "Take it easy. I don't want to have to chase you across the expanse again."

Phina shrugged his hand off, adrenaline pumping through her body. "Bethany Anne doesn't know it moves around. It won't be there, and every minute we spend talking means the trail gets colder."

>>**She knows now,**<< ADAM interjected.

The roamer pulled into a charging dock and they hurried to the situation room, where Bethany Anne was sitting alone at the head of the table.

"We will make this quick," Bethany Anne told them as they took their seats. "We have data on other factory locations from the communication logs the breach teams recovered. Spy Corps isn't needed to find more; we know what to look for. I want your people to search for the temple. Reynolds, you have the most experience with operations outside the Federation. I want you to stay with Phina and Link and provide whatever support they need."

Phina covered her mouth with her hands. "Thank you. All I've wanted since Todd died is to prove Glo…I mean, Gödel caused it."

Bethany Anne took Phina's hand, putting all the faith she had in her spy into her smile. "I know this is personal for you. It's your time, Phina. Find the temple. Find Gödel so I can end this."

EPILOGUE

Kurtherian Territory, QSD *Baba Yaga*, (Thirty-Five Years Later)

Izanami was adjusting their heading in preparation for Bethany Anne's next planned incursion when she received a video link from Plato.

Curious as to why he was contacting them out of the blue, she opened the link and was surprised to find the origin of the call was Earth. She connected the link to the viewscreen and a number of humans appeared, most of whom should not have been where they were.

One of the two identical blonde women Izanami didn't recognize stared at the bridge. "So much technology," she murmured.

Izanami smiled at her before addressing the highest-ranking person in the group. "The Queen is indisposed at the moment. How may I help you, Colonel Walton?"

"Not me, Izanami," Terry Henry replied. "My grand-daughters on Earth."

Izanami's eyes widened. This was worth disturbing

Bethany Anne for. She transferred the call to Bethany Anne's ready room and told her Queen what she knew.

Bethany Anne's heart dropped at the mention of a problem on Earth. The fear Gödel would find it and take revenge on the people for her losses had kept her awake too many nights. She put the call onscreen and saw TH, Char, Ted, Felicity, a man who looked like Timmons on steroids, and two almost-identical women she assumed were TH's and Char's granddaughters, Sarah Jennifer and Sylvia.

>>I just received a ton of raw data from Plato,<< ADAM informed Bethany Anne.

Hold it for now, Bethany Anne instructed. "What about Earth? Lay it out for me," she began without wasting time on introductions.

"Here's what I have so far," Ted announced. "The nanocytes you saturated the Earth with have malfunctioned in humans and a number of other species. There's barely any information because nobody wants to help me get a sample of the Madness-infected nanocytes."

Bethany Anne didn't respond to Ted's complaint. She sat back in her chair, annoyed that she hadn't had the foresight to consider the issue. "Well, fuck. That wasn't what I intended."

"No kidding," one of the twins muttered.

"Not helpful, Sylvie." Sarah Jennifer shot her sister an annoyed glance. She turned back to Bethany Anne on the screen. "What do I call you, Your Highness or something?"

Bethany Anne decided right away that she liked this no-nonsense woman. "You can call me by my name, and tell me what your place in this is."

Sarah Jennifer returned her smile. "Fair enough. I'm building a military to counter the issues humanity is facing. The plan is to revive the infrastructure on what's left of the East Coast—"

"What's left of it?" Bethany Anne interrupted.

Sarah Jennifer lifted her hands without apologizing. "We were invaded by an army of the Mad coming down from the north. Sometimes all you have is a hammer. What Ted hasn't stopped to hear yet is that we have magic-users in Salem. They acted to save more lives being lost when the Madness took Canada."

Bethany Anne raised an eyebrow at Ted's choked protest.

"It's not magic," Sarah Jennifer clarified, soothing Ted with a look he ignored. "But that's what the people who have it call it."

Bethany Anne pointed at Sarah Jennifer. "*That's* what I wanted to gift the world with. Not that fucktacular—what are we calling it, 'Madness?'"

>>**That's not the only problem,**<< ADAM told her. >>**There's an issue with the climate control network.**<<

What issue? Bethany Anne asked, hardly daring to hear the answer.

>>**Give me a minute.**<<

"What can I do to help you with this?" Bethany Anne asked Sarah Jennifer while she waited for ADAM to finish processing the data.

"What can you do from halfway across the universe?" TH asked.

"I can pull you out of retirement and have Nathan assign your ass there for a start," Bethany Anne shot back.

"Keeg Station is secure, and don't think for a moment I won't have Ted take you there."

Char made a face. "Keeg Station is not an issue since we're not there right now." She gestured, and Nathan joined them on the screen for a moment.

He waved at Bethany Anne as he walked by.

Bethany Anne sighed. "You're at Onyx."

Char and TH nodded in unison. "Temporarily," TH replied. "My bar doesn't run itself."

"Neither does the CEREBRO network," Nathan called from offscreen.

Bethany Anne shook her head. "Actually, it does."

Sarah Jennifer grunted in frustration, drawing her attention. "Everyone is missing the point. If the Madness or the Were affliction got off Earth, they would destroy humanity and any aliens who have nanocytes. Your war would be over like that." She snapped her fingers. "Why do you think I was so reluctant to call for help? Bethany Anne, I'm living this. Trust me when I say that I won't rest until humanity is safe. We have magic, we have Lilith, and we have the Werepower and the willpower to rebuild. Humanity is going to save itself. I'm just the coordinator."

"Lilith?" Bethany Anne raised an eyebrow. "Well, that changes things."

"She's in a bind right now, but we're working on getting to New Romanov," Sarah Jennifer explained. "Once we get there, making our way into the heart of Europe will be a cakewalk."

Bethany Anne's expression shifted. "A cakewalk with zombies."

"Not zombies," Ted corrected. "This is real life, not a

horror movie."

"If it walks the Earth looking for brains to eat, it's a zombie," Sylvia argued.

"Enough, both of you," Sarah Jennifer snapped when Sylvia and Ted started shouting over each other. "This isn't a joke or a scary story for a dark night. Millions of lives are at stake."

Bethany Anne agreed with her entirely. "What are you suggesting? I don't like the idea of leaving Earth to fix a problem caused by my technology."

"Sarah never was one to hold back when she had a plan," Terry Henry cut in.

Char smiled, her eyes sparkling. "That's the nicest way you could have said she's going to do what she thinks is right regardless of what we say."

Bethany Anne had no problem with a Walton taking the reins if that was the case. "Is that true?"

Sarah Jennifer shrugged. "They know me better than anyone. I'm not going to stand aside and let everyone die. I'm not saying we couldn't use some help, especially with tech, but we've got this. When you come back to Earth, it will be filled with magic, not horror."

Bethany Anne listened, then was silent for a moment while she deliberated the best course of action. "Okay, this is where we're at. We have two potentially devastating nanocyte issues that cannot be allowed to spread past Earth. Right now, whether they're connected isn't our concern. That will come after the contagion has been secured. I have no choice but to put the planet under quarantine. It's the only way to protect everyone." She straightened in her chair. "Everyone except for Sarah can leave for now. Ted, Felicity, I want you both in Pod-docs immediately. If there's any chance either of you is infected with either virus, we need to know. If you are both clear, you will leave the planet immediately after unloading anything that will help Sarah while I arrange for a care package to be delivered."

She didn't need to say what would happen if either of them were infected.

Ted opened his mouth to argue. "I can't go into the Pod-doc while you all dismantle my labs! I have vital projects going on."

"Do you also have non-essential experiments running?" Bethany Anne asked. She didn't want to delay his vital work, but Sarah's need was greater at the moment.

Charumati spoke up when Ted declined to answer, her tone apologetic. "I'm sorry you ended up back in a situation where you have to obey orders, but there's no option. Please, Ted. Be logical about this."

Felicity took his arm. "Plato will make sure nobody touches your essential projects, and we'll figure the rest out." She nodded at Bethany Anne. "We have a bunch of printers, biomass, and God only knows what all else in our stores to run on them."

"Can they print power packs?" Sarah Jennifer asked hopefully.

Felicity looked pointedly at Ted, who nodded. She glanced at Bethany Anne. "We can give them our Pod-doc, right?"

Bethany Anne nodded. "Make sure it only operates on Sarah's instructions."

Ted acquiesced, allowing Felicity to guide him off the

bridge. He whispered furiously as the door swished shut.

TH and Char signed off after extracting a promise from both Sarah Jennifer and Sylvia to call again soon.

Bethany Anne felt Sarah Jennifer's sudden nervousness and smiled to put the younger woman at ease. "You seem lost for words."

"I suppose I am," Sarah Jennifer admitted. "The stories I've heard about you make me feel inadequate."

"You've taken on responsibility for the human race on Earth," Bethany Anne replied. "Don't sell yourself short. I don't know you at all, but I know this. What you've taken on is a life of sacrificing yourself for the sake of everyone else. There aren't many who have what it takes to be the leader people need in dark times. Holding yourself to a higher principle is a hard road to take."

Sarah Jennifer nodded as she took a seat. "Too hard, it feels like some days. But I know it's survivable. You've been where I am now, and you got through it."

Bethany Anne's smile radiated her empathy across the galaxies. "As will you, with my support. Tech is not a problem. I can arrange for no-contact drops to be made. Your military will need equipping, and that's also easily solved. Transport. What do you have?"

Sarah Jennifer told her about the few vehicles they had in the motor pool and their plans to convert a Boeing Dreamliner into an Etheric-powered anti-gravitic airship. "Ted's going to build us an EI that can be run on any system we come up with, starting with the airship."

Bethany Anne nodded. "Okay. You need more and better transport. I'm going to assume medical care is primitive?"

"We have healers and common sense," Sarah Jennifer informed her, "But nothing like a Pod-doc. That tech died out when Akio left."

>>**At the very least, we have to get the climate modules repaired,**<< ADAM cut in. >>**I've finished going through the data Ted sent, and it looks like the station at Norrköping has suffered a failure.**<<

"Got it." Bethany Anne listed some of the equipment she could have shipped to Earth. "Some of it could be difficult to deliver, but if you need it, you're getting it."

Sarah Jennifer's expression wavered. "We don't have the infrastructure to support all this space-tech," she admitted. "Hell, we don't even have roads yet. People outside of the Defense Force are farmers and artisans. Academics and engineers are few and far between. We're lacking people with technical knowledge, although we have one man with a mind for engineering teaching others while he learns, and every recruit in the Defense Force is also required to learn a trade if they don't already have one."

She paused. "I know there are rules against it, but I want to upgrade my chief engineer in the Pod-doc with your permission. He's getting old, and we can't afford to lose him. I was considering allowing him to be turned Were before they started having trouble shifting."

Bethany Anne needed her to think bigger. "You have my permission to give all of the vital people you trust the upgrade to lengthen their lives and protect them from disease or severe injury. It gives you a solution for the Weres as well, right?"

"Ted's solution is to remove all the affected Weres' nanocytes and give them a new set," Sarah Jennifer explained. "We'll see how that works when Linus is done cooking." She paused. "Are you going to make Ted and Felicity stay on Earth if they're infected?"

Bethany Anne nodded. "Without hesitation. You're right, we cannot afford for this to get into the intergalactic population. As long as they're clear, they can sterilize their ship and go on their way. We will have to establish a protocol for contact. I doubt I will be able to prevent Ted from returning to study this."

Sarah Jennifer chuckled. "He's going to love that."

Bethany Anne lifted a shoulder. "He can love it, or he can stay away from Earth, and I'll send Eve instead."

Sarah Jennifer smiled. "I think he'll be fine. He's pretty taken by this mystery."

"He needs that sample to get started," Bethany Anne told Sarah Jennifer.

"All respect, it's not possible right now," Sarah Jennifer replied. She explained a little about the historic rivalry between the pack and the council. "This new era of cooperation is still in its infancy. I've spent the past few months back and forth from Salem, but that's got to change while the Weres we rescued from the prison get integrated into the community. Same for Esme."

Bethany Anne tilted her head, unfamiliar with the name. "Who?"

"She's the lead witch and my good friend." Sarah Jennifer recapped Esme's story for Bethany Anne.

"I can't say I remember her," Bethany Anne admitted. "She has the right idea about will and nanocytes. Listen to her."

"You never met." Sarah Jennifer grinned. "Trust me, I

listen. Her experience working for TQB and her ability to manipulate Etheric energy are invaluable when it comes to the logistics of getting the cure to everyone, but she has to keep the magic-users in line while the committees are formed to manage the rebuilding of our infrastructure. Our plan took that into account, as well as the time it's going to take the engineering corps to get the Dreamliner airborne."

She sighed, pushing her hair back. "If we had your capabilities, we'd be able to fix this with no problem. As it stands, while I'm grateful you're offering so much, we don't need anything so much as we need people."

Bethany Anne tapped a finger on her lips. "The one thing I can't provide. I see your predicament."

Sarah Jennifer sat back and folded her hands behind her head. "We've got that covered too, believe it or not. This part of the world runs on favors and barter. The key is trade; it always is. Once the Defense Force stamps out the blood trade and opens the roads again, civilization will bloom. Just wait and see."

Bethany Anne chuckled. "Then you'll have no problem fitting in a little job for me." Her amusement at Sarah Jennifer's curiosity blossomed and faded in the blink of an eye. "I need you to go to Sweden. I need eyes on a situation there."

"Something is wrong with the BYPS, right?" Sarah Jennifer offered. "I can't pretend to understand how it works beyond there are satellites above the planet that will defend us from attacks from space."

Bethany Anne nodded. "One of the satellites was damaged and rejected by the network. Its final transmission was received by a ground station on the climate control network—something else that's not working the way it should be—in what used to be Östergötland, Sweden. That malfunction is what's causing the ice age you're experiencing."

"You can't get Ted to access it remotely?" Sarah Jennifer asked.

Bethany Anne shook her head. "It looks like the station went offline around thirty years ago. Even without the risk of him getting infected—a risk I'm not willing to allow him to take—Ted's not equipped to handle the situation on the ground without his pack. Whatever monsters this malfunction is turning people into, it can be reversed. I'm trusting you because you're a Walton. I know you'll get the job done."

Sarah Jennifer sighed. "I'm going to need the locations of the ground stations. Europe is a mess. I'm not willing to risk my people by going in before we're ready. The priority right now is finding the route the Mad are taking into Canada and blocking it, then getting to Archangelsk."

"How do you plan to block the land bridge?" Bethany Anne asked skeptically. "As far as I can see, the ice shelf has extended as far as Japan."

"Witch power," Sarah Jennifer promised. "As for stopping the Mad, Ted has a six-person Pod. If we have that, we won't have to wait for the airship to start making a difference beyond the East Coast."

Bethany Anne nodded. "Understood. Do what you can. I appreciate that you're working around the limitations of your situation."

"I'm going to establish a garrison on the ice shelf. The

Weres will protect the magic-users while they work the landscape to put up a physical border. I just have to live with the death toll to the infected in the meantime." Sarah Jennifer shook her head, her expression severe. "Believe me, it's a motivator. When we release the cure, will the infected survive it? Will they be healed?"

"If their brains are not beyond repair." Bethany Anne closed her eyes, knowing not everyone would be so lucky. "Not all of them will make it."

Sarah Jennifer nodded somberly. "It's not all bad. We have more than a fighting chance, thanks to you. The time-frame for rebuilding has to be recalculated to account for your assistance, so I'll make Sweden the next stop on my list after getting to Lilith. Her power source is failing."

"I thought she had longer?" Bethany Anne asked. "Her power source should be good for another couple hundred years, at least."

"She's pushed herself too far too many times," Sarah Jennifer told her with regret. "Guiding me to Salem was a monumental effort for her. My psychic ability was still latent, but she persisted until she found a way to drive me across the country, regardless of the cost to herself. She's hibernating to conserve energy until we can get to her."

Bethany Anne was filled with sadness at the thought of losing Lilith. "There's nothing more important. Save Lilith. Sweden can wait."

She remained at her desk after the call ended, her thoughts turning on the plight of Earth. Humanity had a champion in the form of Sarah Jennifer Walton. All she could do was give what assistance she could from a distance.

Izanami interrupted her thoughts, appearing in a spray of red-gold sparkles by the desk. "We have a report from Phina. She has located the temple."

Temple of the Ascension Path

The armada Gated into the system in formation, surrounding the floating city on all sides. The underside of the base trailed massive tree roots from between jagged inverted peaks, the debris swept up by the atmosphere. Topside, shining towers crowded rolling hills, surrounded by forests and lakes.

Bethany Anne felt a surge of emotion from TOM as the conglomeration of spires lit up in reaction to their arrival. ***What is it?*** she asked, her attention captured for the moment by the gigantic engines secreted in the underside of the city.

We are looking at the Azzhur clan's capital city, TOM answered. **This used to be part of a planet. She... She tore it out?**

Why am I not shocked that Gödel took it for herself? Bethany Anne picked up a brief flash of urgency in the mindspace. It was gone before she could do more than discern it had come from the tallest tower on the highest hill, and that it was Phina who had broadcast it.

Bethany Anne reached out for Michael as she got to her feet. ***Meet me in the armory.*** "Phina needs backup," she told Alexis. "Your father and I are going in."

"The atmosphere is artificial," Alexis informed her. "A well-placed strike would damage the generators and cause a panic."

"Not yet," Bethany Anne told her. "There are thousands of slaves here, according to Phina's report. They need to be freed before we start dismantling the city."

Alexis frowned as hundreds of battleships rose from the towers. "I'll run point for the ground troops from here. Gabriel is with John and Gabrielle, and they're about to head out in the scout fighters. Good luck down there, Mom."

Bethany Anne squeezed Alexis' shoulder. "Same to you, sweetheart. Give them hell."

While the battle in space raged, Bethany Anne and Michael cut through the Etheric to get to the surface. After confirming their surroundings were clear, Bethany Anne informed Alexis that they had made their entry undetected.

Nobody comes down here until Michael and I have made sure it's not a trap, she instructed.

Nothing will get in or out of the city without my permission, Alexis assured her. *We have Etheric jammers moving into position to prevent the Kurtherian fleet from slipping away.*

Bethany Anne looked around, seeing nothing but the tree-covered hills filling her horizon. "Where is the temple?"

Michael pointed at a group of seven towers on a peak kilometers away that rose above the rest. "How do you want to approach this?"

Bethany Anne focused on the towers for a moment before retrieving a nanoswarm capsule from her armor. She pushed the button to release what looked like a handful of dust but was actually a hundred thousand miniscule camera drones programmed to blanket their target and send back images.

The swarm fell a few centimeters, then hung suspended, awaiting instructions. She sent it ahead to map the temple. "I *want* to motherpuck this place into nonexistence," she told him tersely. "I can't do that without killing thousands of innocent slaves."

Bethany Anne clenched her hands into fists as she tamped down her urge to destroy, focusing instead on circumventing the problem while they waited for the drone data. "How do we get them out of there? I don't want to kill people who have been forced to attack us."

"They have no idea we're not here for them," Michael told her. "We have to be prepared for unavoidable casualties."

"I don't like it, but we aren't the ones who put them in harm's way." Bethany Anne was torn. Gödel was here somewhere, and Phina was possibly—no, make that probably—in danger. "How many times over the last three and a half decades have we avoided all-out violence because we took the time to talk to the people? There's no *time,* fuckdammit."

"The plan." Michael pressed her gently, knowing she would add those deaths to the weight on her conscience. "We know Gödel isn't the type to share her power. The soldiers we captured on Belaria were armed with Etheric-powered weapons."

"Her Chosen," Bethany Anne ground out, decision made. "She has to give power to the ones protecting her ass. We launch a frontal assault to let Gödel know we don't give a shit how powerful she is. She's no match for Saint Payback."

Their HUDs pinged. The nanoswarm had begun sending data.

>>**I'm building the map,**<< ADAM announced so Michael also heard him.

Good. Bethany Anne created a bubble of solid energy around her and Michael and lifted them both above the tree line. ***Then we're going in.***

Michael flexed his gauntlets as the bubble rose, activating their draw on the Etheric. *How much of a scene do you want to cause?*

Bethany Anne's eyes blazed red as she stared straight ahead at the temple. ***Shock and awe have never failed me.*** She released her camera drones as she took the bubble above the treetops and sent it toward the seven towers of the temple at high speed.

As they got closer, Bethany Anne made out larger than life carvings around the temple entrance depicting Kurtherians in various poses. ***TOM, was this place always a temple?***

I don't know, I'm afraid, TOM told her with regret. **I recognize the entrance from an image in a book.**

It looks almost Egyptian, Michael remarked.

>>**I have the entrance level mapped.**<< ADAM activated the map in their HUDs. >>**I'll keep adding to it as the swarm makes progress.**<<

Bethany Anne counted the red dots in her HUD map, noting that there were several groups inside the walls of a huge, pillared space beyond the atrium. ***The drones have IR?***

>>**Yes,**<< ADAM confirmed.

They think they're ready for an attack. Michael let a wry smile slip. *Let's disabuse them of the notion that any amount of preparation could be enough to stop us now we've found this place.*

Bethany Anne drew her Jean Dukes Specials as they rocketed toward the temple. ***Starting with making an entrance.*** She adjusted the bubble so they weren't in contact with the skin of energy and set it ablaze. ***Justice awaits.***

It would be rude of us to keep the lady waiting, Michael replied, flourishing his hands to electrify the bubble with lightning from his gauntlets.

Bethany Anne laughed as they crashed into the temple in a ball of flames and smashed pillars.

The Kurtherians were literally blown away when they burst in, washing the atrium with a blaze of fire and lightning. Debris flying on the wave of concussive energy ripped right through the first line of defenders, taking them out.

Bethany Anne winced when two of the central pillars looked like they were going to collapse from the impact. She was about to act when the temple's defenses came online and shored up the damaged columns with some kind of shielding.

Satisfied the roof wasn't going to fall and crush them, Bethany Anne released the flaming bubble and flung the energy outward as the Chosen ran for barricades they'd placed strategically between the pillars to impede entry to the throne room.

The Chosen were heavily armored, wielding Etheric-enabled weaponry from behind the barricades. Bethany Anne threw up more shielding around her and Michael to repel the torrent of Etheric energy they discharged at them.

Do they all look kind of the same to you? Michael asked as he shot a Chosen with the same kinked mandible he'd noticed on a few of the others.

Like clones? Bethany Anne replied, catching his meaning when two identical Kurtherians attacked her. ***You think they're reckless enough to replicate themselves?***

I'd be interested to know what TOM thinks about it, Michael told her. *When we are not fighting, that is.*

Bethany Anne leapt onto the nearest barricade and kicked the Kurtherian who'd jumped up to defend himself in the face. She shot the ones retreating in the backs.

The temple glowed with licking flames, the air thick with black smoke as the fire spread to the painted walls. The barricades were burning, yet the Kurtherians kept coming. More clones, more weapons.

We could come back for these later, Michael suggested as he retaliated against the Chosen shooting at him by targeting the glowing red jewels in their weapons with bolts of lightning. *Gödel is the prize.*

Michael's distraction worked. They progressed to the next pillar as the Chosens' weapons exploded, showering their owners with shards of the molten jewels.

Gödel isn't going any-fucking-where, Bethany Anne stated, her eyes glowing with righteous fury. ***I'm done with this shit. Every Kurtherian in this temple dies today. ADAM, it's time. Get the virus ready.***

>>Are you sure? There's no going back from this.<<

It's taken us thirty-five long fucking years to find this place, Bethany Anne told him as she drew hard on the

Etheric to encase the remaining barricades in impermeable energy. ***If Gödel wants to fight dirty, she's going to see how dirty I can get when I'm all out of fucks to give.***

The Chosen whose air she'd just stolen fought to escape their prisons.

>>**It's ready,**<< ADAM told her as the Chosen ceased firing, preoccupied with their dwindling ability to draw breath.

Bethany Anne had not one shred of pity for the Kurtherian clones as she released the virus into the enclosed spaces. She put a hand on Michael's arm when he made to move on, pointing at the camera drones. "Wait. I have no stomach for suffering, but I need to witness this. People need to know Kurtherians bleed, same as the rest of us."

Michael nodded and stood beside her with his hand on her shoulder. "Perhaps it would be prudent to inform the people that this extreme measure is only available to us because of the mistrust Gödel has for her own people."

Bethany Anne was barely listening. She felt the Chosen's rising panic as the virus entered them via the backdoor Gödel had built into their nanocytes and got to work stripping those nanocytes of function, replacing the code for extra strength, speed, and agility with instructions to terminate the host with prejudice.

Michael dropped his hand when the enclosures around them were coated with biomatter from the inside as the sound of Kurtherians exploding like popcorn kernels filled the air.

"That's enough. The Chosen are no longer an issue." Bethany Anne strode ahead of Michael to the massive doors barring the throne room. Seeing they opened outward, she seized the energy in the air surrounding the doors and wrenched them apart.

Michael glanced up when a movement caught his eye as they entered the ornate room. *Above us!*

Bethany Anne had been distracted by a robed figure slipping through a door behind the dais. She ducked the fireball that came from a gallery above. Before the burning energy impacted the doors behind her, she took control of it and flung it right back at the robed combatants entrenched behind a barricade on the gallery.

Dammit, more Chosen. Michael sprang into action, spraying the gallery with a hail of explosive darts from his Jean Dukes Specials.

More clones, too. Bethany Anne increased her shield's area as the Chosen formed a loose circle around them. ***I guess they're not going to make this easy for us.***

Michael added his touch, electrifying the shield with a flourish of his gauntlets as portions of the walls slid back and more armored Chosen poured out of the passages in the walls.

Bethany Anne cursed aloud. ***We decided these guys don't have direct control of the Etheric, right?***

It doesn't look that way, Michael agreed. I'm not sensing they have a connection at all.

Bethany Anne tweaked the shield to deflect Etheric energy as the Chosen prepared to fire. ***They can't be that stupid, surely.***

You're mistaking the blinkers of their superiority complex for stupidity, Michael commented with a shake of his head. *They've been dominant for so long they believe they can take us.*

Yeah, HELL, no, Bethany Anne retorted.

The Chosen displayed their "superiority" by opening fire on Bethany Anne's shield, killing themselves and each other when the energy streams bounced back at them.

That's... She laughed in disbelief. ***I've met fungi with more intelligence.***

Bethany Anne and Michael stepped over the corpses and searched the back of the dais for the hidden door's mechanism. She quickly lost patience and kicked a hole in the wall beside the door.

Michael pulled on the wall, widening the hole enough for them to see a torchlit passage beyond.

I'm not picking up Phina's mental signature. Can you sense her? Bethany Anne asked Michael as they ducked one at a time through the hole.

Not yet, Michael told her. *Wherever she is, she's either cut off, or she's blocking all telepathic connections.*

Bethany Anne indicated the sloping passage. ***I saw Gödel. I think. She has to have gone this way.***

They followed the passage into a downward spiraling tunnel held up by twisting tree roots that had been trained to form stairs. Humidity from the increasing damp rose the farther they descended. The walls changed from stone to crumbling earth, and they saw insects that had managed to hang on despite the roots of their homes being exposed to space.

Bethany Anne ignored the showers of small bugs that periodically erupted from the roof of the tunnel. She was wondering how close they were to the great engines she'd seen on their approach when they came to a metal slab that blocked the tunnel.

She laid a hand on the metal and found it was chilled despite the natural hot box they were standing in.

There is a chamber of some kind, Michael told her, sensing the enclosed space within.

Bethany Anne nodded. ***Can you feel the energy being generated in there? Something is sucking up a hell of a lot of power.***

They sensed Phina's psyche crash through the mind-space at the same time.

Bethany Anne reacted without thinking and cut through the Etheric to get inside the chamber. She emerged with an energy ball in each hand, letting them dissipate when she saw Phina sprawled on the floor by a solitary computer terminal in a pool of pale blue light.

She ran through the glowing stacks to where Phina lay and dropped to the floor to press two fingers to her throat.

Michael exited the Etheric beside Bethany Anne as she pulled Phina onto her lap. He released the energy sparking over his gauntlets when he saw the woman's state.

She has a pulse. It's weak, but it's there. Bethany Anne put Phina down gently. ***ADAM, wake her up.***

>>**Her neurochemistry is telling me she suffered a serious shock,**<< ADAM told Bethany Anne. >>**I don't think waking her is a good idea.**<<

I don't want to leave her here unprotected. Bethany Anne got to her feet, recalling Tabitha's measures to hide Todd when their ship was under attack. ***Stay with her. I'm going to find somewhere to hide her for the time being. We'll pick her up on our way out.***

Bethany Anne made her way into the stacks, searching

for a recess away from the light. She was drawn to a section of the room that glowed less brightly than the rest.

These are memory crystals, TOM told her.

Bethany Anne paused and stared at the crystals standing more than double her height. ***Seriously?***

A flash of gilt on one of the crystals caught her eye. ***Wait. I see something.***

Bethany Anne drew her Jean Dukes Specials and approached cautiously. The gold she'd seen was a scrap of fabric stuck to the crystal with a spot of blood. Closer inspection of the row revealed that this section of the stacks was dimmer than the rest because the crystals along the row had an eight-foot layer of blood, brain matter, and other fine gore coating them.

She spotted a mess of tattered clothing and jewelry strewn on the floor. Realizing what had happened, she lowered her weapon and spoke aloud. "Michael."

He was by her side in an instant. "This was not Gödel."

Bethany Anne shook her head. "No, it was a clone. Phina must have given it the virus." She shook her head. "Gödel doesn't even trust herself. The virus can't do a thing without her backdoor."

Michael felt Phina's consciousness stirring. "This is still a victory."

Bethany Anne smiled. "Damn straight, it's a victory. We have just captured the sum of Kurtherian knowledge. No more mysteries. We have what we need to dismantle everything Gödel has built."

AUTHOR NOTES - MICHAEL ANDERLE
SEPTEMBER 6, 2020

THANK YOU for reading not only the story, but all the way to the back of the book to these author notes as well!

I'm always touched when I hear Bethany Anne or any of the other characters in the universe has been there for someone going through a hard time. Life is hard for everyone right now. Whatever comfort you find in our stories, all of us who are part of bringing you these stories are glad to have given it.

THE FUTURE (in a few books)

I was chatting about the 20Books London convention where I met Nat Roberts a few days ago. It hit me that it wasn't all that long ago that I was getting close to completing the first twenty-one books of *The Kurtherian Gambit*, and Bethany Anne was just getting started on the events that set *Endgame* in motion.

The universe was expanding as quickly as LMBPN was growing.

As you might have guessed, LMBPN is *still* growing,

and the universe is going through another expansion. We're getting close to the conclusion of *Endgame,* but Bethany Anne's story isn't done. You might have noticed that we skipped a few decades to get to the epilogue.

We're about to skip another hundred years or so to get to book 10.

Part of this is to keep Bethany Anne's story focused on the battle with Gödel and the Kurtherians. Another reason is to make space for other authors to tell their stories. These stories have changed lives. Another thing that was happening around the time of 20Books London was Fans Write. The project gave us a whole new wave of authors.

This universe has been a fantastic collaborative effort, and while the main focus is Bethany Anne's war against the Kurtherians, the stories of individual characters have spoken to so many people.

NEW SERIES COMING AT YA! (or recently dropped and more coming...)

Promises Kept introduced Phina Waters for those of you who missed the Fans Write story by Sarah (S.E.) Weir. Phina's story will open up during the Leath War and continue into the Leath War gap. Sarah is nearing completion of her first arc, so keep your eyes peeled in the next few months. You won't want to miss this series! (And please check out the short preview of Phina's story after these author notes!)

We have Charles Tillman writing *way* back in the Second Dark Ages. Another Fans Write graduate, his first arc of Akio's story has quickly become a fan favorite. We can confirm a second arc is being written.

Over in the Age of Madness, Nat (N.D.) Roberts is continuing work on the second book in the Birth of Magic series. We touched base with Sarah Jennifer Walton in the epilogue. Nat will be covering the time between then and the beginning of the Age of Magic in her next two books.

Last but not least, we have Peter Glenn writing over in the Age of Magic in The Sariah Chronicles where a young woman finds a way out of her half-starved life. Or did she?

By the time Bethany Anne returns, the Age of Madness will be long over, and we'll be getting into her part in The Rise of Magic - Hannah's story.

I sincerely appreciate ALL that you have done to help those of us who put together these stories, the art, the editing, and the operations teams who allow our stories to make it out to you. Without your support, we wouldn't get to do what we are blessed to do!

Reviews are still just as important as they were when I asked for your help to get to fifty reviews for *Death Becomes Her*...oh, too long ago. PLEASE let us know how we're doing!

If you can take a moment to leave a few words about what you liked in the story is fantastic.

(Or heck, just a star rating by itself is now an option for those who are more introverted is also appreciated.)

Ad Aeternitatem,

Michael Anderle

PS: Turn the page for Chapter One of the first book featuring Phina Waters, *Diplomatic Recruit*.

CHAPTER ONE OF DIPLOMATIC RECRUIT

QBBS *Meredith Reynolds*, Lance Reynolds' Office

"So," Anna Elizabeth Hauser finished. "The question, Seraphina Waters, is what should we do with you?" She tapped her fingertips on the desk as she watched Phina closely.

Phina didn't know what the elegant woman expected to see on her face. She'd never thought of herself as anything special in appearance, being more concerned about her skills. Her mid-length wavy dark hair was easy to brush or pull back into a braid when needed. Her startling green eyes, dusky skin, and the chin her aunt had told her often was far too stubborn for her own good gave her character in her opinion.

She cleared her throat as Anna clasped her hands together. "Just call me Phina, please. What *are* you going to do with me, uh, ma'am?"

She expected it to be bad news. After all, she had only hacked into the system for information, stolen...ahem, *borrowed* the workout clothes she currently wore, created a fake key pass, and broken into the Marine and Guardian workout room with her best friend before being escorted to General Lance Reynold's office by John Grimes, and the serious conversation that had just taken place. And that was just in the last twenty-four hours.

Anna winced. Was is something Phina had said? *All right,* she thought. *No calling Anna, "ma'am." That's good to know.*

"I thought that answer would be obvious, as smart as you are, Phina. You are a bored hyper-intelligent woman in need of a challenge. You exhibit compassion, loyalty, ethics, and morality in quantities unusual for your age. You obviously know how to hack a system since you did it to ours. You catch on to other languages quickly and in an interesting way, and you have learned to sneak into various secure places with your skills. You will need to join classes and train hard in several different areas, particularly hand-to-hand and weapons."

The woman tilted her head before she went on, spreading her hands as she smiled. "Phina, we are going to give you a job."

Phina's eyes widened, and her heart began to race. She was afraid to hope she could continue to fulfill the vow she had made to her parents' memory. "May I ask what kind of job?"

Anna raised her eyebrows, though Phina saw a small twinkle of amusement in her eyes. "I am putting together a small diplomatic and intelligence team. With your language skills, I think you would be a perfect fit." She leaned forward expectantly.

"Diplomatic team?" Phina's heart sank. Diplomacy, as in talking to people she didn't know? That wasn't the kind of work she wanted, but it was better than being arrested—or thrown out an airlock. She had heard stories of Empress Bethany Anne's temper and what she did to those who purposely went against the needs of the Empire. Phina shuddered, then let out a breath.

"And intelligence." Anna Elizabeth smiled as if she knew the thoughts floating through Phina's head. "The job comes with some side work that will keep you from being bored."

Hmm... Diplomacy and intelligence didn't sound *too* bad. "What kind of side work?"

Anna grinned. "What else? Stealthy information acquisitions. When the team isn't being used for diplomacy, it will gather intelligence for the Empire. Often it will be both."

Phina's eyes lit as she heard her favorite term for being a spy, and she grinned back.

Anna tilted her head, assessing. "There is a catch."

Her hope withered as her smile dimmed. Phina knew the offer had been too good to be true. "What kind of catch?"

Threading her fingers together, Anna straightened, looking Phina straight in the eye. "This team needs time to develop, just as you need time to learn and train. I see it coming together sometime after you graduate."

Phina's eyes widened. "Graduate?"

The elegant woman smiled as she nodded, but her eyes showed the seriousness of the situation. "From the Diplomatic Institute. I would like you to join the Diplomatic

Corps prior to joining the team. The Institute is now newly revamped as of last year to initiate and continue training our diplomats. The first semester of the new year begins in three weeks."

Anna Elizabeth searched Phina's face. "What do you think? Would you like to join our Diplomatic Corps?"

Phina wondered what would happen if she said no. Would Anna just tell Phina, "Off you go, angel." as her mother had often done when she had been alive? She felt a deep pang in her chest at the thought. Or would Anna get the disappointed look on her face that Phina often saw on her Aunt Faith? Not so fun, but Phina had grown used to it. Or would she forget all about being nice and have security escort her to the nearest airlock? That option guaranteed pain as well as death.

Diplomacy still didn't sound like much fun—she envisioned people sitting around an elaborate table using fancy words she would never use in normal conversation—but if gathering intelligence would still be in the picture, even in the future, then it might be worth it.

"What happens if I say no?"

Anna looked thoughtful before she responded, "What do you see yourself doing for the rest of your life, Phina? Finding some way to earn money while you travel around gathering information that *might* be compromising for the Empire, then sending warnings to us?"

Since that had more or less been what Phina had envisioned, her eyes widened in surprise. Still watching Anna, she slowly nodded.

Anna gave her a small smile as she leaned forward. "I

understand the Corps isn't exactly what you envisioned. However, if you agree, I think you will find yourself pleasantly surprised, and before too long, you will have a satisfying career ahead of you."

Phina's gaze fell to her fidgeting fingers as she tried to process her disappointment and this new direction. If she wasn't in an avenue related to spying now, how would she have time to search out information harmful to the Empire? Would she still have time between doing the diplomatic courses Anna wanted her to learn?

"I'll make a deal with you." Phina started at Anna's words and glanced up to meet the woman's serious eyes. "If you agree and join the Corps, in six months you can go do whatever you like with the Empire's full support if that's what you still want."

Phina's eyes grew huge as she realized Anna had basically offered her a blank check. She just needed to suffer through six months of boring diplomat school, and then she was more than free. She would be set for the life she had dreamed about.

Taking a deep breath, she nodded. "All right, I'll give it a try."

Anna smiled. Was that relief in her eyes? Her shoulders did relax. That set Phina wondering until Anna spoke.

"I'm happy to hear it. Welcome to the Corps, Phina."

Phina blinked and straightened in her chair. "You are part of the Corps too?"

The woman nodded, appearing every bit as poised and put together as the first moment Phina had seen her well over an hour ago. "Yes, I'm the Dean of the Diplomatic

Institute and Head Diplomat of the Diplomatic Corps." When she saw Phina frown in confusion, she clarified, "Basically, I'm in charge of everything related to diplomacy. You are on the young side compared to most of our students, but I have full confidence you will fit the Corps just fine."

She considered for a moment while Phina absently rubbed her sore stomach, then her arms. Todd punched hard, or maybe her muscles were just soft. It didn't hurt as much as it had earlier. Anna's words pulled her from her musings. "Which brings me to my next question. How do you think your aunt will react to this news?"

The question caused Phina's arm to drop as she gave a loud sigh. "Honestly? I'm not sure. She responds differently every time I approach her about something. It's like an extreme case of moodiness. Also, even if she initially approves something, she might very easily change her mind later."

Anna's blue eyes showed sympathy Phina wasn't expecting. How much did this woman know about her and Aunt Faith? She thought back to the General's comment earlier when he introduced Anna Elizabeth before he left the room. "She now knows everything I know." Crumbs, did the General know? If he knew, then from what they said earlier, ADAM knew. If ADAM knew... Phina stopped that line of thinking. If Empress Bethany Anne knew every tiny factoid about her life, she didn't want to know. The Empress had been far too intimidating at her last appearance for Phina to feel comfortable with completing the thought.

Her attention was pulled back when Anna sighed.

"Unfortunately, I'm not surprised. However, classes are three weeks away, so you will have time to acclimate her to the idea. You can decide when it's best to inform her."

Phina nodded. With her eighteenth birthday only thirty-six hours away, the smartest move might be to wait until then. That way, Phina would be a legal adult, and her aunt couldn't legally ship her off to Estaria, the rumored new home for those humans wanting a life on an established planet, or somewhere equally out in the middle of nowhere and away from everything Phina wanted to accomplish. She *could* come right back after her birthday, but why create unnecessary expense and headache when it was easily avoided just by being patient?

"I'll send you a message on your tablet so you know when and where your classes begin." Anna smiled encouragingly. "Until then, you have time to reassure your friend Alina, break the news to your aunt, and get ready."

Phina understood the first two things. Alina had been sent back to her apartment when Phina had been brought here to meet the General, and she would be a nervous wreck until she knew Phina wasn't in trouble for their adventure this morning. Her Aunt Faith would need some time to get used to the idea. But... "Get ready? Is there something I need to do to prepare?" Visions of new workouts, tests, and acquiring new skills flew through her head.

She received a grin. "Get ready for your life to change. Trust me, Phina, you won't be the same person by the end of your time in the Corps. Better to brace yourself now."

Phina nodded slowly, wondering just how the woman expected things to be different by the end. She heard a light cough and looked up.

Anna raised her eyebrows, eyes amused, then waved toward the door.

"Oh. Right. Ok, I'll see you later." Phina pushed herself up and headed for the door. With one last glance at Anna Elizabeth, who still looked elegant and beautiful sitting in the General's chair, she left the room.

Though Phina remained lost in thought as she walked back down the hallway to the more public areas, she couldn't help noticing John Grimes, the personal guard of the Empress, with his large frame in front of one of the doors, eyes tracking her movements. Her heart began to pound. The Empress must be behind that door.

As she passed him, looking everywhere except at the man in her nervousness, she heard his deep voice. "Happy Birthday, Phina." She paused, then turned in time to see his wink. "Try to stay out of trouble."

Surprised by the whole situation, Phina could only nod and say thank you. She was in a daze. These important and famous people in the Empire all seemed to know about her. She was joining a group that would be pivotal to the future of the Empire. Though not enamored with the idea of diplomatic talks, Phina had been aware of just how strategically important the Corps could be. No matter what she thought of the work they did when it came to her personally, she knew if the diplomats did their job right, they would better the future of the Empire, even though most people might never know their names.

Who was Phina to become part of that? Still, she hoped there would be some spying soon, or she might space herself to escape.

She left the office area, but instead of heading straight

for home, she meandered toward the main areas. The ache in her stomach and arms was easing, and Phina liked to walk around when she had things on her mind and needed to clear her head. As of this morning, she had more on her mind than she knew what to do with.

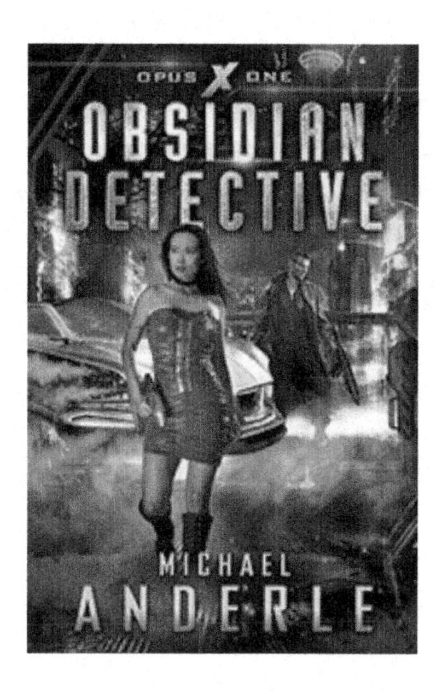

Two Rebels whose Worlds Collide on a Planetary Level.

On the fringes of human space, a murder will light a fuse and send two different people colliding together.

She lives on Earth, where peace among the population is a given. He is on the fringe of society where authority is how much firepower you wield.

She is from the powerful, the elite. He is with the military.

Both want the truth – but is revealing the truth good for society?

Two years ago, a small moon in a far off system was

set to be the location of the first intergalactic war between humans and an alien race.

It never happened. However, something was found many are willing to kill to keep a secret.

Now, they have killed the wrong people.

How many will need to die to keep the truth hidden?

As many as is needed.

He will have vengeance no matter the cost. *She will dig for the truth. No matter how risky the truth is to reveal.*

BOOKS BY MICHAEL ANDERLE

For a complete list of books by Michael Anderle, please visit:

www.lmbpn.com/ma-books/

CONNECT WITH MICHAEL ANDERLE

Connect with Michael Anderle

Website: http://lmbpn.com

Email List: http://lmbpn.com/email/

Social Media:

www.facebook.com/TheKurtherianGambitBooks/

https://twitter.com/lmbpn

https://www.instagram.com/lmbpn_publishing/

https://www.bookbub.com/authors/michael-anderle

Made in the USA
Middletown, DE
07 October 2020

21322434R00255